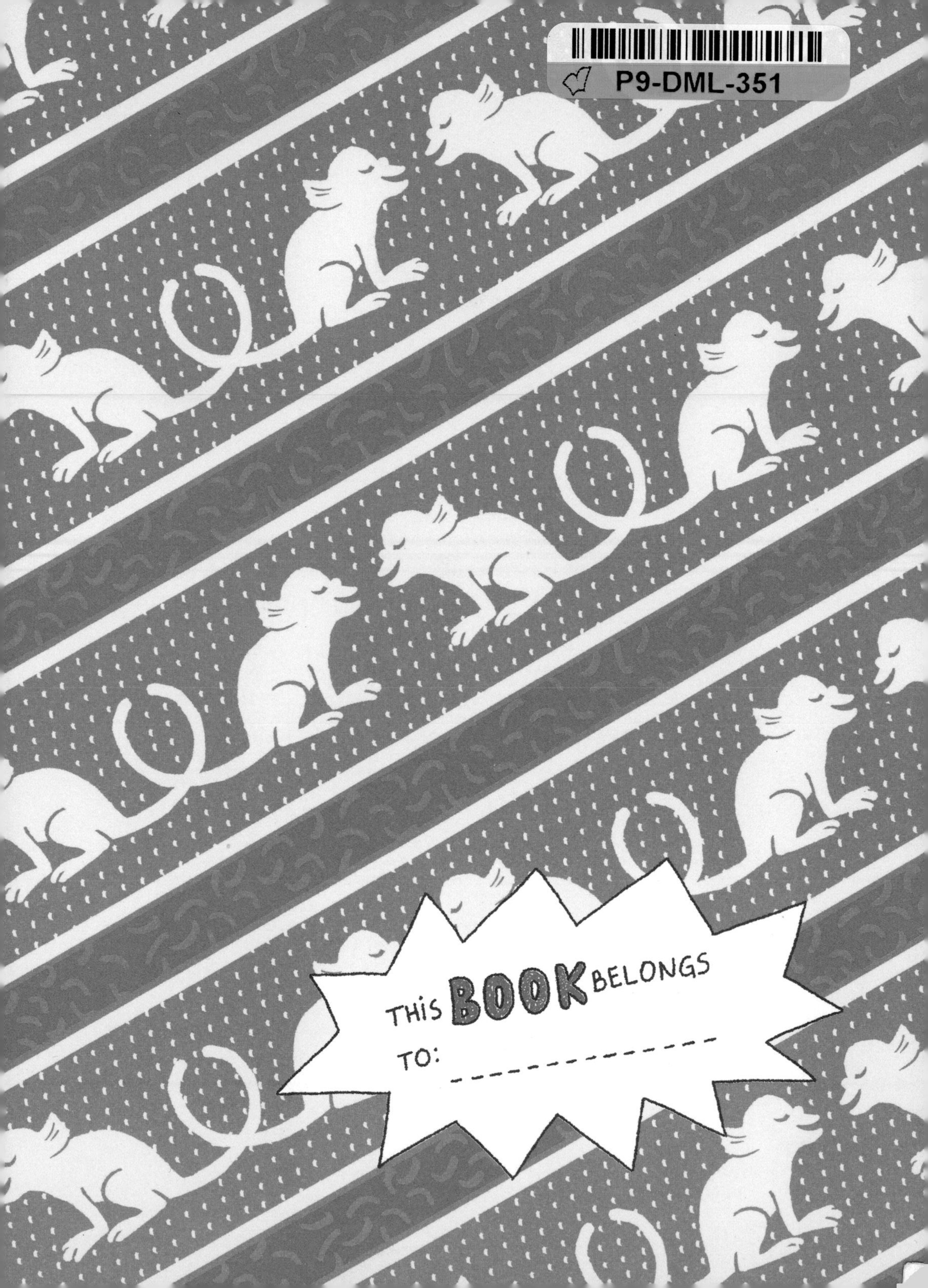
THIS BOOK BELONGS
TO: ______________

First published in English in 2019 by Flying Eye Books,
an imprint of Nobrow Ltd. 27 Westgate Street, London E8 3RL.

Akissi 4: Rentrée Musclée, by Marguerite Abouet and Mathieu Sapin© Gallimard Jeunesse, France, 2013.
Akissi 5: Mixture Magique, by Marguerite Abouet and Mathieu Sapin© Gallimard Jeunesse, France, 2014.
Akissi 6: Sans Amis, by Marguerite Abouet and Mathieu Sapin© Gallimard Jeunesse, France, 2015.

Published in agreement with Éditions Gallimard Jeunesse.

Text by Marguerite Abouet. Illustrations by Mathieu Sapin.

Marguerite Abouet and Mathieu Sapin have asserted their rights under the Copyright,
Designs and Patents Act, 1988, to be identified as the Author and Illustrator of this Work.

Translation by Marie Bédrune.

1 3 5 7 9 10 8 6 4 2

Published in the US by Nobrow (US) Inc.
Printed in Poland on FSC® certified paper.

ISBN: 978-1-912497-17-1
www.flyingeyebooks.com

Abouet & Sapin

Akissi

MORE TALES OF MISCHIEF

FLYING EYE BOOKS

LONDON | NEW YORK

INTRODUCTION

Initially, Akissi was born out of my desire to tell the story of my homeland and the happy memories of being a young Ivorian girl, who would leave her home too soon and head for France without her parents. Akissi was also a product of wanting to show a different view of Africa than the one we are usually shown. An Africa that is full of life, rather than sorrow. The Akissi stories are above all about the need to not focus – like most children's books and animated films do – on the folktales and legends that come from Africa that don't represent the actual day to day lives of modern Africans.

The character of Akissi was just like me when I was young. The whole neighbourhood was my playground and the people that lived in it were my family. With her braids and cute, expressive face, Akissi encourages her friends and all the local children to become urban explorers. She shows that kindness and courage are what is needed for forging friendships and taking on everyday challenges. Akissi treats everyone just the same, without any judgement or prejudice regarding race, religion, ability, gender identity or age.

The stories I tell simply show Africa through the eyes of a child that has grown up there. The characters are positive-minded for the most part. They are full of imperfections at times but always joyful and lively, and children from all across the globe can identify with them.

Come on board and visit a welcoming and fun-filled land and discover an Africa that is so close, and yet so far.

Welcome to my childhood!

Marguerite Abouet

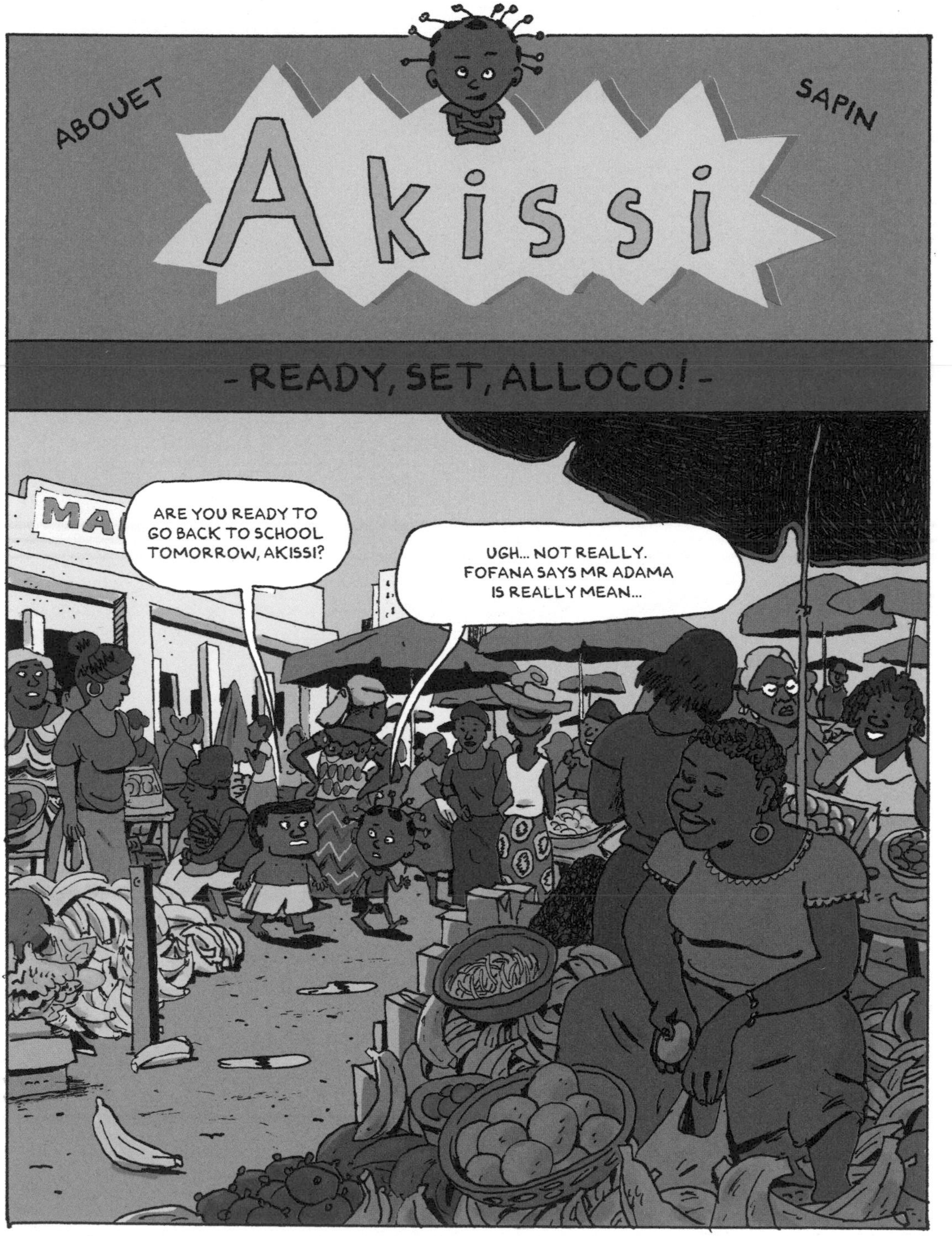
ABOUET
SAPIN
Akissi
- READY, SET, ALLOCO! -
MA
ARE YOU READY TO GO BACK TO SCHOOL TOMORROW, AKISSI?
UGH... NOT REALLY. FOFANA SAYS MR ADAMA IS REALLY MEAN...

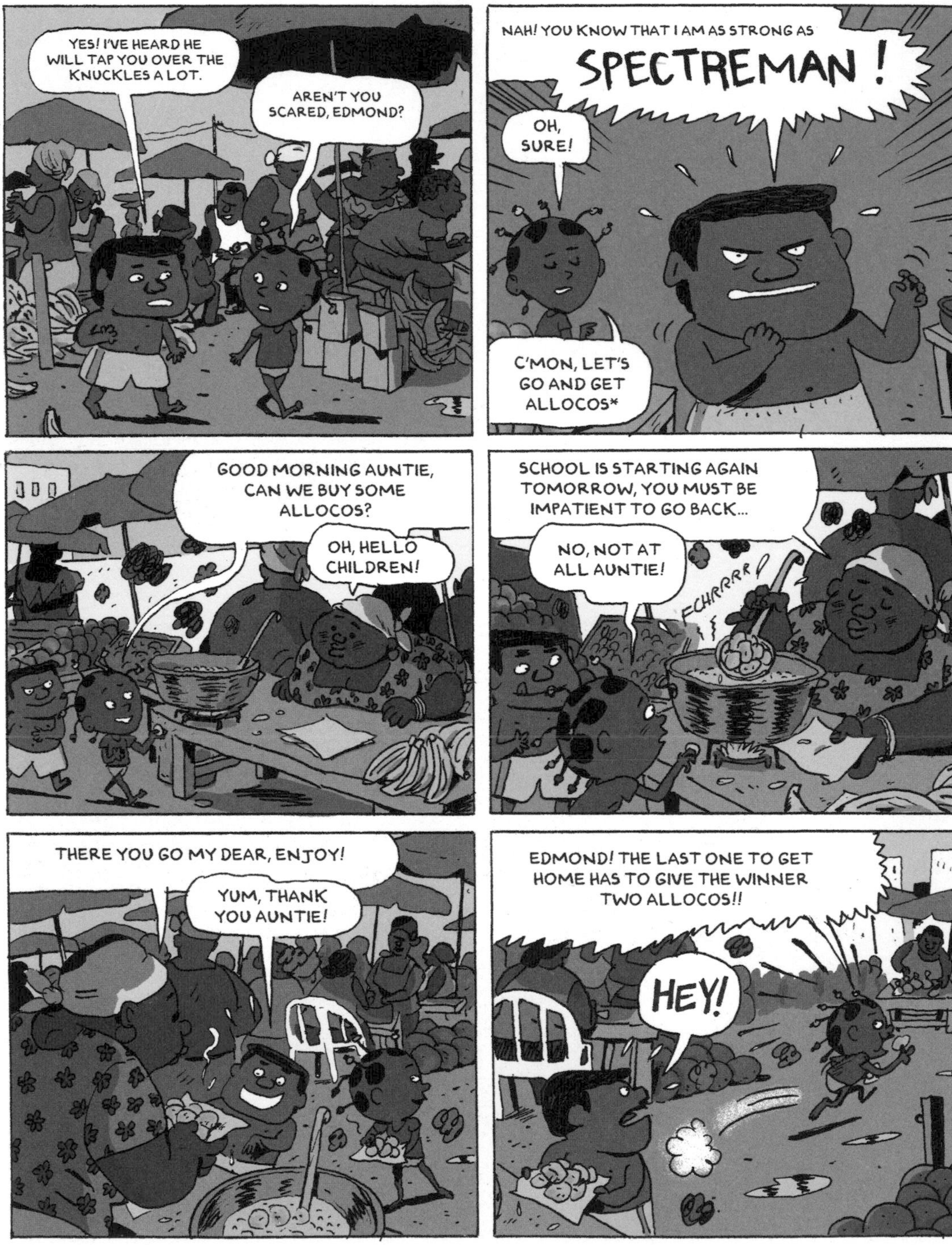
YES! I'VE HEARD HE WILL TAP YOU OVER THE KNUCKLES A LOT.
AREN'T YOU SCARED, EDMOND?
NAH! YOU KNOW THAT I AM AS STRONG AS
SPECTREMAN!
OH, SURE!
C'MON, LET'S GO AND GET ALLOCOS*
GOOD MORNING AUNTIE, CAN WE BUY SOME ALLOCOS?
OH, HELLO CHILDREN!
SCHOOL IS STARTING AGAIN TOMORROW, YOU MUST BE IMPATIENT TO GO BACK...
NO, NOT AT ALL AUNTIE!
FCHRRRR
THERE YOU GO MY DEAR, ENJOY!
YUM, THANK YOU AUNTIE!
EDMOND! THE LAST ONE TO GET HOME HAS TO GIVE THE WINNER TWO ALLOCOS!!
HEY!

*ALLOCOS = FRIED PLANTAINS

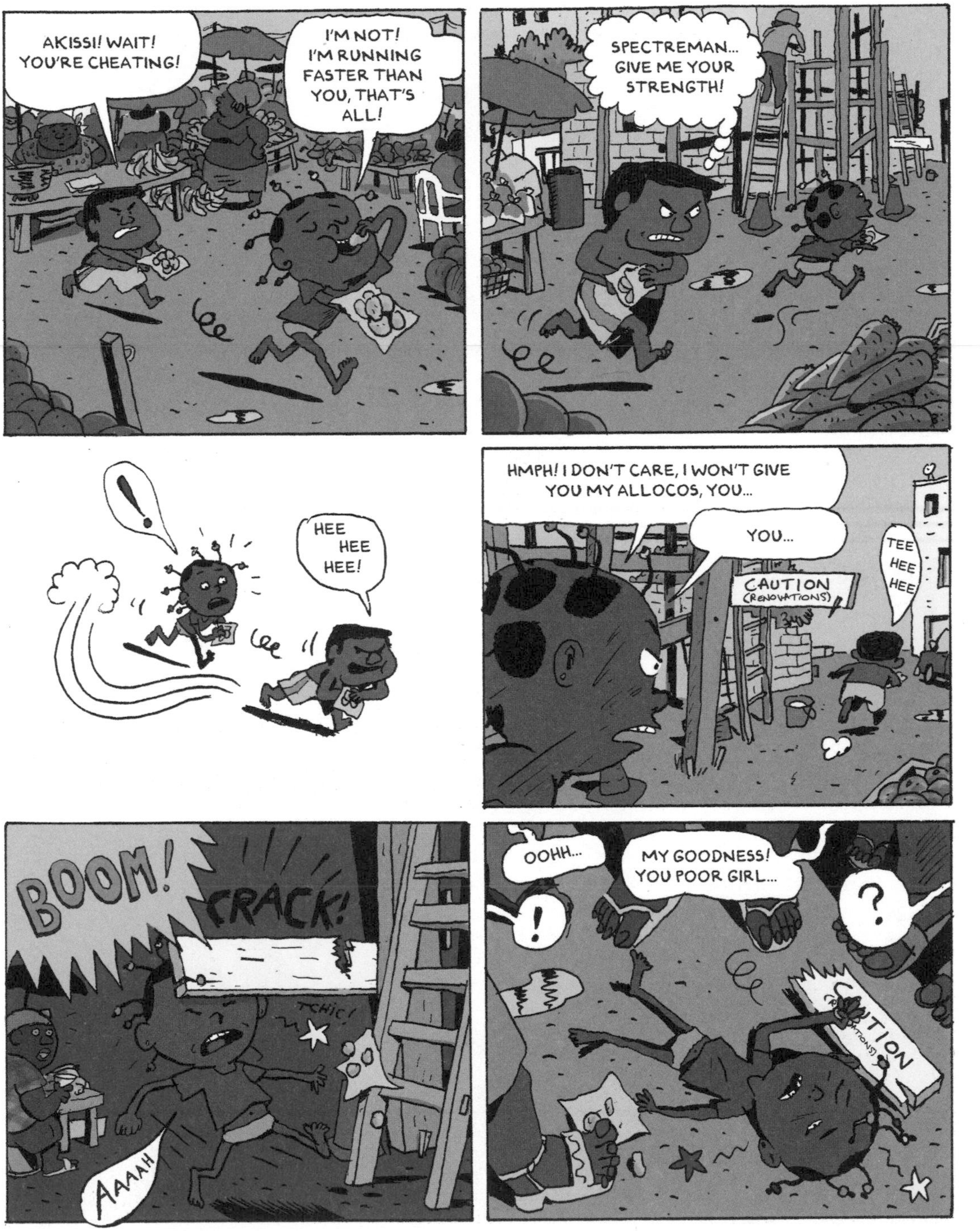
AKISSI! WAIT! YOU'RE CHEATING!
I'M NOT! I'M RUNNING FASTER THAN YOU, THAT'S ALL!
SPECTREMAN... GIVE ME YOUR STRENGTH!
!
HEE HEE HEE!
HMPH! I DON'T CARE, I WON'T GIVE YOU MY ALLOCOS, YOU...
YOU...
TEE HEE HEE
CAUTION (RENOVATIONS)
BOOM!
CRACK!
TCHIC!
AAAAH
OOHH...
MY GOODNESS! YOU POOR GIRL...
!
?
CAUTION (RENOVATIONS)

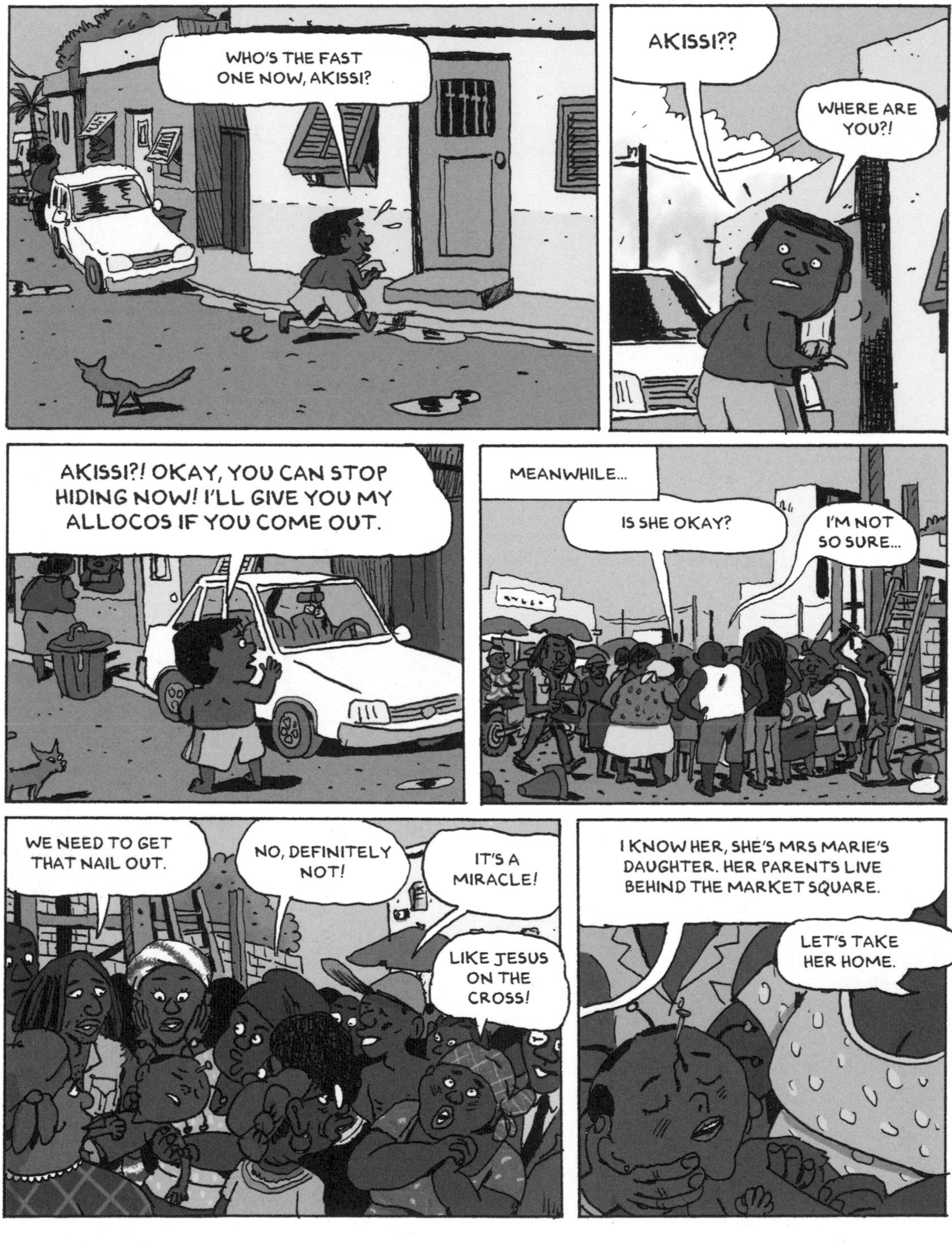
WHO'S THE FAST ONE NOW, AKISSI?
AKISSI??
WHERE ARE YOU?!
AKISSI?! OKAY, YOU CAN STOP HIDING NOW! I'LL GIVE YOU MY ALLOCOS IF YOU COME OUT.
MEANWHILE...
IS SHE OKAY?
I'M NOT SO SURE...
WE NEED TO GET THAT NAIL OUT.
NO, DEFINITELY NOT!
IT'S A MIRACLE!
LIKE JESUS ON THE CROSS!
I KNOW HER, SHE'S MRS MARIE'S DAUGHTER. HER PARENTS LIVE BEHIND THE MARKET SQUARE.
LET'S TAKE HER HOME.

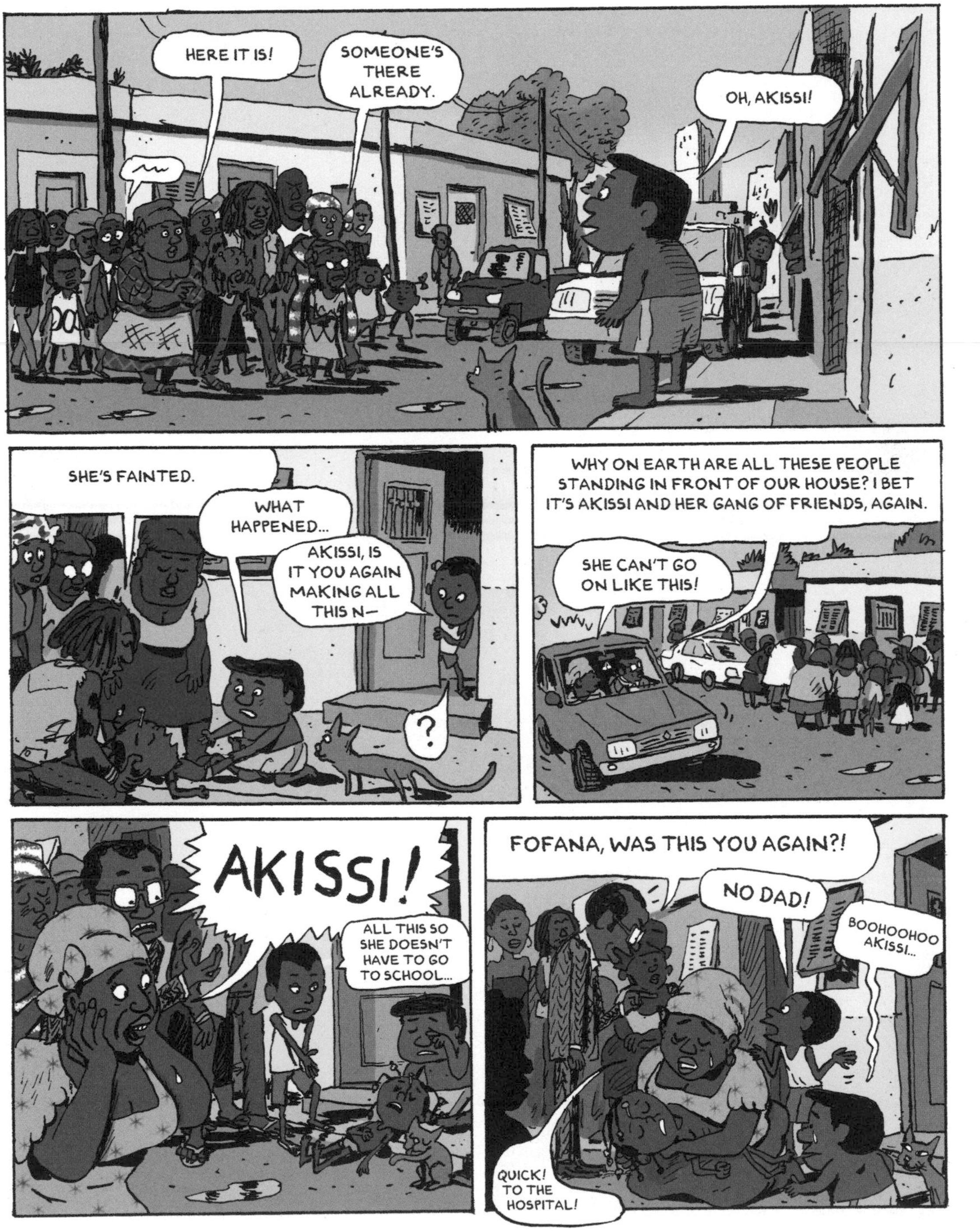
HERE IT IS!
SOMEONE'S THERE ALREADY.
OH, AKISSI!
SHE'S FAINTED.
WHAT HAPPENED...
AKISSI, IS IT YOU AGAIN MAKING ALL THIS N—
?
WHY ON EARTH ARE ALL THESE PEOPLE STANDING IN FRONT OF OUR HOUSE? I BET IT'S AKISSI AND HER GANG OF FRIENDS, AGAIN.
SHE CAN'T GO ON LIKE THIS!
AKISSI!
ALL THIS SO SHE DOESN'T HAVE TO GO TO SCHOOL...
FOFANA, WAS THIS YOU AGAIN?!
NO DAD!
BOOHOOHOO AKISSI...
QUICK! TO THE HOSPITAL!

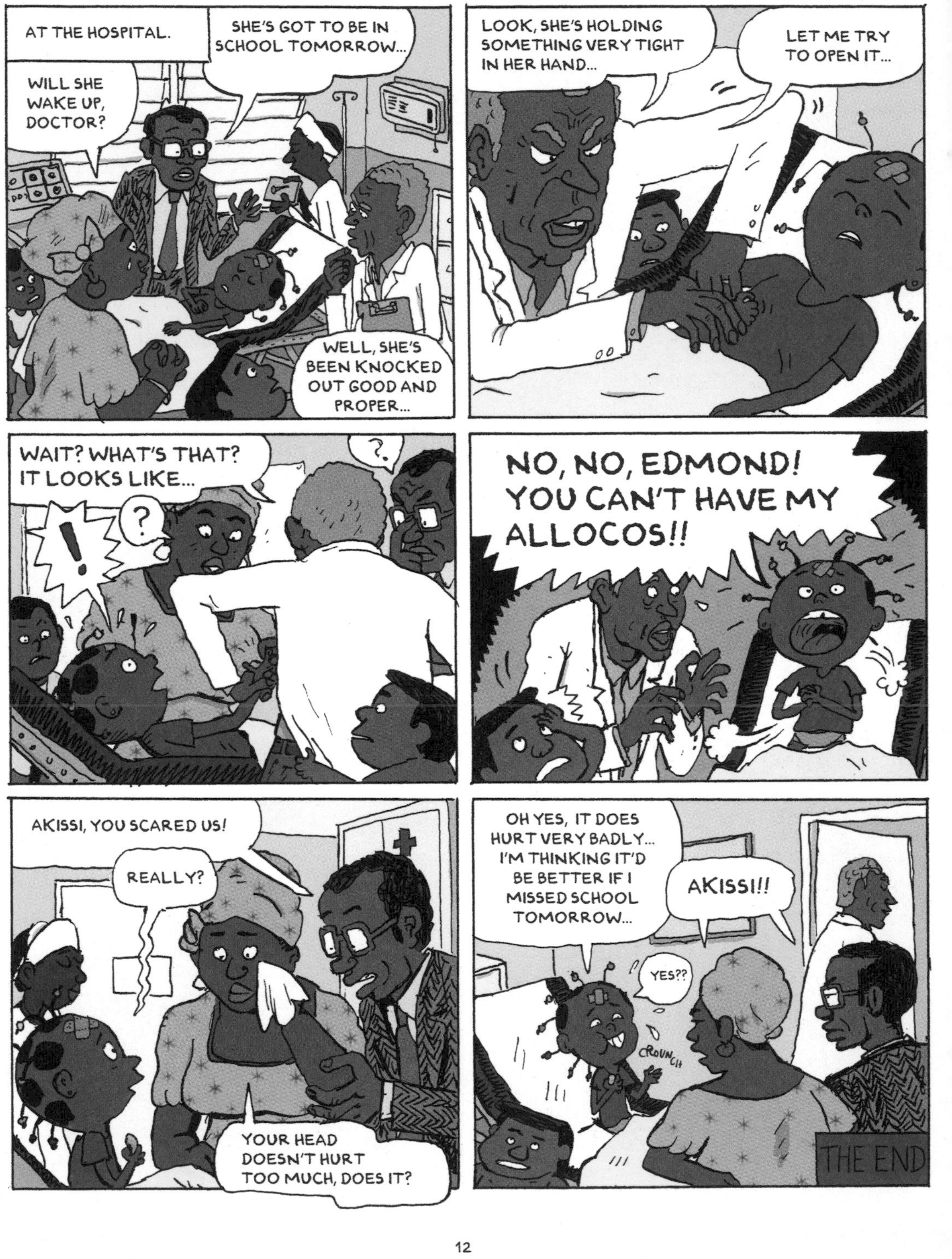
AT THE HOSPITAL.
SHE'S GOT TO BE IN SCHOOL TOMORROW...
WILL SHE WAKE UP, DOCTOR?
WELL, SHE'S BEEN KNOCKED OUT GOOD AND PROPER...
LOOK, SHE'S HOLDING SOMETHING VERY TIGHT IN HER HAND...
LET ME TRY TO OPEN IT...
WAIT? WHAT'S THAT? IT LOOKS LIKE...
?
!
?
NO, NO, EDMOND! YOU CAN'T HAVE MY ALLOCOS!!
AKISSI, YOU SCARED US!
REALLY?
YOUR HEAD DOESN'T HURT TOO MUCH, DOES IT?
OH YES, IT DOES HURT VERY BADLY... I'M THINKING IT'D BE BETTER IF I MISSED SCHOOL TOMORROW...
AKISSI!!
YES??
CROUNCH
THE END

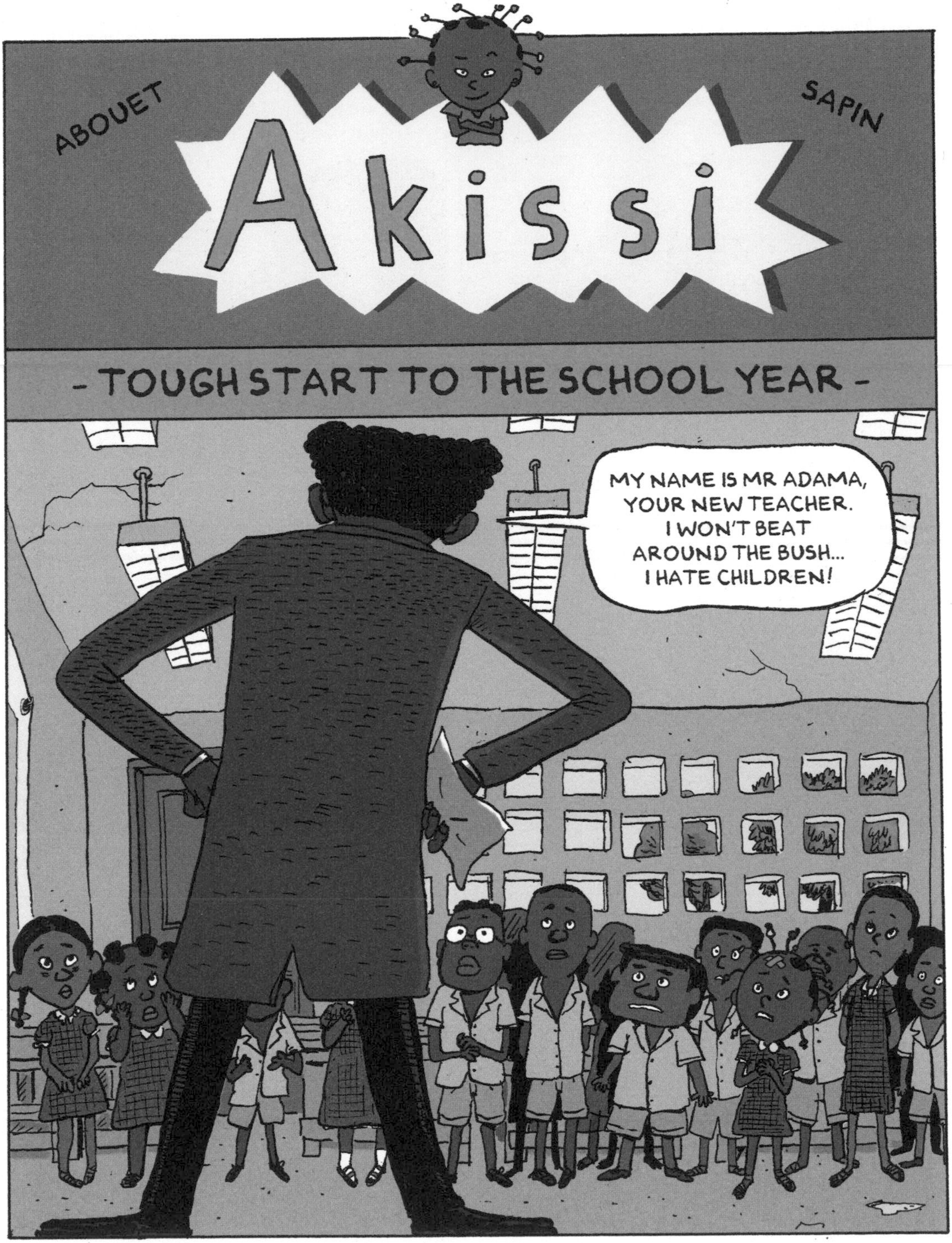
ABOUET
SAPIN
Akissi
- TOUGH START TO THE SCHOOL YEAR -
MY NAME IS MR ADAMA, YOUR NEW TEACHER. I WON'T BEAT AROUND THE BUSH... I HATE CHILDREN!

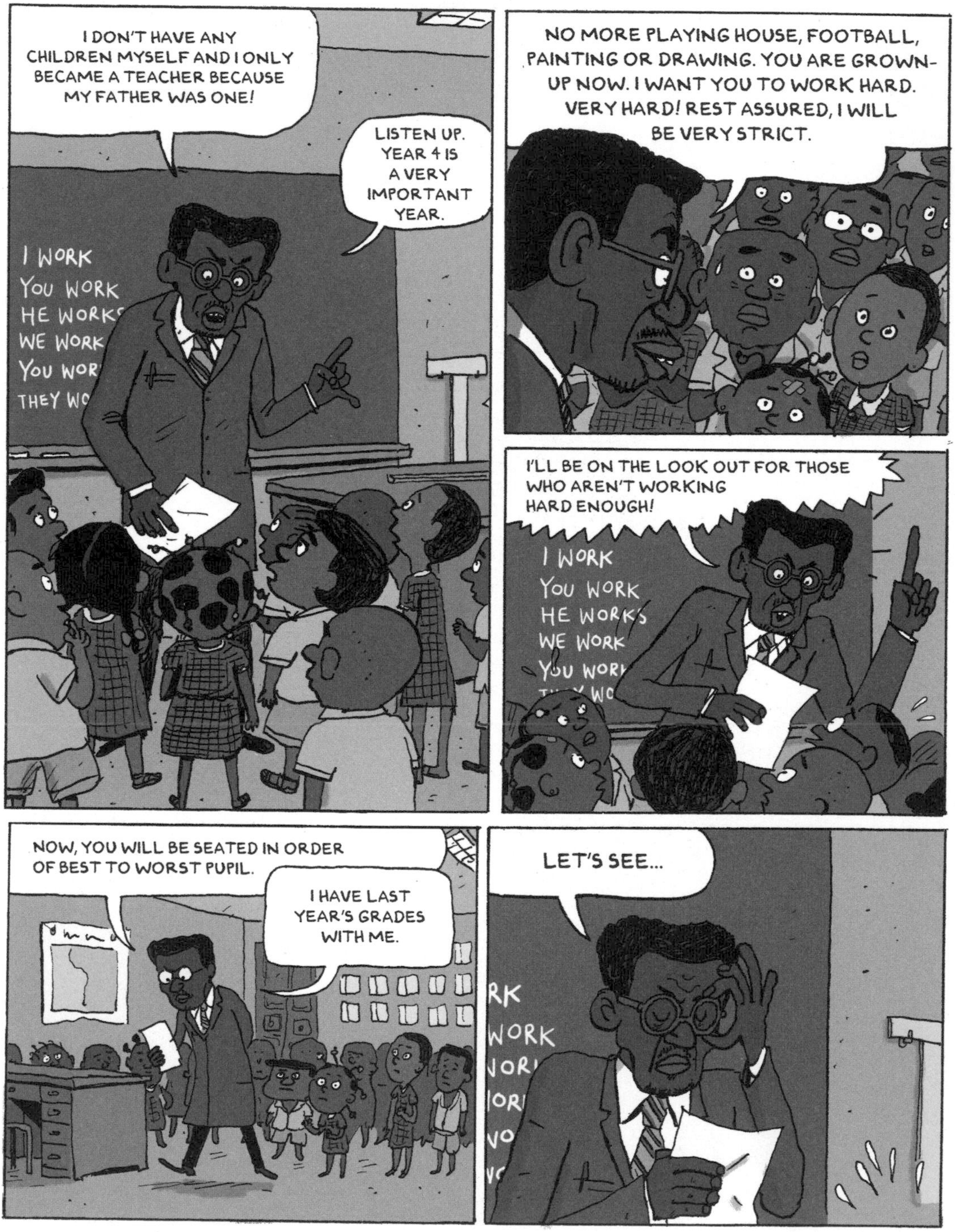
I DON'T HAVE ANY CHILDREN MYSELF AND I ONLY BECAME A TEACHER BECAUSE MY FATHER WAS ONE!
LISTEN UP. YEAR 4 IS A VERY IMPORTANT YEAR.
I WORK
YOU WORK
HE WORKS
WE WORK
NO MORE PLAYING HOUSE, FOOTBALL, PAINTING OR DRAWING. YOU ARE GROWN-UP NOW. I WANT YOU TO WORK HARD. VERY HARD! REST ASSURED, I WILL BE VERY STRICT.
I'LL BE ON THE LOOK OUT FOR THOSE WHO AREN'T WORKING HARD ENOUGH!
I WORK
YOU WORK
HE WORKS
WE WORK
NOW, YOU WILL BE SEATED IN ORDER OF BEST TO WORST PUPIL.
I HAVE LAST YEAR'S GRADES WITH ME.
LET'S SEE...

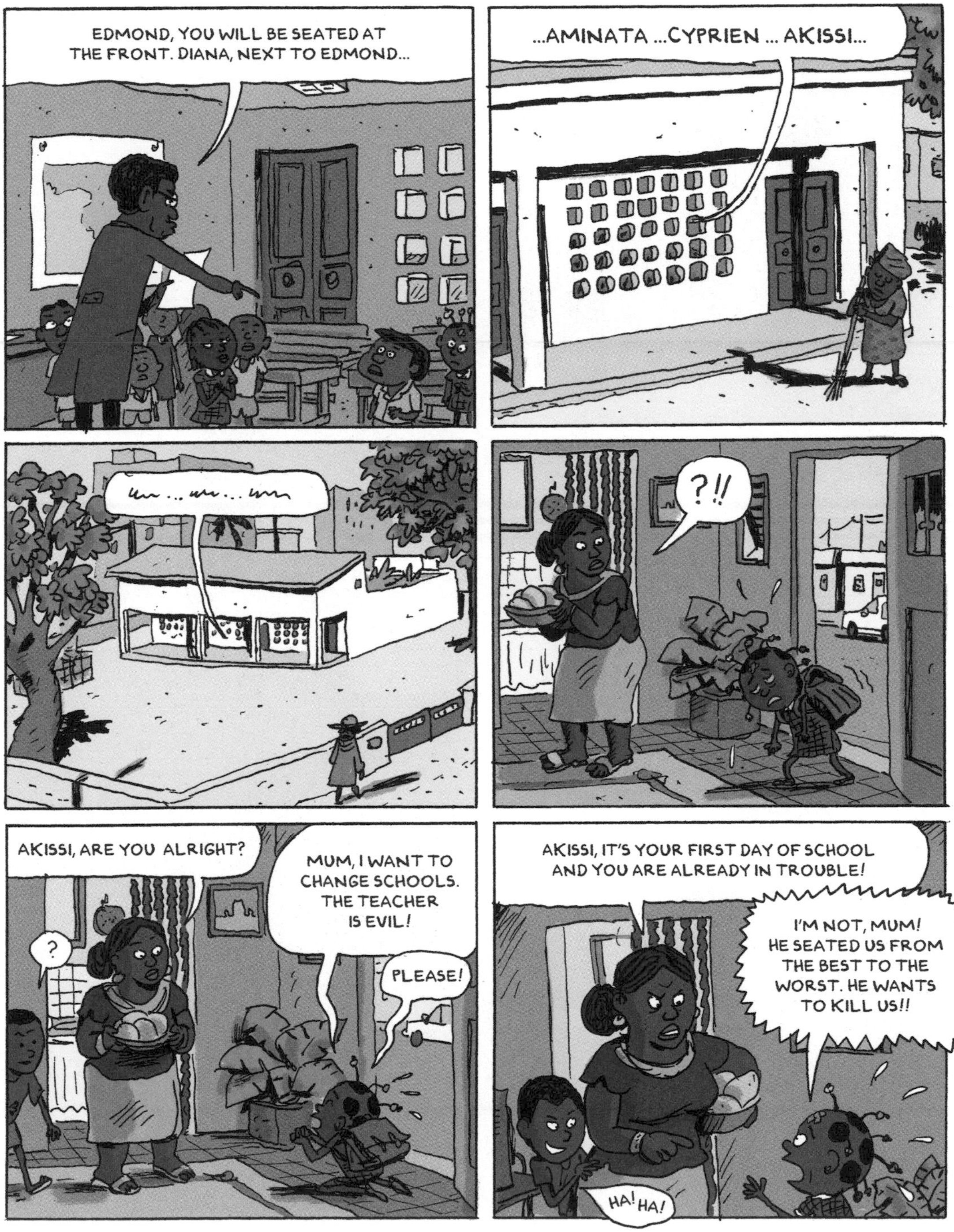
EDMOND, YOU WILL BE SEATED AT THE FRONT. DIANA, NEXT TO EDMOND...
...AMINATA ...CYPRIEN ... AKISSI...
?!!
AKISSI, ARE YOU ALRIGHT?
?
MUM, I WANT TO CHANGE SCHOOLS. THE TEACHER IS EVIL!
PLEASE!
AKISSI, IT'S YOUR FIRST DAY OF SCHOOL AND YOU ARE ALREADY IN TROUBLE!
I'M NOT, MUM! HE SEATED US FROM THE BEST TO THE WORST. HE WANTS TO KILL US!!
HA! HA!

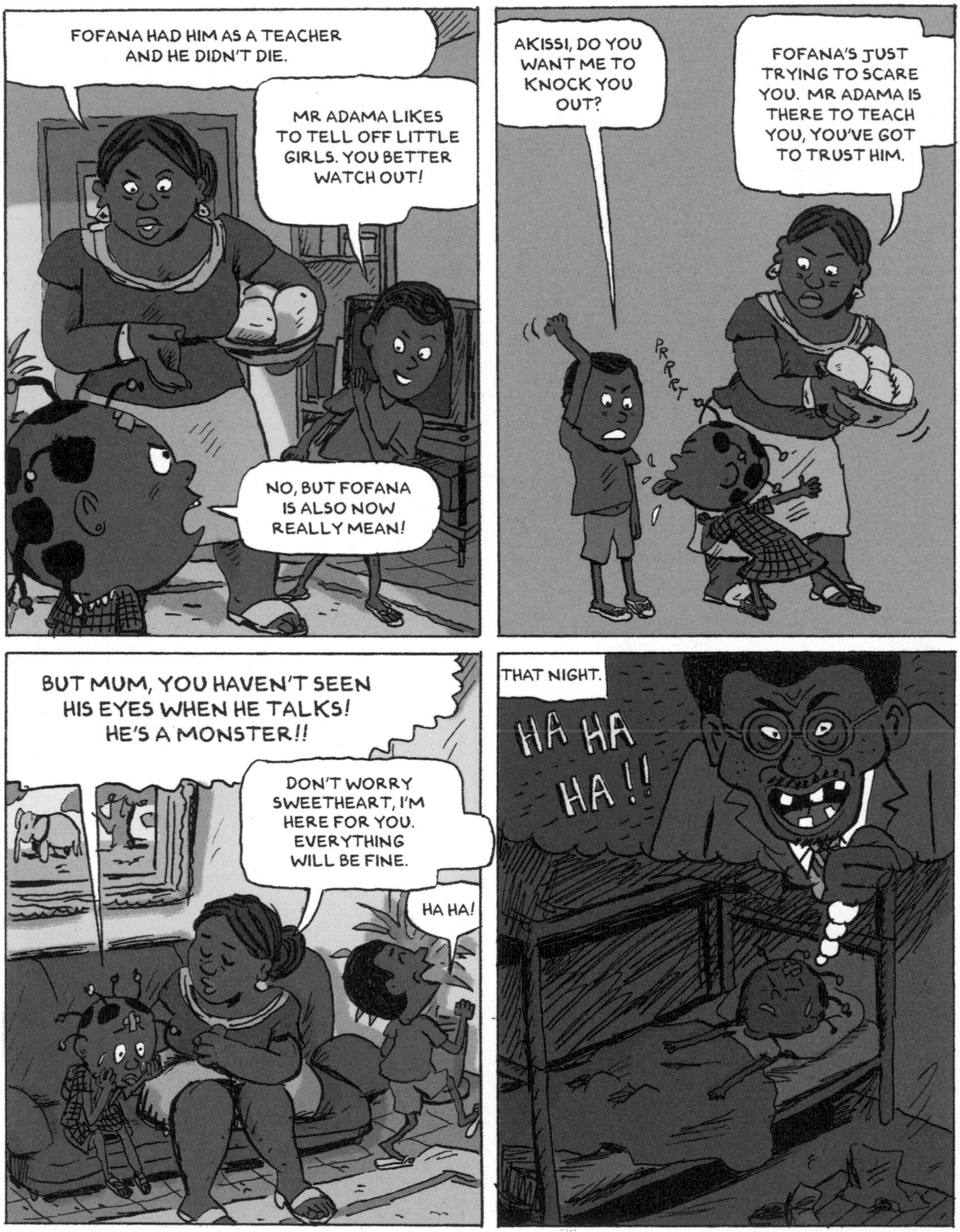
FOFANA HAD HIM AS A TEACHER AND HE DIDN'T DIE.
MR ADAMA LIKES TO TELL OFF LITTLE GIRLS. YOU BETTER WATCH OUT!
NO, BUT FOFANA IS ALSO NOW REALLY MEAN!
AKISSI, DO YOU WANT ME TO KNOCK YOU OUT?
PRRRT
FOFANA'S JUST TRYING TO SCARE YOU. MR ADAMA IS THERE TO TEACH YOU, YOU'VE GOT TO TRUST HIM.
BUT MUM, YOU HAVEN'T SEEN HIS EYES WHEN HE TALKS! HE'S A MONSTER!!
DON'T WORRY SWEETHEART, I'M HERE FOR YOU. EVERYTHING WILL BE FINE.
HA HA!
THAT NIGHT.
HA HA HA!!

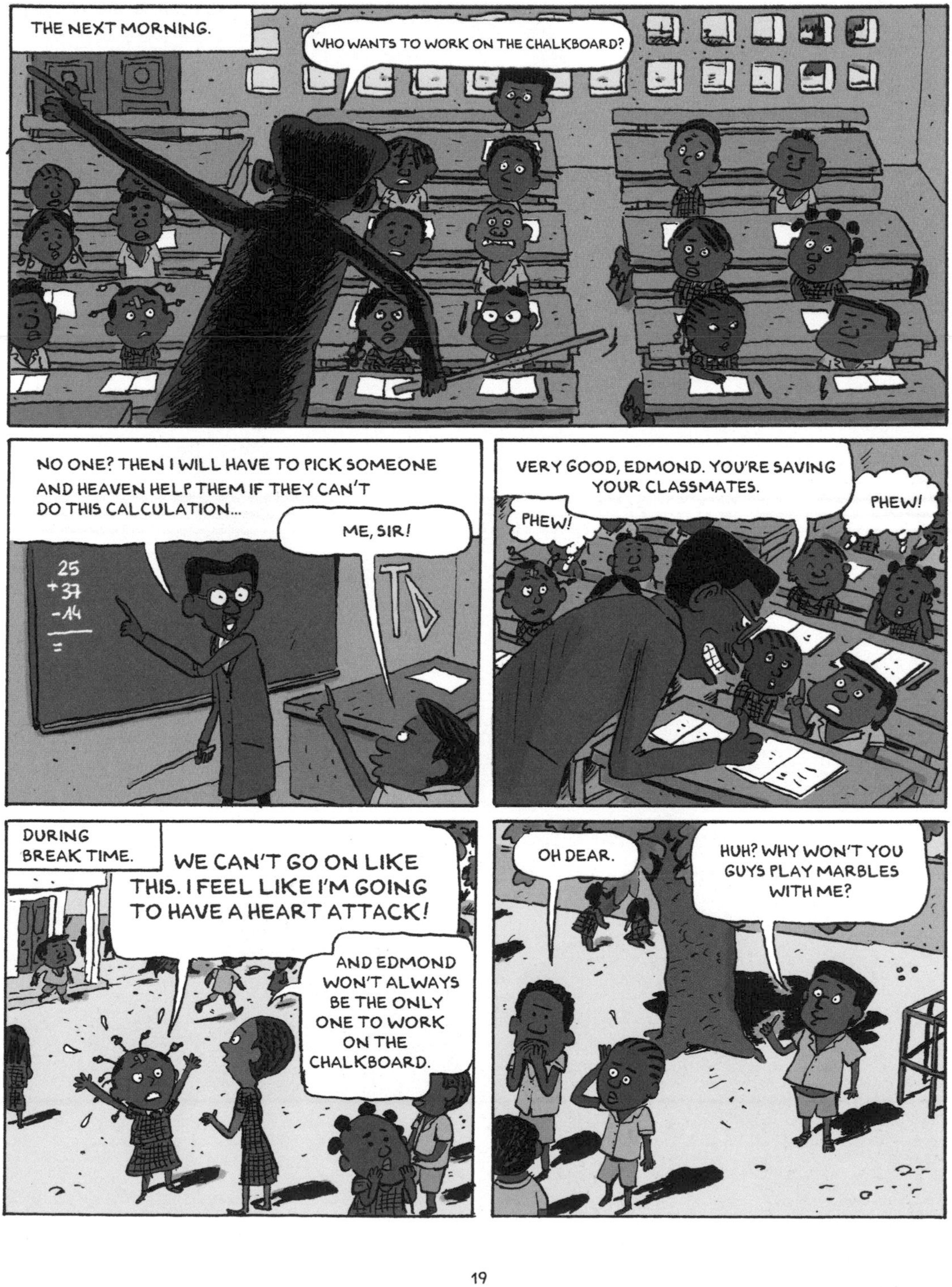
THE NEXT MORNING.
WHO WANTS TO WORK ON THE CHALKBOARD?
NO ONE? THEN I WILL HAVE TO PICK SOMEONE AND HEAVEN HELP THEM IF THEY CAN'T DO THIS CALCULATION...
ME, SIR!
25
+37
-14
=
VERY GOOD, EDMOND. YOU'RE SAVING YOUR CLASSMATES.
PHEW!
PHEW!
DURING BREAK TIME.
WE CAN'T GO ON LIKE THIS. I FEEL LIKE I'M GOING TO HAVE A HEART ATTACK!
AND EDMOND WON'T ALWAYS BE THE ONLY ONE TO WORK ON THE CHALKBOARD.
OH DEAR.
HUH? WHY WON'T YOU GUYS PLAY MARBLES WITH ME?

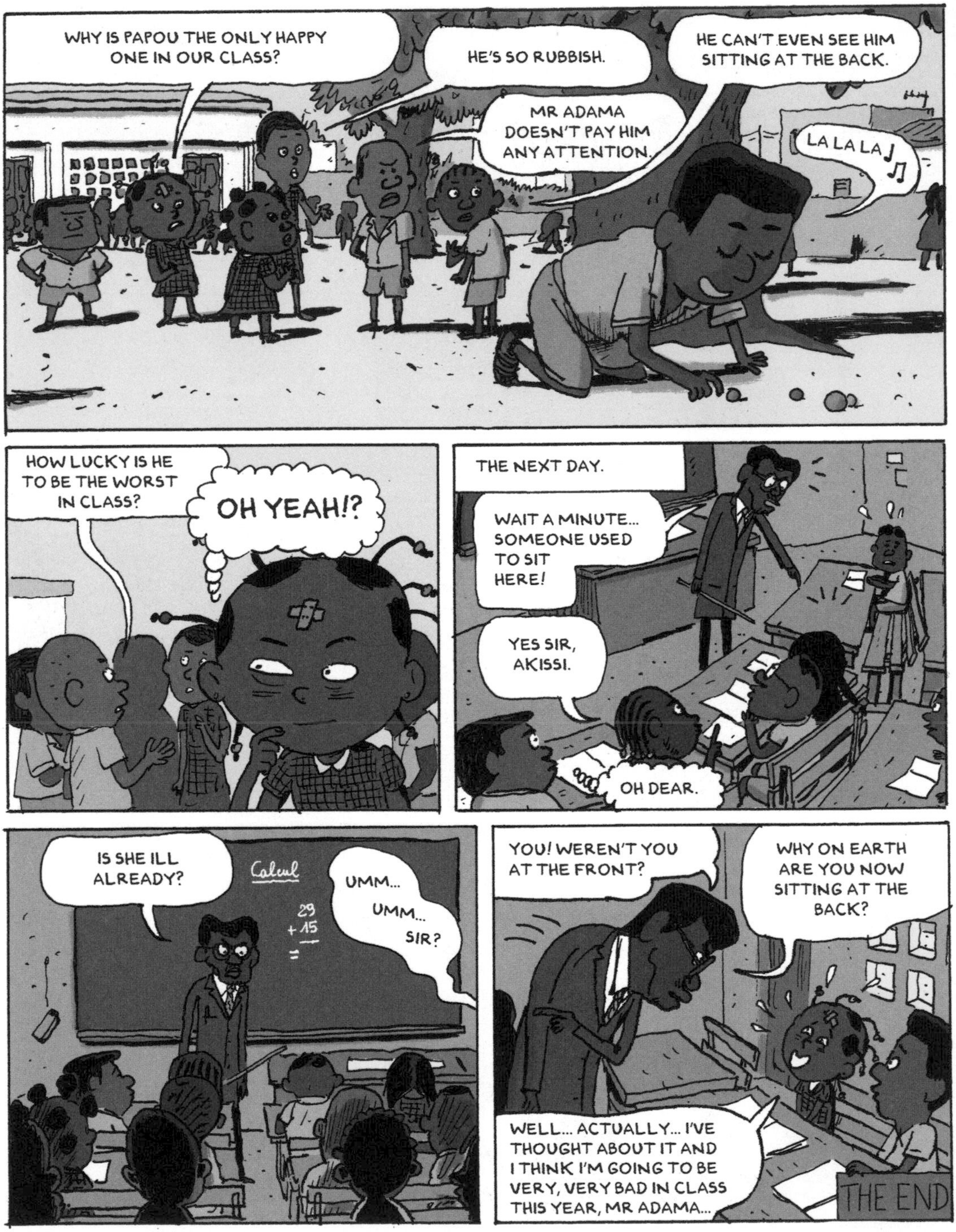
WHY IS PAPOU THE ONLY HAPPY ONE IN OUR CLASS?
HE'S SO RUBBISH.
MR ADAMA DOESN'T PAY HIM ANY ATTENTION.
HE CAN'T EVEN SEE HIM SITTING AT THE BACK.
LA LA LA
HOW LUCKY IS HE TO BE THE WORST IN CLASS?
OH YEAH!?
THE NEXT DAY.
WAIT A MINUTE... SOMEONE USED TO SIT HERE!
YES SIR, AKISSI.
OH DEAR.
IS SHE ILL ALREADY?
Calcul
29
+ 15
=
UMM...
UMM...
SIR?
YOU! WEREN'T YOU AT THE FRONT?
WHY ON EARTH ARE YOU NOW SITTING AT THE BACK?
WELL... ACTUALLY... I'VE THOUGHT ABOUT IT AND I THINK I'M GOING TO BE VERY, VERY BAD IN CLASS THIS YEAR, MR ADAMA...
THE END

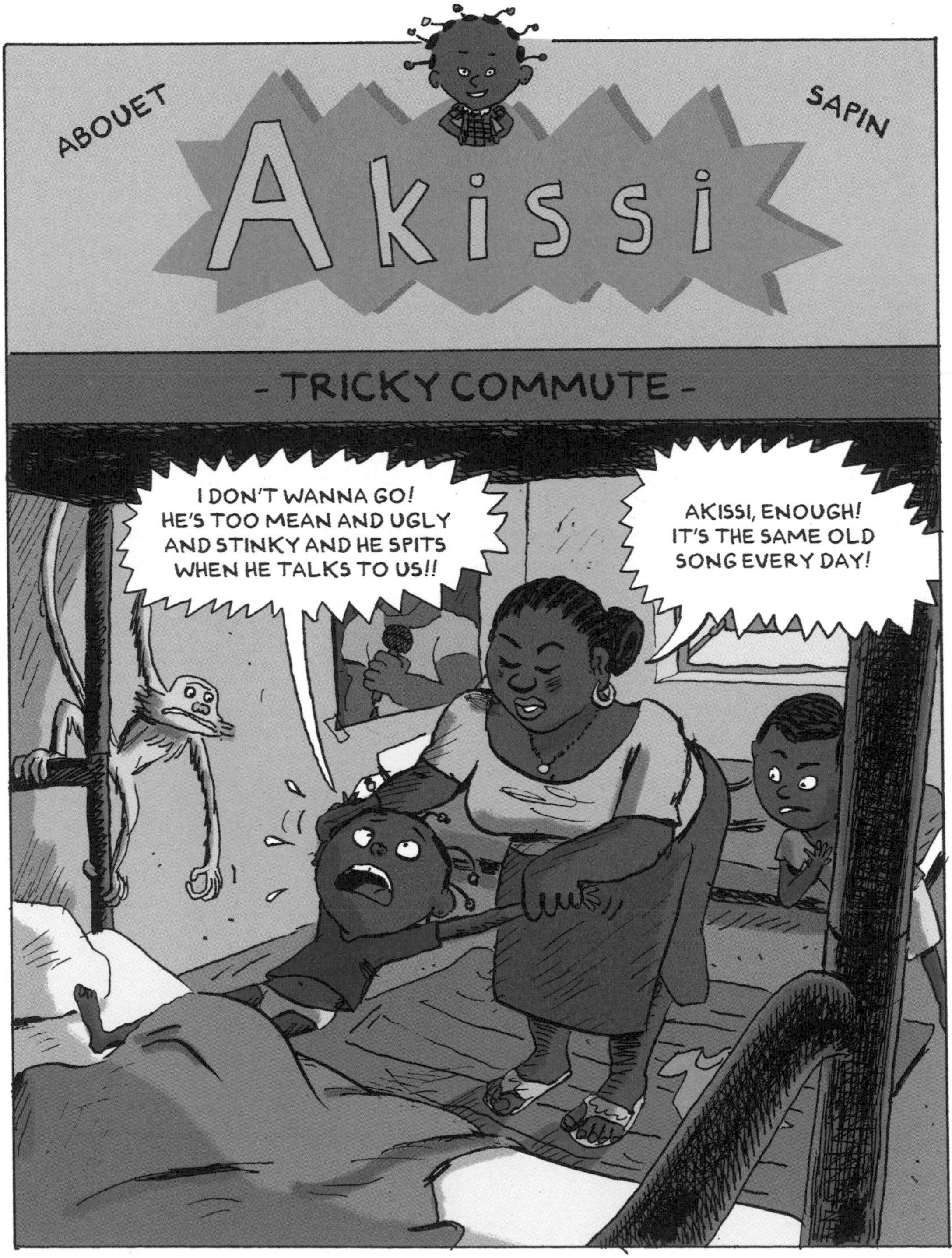
ABOUET
SAPIN
Akissi
- TRICKY COMMUTE -
I DON'T WANNA GO! HE'S TOO MEAN AND UGLY AND STINKY AND HE SPITS WHEN HE TALKS TO US!!
AKISSI, ENOUGH! IT'S THE SAME OLD SONG EVERY DAY!

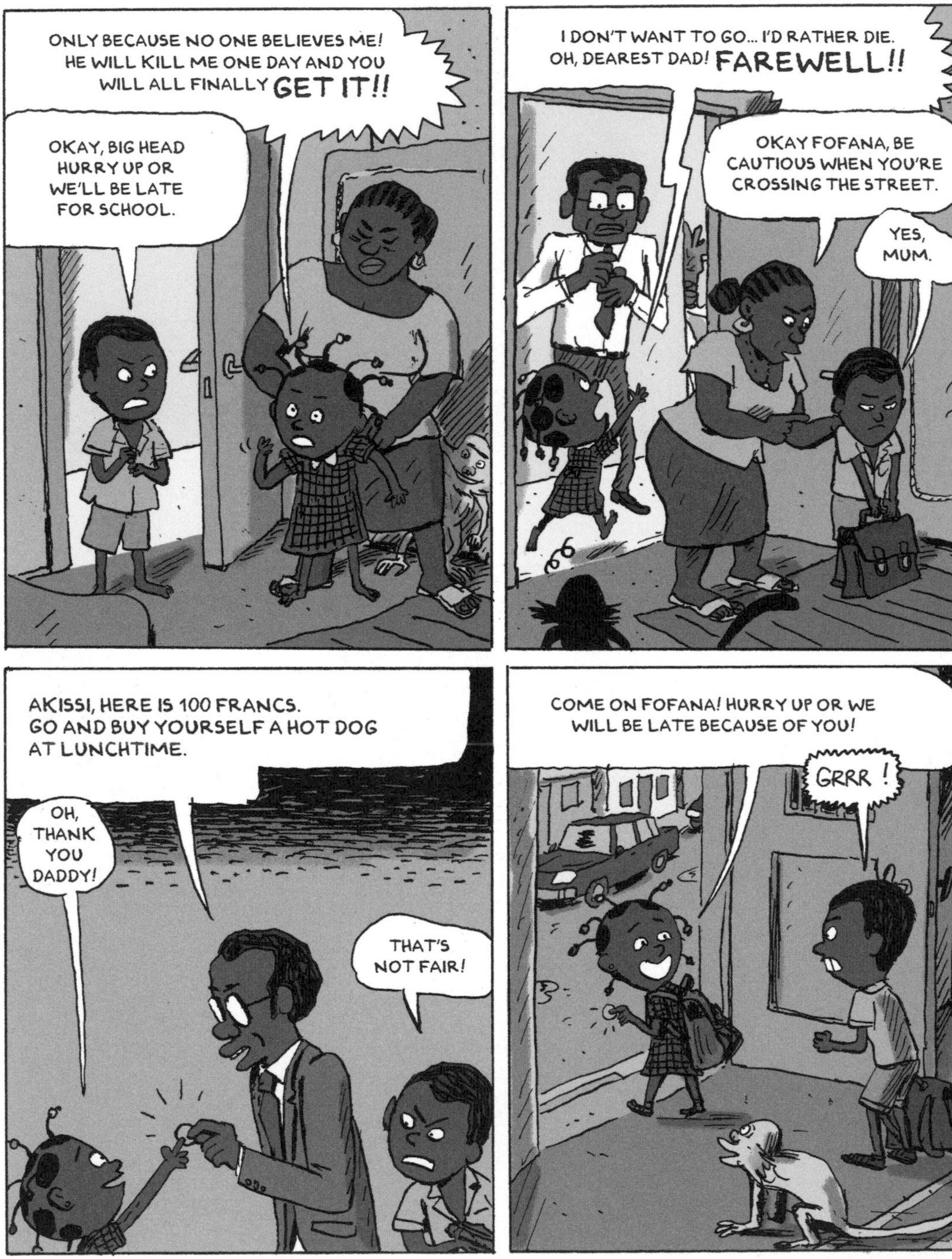
ONLY BECAUSE NO ONE BELIEVES ME! HE WILL KILL ME ONE DAY AND YOU WILL ALL FINALLY GET IT!!
OKAY, BIG HEAD HURRY UP OR WE'LL BE LATE FOR SCHOOL.
I DON'T WANT TO GO... I'D RATHER DIE. OH, DEAREST DAD! FAREWELL!!
OKAY FOFANA, BE CAUTIOUS WHEN YOU'RE CROSSING THE STREET.
YES, MUM.
AKISSI, HERE IS 100 FRANCS. GO AND BUY YOURSELF A HOT DOG AT LUNCHTIME.
OH, THANK YOU DADDY!
THAT'S NOT FAIR!
COME ON FOFANA! HURRY UP OR WE WILL BE LATE BECAUSE OF YOU!
GRRR !

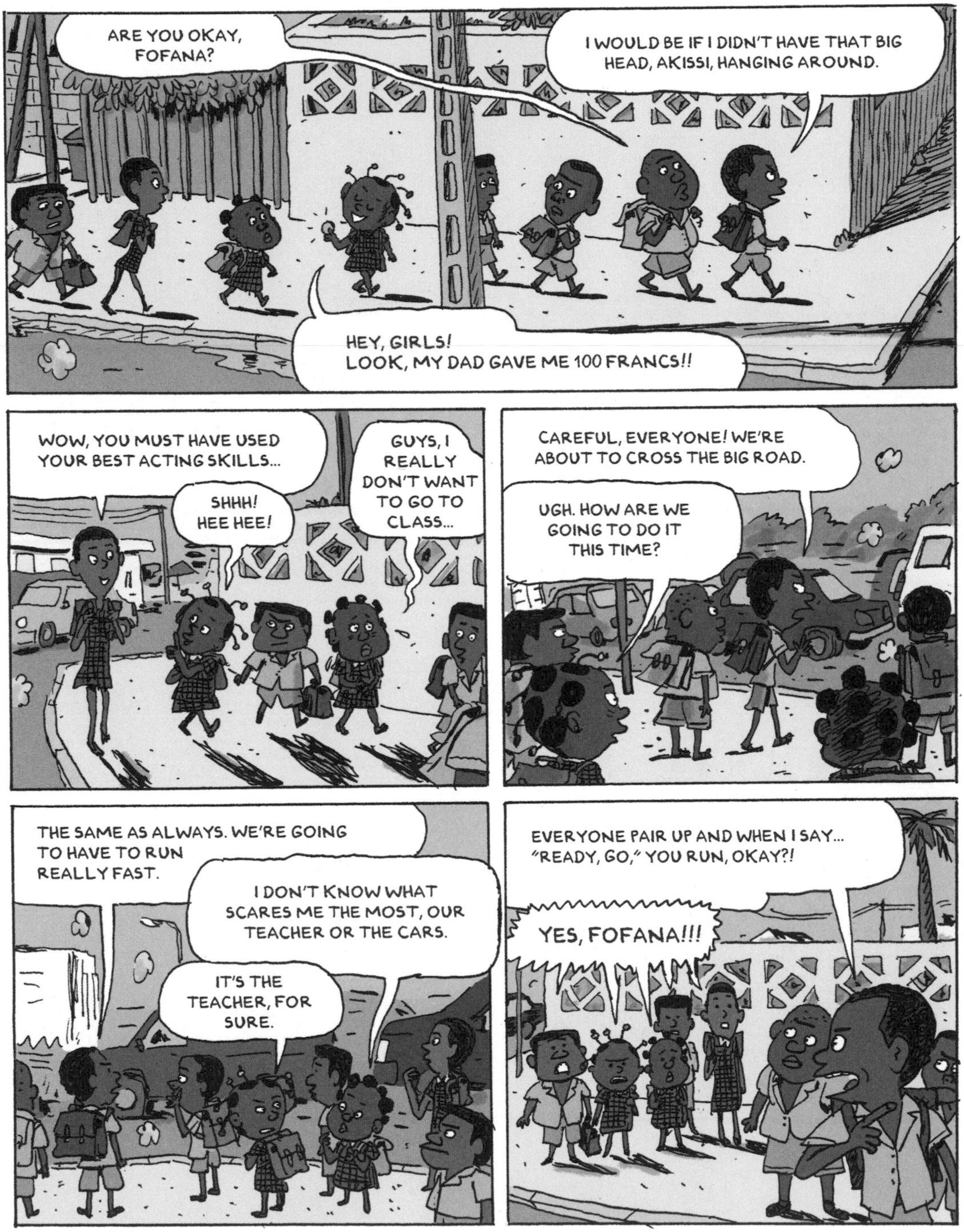
ARE YOU OKAY, FOFANA?
I WOULD BE IF I DIDN'T HAVE THAT BIG HEAD, AKISSI, HANGING AROUND.
HEY, GIRLS! LOOK, MY DAD GAVE ME 100 FRANCS!!
WOW, YOU MUST HAVE USED YOUR BEST ACTING SKILLS...
SHHH! HEE HEE!
GUYS, I REALLY DON'T WANT TO GO TO CLASS...
CAREFUL, EVERYONE! WE'RE ABOUT TO CROSS THE BIG ROAD.
UGH. HOW ARE WE GOING TO DO IT THIS TIME?
THE SAME AS ALWAYS. WE'RE GOING TO HAVE TO RUN REALLY FAST.
I DON'T KNOW WHAT SCARES ME THE MOST, OUR TEACHER OR THE CARS.
IT'S THE TEACHER, FOR SURE.
EVERYONE PAIR UP AND WHEN I SAY... "READY, GO," YOU RUN, OKAY?!
YES, FOFANA!!!

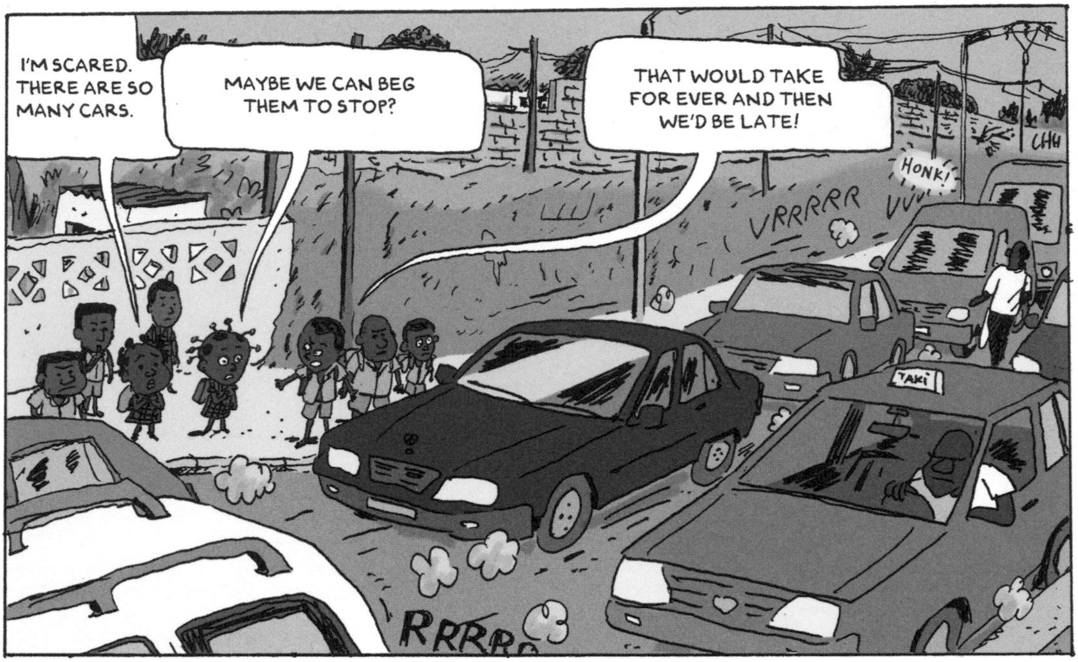
I'M SCARED. THERE ARE SO MANY CARS.
MAYBE WE CAN BEG THEM TO STOP?
THAT WOULD TAKE FOR EVER AND THEN WE'D BE LATE!
HONK!
VRRRRR
VVV
TAXI
RRRRR

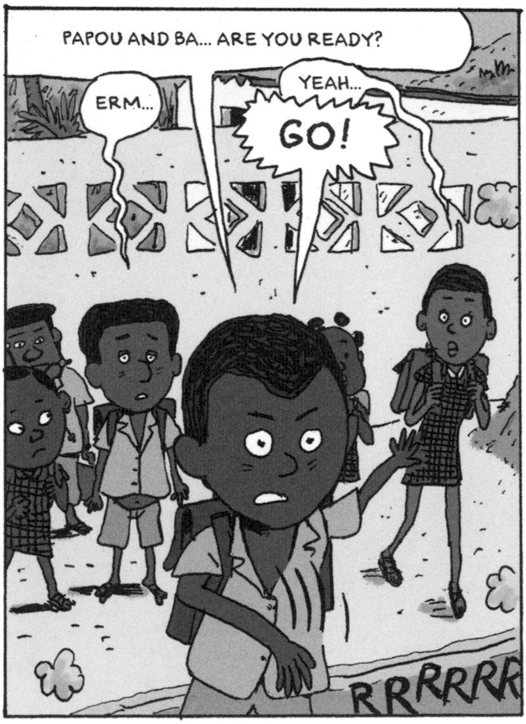
PAPOU AND BA... ARE YOU READY?
ERM...
YEAH...
GO!
RRRRRR

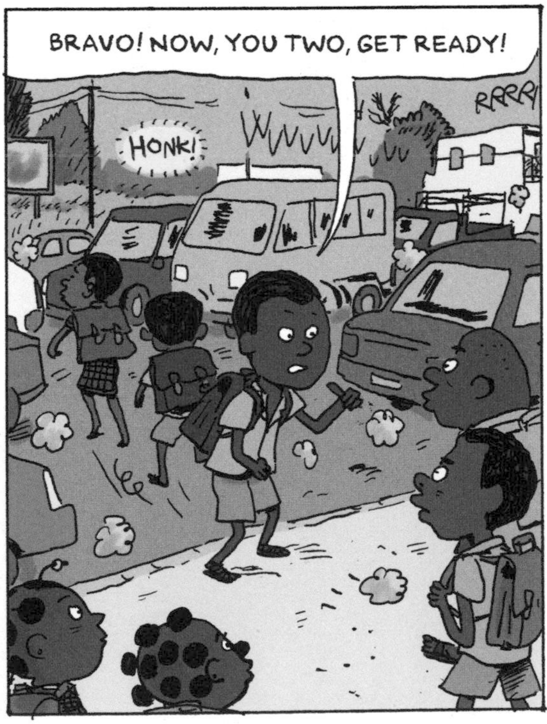
BRAVO! NOW, YOU TWO, GET READY!
HONK!
RRRR
WVVVV

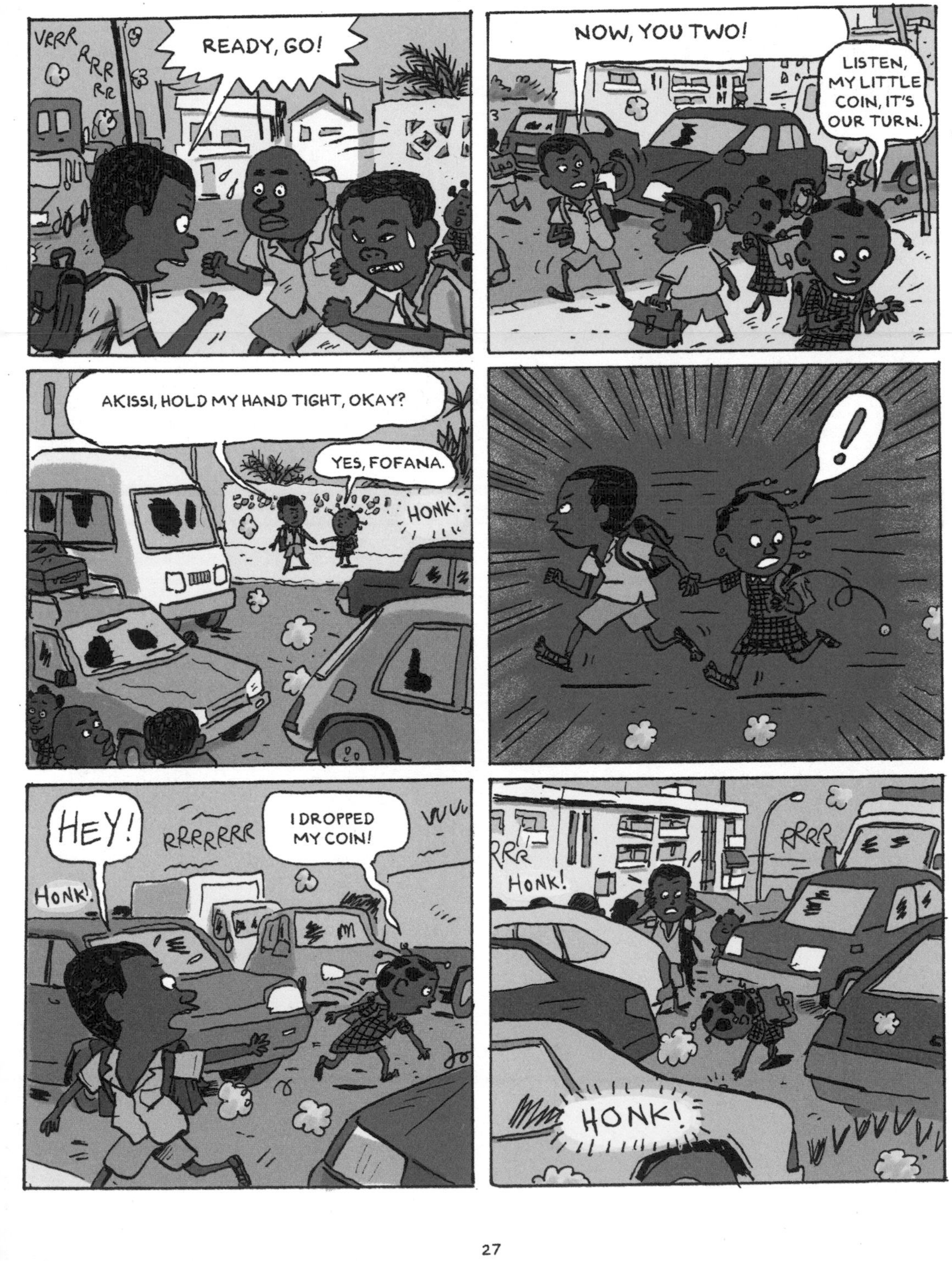
VRRR
RRR
RR
READY, GO!
NOW, YOU TWO!
LISTEN, MY LITTLE COIN, IT'S OUR TURN.
AKISSI, HOLD MY HAND TIGHT, OKAY?
YES, FOFANA.
HONK!
!
HEY!
RRRRRRR
I DROPPED MY COIN!
HONK!
RRRR
RRR
HONK!
HONK!

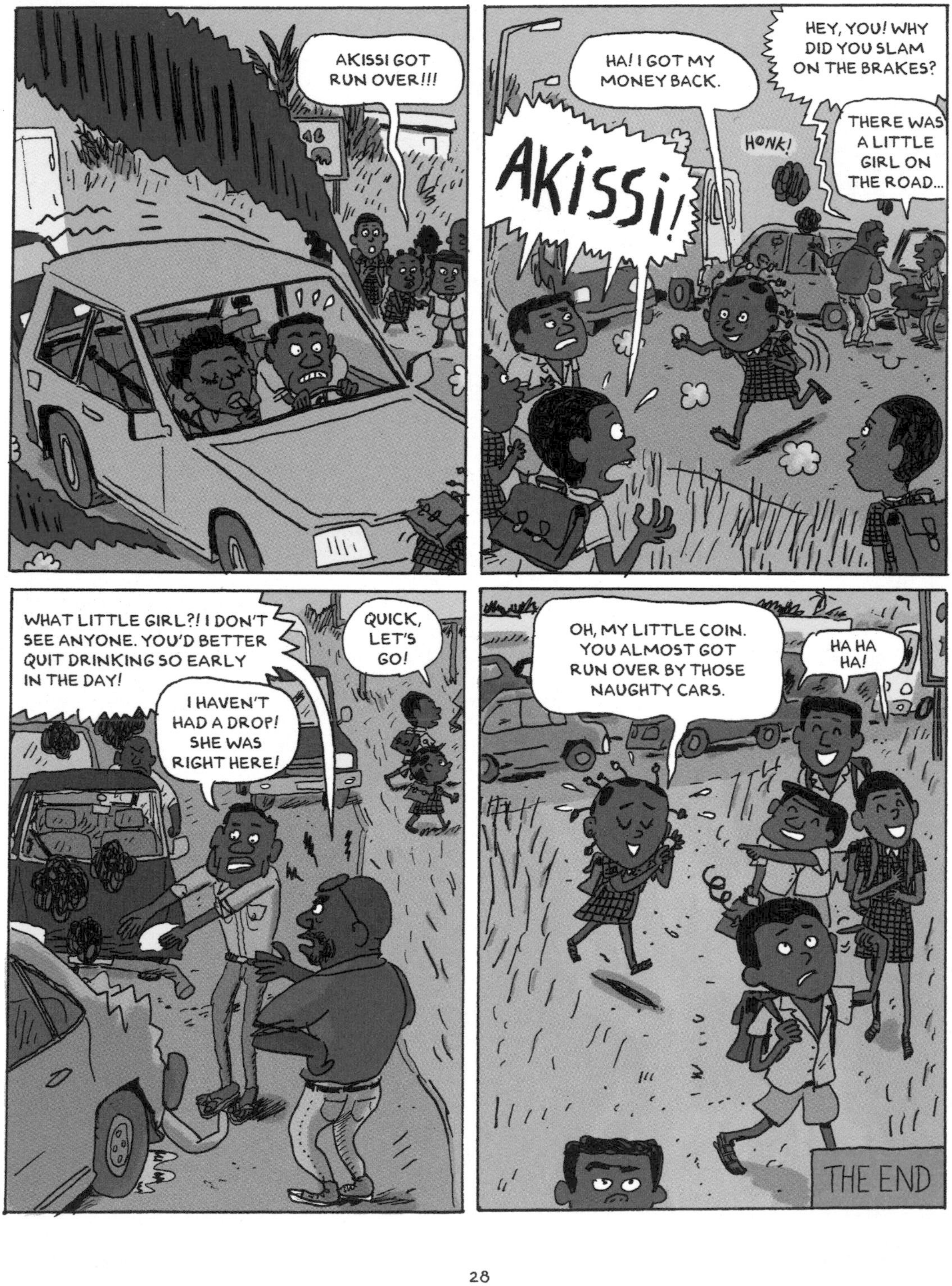
AKISSI GOT RUN OVER!!!
HA! I GOT MY MONEY BACK.
AKISSI!
HEY, YOU! WHY DID YOU SLAM ON THE BRAKES?
HONK!
THERE WAS A LITTLE GIRL ON THE ROAD...
WHAT LITTLE GIRL?! I DON'T SEE ANYONE. YOU'D BETTER QUIT DRINKING SO EARLY IN THE DAY!
I HAVEN'T HAD A DROP! SHE WAS RIGHT HERE!
QUICK, LET'S GO!
OH, MY LITTLE COIN. YOU ALMOST GOT RUN OVER BY THOSE NAUGHTY CARS.
HA HA HA!
THE END

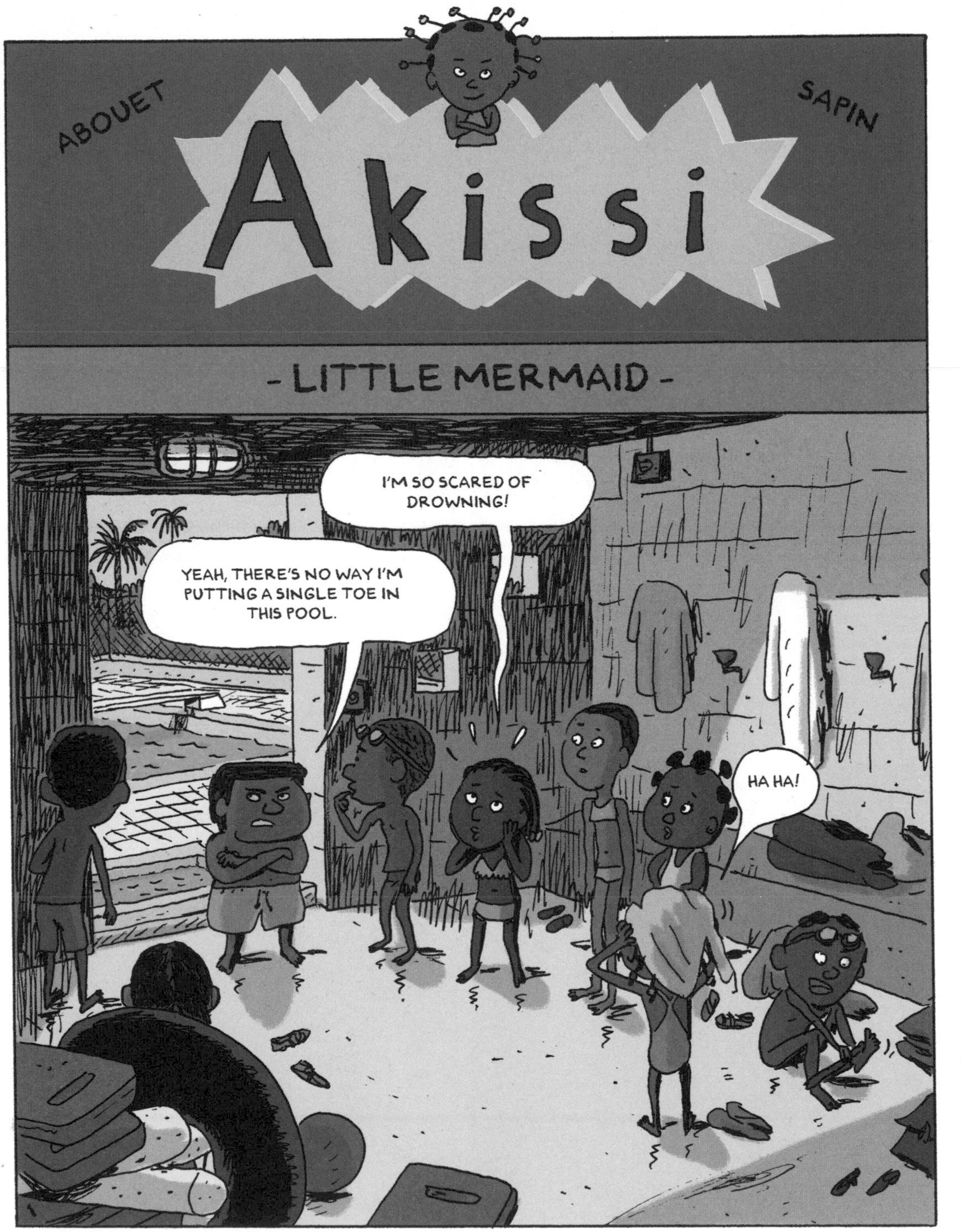
ABOUET
Akissi
SAPIN
- LITTLE MERMAID -
I'M SO SCARED OF DROWNING!
YEAH, THERE'S NO WAY I'M PUTTING A SINGLE TOE IN THIS POOL.
HA HA!

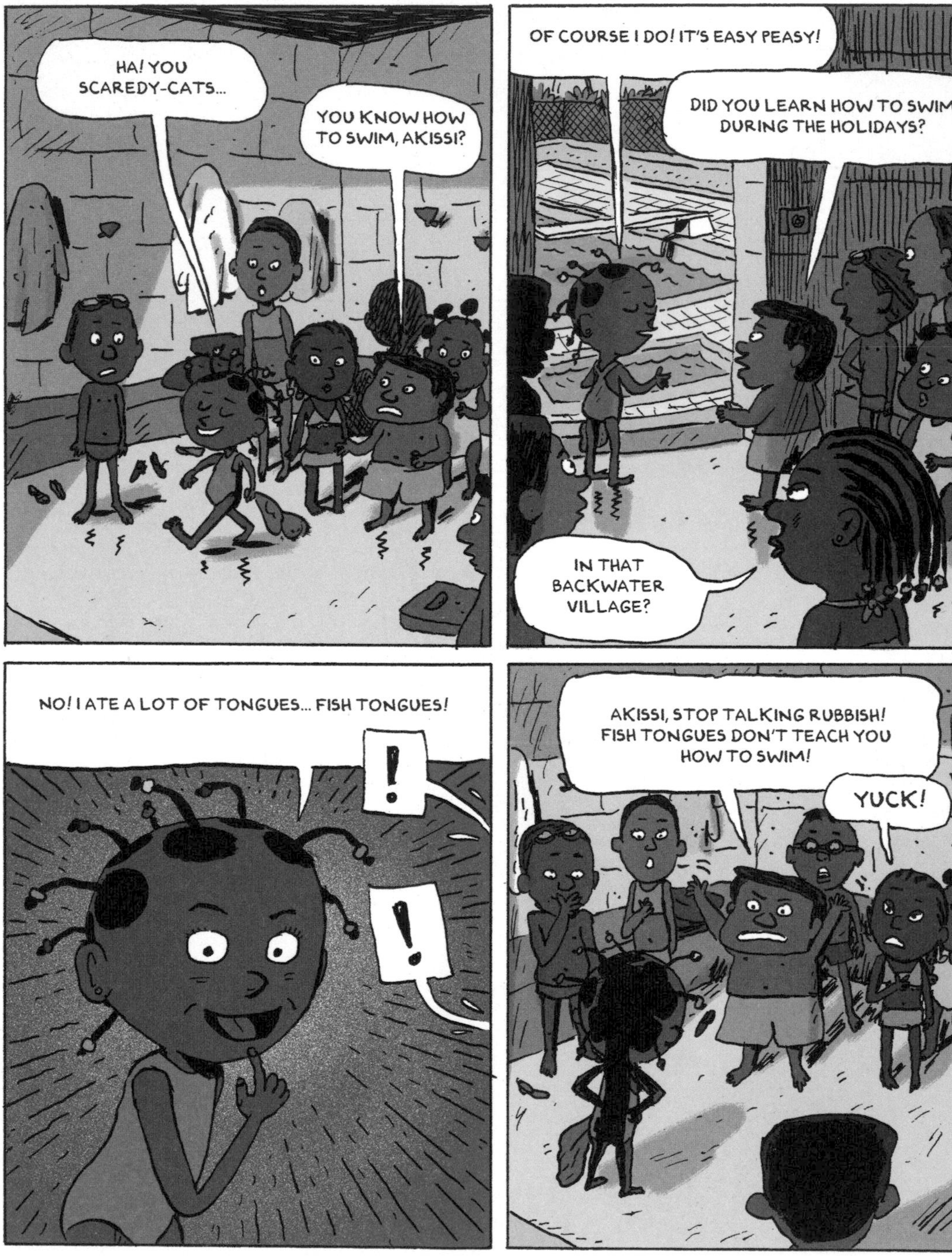
HA! YOU SCAREDY-CATS...
YOU KNOW HOW TO SWIM, AKISSI?
OF COURSE I DO! IT'S EASY PEASY!
DID YOU LEARN HOW TO SWIM DURING THE HOLIDAYS?
IN THAT BACKWATER VILLAGE?
NO! I ATE A LOT OF TONGUES... FISH TONGUES!
!
!
AKISSI, STOP TALKING RUBBISH! FISH TONGUES DON'T TEACH YOU HOW TO SWIM!
YUCK!

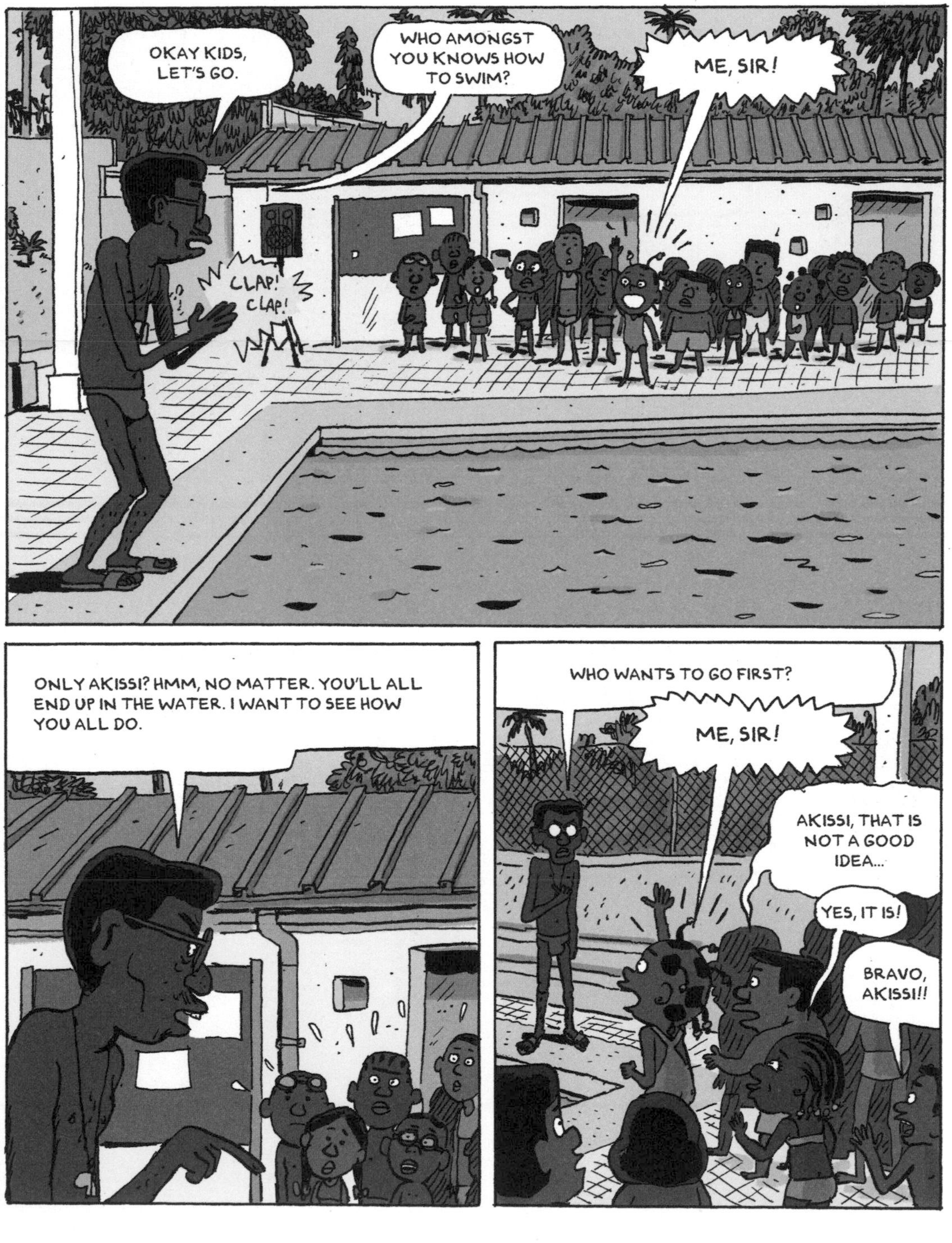
OKAY KIDS, LET'S GO.
WHO AMONGST YOU KNOWS HOW TO SWIM?
ME, SIR!
CLAP! CLAP!
ONLY AKISSI? HMM, NO MATTER. YOU'LL ALL END UP IN THE WATER. I WANT TO SEE HOW YOU ALL DO.
WHO WANTS TO GO FIRST?
ME, SIR!
AKISSI, THAT IS NOT A GOOD IDEA...
YES, IT IS!
BRAVO, AKISSI!!

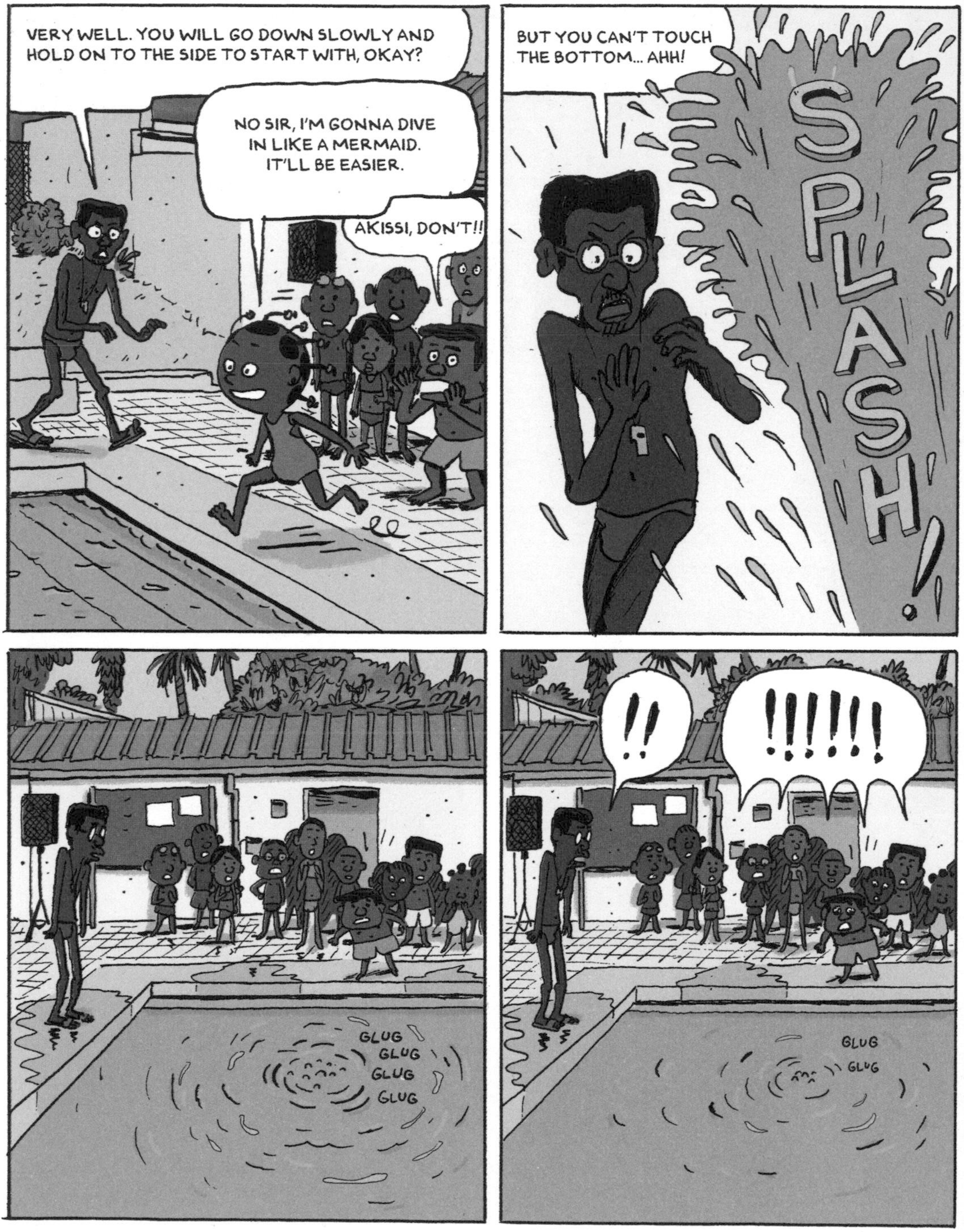
VERY WELL. YOU WILL GO DOWN SLOWLY AND HOLD ON TO THE SIDE TO START WITH, OKAY?
NO SIR, I'M GONNA DIVE IN LIKE A MERMAID. IT'LL BE EASIER.
AKISSI, DON'T!!
BUT YOU CAN'T TOUCH THE BOTTOM... AHH!
SPLASH!
GLUG GLUG GLUG GLUG
!!
!!!!!!
GLUG GLUG

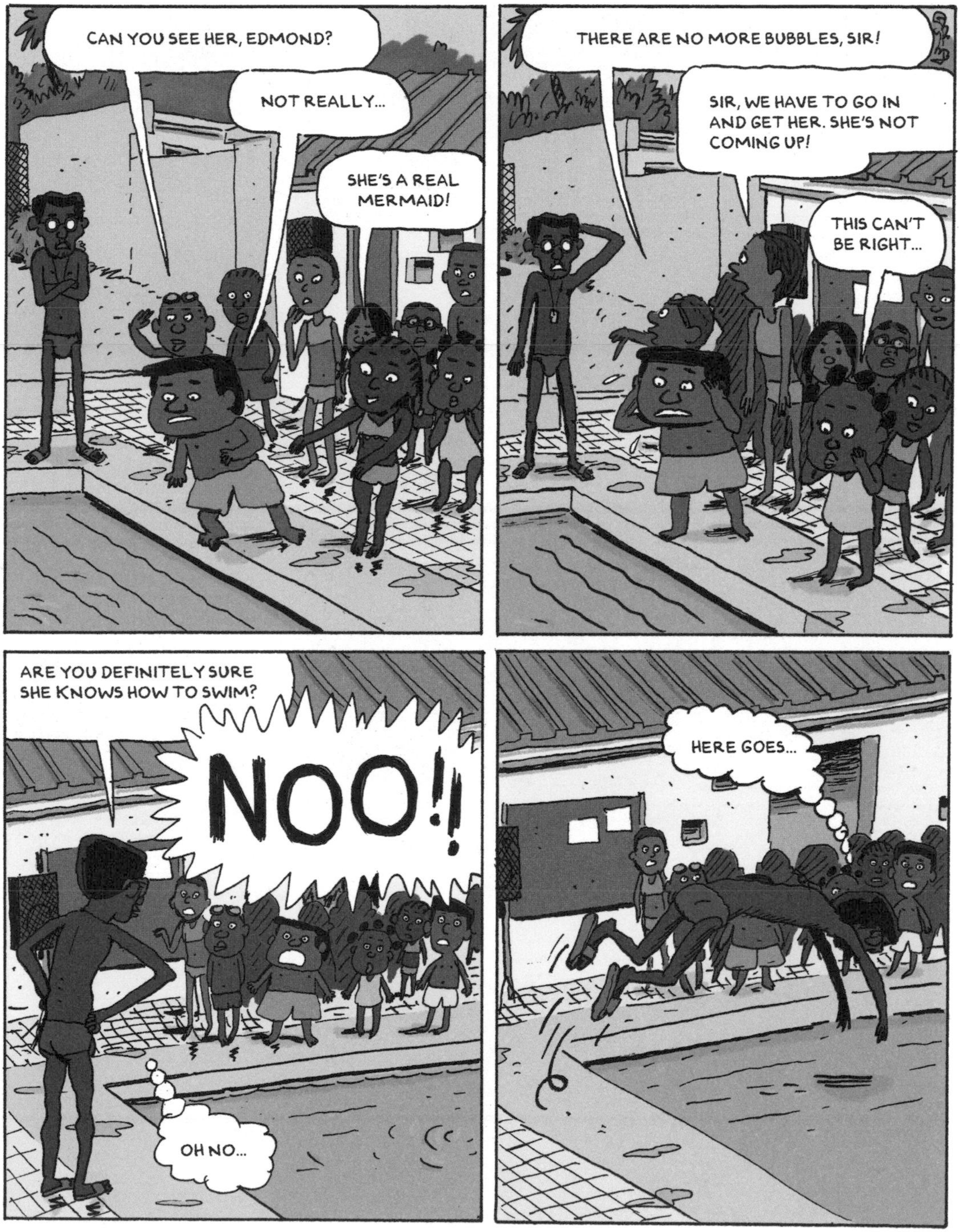
CAN YOU SEE HER, EDMOND?
NOT REALLY...
SHE'S A REAL MERMAID!
THERE ARE NO MORE BUBBLES, SIR!
SIR, WE HAVE TO GO IN AND GET HER. SHE'S NOT COMING UP!
THIS CAN'T BE RIGHT...
ARE YOU DEFINITELY SURE SHE KNOWS HOW TO SWIM?
NOO!!
OH NO...
HERE GOES...

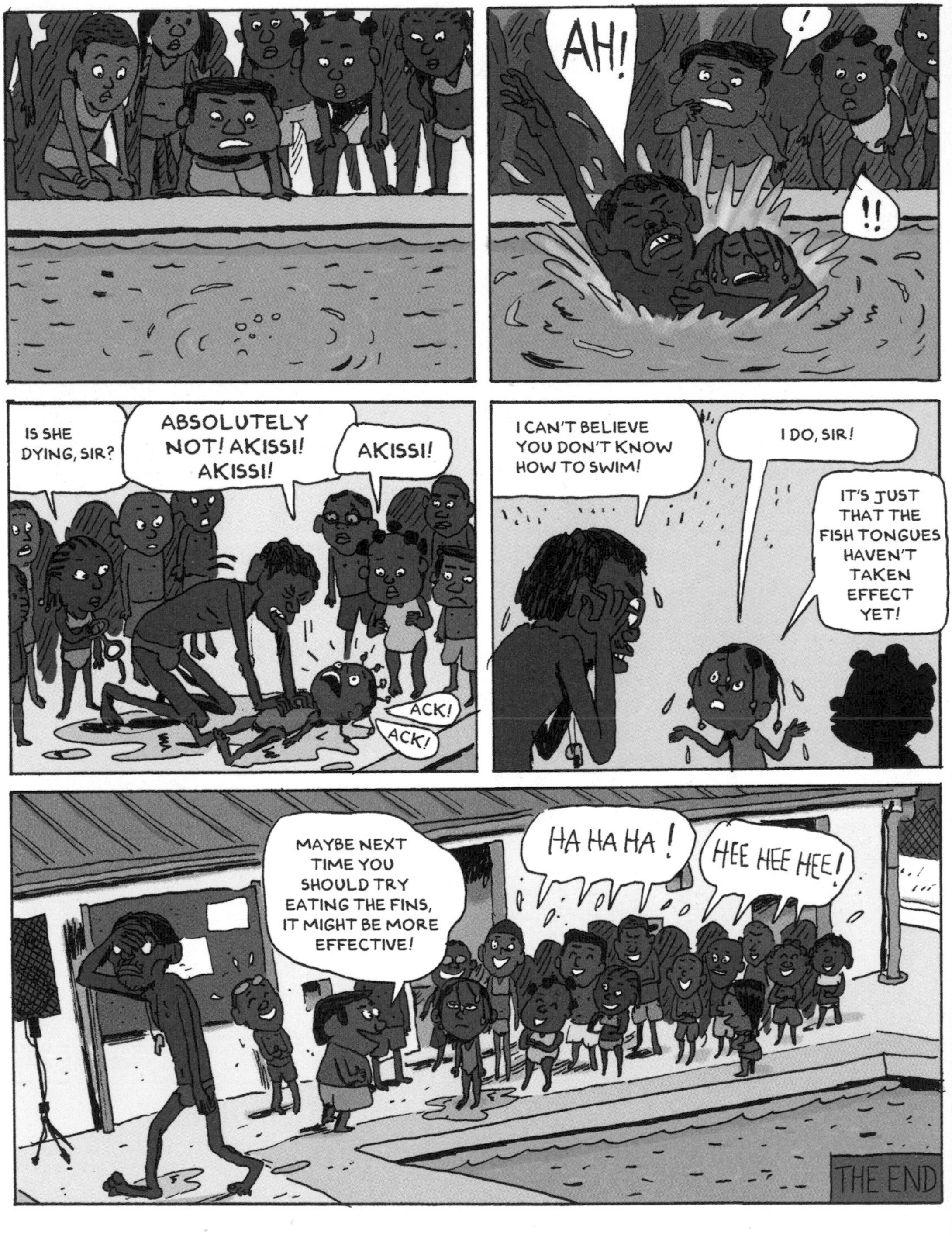
AH!
!
!!
IS SHE DYING, SIR?
ABSOLUTELY NOT! AKISSI! AKISSI!
AKISSI!
ACK!
ACK!
I CAN'T BELIEVE YOU DON'T KNOW HOW TO SWIM!
I DO, SIR!
IT'S JUST THAT THE FISH TONGUES HAVEN'T TAKEN EFFECT YET!
MAYBE NEXT TIME YOU SHOULD TRY EATING THE FINS, IT MIGHT BE MORE EFFECTIVE!
HA HA HA!
HEE HEE HEE!
THE END

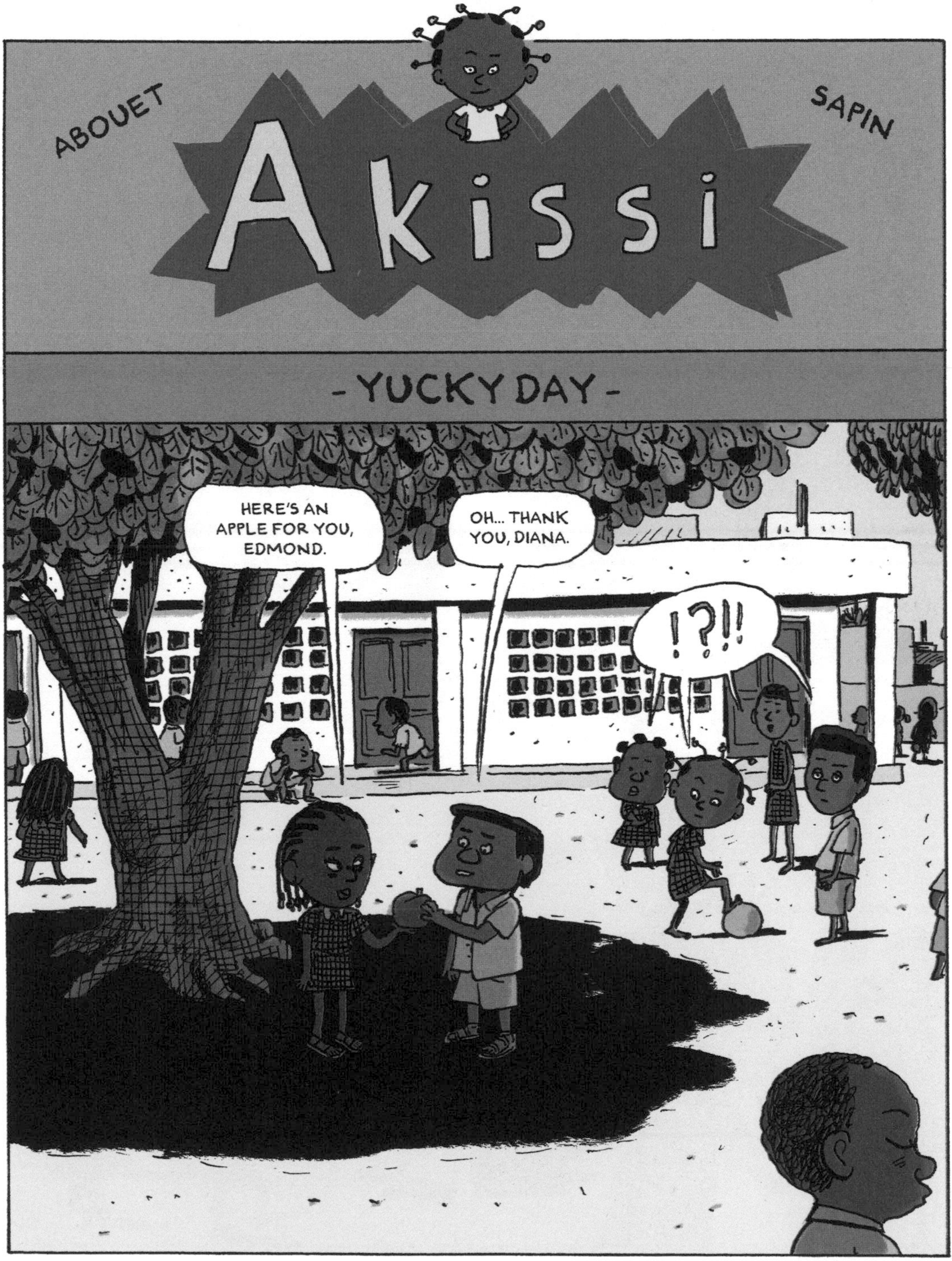
ABOUET
Akissi
SAPIN
- YUCKY DAY -
HERE'S AN APPLE FOR YOU, EDMOND.
OH... THANK YOU, DIANA.
!?!!

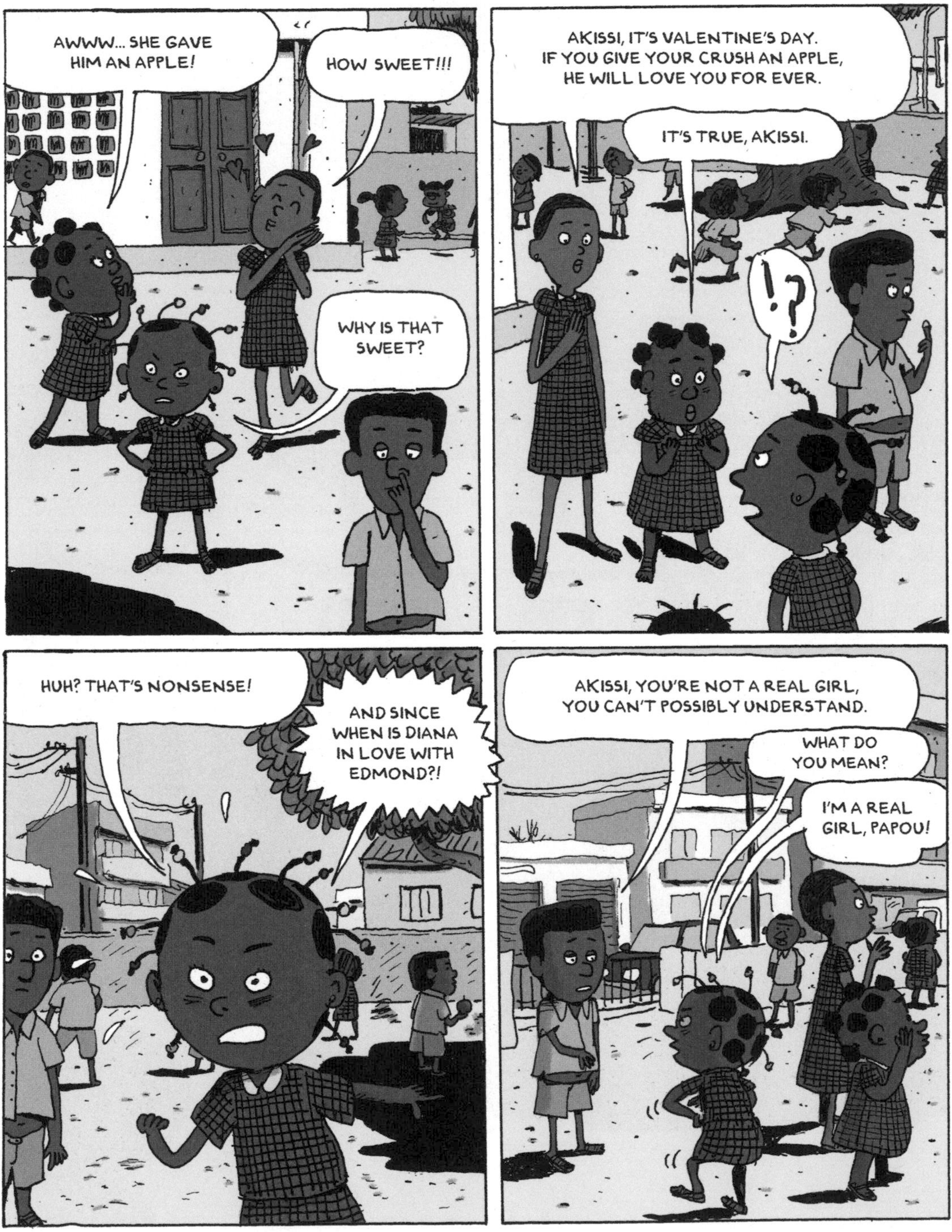
AWWW... SHE GAVE HIM AN APPLE!
HOW SWEET!!!
WHY IS THAT SWEET?
AKISSI, IT'S VALENTINE'S DAY. IF YOU GIVE YOUR CRUSH AN APPLE, HE WILL LOVE YOU FOR EVER.
IT'S TRUE, AKISSI.
!?
HUH? THAT'S NONSENSE!
AND SINCE WHEN IS DIANA IN LOVE WITH EDMOND?!
AKISSI, YOU'RE NOT A REAL GIRL, YOU CAN'T POSSIBLY UNDERSTAND.
WHAT DO YOU MEAN?
I'M A REAL GIRL, PAPOU!

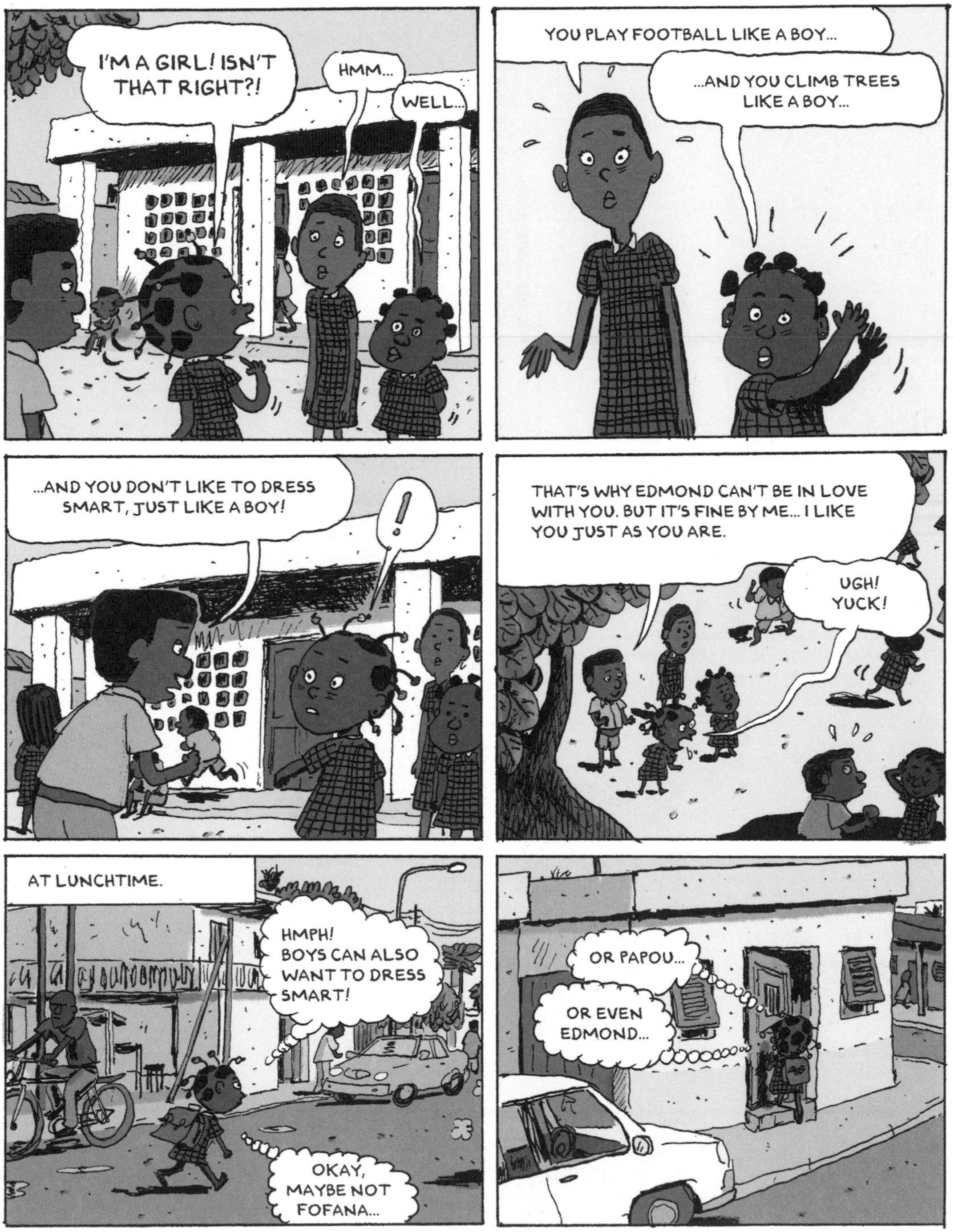
I'M A GIRL! ISN'T THAT RIGHT?!
HMM...
WELL...
YOU PLAY FOOTBALL LIKE A BOY...
...AND YOU CLIMB TREES LIKE A BOY...
...AND YOU DON'T LIKE TO DRESS SMART, JUST LIKE A BOY!
!
THAT'S WHY EDMOND CAN'T BE IN LOVE WITH YOU. BUT IT'S FINE BY ME... I LIKE YOU JUST AS YOU ARE.
UGH! YUCK!
AT LUNCHTIME.
HMPH! BOYS CAN ALSO WANT TO DRESS SMART!
OKAY, MAYBE NOT FOFANA...
OR PAPOU...
OR EVEN EDMOND...

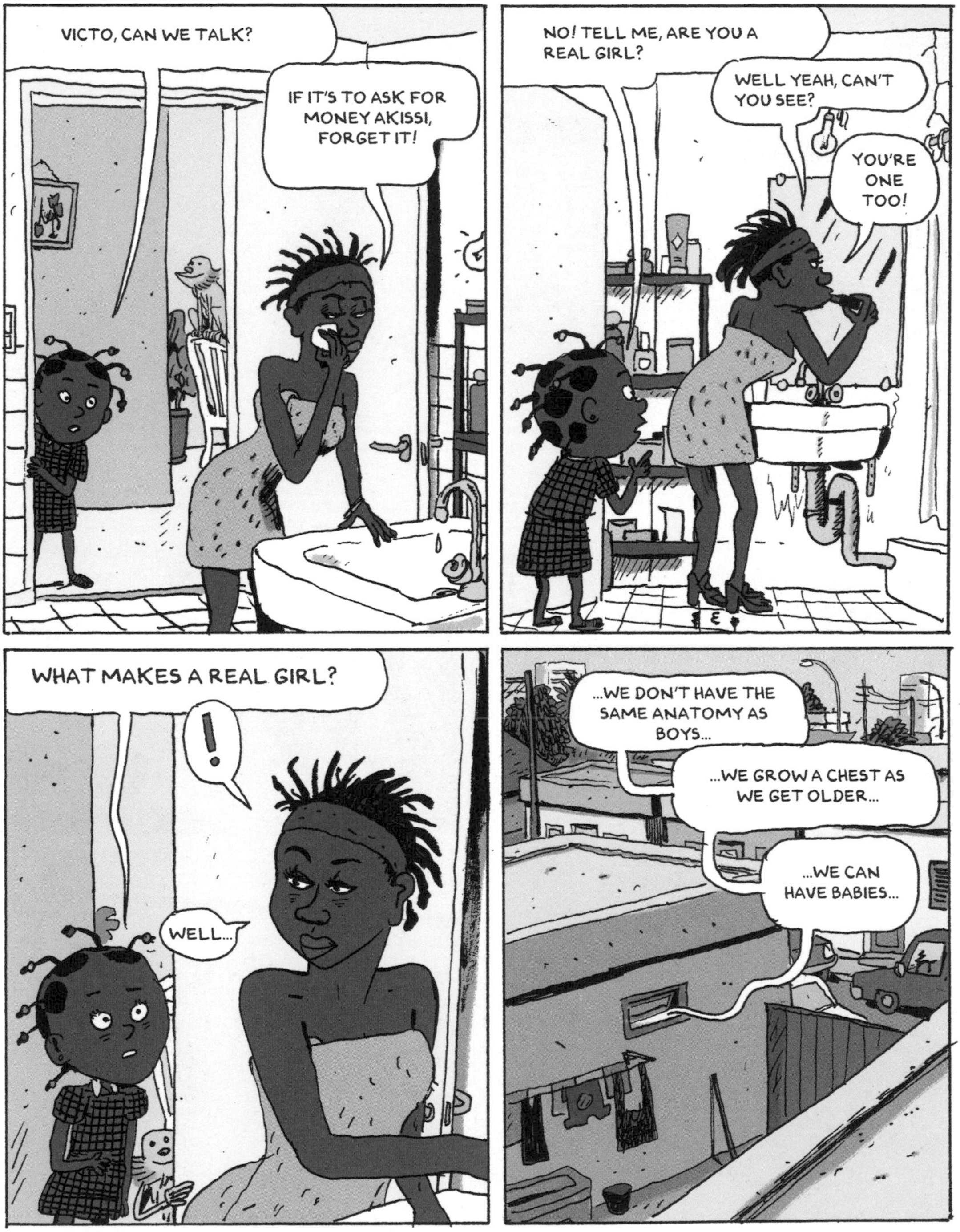
VICTO, CAN WE TALK?
IF IT'S TO ASK FOR MONEY AKISSI, FORGET IT!
NO! TELL ME, ARE YOU A REAL GIRL?
WELL YEAH, CAN'T YOU SEE?
YOU'RE ONE TOO!
WHAT MAKES A REAL GIRL?
!
WELL...
...WE DON'T HAVE THE SAME ANATOMY AS BOYS...
...WE GROW A CHEST AS WE GET OLDER...
...WE CAN HAVE BABIES...

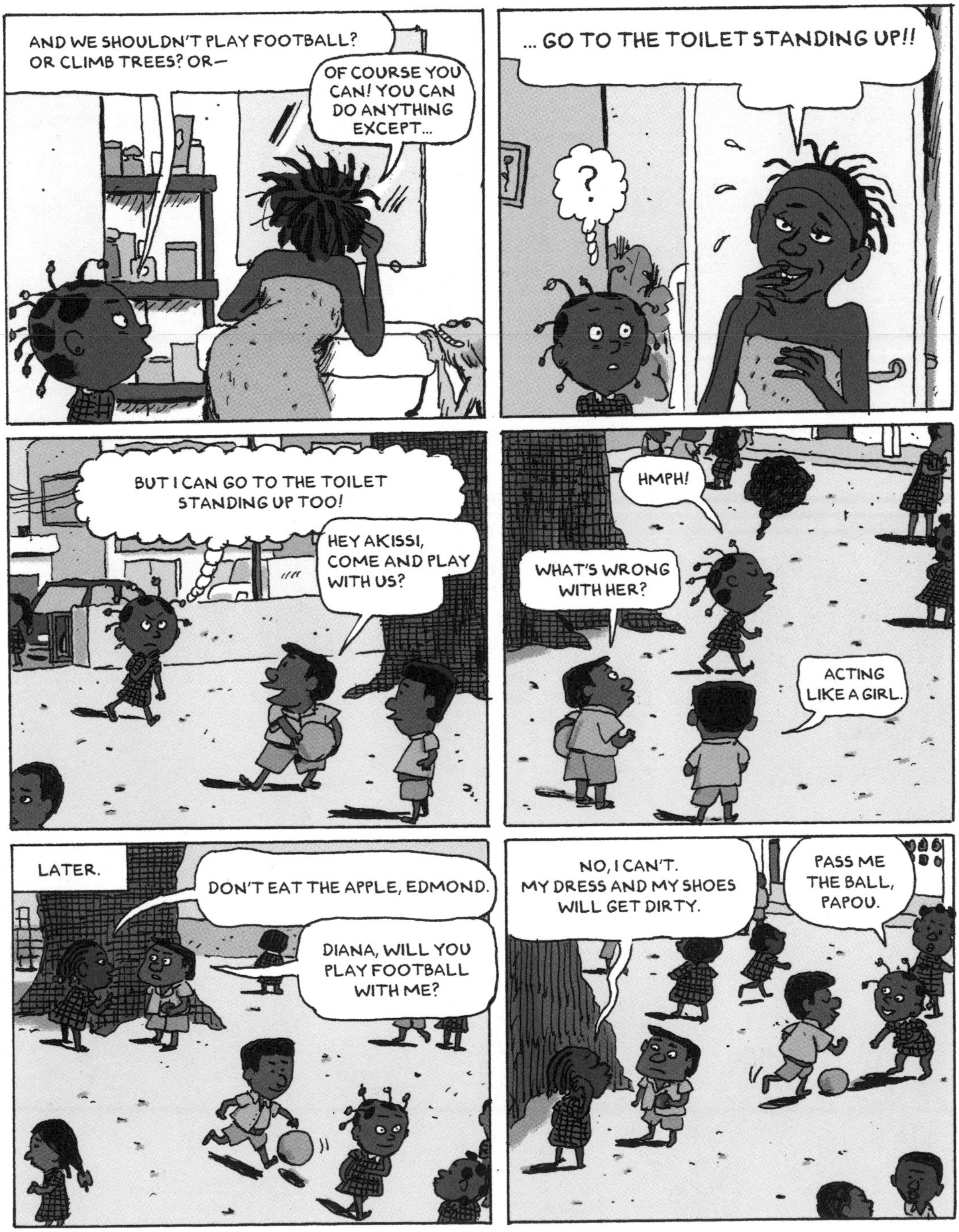
AND WE SHOULDN'T PLAY FOOTBALL? OR CLIMB TREES? OR—
OF COURSE YOU CAN! YOU CAN DO ANYTHING EXCEPT...
... GO TO THE TOILET STANDING UP!!
?
BUT I CAN GO TO THE TOILET STANDING UP TOO!
HEY AKISSI, COME AND PLAY WITH US?
HMPH!
WHAT'S WRONG WITH HER?
ACTING LIKE A GIRL.
LATER.
DON'T EAT THE APPLE, EDMOND.
DIANA, WILL YOU PLAY FOOTBALL WITH ME?
NO, I CAN'T. MY DRESS AND MY SHOES WILL GET DIRTY.
PASS ME THE BALL, PAPOU.

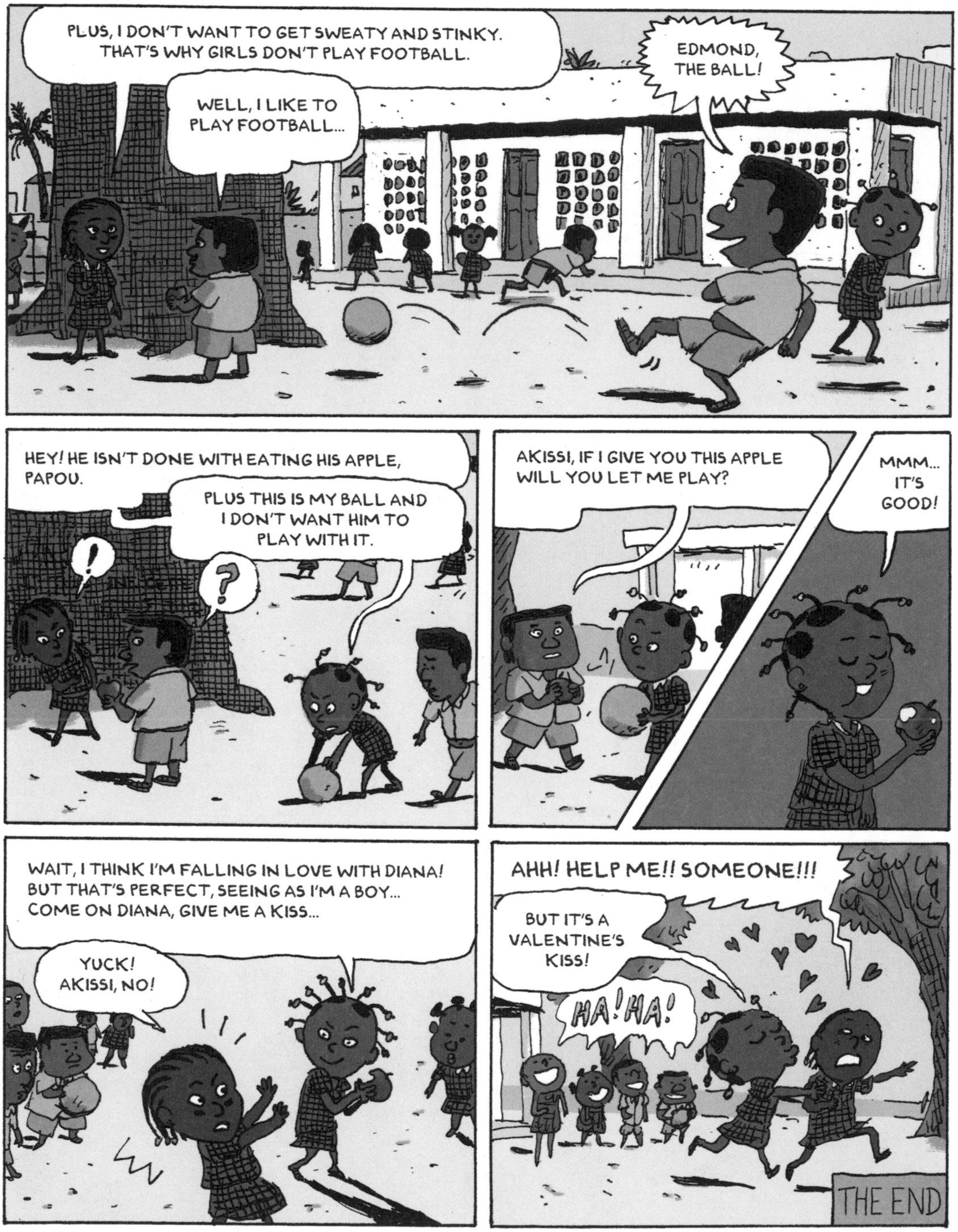
PLUS, I DON'T WANT TO GET SWEATY AND STINKY. THAT'S WHY GIRLS DON'T PLAY FOOTBALL.
WELL, I LIKE TO PLAY FOOTBALL...
EDMOND, THE BALL!
HEY! HE ISN'T DONE WITH EATING HIS APPLE, PAPOU.
PLUS THIS IS MY BALL AND I DON'T WANT HIM TO PLAY WITH IT.
!
?
AKISSI, IF I GIVE YOU THIS APPLE WILL YOU LET ME PLAY?
MMM... IT'S GOOD!
WAIT, I THINK I'M FALLING IN LOVE WITH DIANA! BUT THAT'S PERFECT, SEEING AS I'M A BOY... COME ON DIANA, GIVE ME A KISS...
YUCK! AKISSI, NO!
AHH! HELP ME!! SOMEONE!!!
BUT IT'S A VALENTINE'S KISS!
HA! HA!
THE END

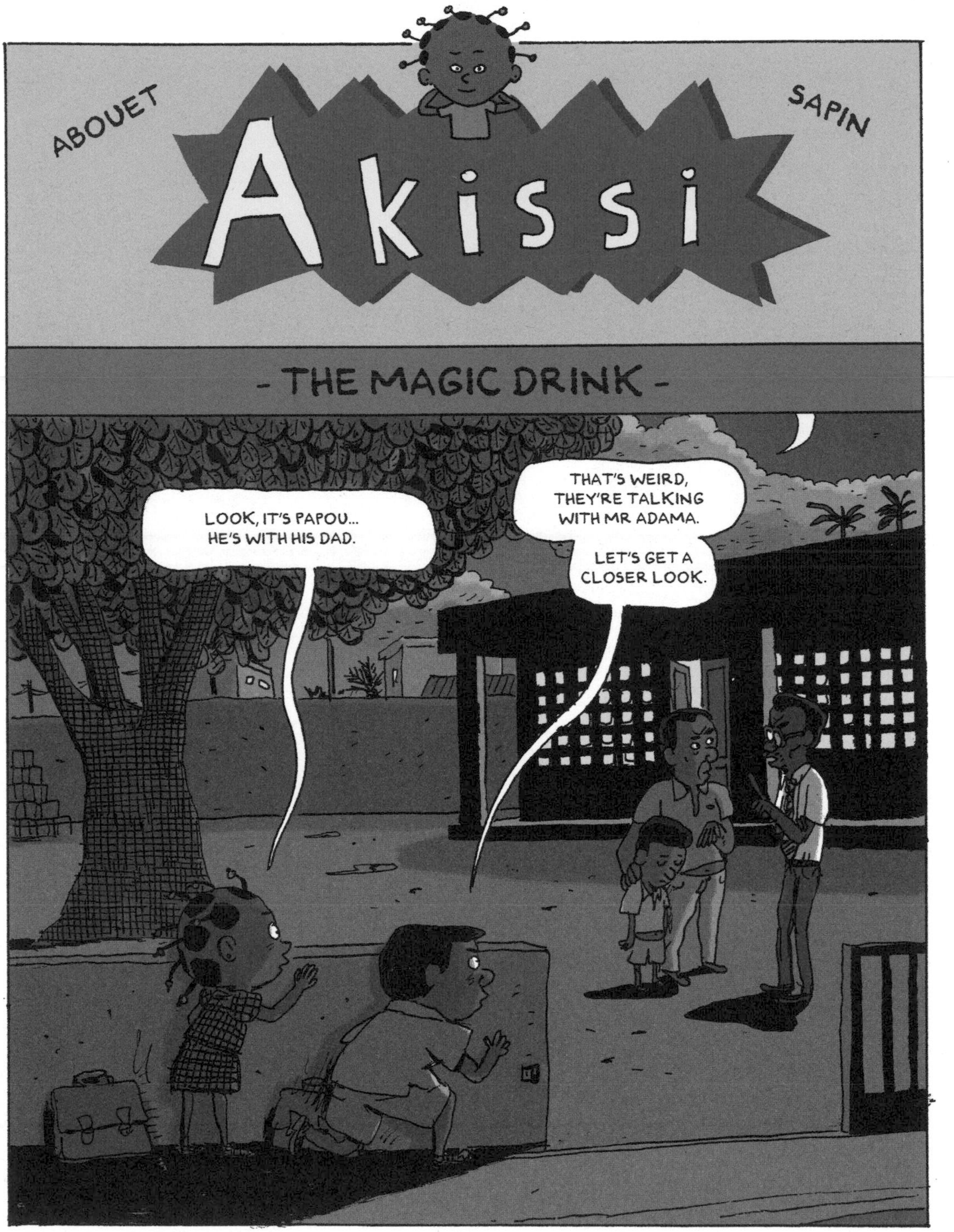
ABOUET
SAPIN
Akissi
- THE MAGIC DRINK -
LOOK, IT'S PAPOU... HE'S WITH HIS DAD.
THAT'S WEIRD, THEY'RE TALKING WITH MR ADAMA.
LET'S GET A CLOSER LOOK.

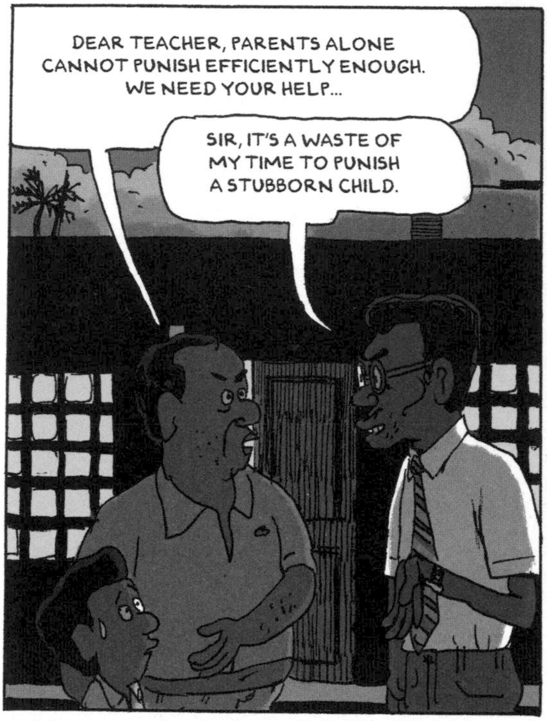
DEAR TEACHER, PARENTS ALONE CANNOT PUNISH EFFICIENTLY ENOUGH. WE NEED YOUR HELP...
SIR, IT'S A WASTE OF MY TIME TO PUNISH A STUBBORN CHILD.

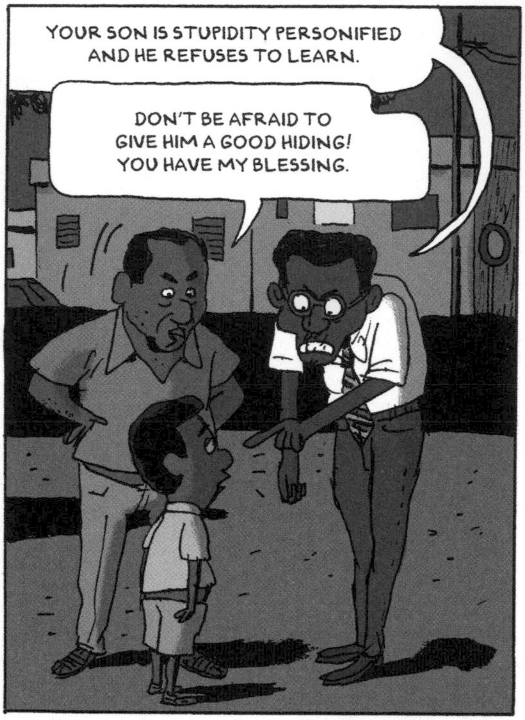
YOUR SON IS STUPIDITY PERSONIFIED AND HE REFUSES TO LEARN.
DON'T BE AFRAID TO GIVE HIM A GOOD HIDING! YOU HAVE MY BLESSING.

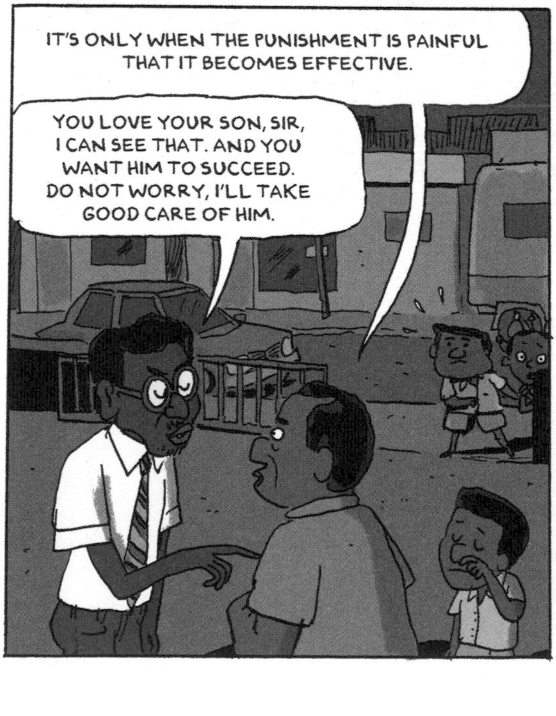
IT'S ONLY WHEN THE PUNISHMENT IS PAINFUL THAT IT BECOMES EFFECTIVE.
YOU LOVE YOUR SON, SIR, I CAN SEE THAT. AND YOU WANT HIM TO SUCCEED. DO NOT WORRY, I'LL TAKE GOOD CARE OF HIM.

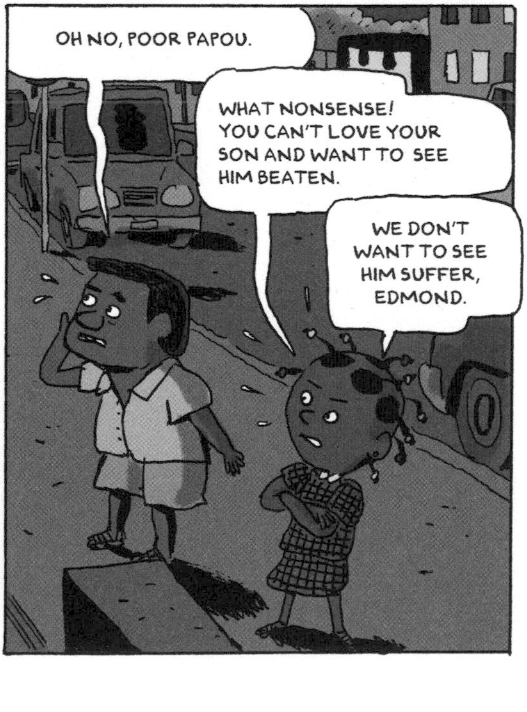
OH NO, POOR PAPOU.
WHAT NONSENSE! YOU CAN'T LOVE YOUR SON AND WANT TO SEE HIM BEATEN.
WE DON'T WANT TO SEE HIM SUFFER, EDMOND.

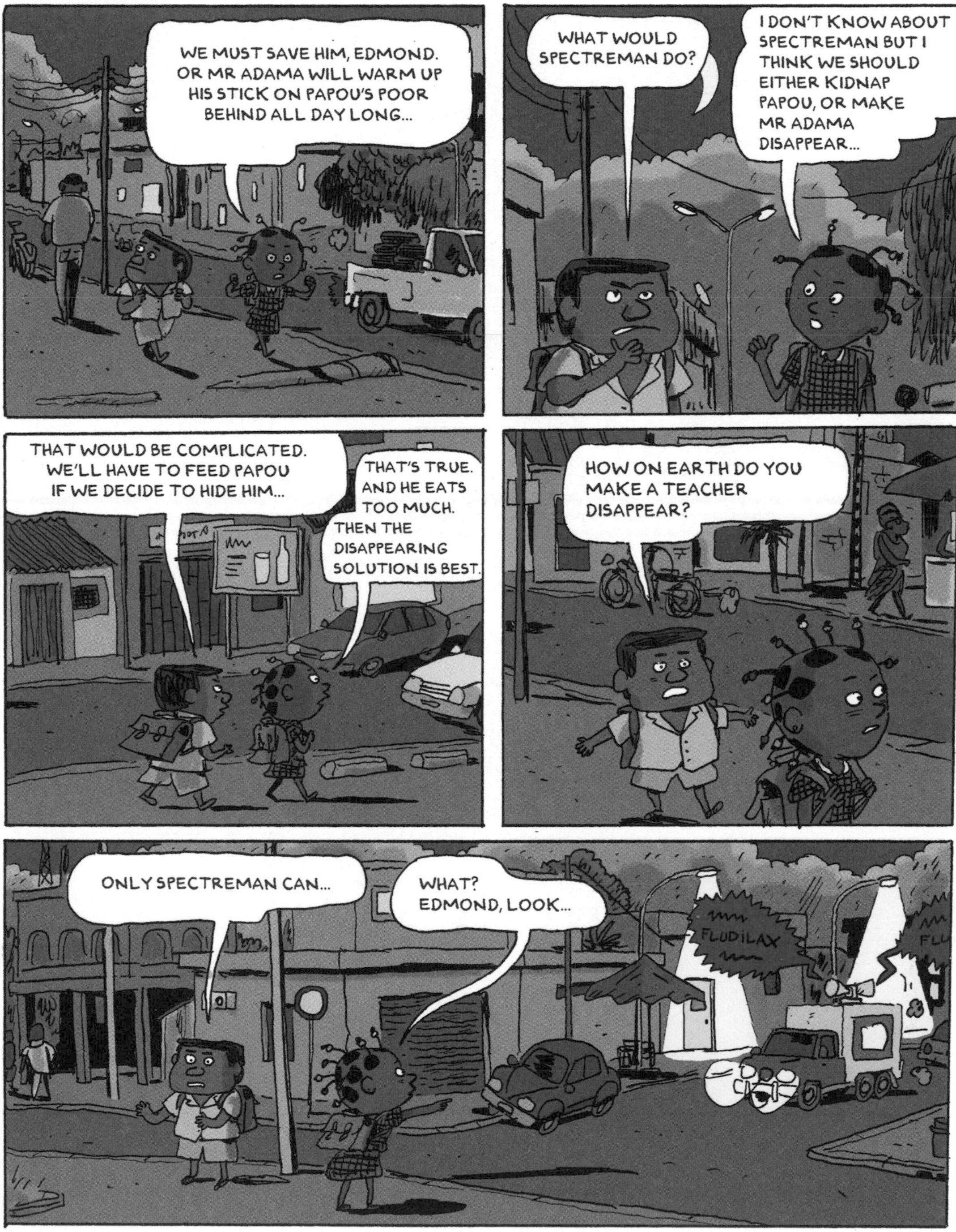
WE MUST SAVE HIM, EDMOND. OR MR ADAMA WILL WARM UP HIS STICK ON PAPOU'S POOR BEHIND ALL DAY LONG...
WHAT WOULD SPECTREMAN DO?
I DON'T KNOW ABOUT SPECTREMAN BUT I THINK WE SHOULD EITHER KIDNAP PAPOU, OR MAKE MR ADAMA DISAPPEAR...
THAT WOULD BE COMPLICATED. WE'LL HAVE TO FEED PAPOU IF WE DECIDE TO HIDE HIM...
THAT'S TRUE. AND HE EATS TOO MUCH. THEN THE DISAPPEARING SOLUTION IS BEST.
HOW ON EARTH DO YOU MAKE A TEACHER DISAPPEAR?
ONLY SPECTREMAN CAN...
WHAT? EDMOND, LOOK...
FLUDILAX

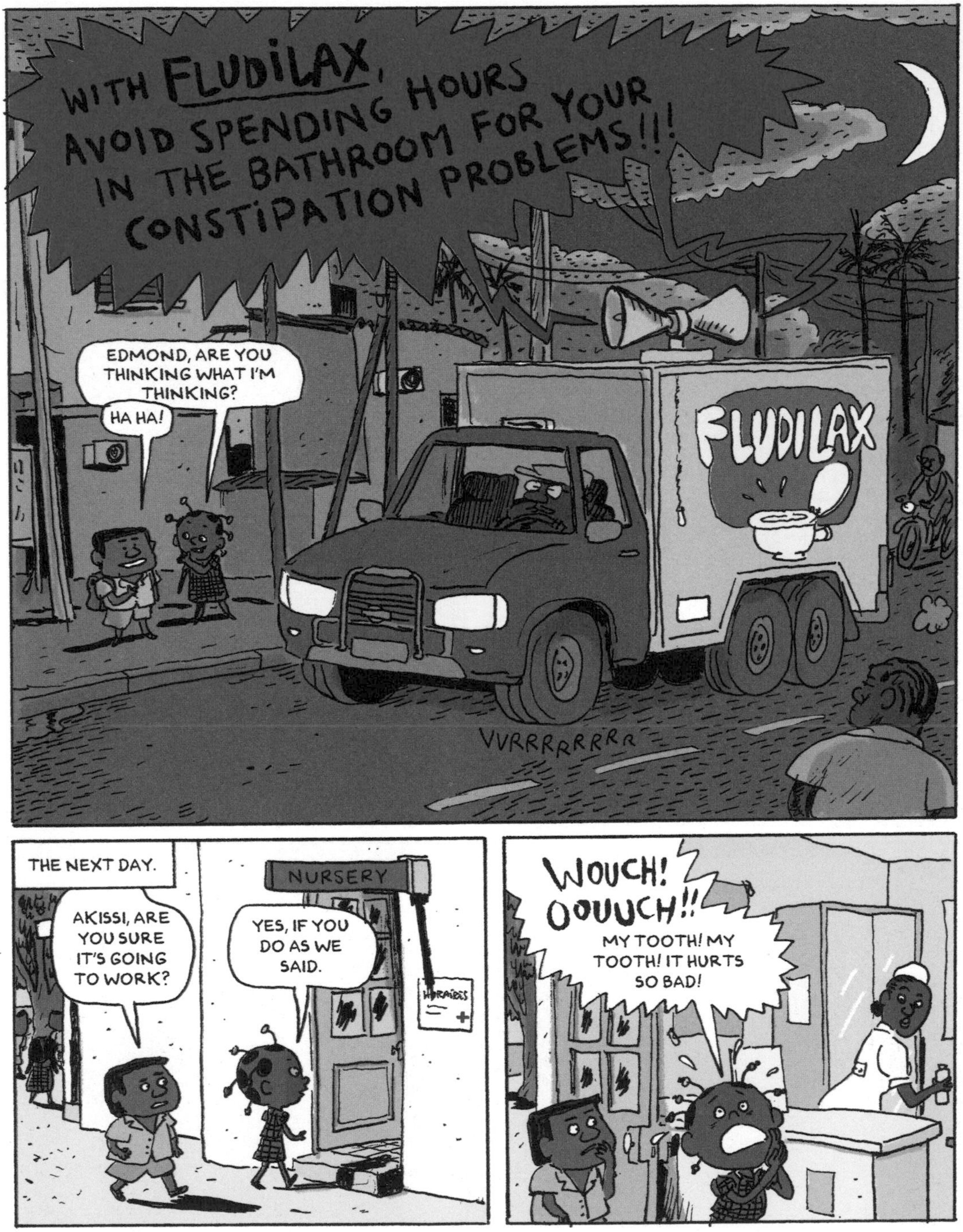
WITH FLUDILAX, AVOID SPENDING HOURS IN THE BATHROOM FOR YOUR CONSTIPATION PROBLEMS!!!
EDMOND, ARE YOU THINKING WHAT I'M THINKING?
HA HA!
FLUDILAX
VVRRRRRRRR
THE NEXT DAY.
NURSERY
AKISSI, ARE YOU SURE IT'S GOING TO WORK?
YES, IF YOU DO AS WE SAID.
WOUCH! OOUUCH!!
MY TOOTH! MY TOOTH! IT HURTS SO BAD!

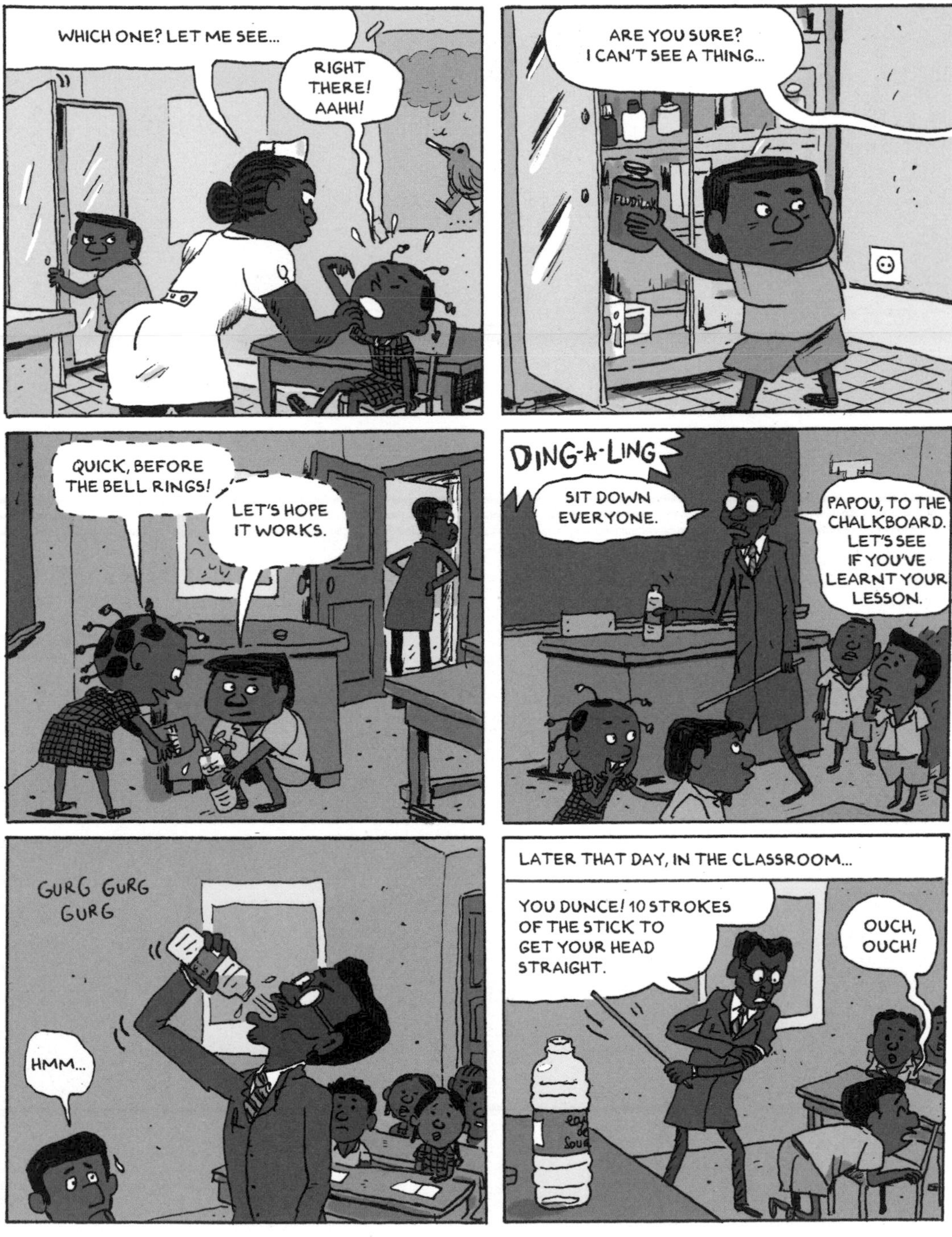
WHICH ONE? LET ME SEE...
RIGHT THERE! AAHH!
ARE YOU SURE? I CAN'T SEE A THING...
QUICK, BEFORE THE BELL RINGS!
LET'S HOPE IT WORKS.
DING-A-LING
SIT DOWN EVERYONE.
PAPOU, TO THE CHALKBOARD. LET'S SEE IF YOU'VE LEARNT YOUR LESSON.
GURG GURG GURG
HMM...
LATER THAT DAY, IN THE CLASSROOM...
YOU DUNCE! 10 STROKES OF THE STICK TO GET YOUR HEAD STRAIGHT.
OUCH, OUCH!

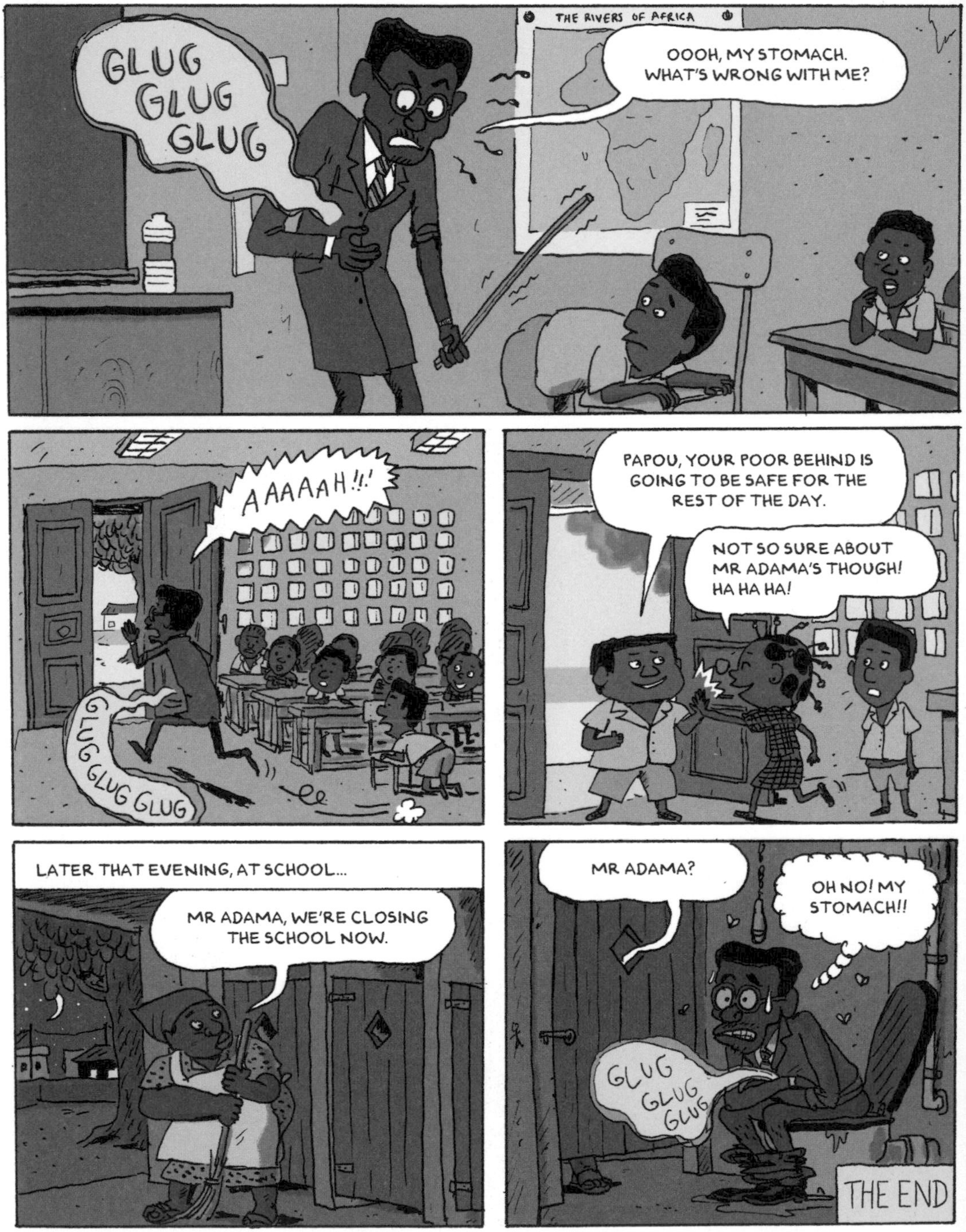
GLUG GLUG GLUG
THE RIVERS OF AFRICA
OOOH, MY STOMACH. WHAT'S WRONG WITH ME?
AAAAAH!!!
GLUG GLUG GLUG
PAPOU, YOUR POOR BEHIND IS GOING TO BE SAFE FOR THE REST OF THE DAY.
NOT SO SURE ABOUT MR ADAMA'S THOUGH! HA HA HA!
LATER THAT EVENING, AT SCHOOL...
MR ADAMA, WE'RE CLOSING THE SCHOOL NOW.
MR ADAMA?
OH NO! MY STOMACH!!
GLUG GLUG GLUG
THE END

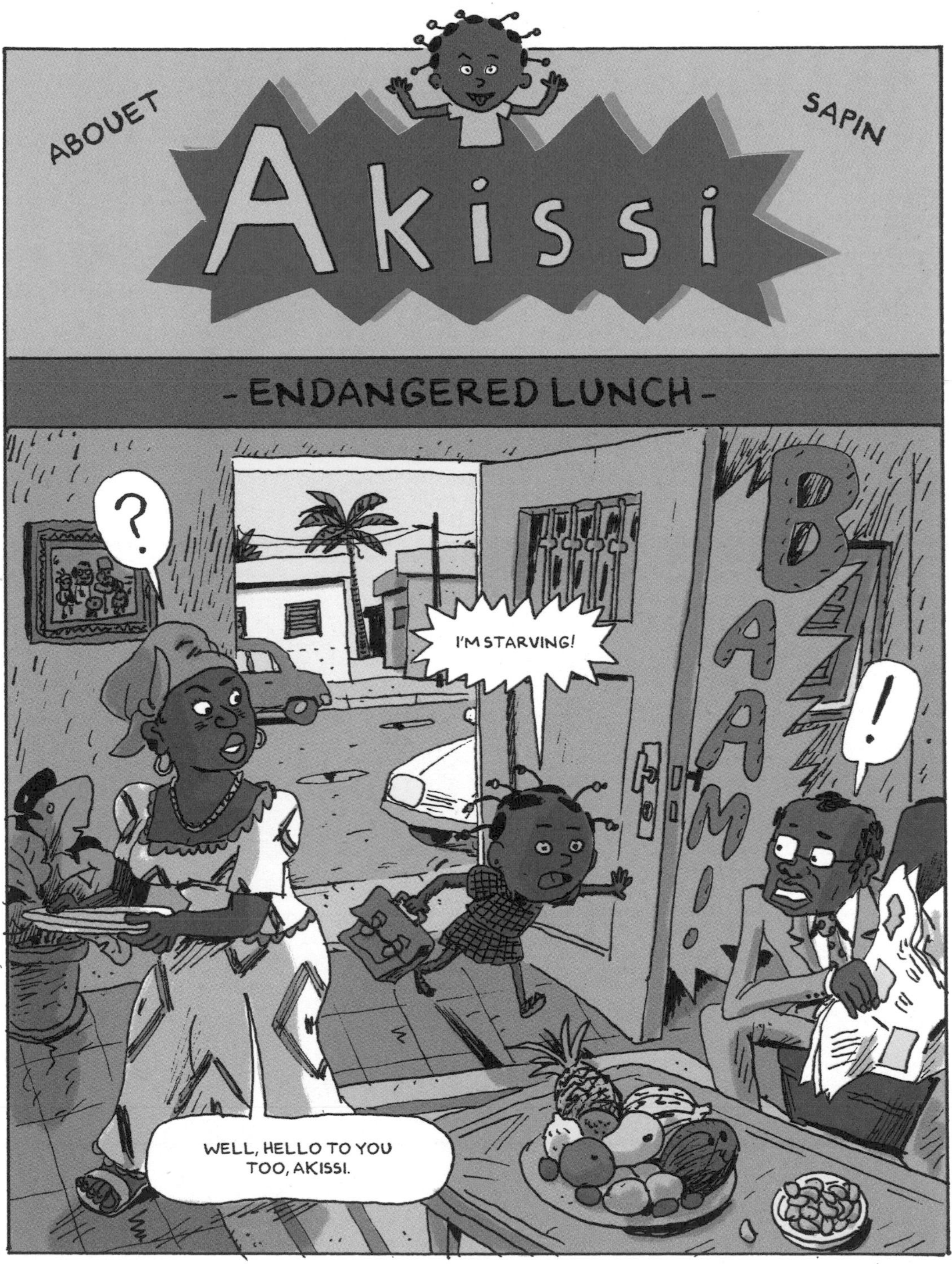
ABOUET
SAPIN
Akissi
- ENDANGERED LUNCH -
?
I'M STARVING!
BAAAM!
!
WELL, HELLO TO YOU TOO, AKISSI.

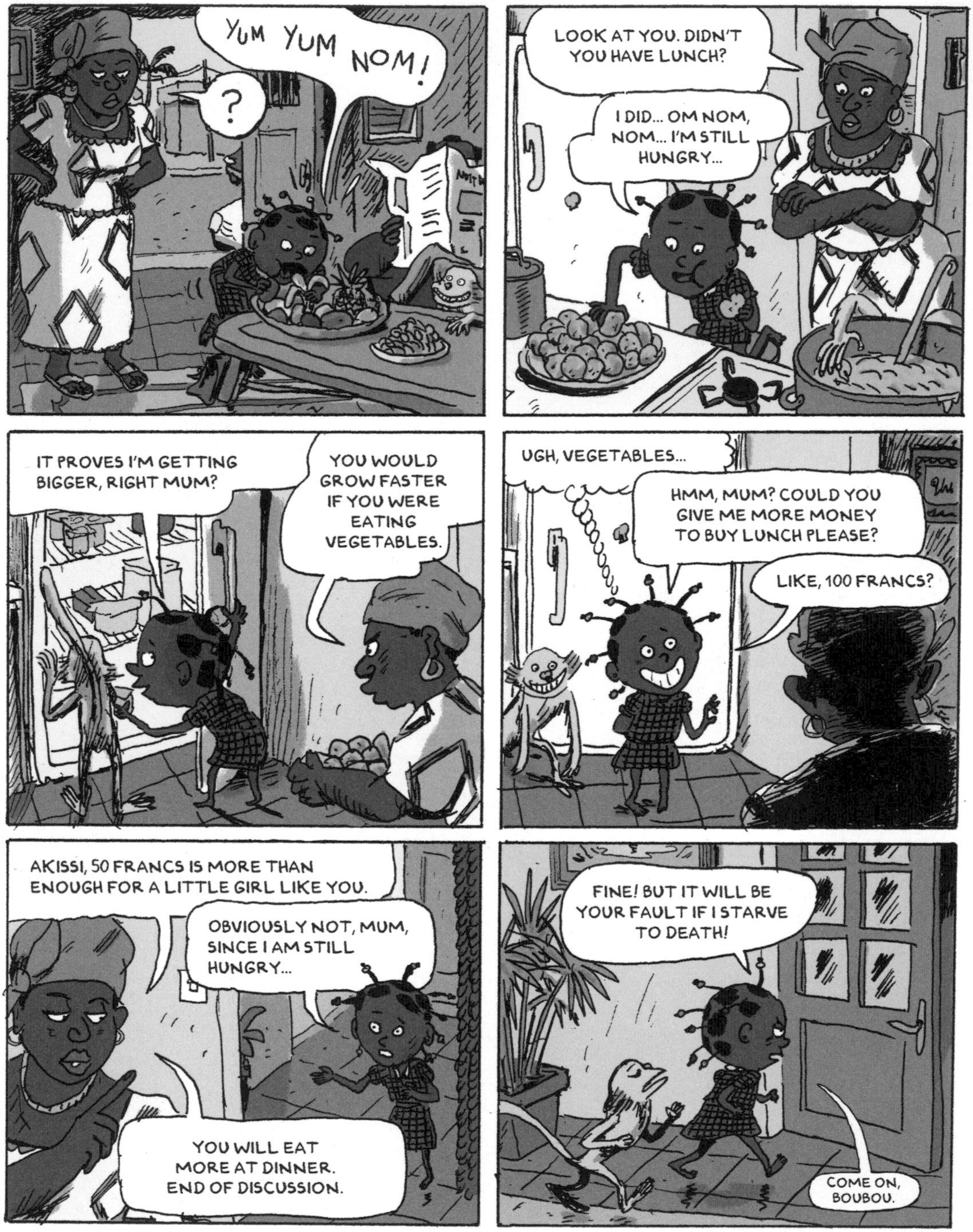
YUM YUM NOM!
?
LOOK AT YOU. DIDN'T YOU HAVE LUNCH?
I DID... OM NOM, NOM... I'M STILL HUNGRY...
IT PROVES I'M GETTING BIGGER, RIGHT MUM?
YOU WOULD GROW FASTER IF YOU WERE EATING VEGETABLES.
UGH, VEGETABLES...
HMM, MUM? COULD YOU GIVE ME MORE MONEY TO BUY LUNCH PLEASE?
LIKE, 100 FRANCS?
AKISSI, 50 FRANCS IS MORE THAN ENOUGH FOR A LITTLE GIRL LIKE YOU.
OBVIOUSLY NOT, MUM, SINCE I AM STILL HUNGRY...
YOU WILL EAT MORE AT DINNER. END OF DISCUSSION.
FINE! BUT IT WILL BE YOUR FAULT IF I STARVE TO DEATH!
COME ON, BOUBOU.

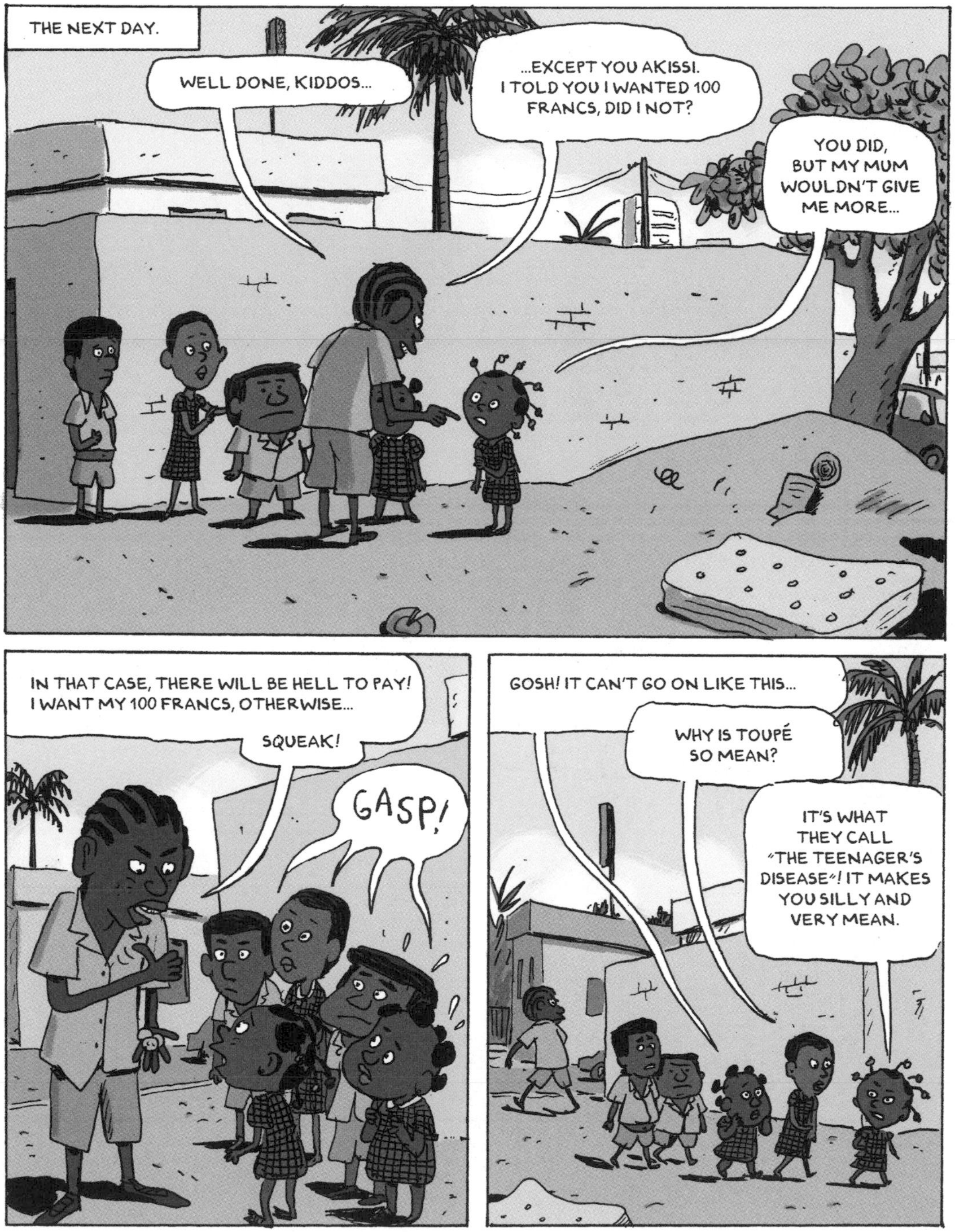
THE NEXT DAY.
WELL DONE, KIDDOS...
...EXCEPT YOU AKISSI. I TOLD YOU I WANTED 100 FRANCS, DID I NOT?
YOU DID, BUT MY MUM WOULDN'T GIVE ME MORE...
IN THAT CASE, THERE WILL BE HELL TO PAY! I WANT MY 100 FRANCS, OTHERWISE...
SQUEAK!
GASP!
GOSH! IT CAN'T GO ON LIKE THIS...
WHY IS TOUPÉ SO MEAN?
IT'S WHAT THEY CALL "THE TEENAGER'S DISEASE"! IT MAKES YOU SILLY AND VERY MEAN.

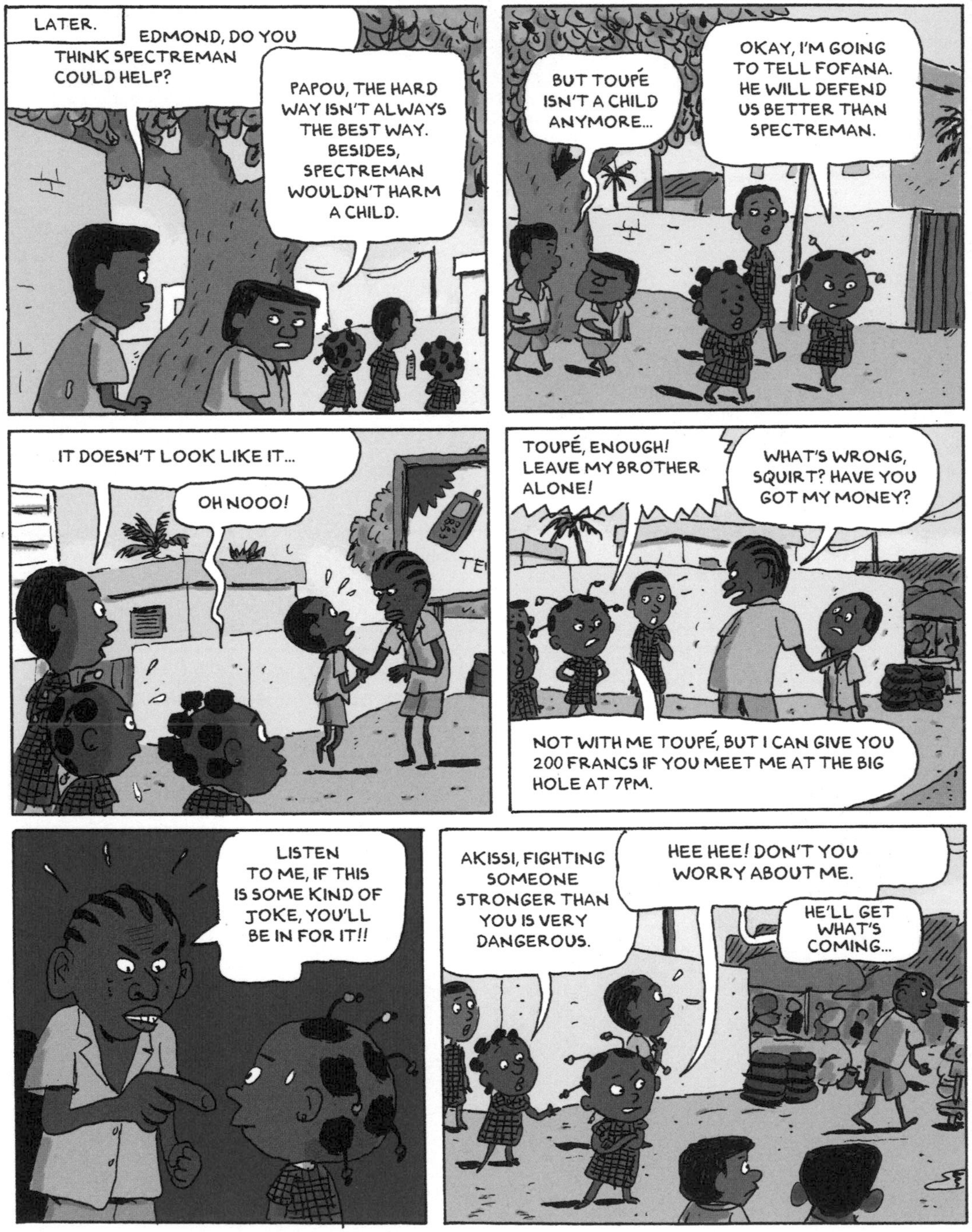

LATER.
EDMOND, DO YOU THINK SPECTREMAN COULD HELP?
PAPOU, THE HARD WAY ISN'T ALWAYS THE BEST WAY. BESIDES, SPECTREMAN WOULDN'T HARM A CHILD.
BUT TOUPÉ ISN'T A CHILD ANYMORE...
OKAY, I'M GOING TO TELL FOFANA. HE WILL DEFEND US BETTER THAN SPECTREMAN.
IT DOESN'T LOOK LIKE IT...
OH NOOO!
TOUPÉ, ENOUGH! LEAVE MY BROTHER ALONE!
WHAT'S WRONG, SQUIRT? HAVE YOU GOT MY MONEY?
NOT WITH ME TOUPÉ, BUT I CAN GIVE YOU 200 FRANCS IF YOU MEET ME AT THE BIG HOLE AT 7PM.
LISTEN TO ME, IF THIS IS SOME KIND OF JOKE, YOU'LL BE IN FOR IT!!
AKISSI, FIGHTING SOMEONE STRONGER THAN YOU IS VERY DANGEROUS.
HEE HEE! DON'T YOU WORRY ABOUT ME.
HE'LL GET WHAT'S COMING...

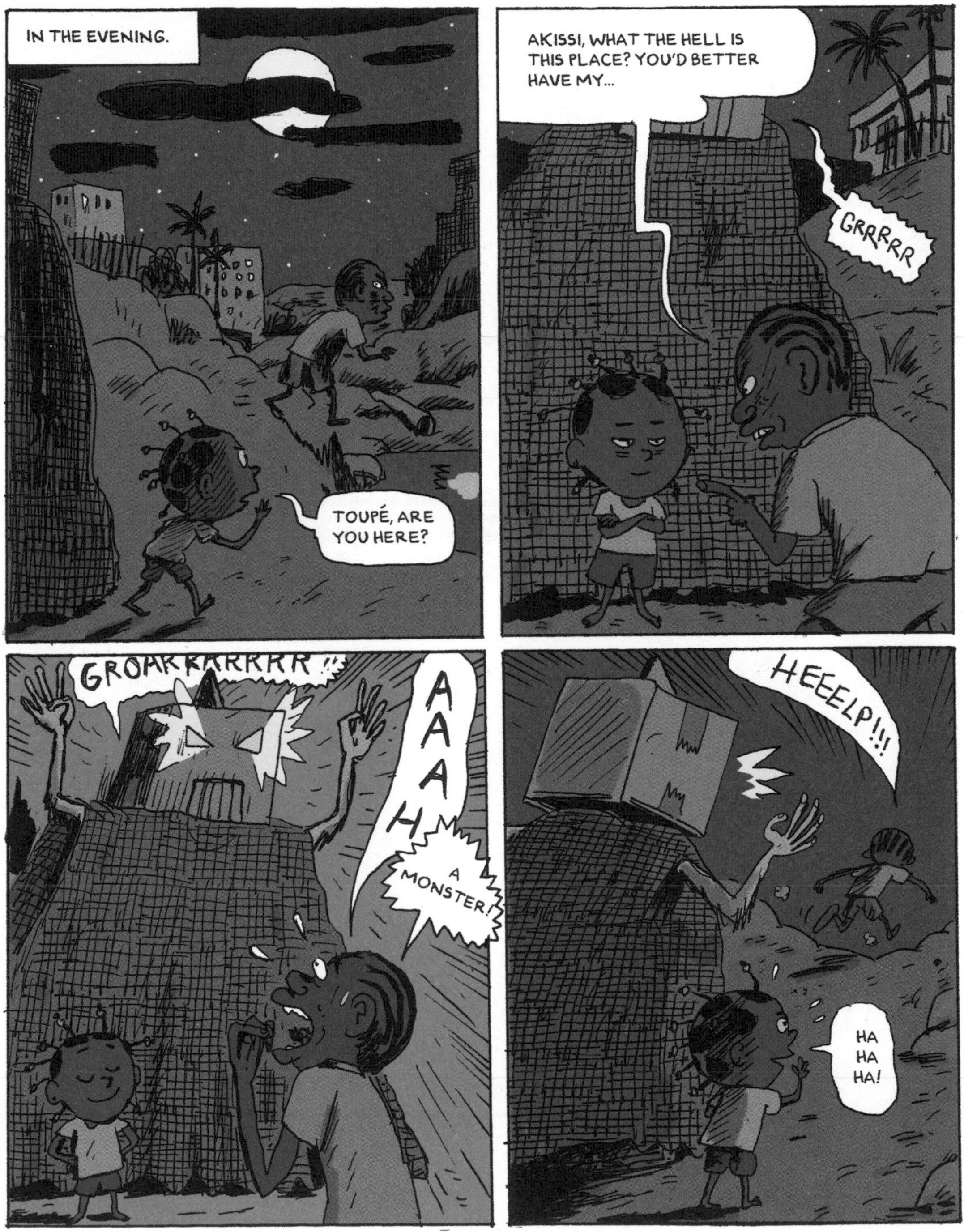
IN THE EVENING.
TOUPÉ, ARE YOU HERE?
AKISSI, WHAT THE HELL IS THIS PLACE? YOU'D BETTER HAVE MY...
GRRRRR
GROARRRRRRR!!
AAAH
A MONSTER!
HEEELP!!!
HA HA HA!

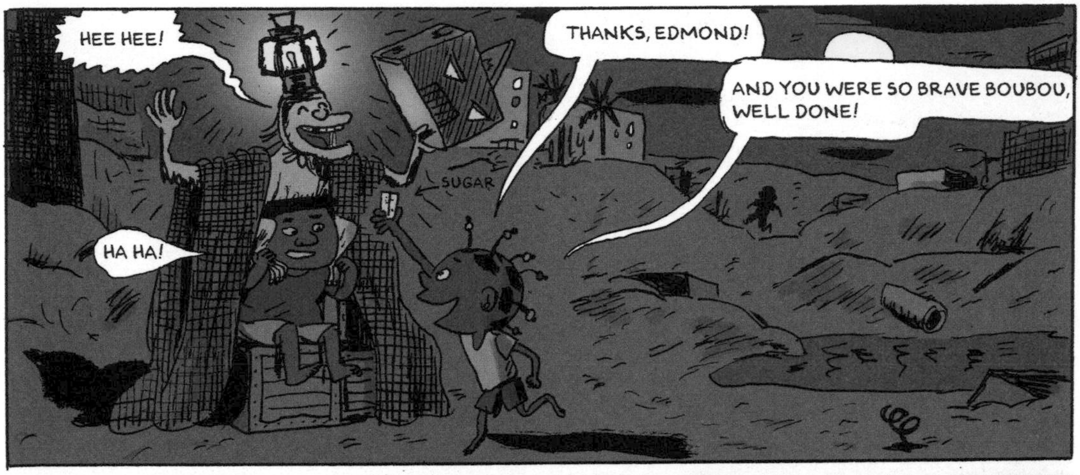
HEE HEE!
HA HA!
SUGAR
THANKS, EDMOND!
AND YOU WERE SO BRAVE BOUBOU, WELL DONE!

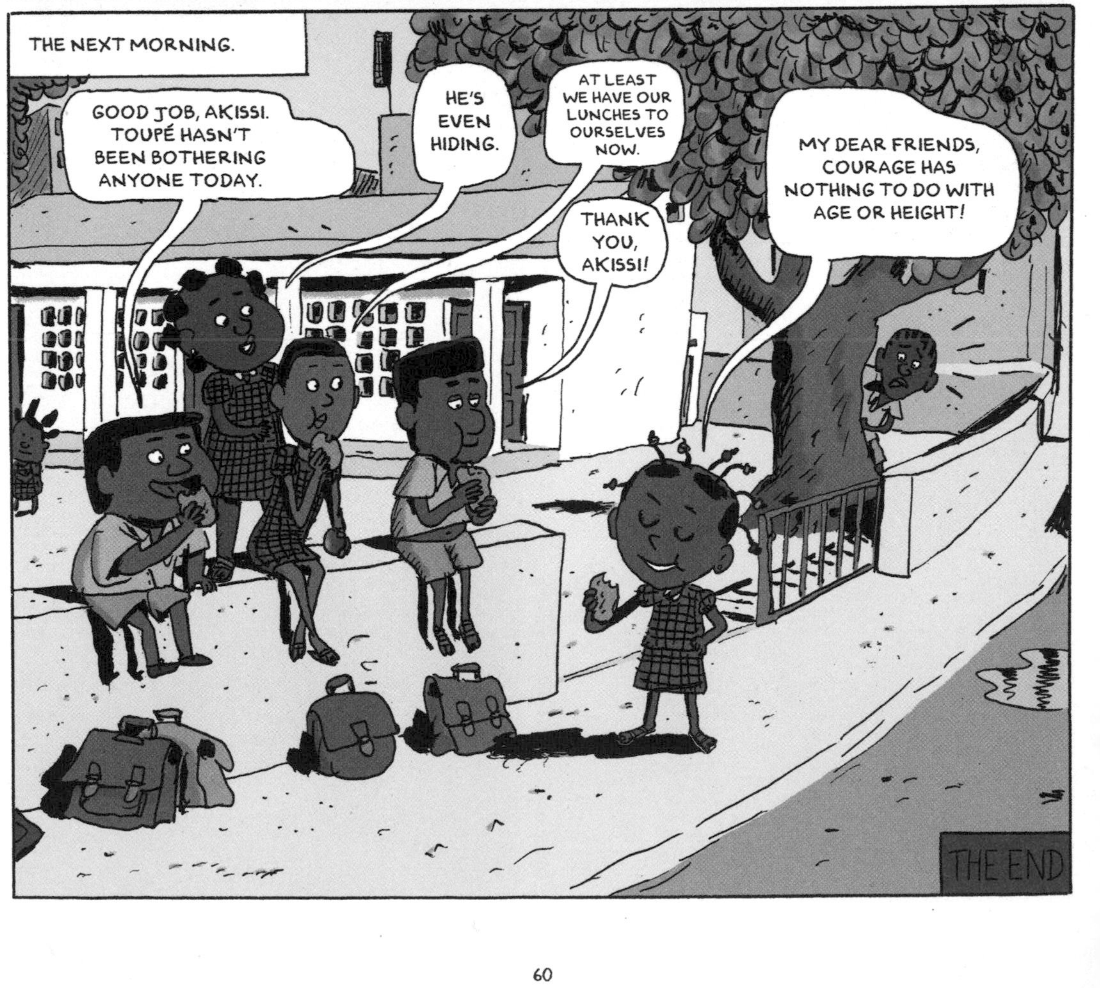
THE NEXT MORNING.
GOOD JOB, AKISSI. TOUPÉ HASN'T BEEN BOTHERING ANYONE TODAY.
HE'S EVEN HIDING.
AT LEAST WE HAVE OUR LUNCHES TO OURSELVES NOW.
THANK YOU, AKISSI!
MY DEAR FRIENDS, COURAGE HAS NOTHING TO DO WITH AGE OR HEIGHT!
THE END

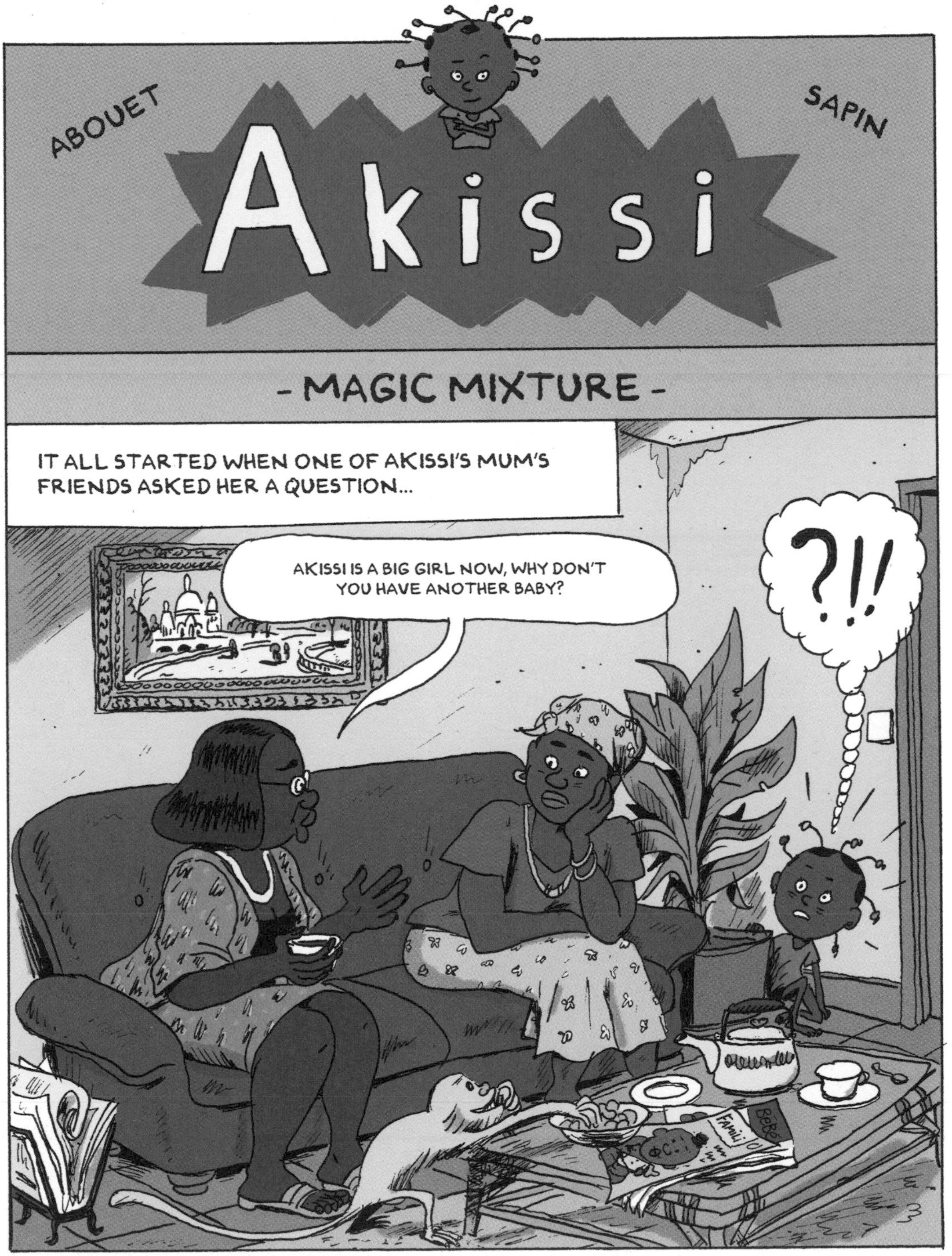
ABOUET
Akissi
SAPIN
- MAGIC MIXTURE -
IT ALL STARTED WHEN ONE OF AKISSI'S MUM'S FRIENDS ASKED HER A QUESTION...
AKISSI IS A BIG GIRL NOW, WHY DON'T YOU HAVE ANOTHER BABY?
?!!

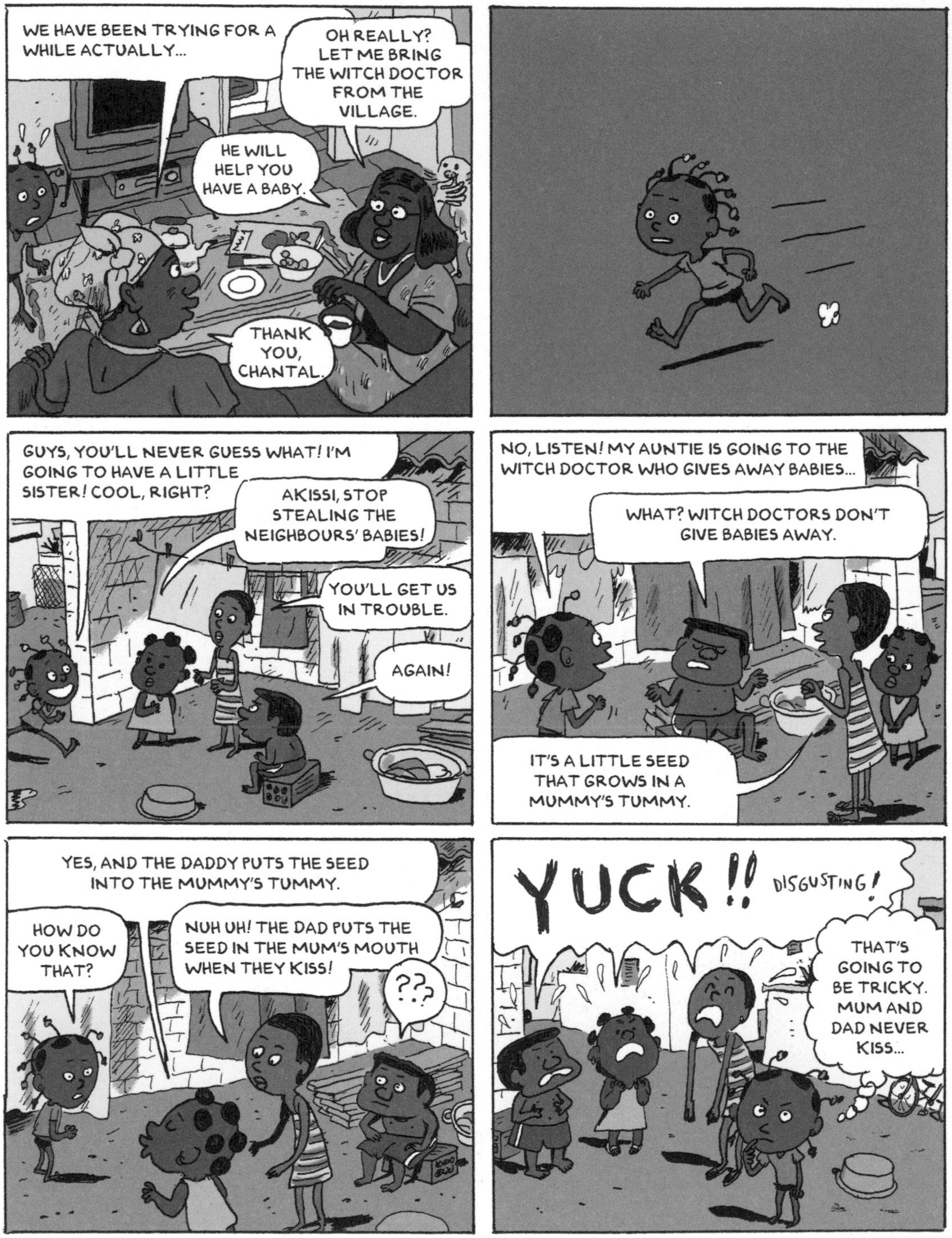
WE HAVE BEEN TRYING FOR A WHILE ACTUALLY...
OH REALLY? LET ME BRING THE WITCH DOCTOR FROM THE VILLAGE.
HE WILL HELP YOU HAVE A BABY.
THANK YOU, CHANTAL.
GUYS, YOU'LL NEVER GUESS WHAT! I'M GOING TO HAVE A LITTLE SISTER! COOL, RIGHT?
AKISSI, STOP STEALING THE NEIGHBOURS' BABIES!
YOU'LL GET US IN TROUBLE.
AGAIN!
NO, LISTEN! MY AUNTIE IS GOING TO THE WITCH DOCTOR WHO GIVES AWAY BABIES...
WHAT? WITCH DOCTORS DON'T GIVE BABIES AWAY.
IT'S A LITTLE SEED THAT GROWS IN A MUMMY'S TUMMY.
YES, AND THE DADDY PUTS THE SEED INTO THE MUMMY'S TUMMY.
HOW DO YOU KNOW THAT?
NUH UH! THE DAD PUTS THE SEED IN THE MUM'S MOUTH WHEN THEY KISS!
???
YUCK!!
DISGUSTING!
THAT'S GOING TO BE TRICKY. MUM AND DAD NEVER KISS...

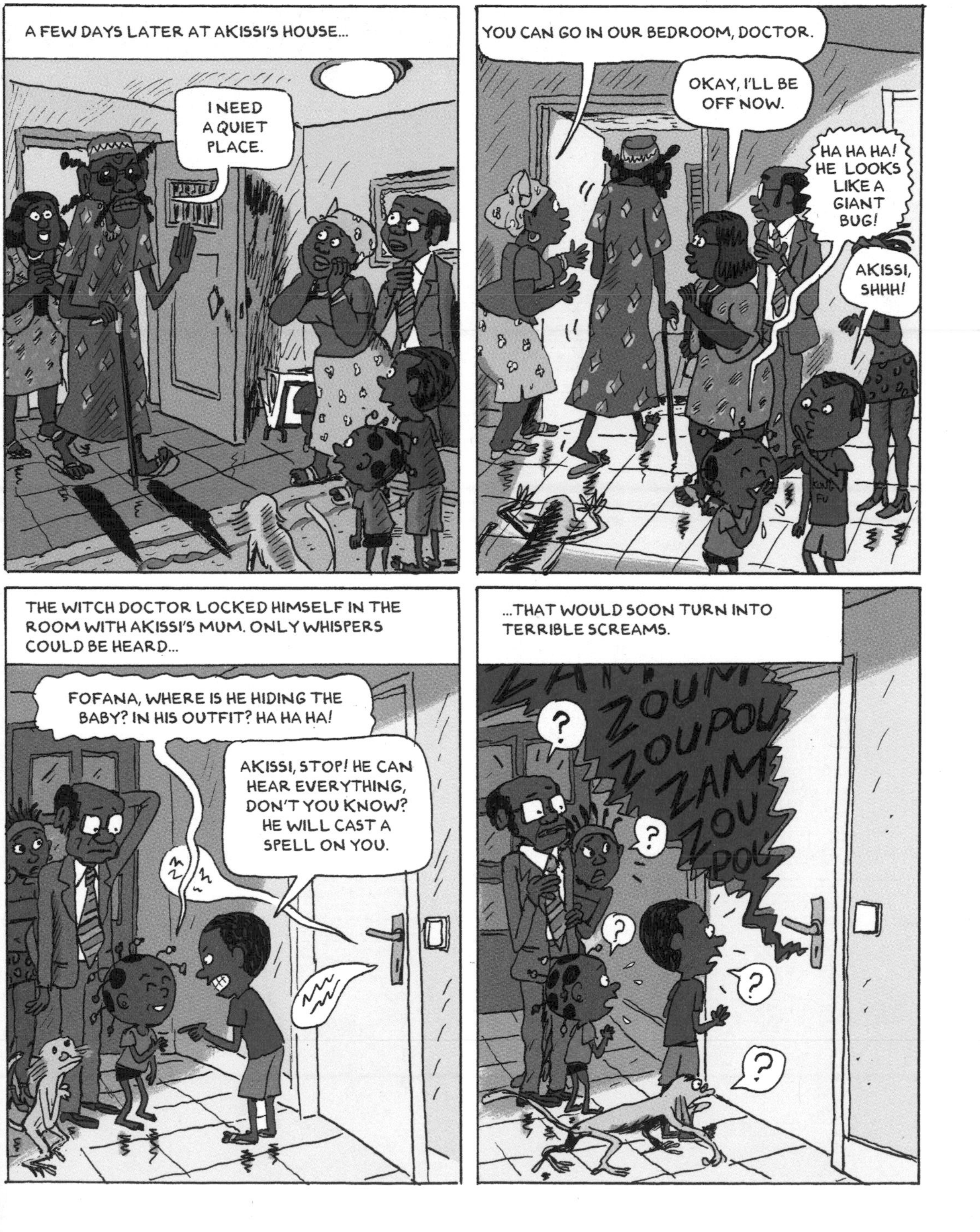
A FEW DAYS LATER AT AKISSI'S HOUSE...
I NEED A QUIET PLACE.
YOU CAN GO IN OUR BEDROOM, DOCTOR.
OKAY, I'LL BE OFF NOW.
HA HA HA! HE LOOKS LIKE A GIANT BUG!
AKISSI, SHHH!
KUNG FU
THE WITCH DOCTOR LOCKED HIMSELF IN THE ROOM WITH AKISSI'S MUM. ONLY WHISPERS COULD BE HEARD...
FOFANA, WHERE IS HE HIDING THE BABY? IN HIS OUTFIT? HA HA HA!
AKISSI, STOP! HE CAN HEAR EVERYTHING, DON'T YOU KNOW? HE WILL CAST A SPELL ON YOU.
...THAT WOULD SOON TURN INTO TERRIBLE SCREAMS.
ZOUM ZOUPOU ZAM ZOU POU
?
?
?
?
?

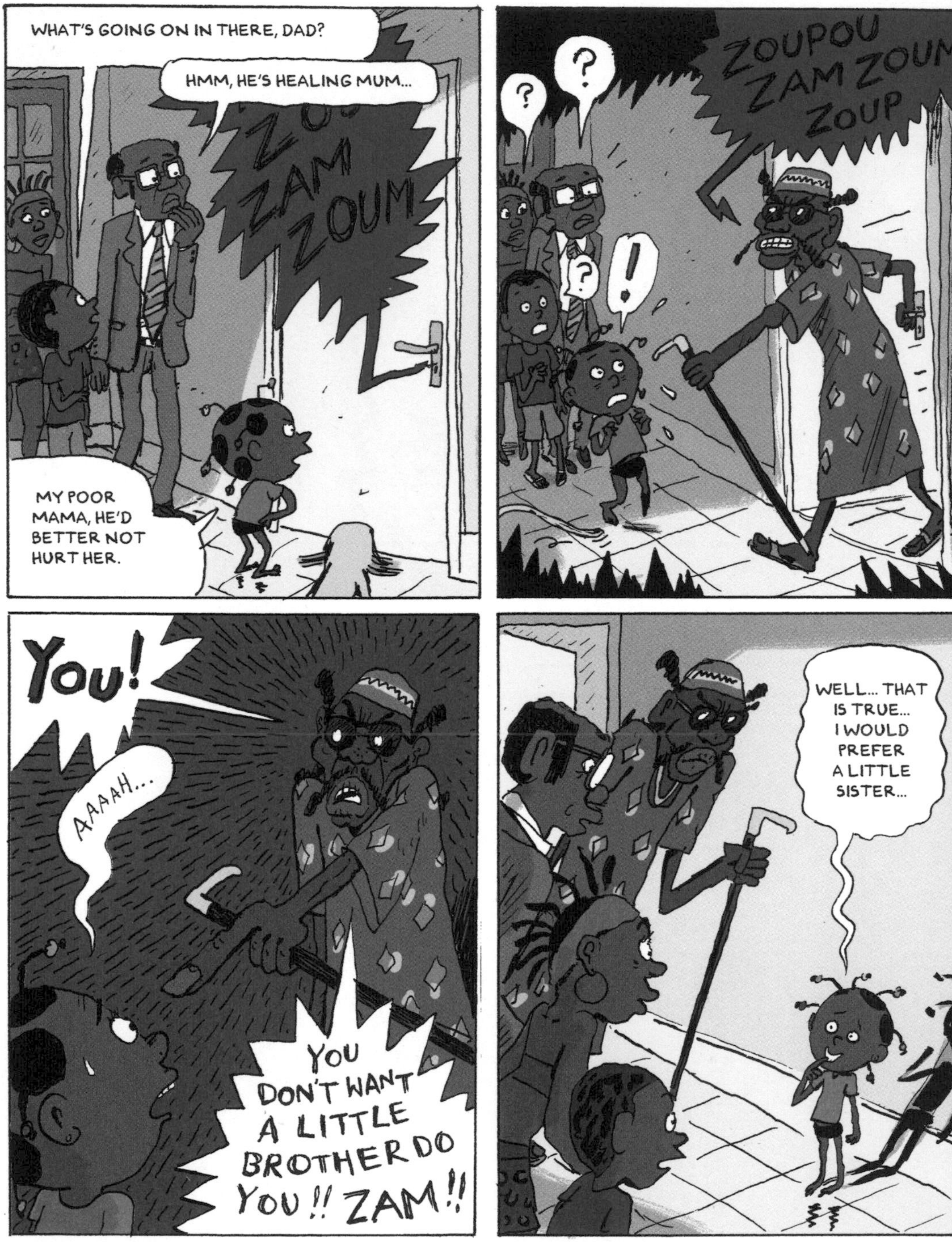
WHAT'S GOING ON IN THERE, DAD?
HMM, HE'S HEALING MUM...
ZAM ZOUM
MY POOR MAMA, HE'D BETTER NOT HURT HER.
?
?
ZOUPOU ZAM ZOUM ZOUP
?
!
YOU!
AAAAH...
YOU DON'T WANT A LITTLE BROTHER DO YOU!! ZAM!!
WELL... THAT IS TRUE... I WOULD PREFER A LITTLE SISTER...

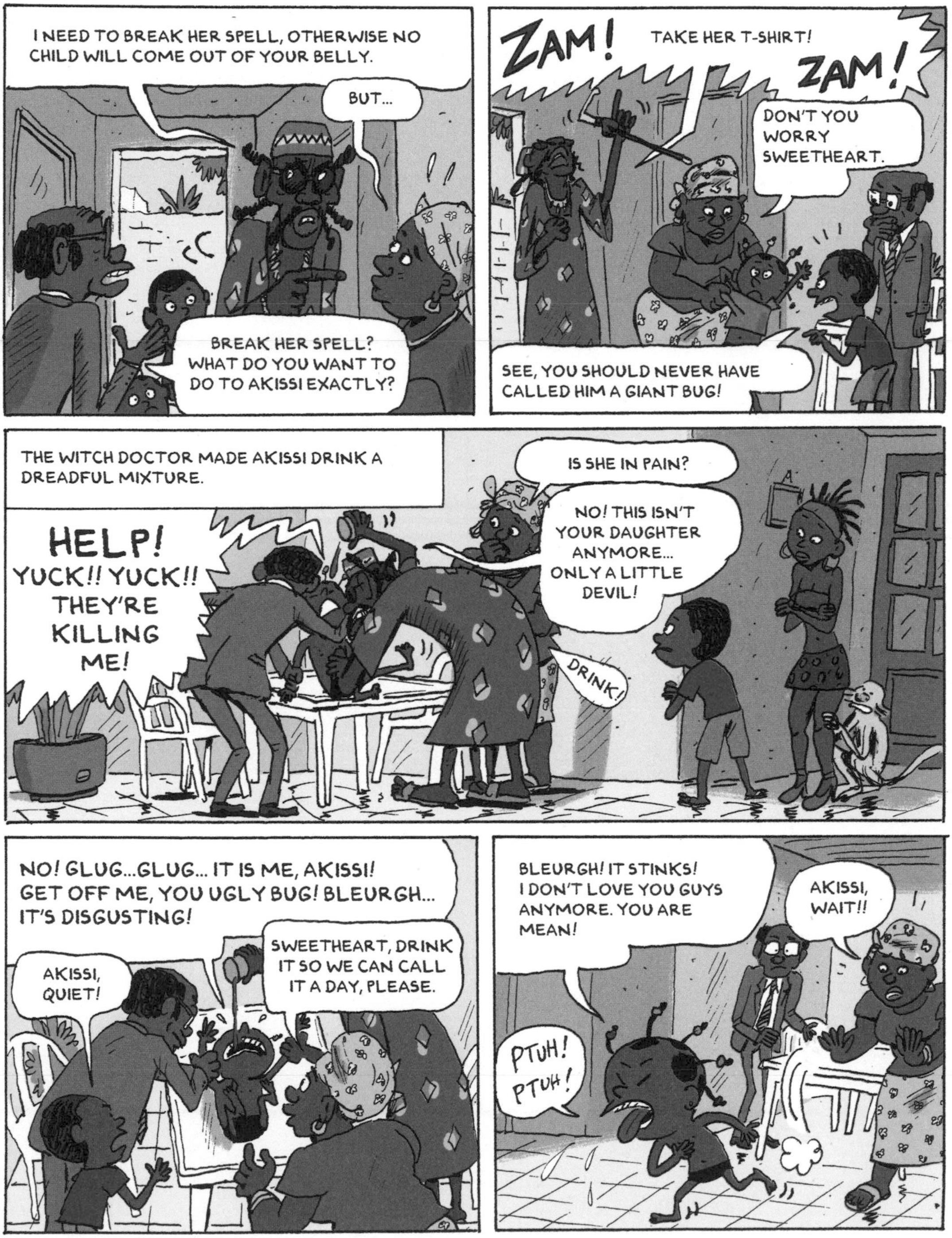
I NEED TO BREAK HER SPELL, OTHERWISE NO CHILD WILL COME OUT OF YOUR BELLY.
BUT...
BREAK HER SPELL? WHAT DO YOU WANT TO DO TO AKISSI EXACTLY?
ZAM!
TAKE HER T-SHIRT!
ZAM!
DON'T YOU WORRY SWEETHEART.
SEE, YOU SHOULD NEVER HAVE CALLED HIM A GIANT BUG!
THE WITCH DOCTOR MADE AKISSI DRINK A DREADFUL MIXTURE.
HELP! YUCK!! YUCK!! THEY'RE KILLING ME!
IS SHE IN PAIN?
NO! THIS ISN'T YOUR DAUGHTER ANYMORE... ONLY A LITTLE DEVIL!
DRINK!
NO! GLUG...GLUG... IT IS ME, AKISSI! GET OFF ME, YOU UGLY BUG! BLEURGH... IT'S DISGUSTING!
AKISSI, QUIET!
SWEETHEART, DRINK IT SO WE CAN CALL IT A DAY, PLEASE.
BLEURGH! IT STINKS! I DON'T LOVE YOU GUYS ANYMORE. YOU ARE MEAN!
AKISSI, WAIT!!
PTUH! PTUH!

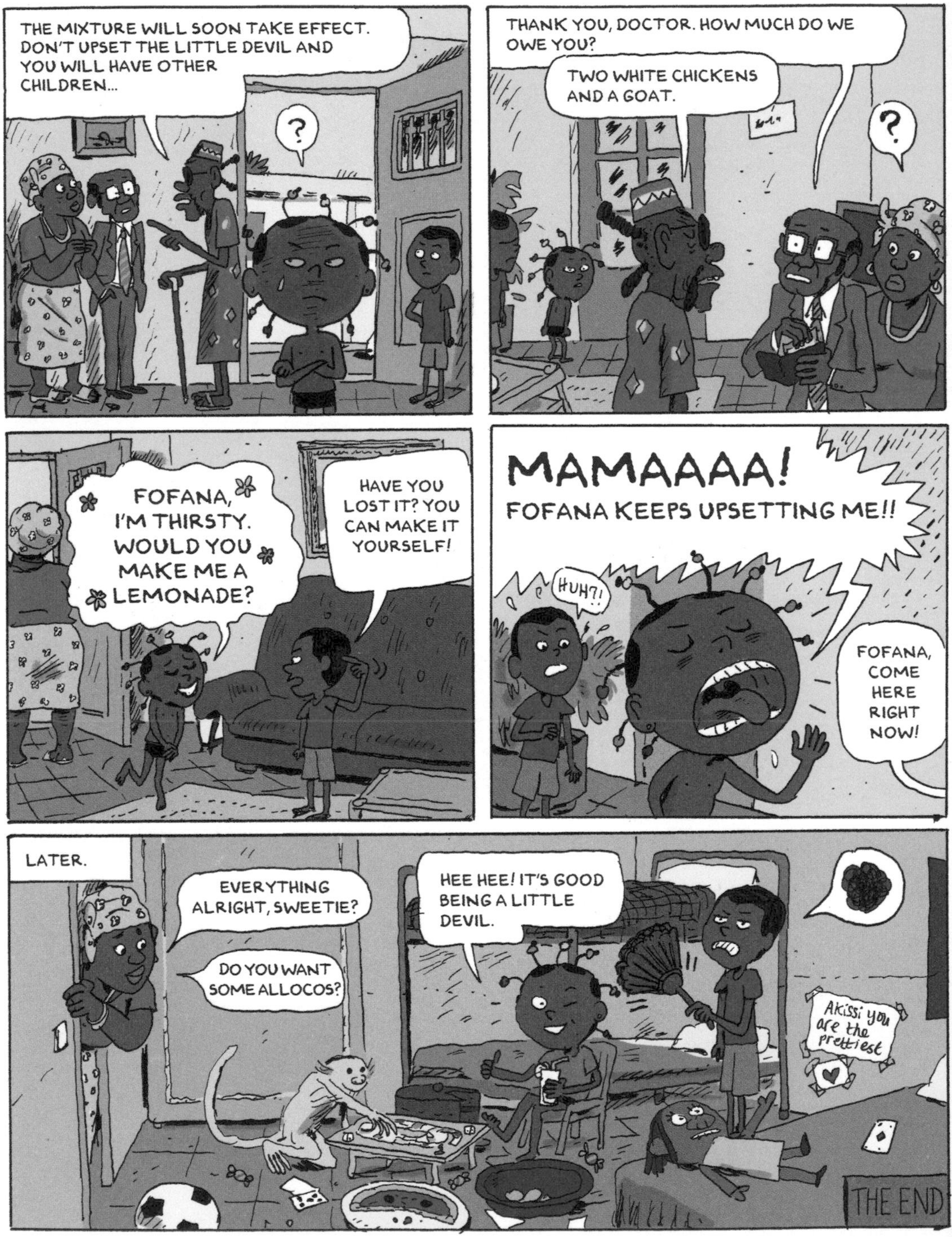
THE MIXTURE WILL SOON TAKE EFFECT. DON'T UPSET THE LITTLE DEVIL AND YOU WILL HAVE OTHER CHILDREN...
?
THANK YOU, DOCTOR. HOW MUCH DO WE OWE YOU?
TWO WHITE CHICKENS AND A GOAT.
?
FOFANA, I'M THIRSTY. WOULD YOU MAKE ME A LEMONADE?
HAVE YOU LOST IT? YOU CAN MAKE IT YOURSELF!
MAMAAAA!
FOFANA KEEPS UPSETTING ME!!
HUH?!
FOFANA, COME HERE RIGHT NOW!
LATER.
EVERYTHING ALRIGHT, SWEETIE?
DO YOU WANT SOME ALLOCOS?
HEE HEE! IT'S GOOD BEING A LITTLE DEVIL.
Akissi you are the prettiest
THE END

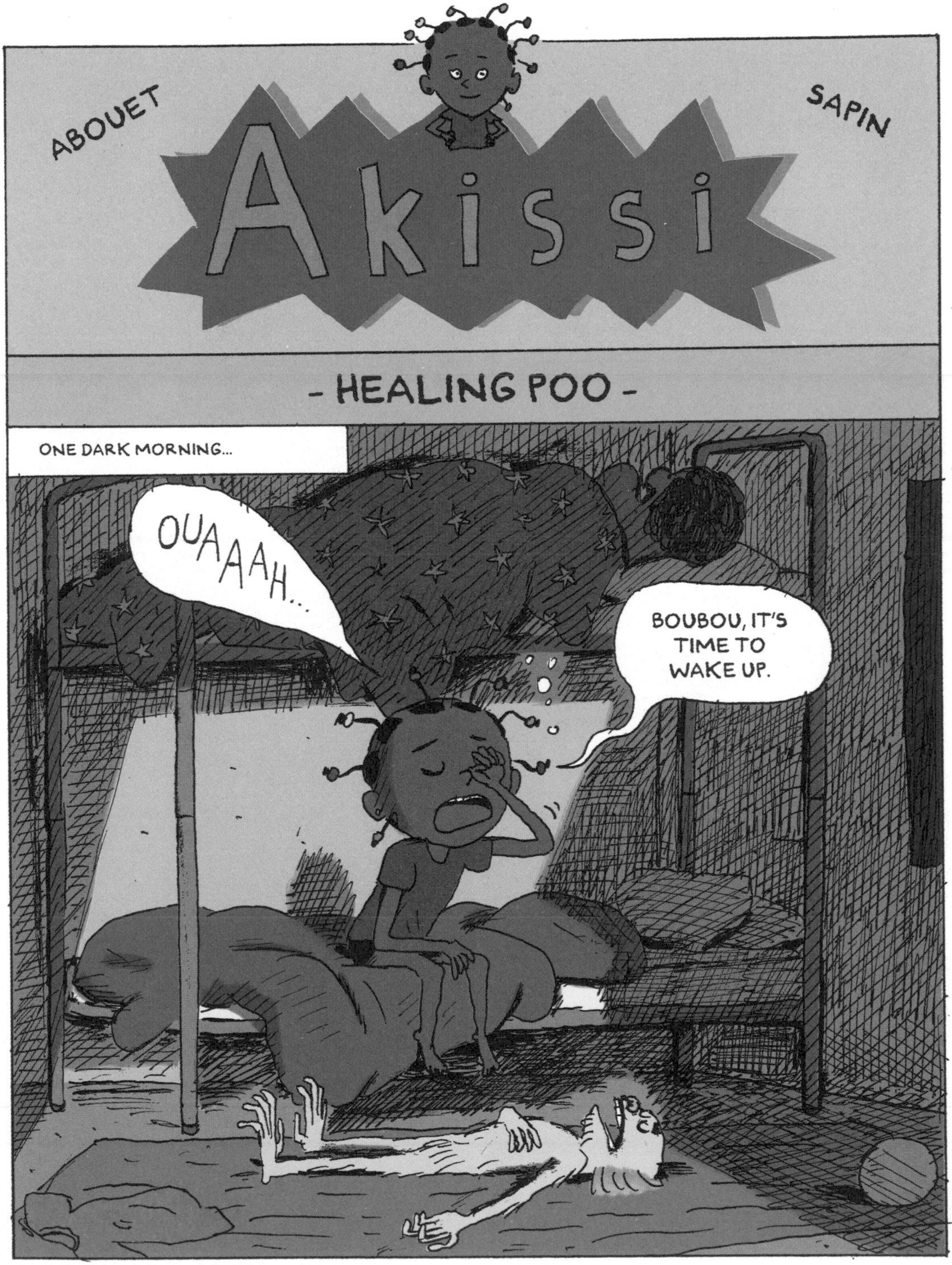
ABOUET
SAPIN
Akissi
- HEALING POO -
ONE DARK MORNING...
OUAAAAH...
BOUBOU, IT'S TIME TO WAKE UP.

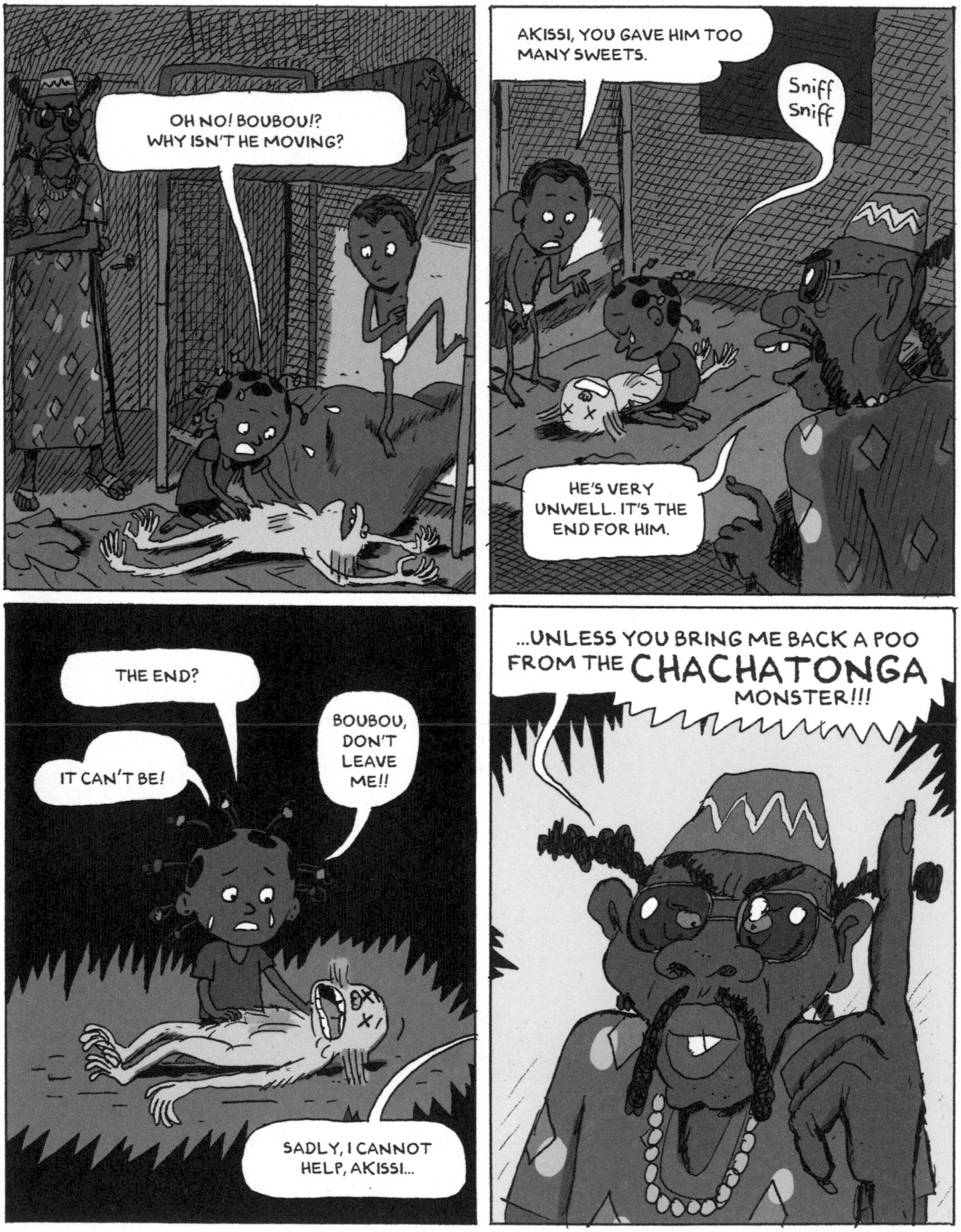
OH NO! BOUBOU!? WHY ISN'T HE MOVING?
AKISSI, YOU GAVE HIM TOO MANY SWEETS.
Sniff Sniff
HE'S VERY UNWELL. IT'S THE END FOR HIM.
THE END?
IT CAN'T BE!
BOUBOU, DON'T LEAVE ME!!
SADLY, I CANNOT HELP, AKISSI...
...UNLESS YOU BRING ME BACK A POO FROM THE CHACHATONGA MONSTER!!!

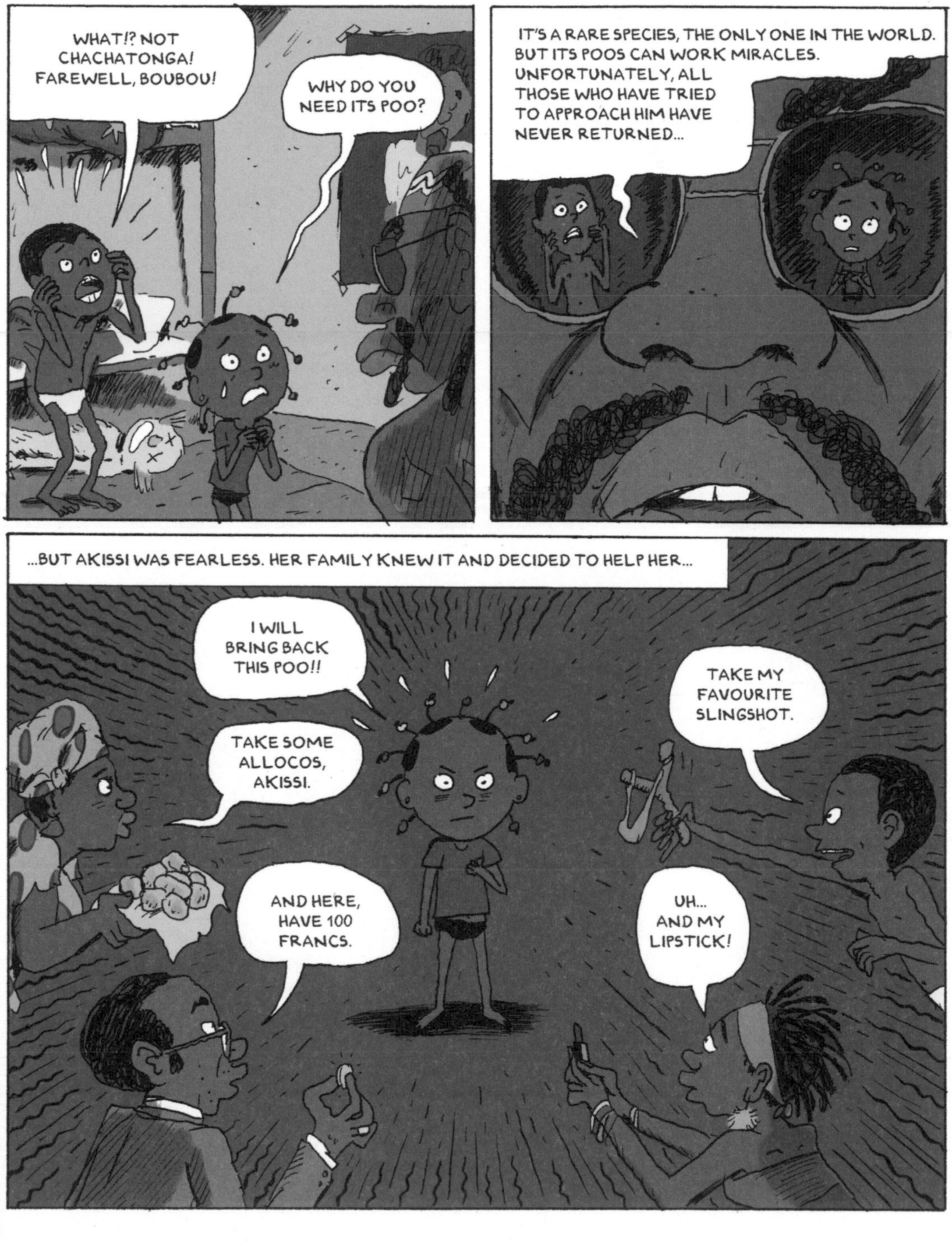
WHAT!? NOT CHACHATONGA! FAREWELL, BOUBOU!
WHY DO YOU NEED ITS POO?
IT'S A RARE SPECIES, THE ONLY ONE IN THE WORLD. BUT ITS POOS CAN WORK MIRACLES. UNFORTUNATELY, ALL THOSE WHO HAVE TRIED TO APPROACH HIM HAVE NEVER RETURNED...
...BUT AKISSI WAS FEARLESS. HER FAMILY KNEW IT AND DECIDED TO HELP HER...
I WILL BRING BACK THIS POO!!
TAKE SOME ALLOCOS, AKISSI.
TAKE MY FAVOURITE SLINGSHOT.
AND HERE, HAVE 100 FRANCS.
UH... AND MY LIPSTICK!

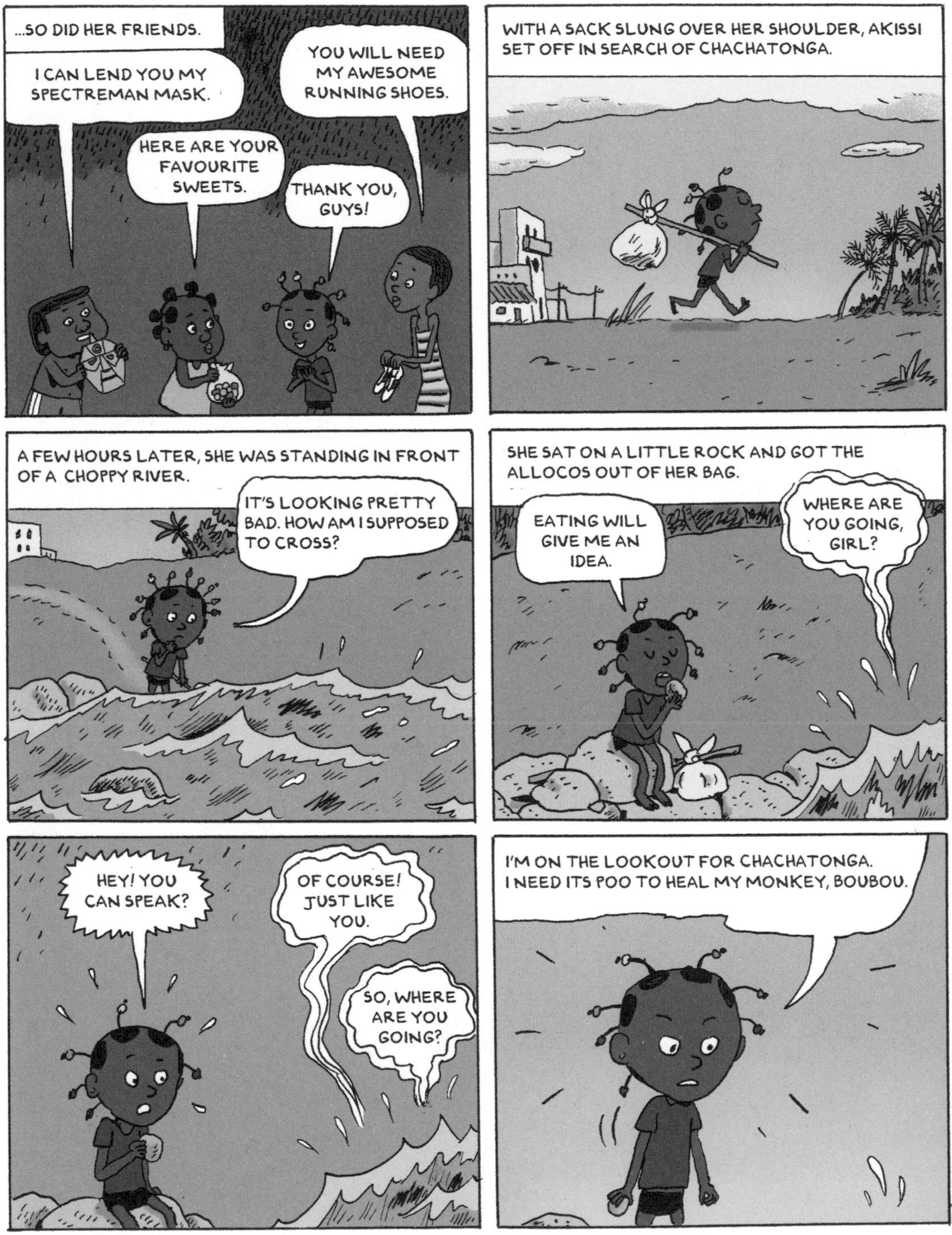
...SO DID HER FRIENDS.
I CAN LEND YOU MY SPECTREMAN MASK.
YOU WILL NEED MY AWESOME RUNNING SHOES.
HERE ARE YOUR FAVOURITE SWEETS.
THANK YOU, GUYS!
WITH A SACK SLUNG OVER HER SHOULDER, AKISSI SET OFF IN SEARCH OF CHACHATONGA.
A FEW HOURS LATER, SHE WAS STANDING IN FRONT OF A CHOPPY RIVER.
IT'S LOOKING PRETTY BAD. HOW AM I SUPPOSED TO CROSS?
SHE SAT ON A LITTLE ROCK AND GOT THE ALLOCOS OUT OF HER BAG.
EATING WILL GIVE ME AN IDEA.
WHERE ARE YOU GOING, GIRL?
HEY! YOU CAN SPEAK?
OF COURSE! JUST LIKE YOU.
SO, WHERE ARE YOU GOING?
I'M ON THE LOOKOUT FOR CHACHATONGA. I NEED ITS POO TO HEAL MY MONKEY, BOUBOU.

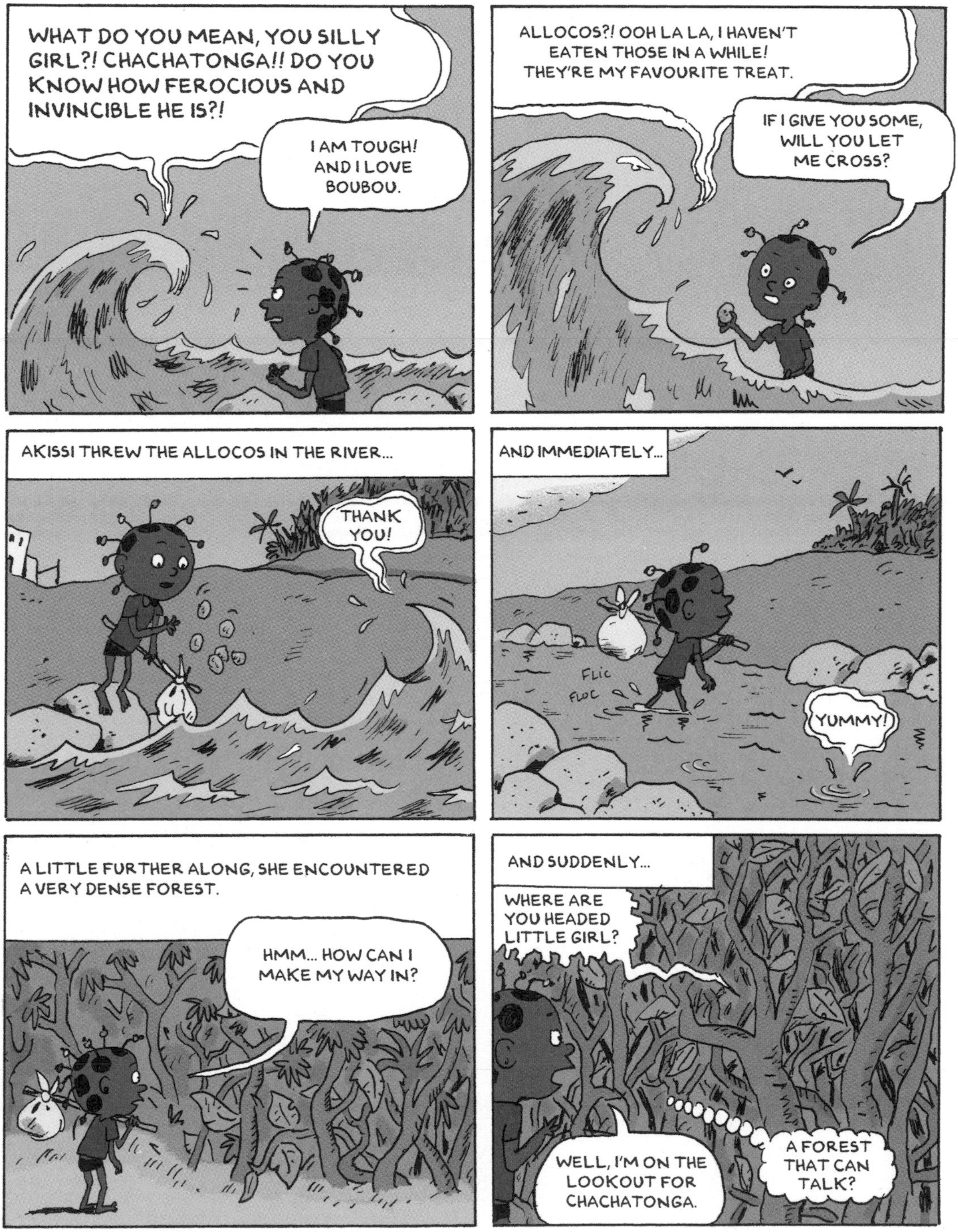

WHAT DO YOU MEAN, YOU SILLY GIRL?! CHACHATONGA!! DO YOU KNOW HOW FEROCIOUS AND INVINCIBLE HE IS?!
I AM TOUGH! AND I LOVE BOUBOU.
ALLOCOS?! OOH LA LA, I HAVEN'T EATEN THOSE IN A WHILE! THEY'RE MY FAVOURITE TREAT.
IF I GIVE YOU SOME, WILL YOU LET ME CROSS?
AKISSI THREW THE ALLOCOS IN THE RIVER...
THANK YOU!
AND IMMEDIATELY...
FLIC
FLOC
YUMMY!
A LITTLE FURTHER ALONG, SHE ENCOUNTERED A VERY DENSE FOREST.
HMM... HOW CAN I MAKE MY WAY IN?
AND SUDDENLY...
WHERE ARE YOU HEADED LITTLE GIRL?
WELL, I'M ON THE LOOKOUT FOR CHACHATONGA.
A FOREST THAT CAN TALK?

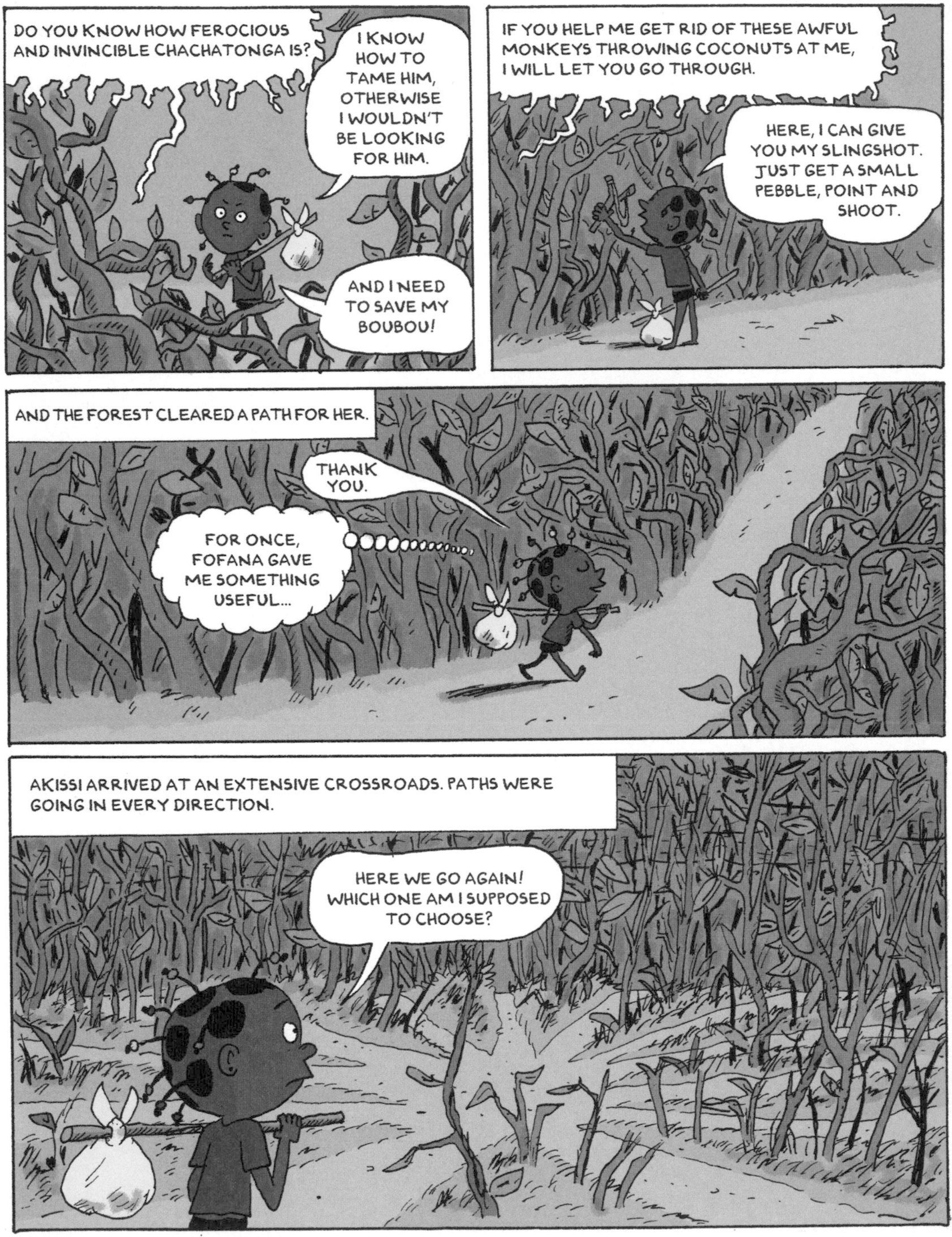

DO YOU KNOW HOW FEROCIOUS AND INVINCIBLE CHACHATONGA IS?
I KNOW HOW TO TAME HIM, OTHERWISE I WOULDN'T BE LOOKING FOR HIM.
AND I NEED TO SAVE MY BOUBOU!
IF YOU HELP ME GET RID OF THESE AWFUL MONKEYS THROWING COCONUTS AT ME, I WILL LET YOU GO THROUGH.
HERE, I CAN GIVE YOU MY SLINGSHOT. JUST GET A SMALL PEBBLE, POINT AND SHOOT.
AND THE FOREST CLEARED A PATH FOR HER.
THANK YOU.
FOR ONCE, FOFANA GAVE ME SOMETHING USEFUL...
AKISSI ARRIVED AT AN EXTENSIVE CROSSROADS. PATHS WERE GOING IN EVERY DIRECTION.
HERE WE GO AGAIN! WHICH ONE AM I SUPPOSED TO CHOOSE?

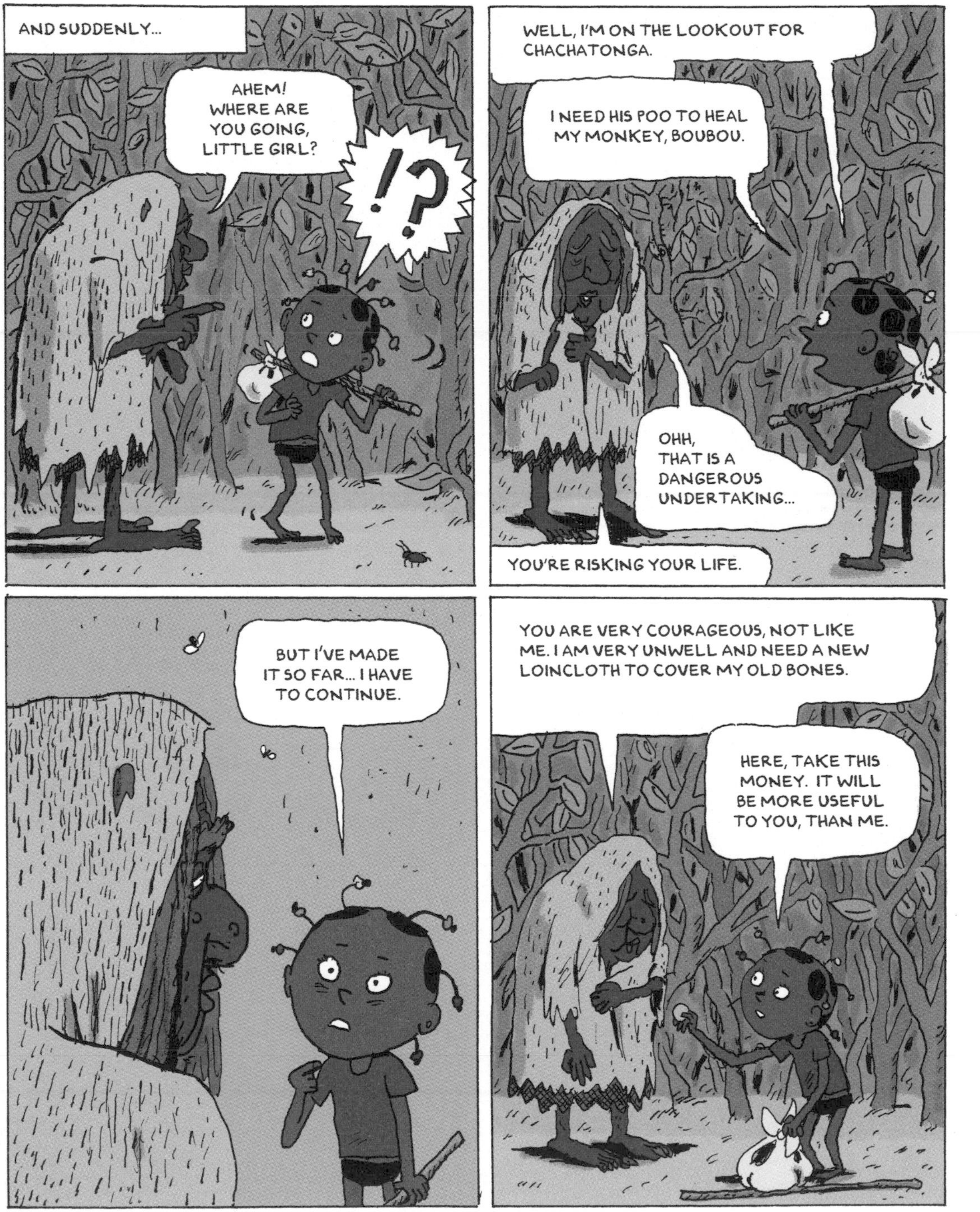
AND SUDDENLY...
AHEM! WHERE ARE YOU GOING, LITTLE GIRL?
!?
WELL, I'M ON THE LOOKOUT FOR CHACHATONGA.
I NEED HIS POO TO HEAL MY MONKEY, BOUBOU.
OHH, THAT IS A DANGEROUS UNDERTAKING...
YOU'RE RISKING YOUR LIFE.
BUT I'VE MADE IT SO FAR... I HAVE TO CONTINUE.
YOU ARE VERY COURAGEOUS, NOT LIKE ME. I AM VERY UNWELL AND NEED A NEW LOINCLOTH TO COVER MY OLD BONES.
HERE, TAKE THIS MONEY. IT WILL BE MORE USEFUL TO YOU, THAN ME.

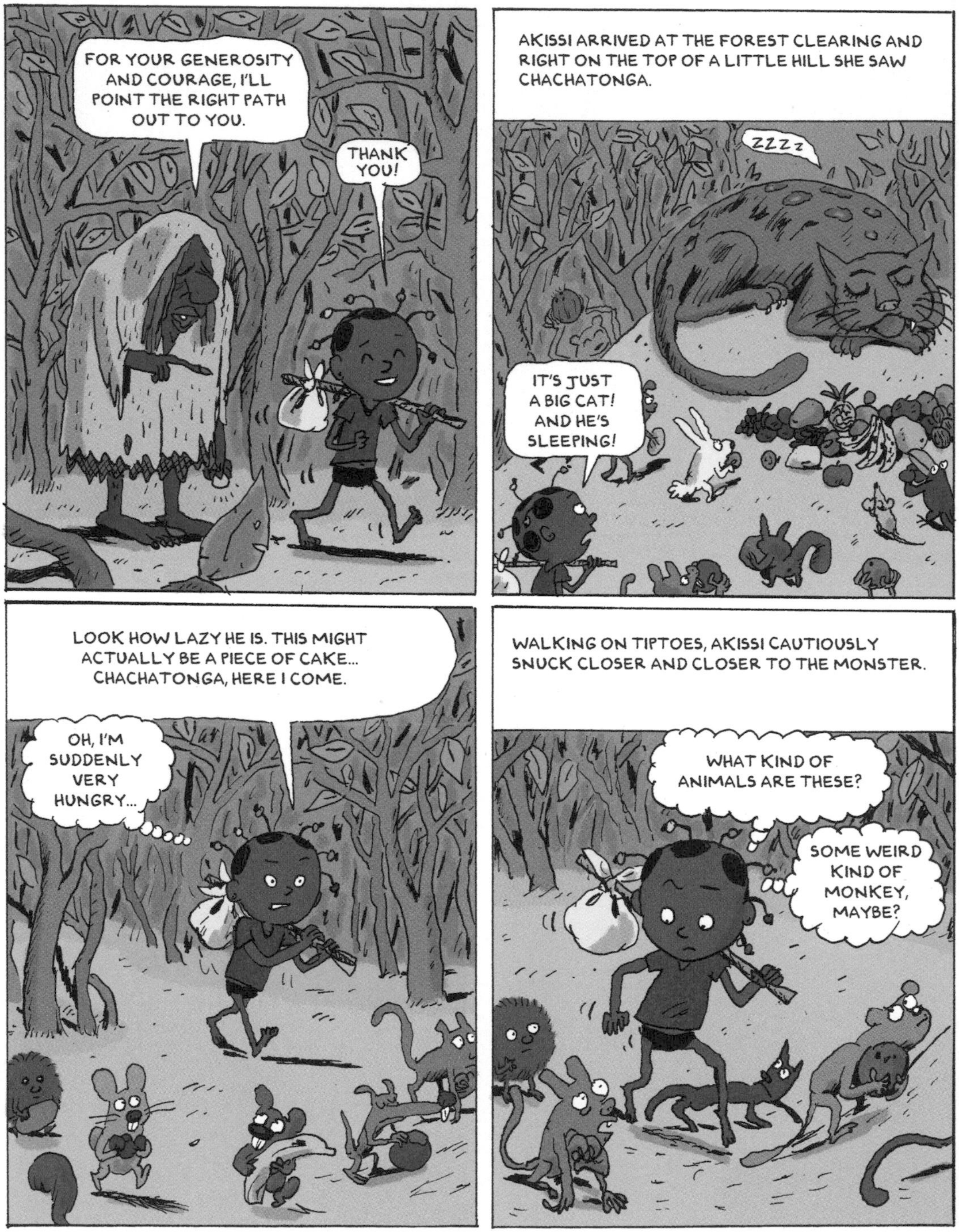
FOR YOUR GENEROSITY AND COURAGE, I'LL POINT THE RIGHT PATH OUT TO YOU.
THANK YOU!
AKISSI ARRIVED AT THE FOREST CLEARING AND RIGHT ON THE TOP OF A LITTLE HILL SHE SAW CHACHATONGA.
ZZZz
IT'S JUST A BIG CAT! AND HE'S SLEEPING!
LOOK HOW LAZY HE IS. THIS MIGHT ACTUALLY BE A PIECE OF CAKE... CHACHATONGA, HERE I COME.
OH, I'M SUDDENLY VERY HUNGRY...
WALKING ON TIPTOES, AKISSI CAUTIOUSLY SNUCK CLOSER AND CLOSER TO THE MONSTER.
WHAT KIND OF ANIMALS ARE THESE?
SOME WEIRD KIND OF MONKEY, MAYBE?

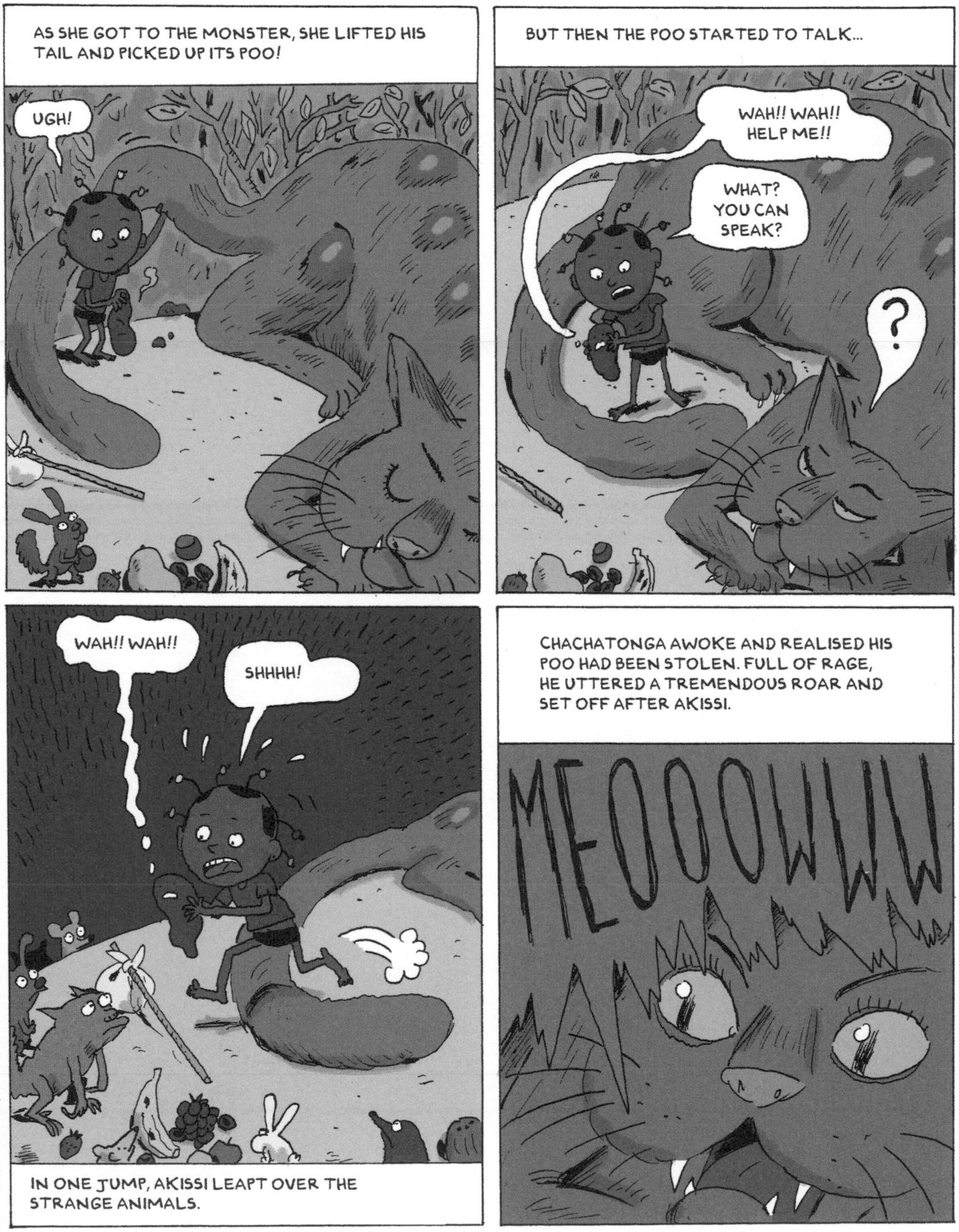
AS SHE GOT TO THE MONSTER, SHE LIFTED HIS TAIL AND PICKED UP ITS POO!
UGH!
BUT THEN THE POO STARTED TO TALK...
WAH!! WAH!! HELP ME!!
WHAT? YOU CAN SPEAK?
?
WAH!! WAH!!
SHHHH!
IN ONE JUMP, AKISSI LEAPT OVER THE STRANGE ANIMALS.
CHACHATONGA AWOKE AND REALISED HIS POO HAD BEEN STOLEN. FULL OF RAGE, HE UTTERED A TREMENDOUS ROAR AND SET OFF AFTER AKISSI.
MEOOOWWW

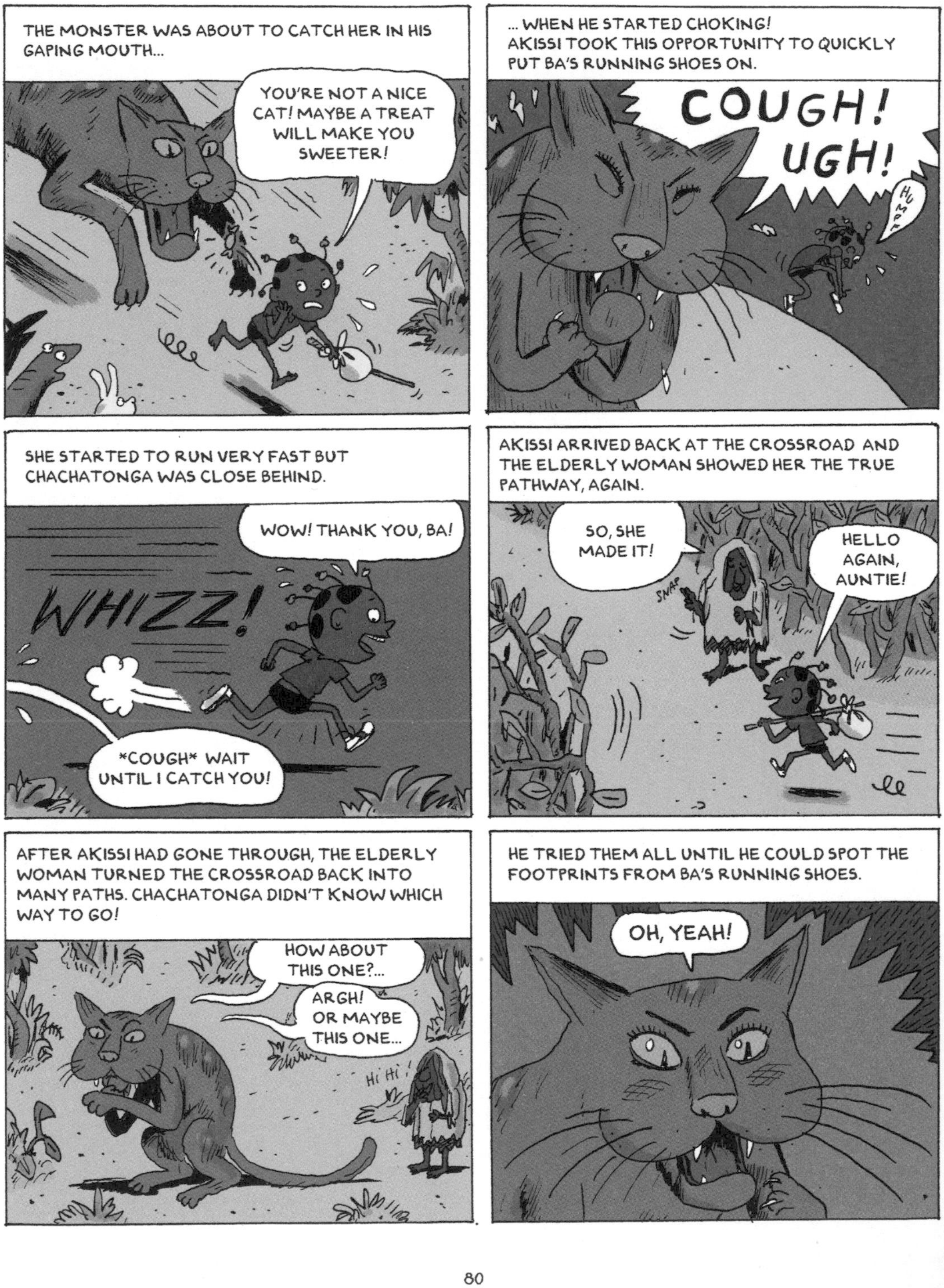
THE MONSTER WAS ABOUT TO CATCH HER IN HIS GAPING MOUTH...
YOU'RE NOT A NICE CAT! MAYBE A TREAT WILL MAKE YOU SWEETER!
... WHEN HE STARTED CHOKING! AKISSI TOOK THIS OPPORTUNITY TO QUICKLY PUT BA'S RUNNING SHOES ON.
COUGH! UGH!
HUMPF
SHE STARTED TO RUN VERY FAST BUT CHACHATONGA WAS CLOSE BEHIND.
WOW! THANK YOU, BA!
WHIZZ!
COUGH WAIT UNTIL I CATCH YOU!
AKISSI ARRIVED BACK AT THE CROSSROAD AND THE ELDERLY WOMAN SHOWED HER THE TRUE PATHWAY, AGAIN.
SO, SHE MADE IT!
SNAP
HELLO AGAIN, AUNTIE!
AFTER AKISSI HAD GONE THROUGH, THE ELDERLY WOMAN TURNED THE CROSSROAD BACK INTO MANY PATHS. CHACHATONGA DIDN'T KNOW WHICH WAY TO GO!
HOW ABOUT THIS ONE?...
ARGH! OR MAYBE THIS ONE...
HI HI
HE TRIED THEM ALL UNTIL HE COULD SPOT THE FOOTPRINTS FROM BA'S RUNNING SHOES.
OH, YEAH!

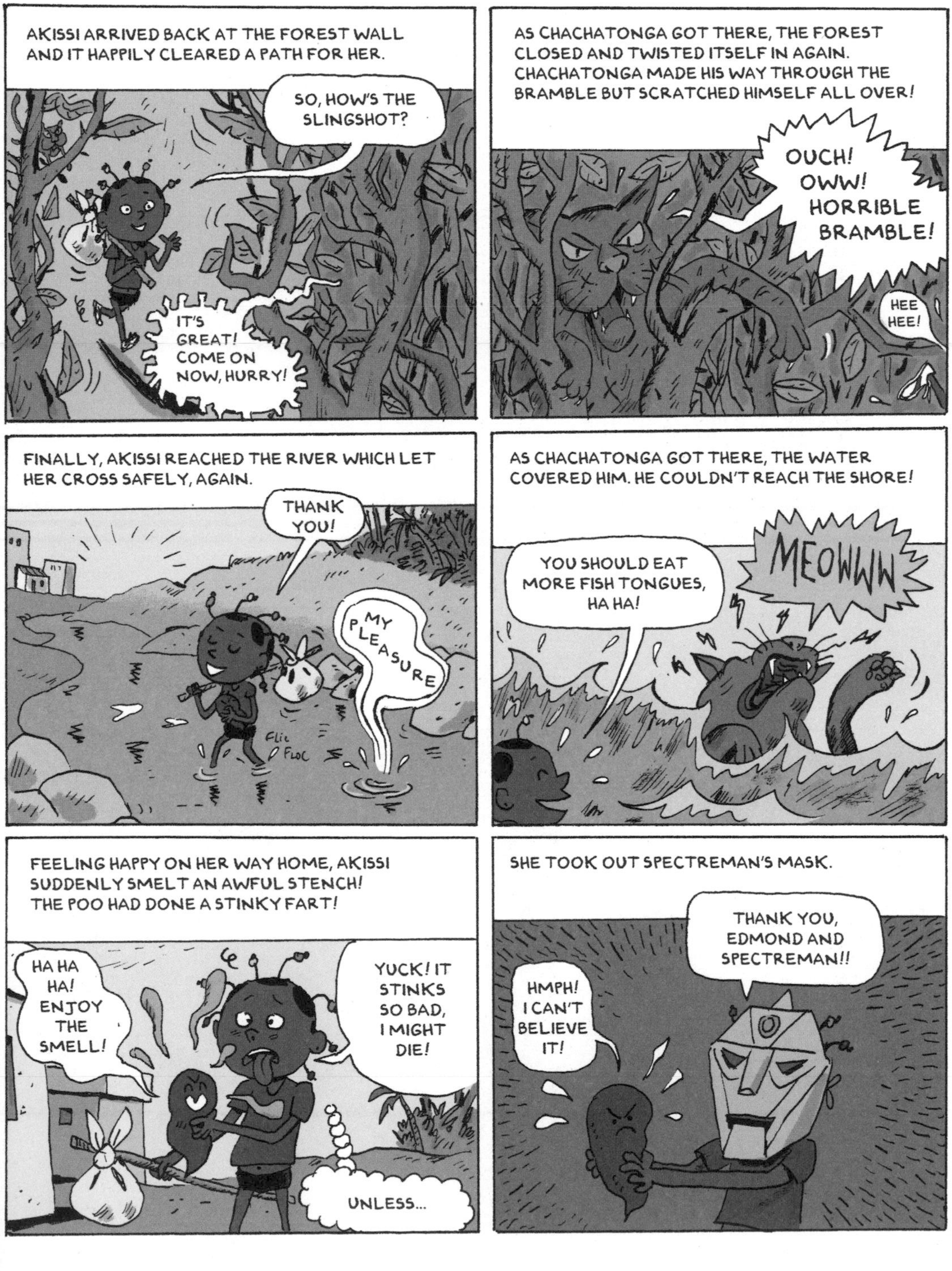
AKISSI ARRIVED BACK AT THE FOREST WALL AND IT HAPPILY CLEARED A PATH FOR HER.
SO, HOW'S THE SLINGSHOT?
IT'S GREAT! COME ON NOW, HURRY!
AS CHACHATONGA GOT THERE, THE FOREST CLOSED AND TWISTED ITSELF IN AGAIN. CHACHATONGA MADE HIS WAY THROUGH THE BRAMBLE BUT SCRATCHED HIMSELF ALL OVER!
OUCH! OWW! HORRIBLE BRAMBLE!
HEE HEE!
FINALLY, AKISSI REACHED THE RIVER WHICH LET HER CROSS SAFELY, AGAIN.
THANK YOU!
MY PLEASURE
Flic
Floc
AS CHACHATONGA GOT THERE, THE WATER COVERED HIM. HE COULDN'T REACH THE SHORE!
YOU SHOULD EAT MORE FISH TONGUES, HA HA!
MEOWWW
FEELING HAPPY ON HER WAY HOME, AKISSI SUDDENLY SMELT AN AWFUL STENCH! THE POO HAD DONE A STINKY FART!
HA HA HA! ENJOY THE SMELL!
YUCK! IT STINKS SO BAD, I MIGHT DIE!
UNLESS...
SHE TOOK OUT SPECTREMAN'S MASK.
THANK YOU, EDMOND AND SPECTREMAN!!
HMPH! I CAN'T BELIEVE IT!

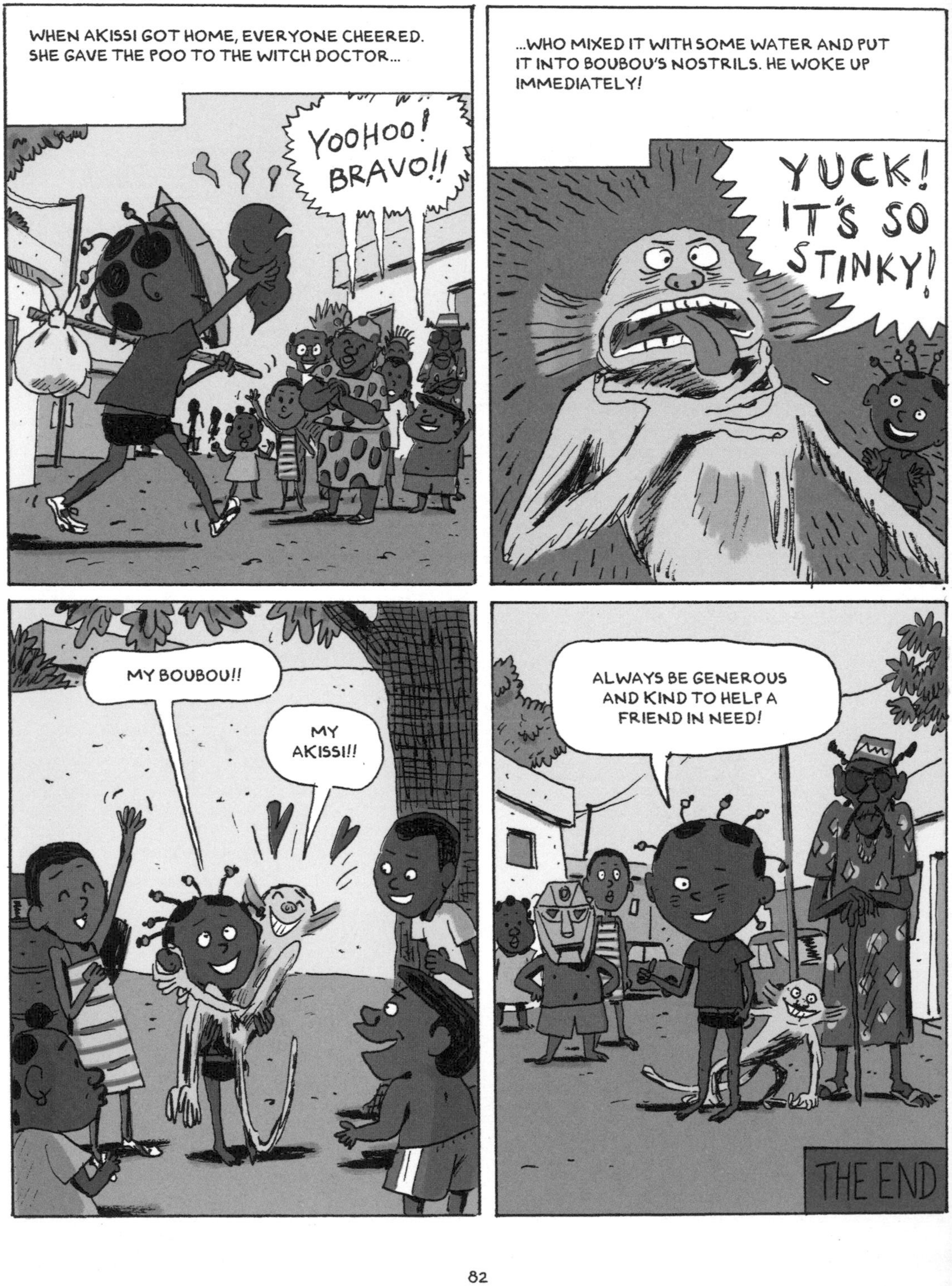
WHEN AKISSI GOT HOME, EVERYONE CHEERED. SHE GAVE THE POO TO THE WITCH DOCTOR...
YOOHOO! BRAVO!!
...WHO MIXED IT WITH SOME WATER AND PUT IT INTO BOUBOU'S NOSTRILS. HE WOKE UP IMMEDIATELY!
YUCK! IT'S SO STINKY!
MY BOUBOU!!
MY AKISSI!!
ALWAYS BE GENEROUS AND KIND TO HELP A FRIEND IN NEED!
THE END

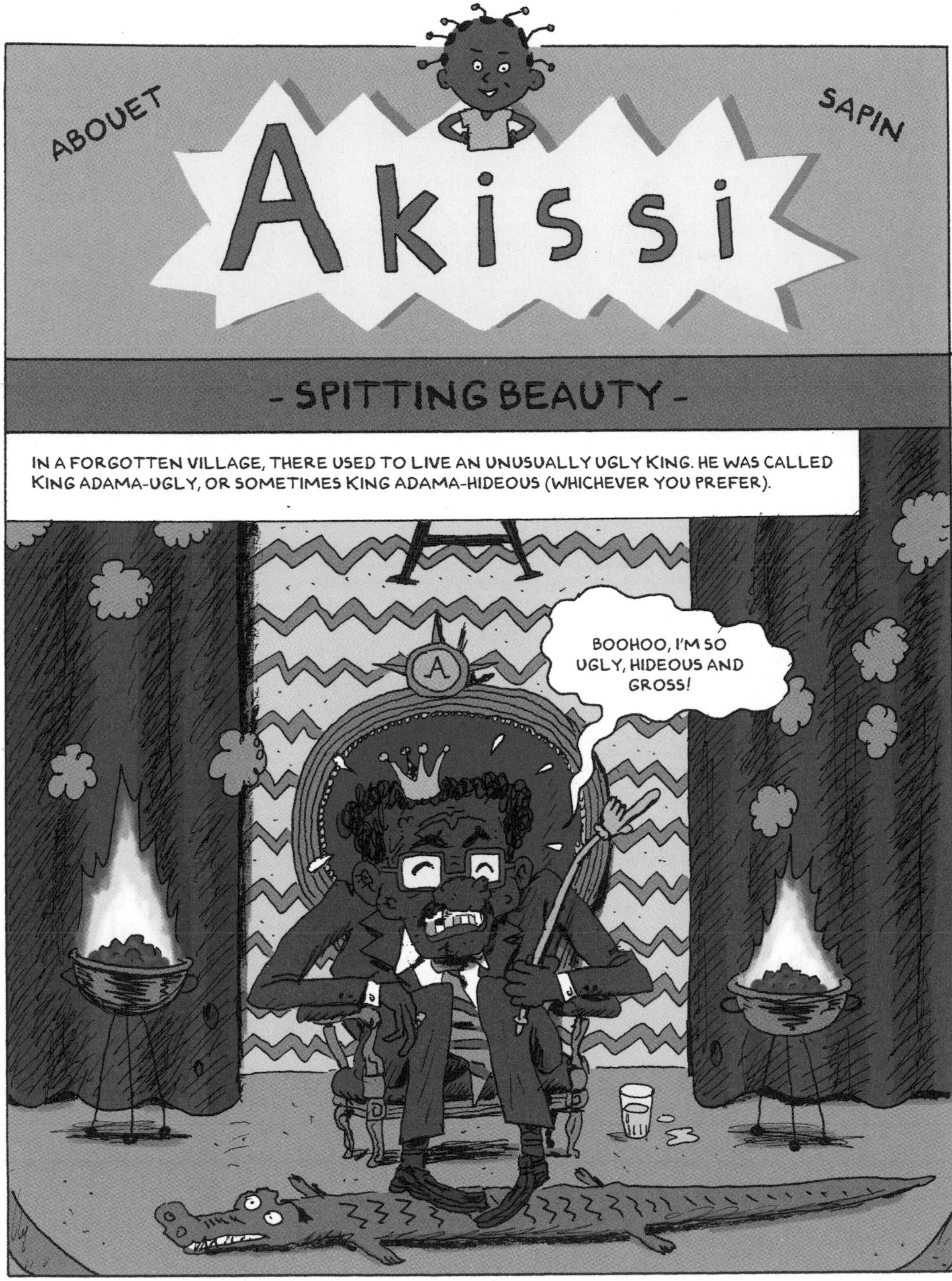
ABOUET
Akissi
SAPIN
- SPITTING BEAUTY -
IN A FORGOTTEN VILLAGE, THERE USED TO LIVE AN UNUSUALLY UGLY KING. HE WAS CALLED KING ADAMA-UGLY, OR SOMETIMES KING ADAMA-HIDEOUS (WHICHEVER YOU PREFER).
BOOHOO, I'M SO UGLY, HIDEOUS AND GROSS!

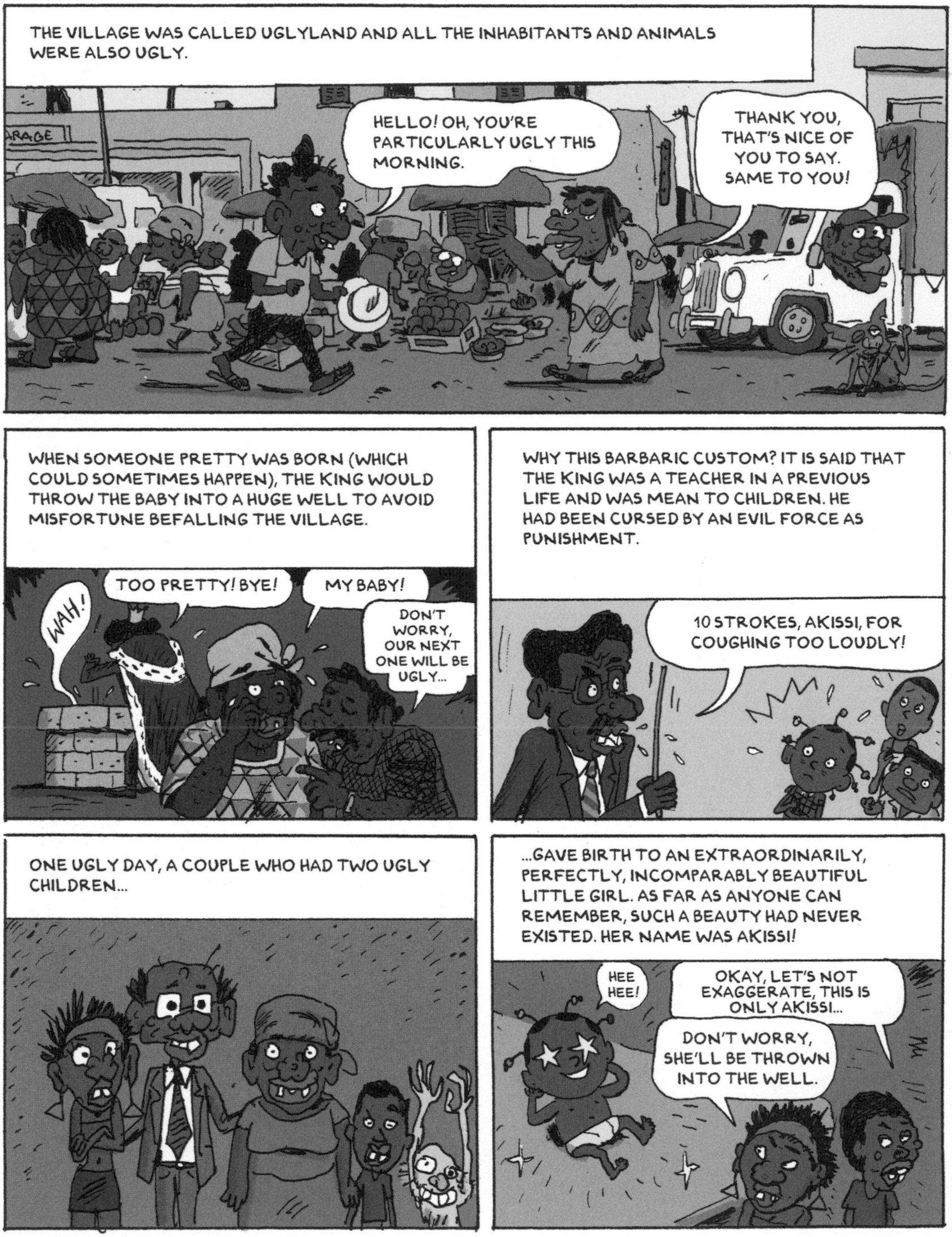
THE VILLAGE WAS CALLED UGLYLAND AND ALL THE INHABITANTS AND ANIMALS WERE ALSO UGLY.
HELLO! OH, YOU'RE PARTICULARLY UGLY THIS MORNING.
THANK YOU, THAT'S NICE OF YOU TO SAY. SAME TO YOU!
WHEN SOMEONE PRETTY WAS BORN (WHICH COULD SOMETIMES HAPPEN), THE KING WOULD THROW THE BABY INTO A HUGE WELL TO AVOID MISFORTUNE BEFALLING THE VILLAGE.
WAH!
TOO PRETTY! BYE!
MY BABY!
DON'T WORRY, OUR NEXT ONE WILL BE UGLY...
WHY THIS BARBARIC CUSTOM? IT IS SAID THAT THE KING WAS A TEACHER IN A PREVIOUS LIFE AND WAS MEAN TO CHILDREN. HE HAD BEEN CURSED BY AN EVIL FORCE AS PUNISHMENT.
10 STROKES, AKISSI, FOR COUGHING TOO LOUDLY!
ONE UGLY DAY, A COUPLE WHO HAD TWO UGLY CHILDREN...
...GAVE BIRTH TO AN EXTRAORDINARILY, PERFECTLY, INCOMPARABLY BEAUTIFUL LITTLE GIRL. AS FAR AS ANYONE CAN REMEMBER, SUCH A BEAUTY HAD NEVER EXISTED. HER NAME WAS AKISSI!
HEE HEE!
OKAY, LET'S NOT EXAGGERATE, THIS IS ONLY AKISSI...
DON'T WORRY, SHE'LL BE THROWN INTO THE WELL.

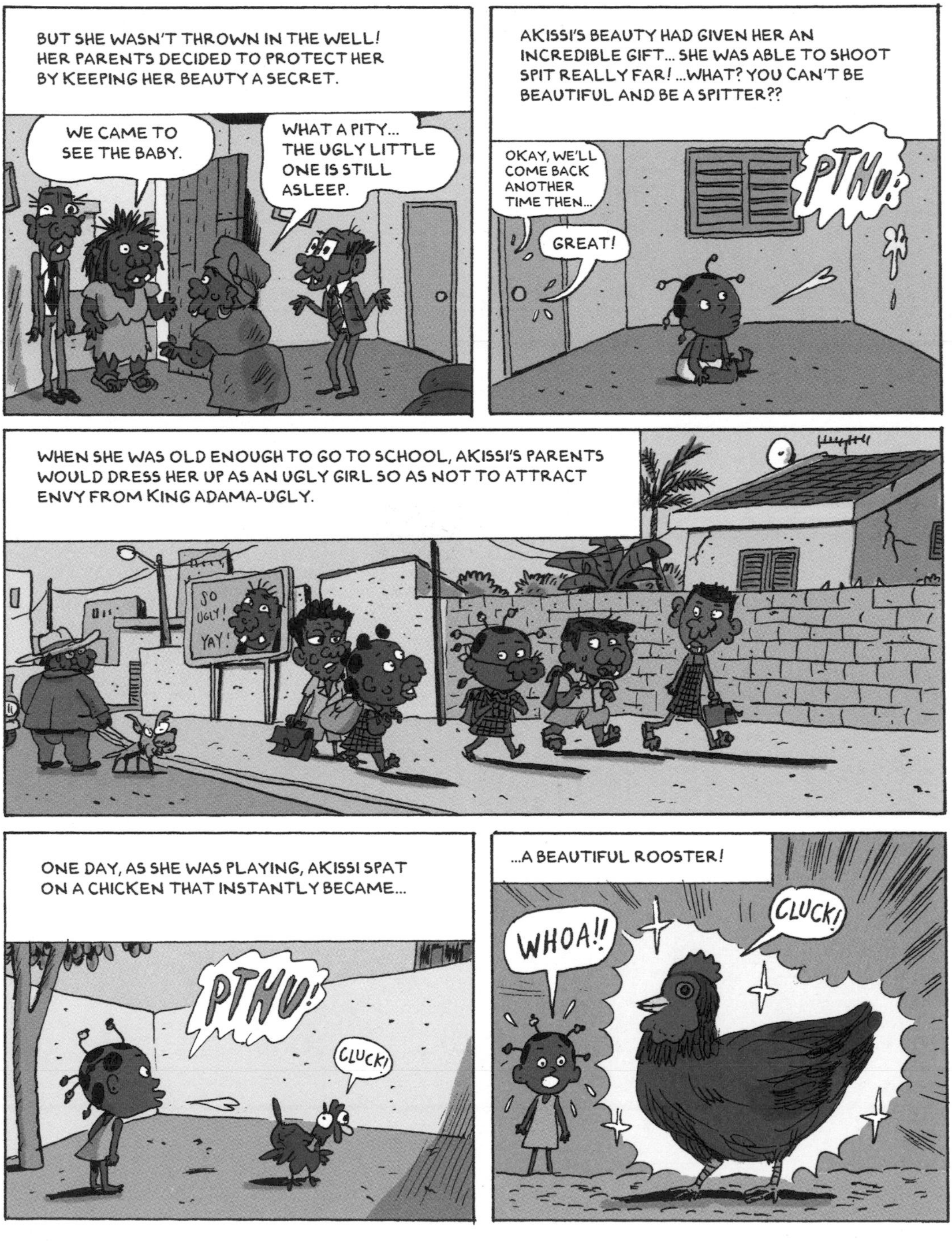
BUT SHE WASN'T THROWN IN THE WELL! HER PARENTS DECIDED TO PROTECT HER BY KEEPING HER BEAUTY A SECRET.
WE CAME TO SEE THE BABY.
WHAT A PITY... THE UGLY LITTLE ONE IS STILL ASLEEP.
AKISSI'S BEAUTY HAD GIVEN HER AN INCREDIBLE GIFT... SHE WAS ABLE TO SHOOT SPIT REALLY FAR! ...WHAT? YOU CAN'T BE BEAUTIFUL AND BE A SPITTER??
OKAY, WE'LL COME BACK ANOTHER TIME THEN...
GREAT!
PTHU!
WHEN SHE WAS OLD ENOUGH TO GO TO SCHOOL, AKISSI'S PARENTS WOULD DRESS HER UP AS AN UGLY GIRL SO AS NOT TO ATTRACT ENVY FROM KING ADAMA-UGLY.
SO UGLY! YAY!
ONE DAY, AS SHE WAS PLAYING, AKISSI SPAT ON A CHICKEN THAT INSTANTLY BECAME...
PTHU!
CLUCK!
...A BEAUTIFUL ROOSTER!
WHOA!!
CLUCK!

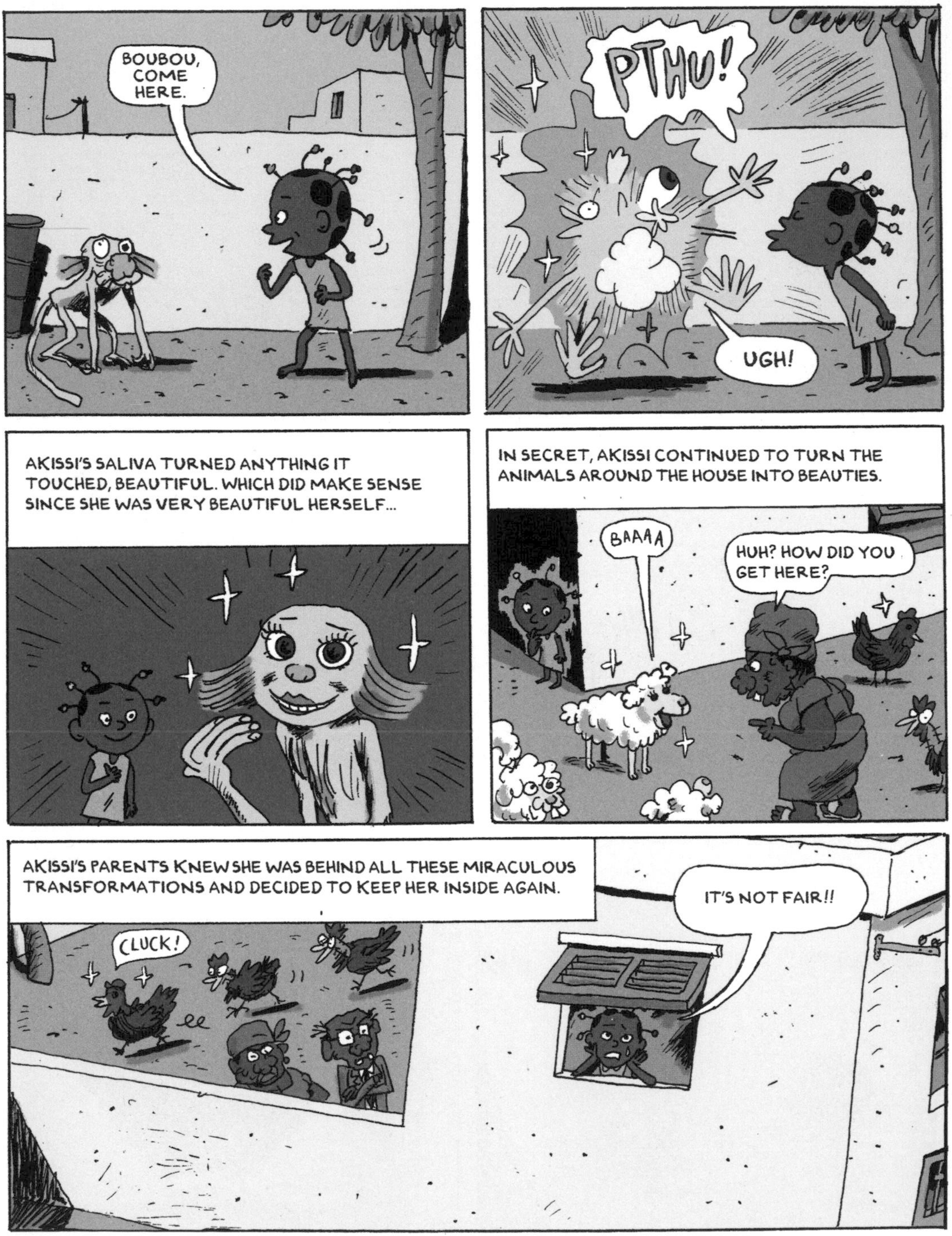
BOUBOU, COME HERE.
PTHU!
UGH!
AKISSI'S SALIVA TURNED ANYTHING IT TOUCHED, BEAUTIFUL. WHICH DID MAKE SENSE SINCE SHE WAS VERY BEAUTIFUL HERSELF...
IN SECRET, AKISSI CONTINUED TO TURN THE ANIMALS AROUND THE HOUSE INTO BEAUTIES.
BAAAA
HUH? HOW DID YOU GET HERE?
AKISSI'S PARENTS KNEW SHE WAS BEHIND ALL THESE MIRACULOUS TRANSFORMATIONS AND DECIDED TO KEEP HER INSIDE AGAIN.
IT'S NOT FAIR!!
CLUCK!

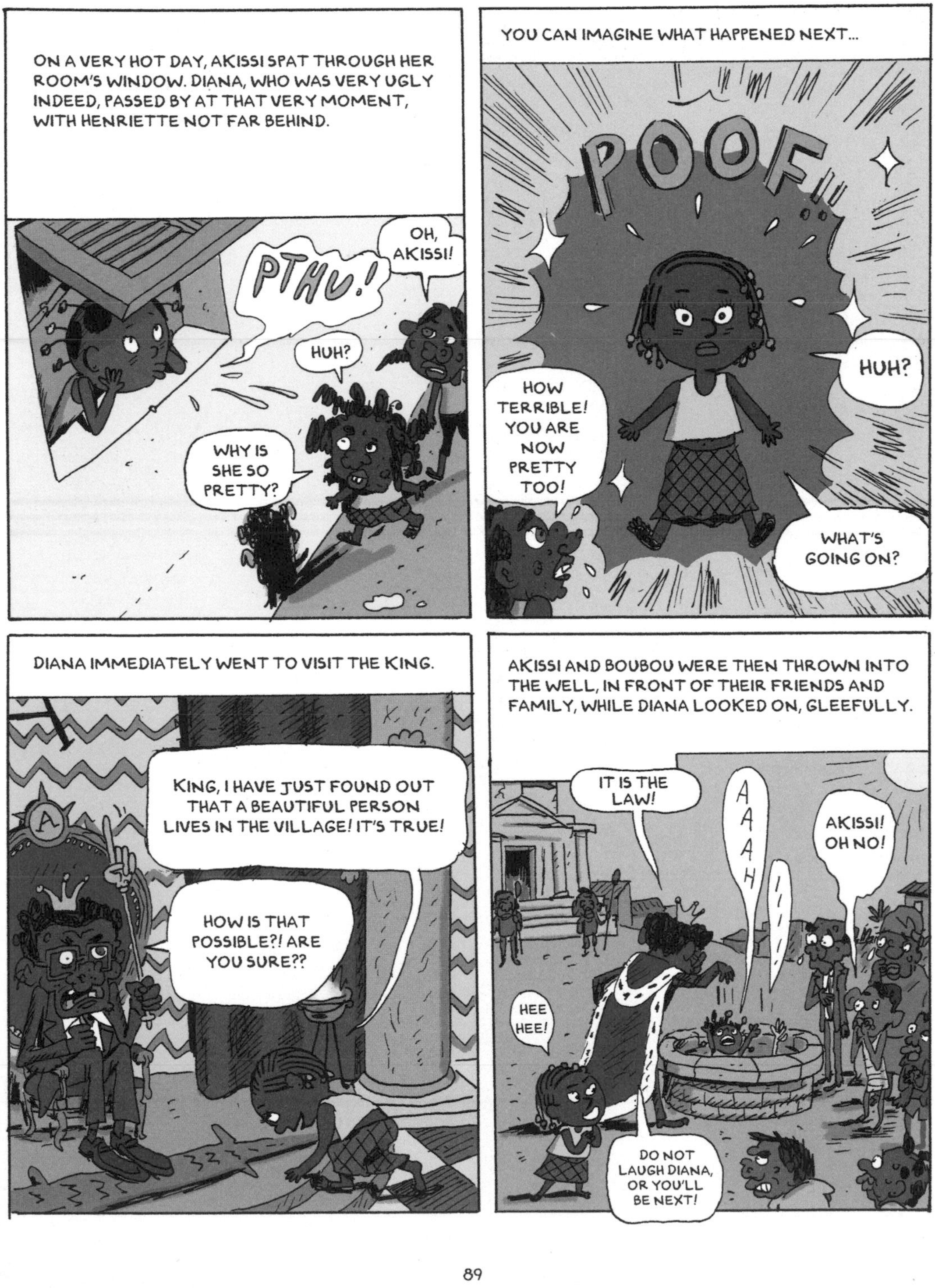
ON A VERY HOT DAY, AKISSI SPAT THROUGH HER ROOM'S WINDOW. DIANA, WHO WAS VERY UGLY INDEED, PASSED BY AT THAT VERY MOMENT, WITH HENRIETTE NOT FAR BEHIND.
PTHU!
OH, AKISSI!
HUH?
WHY IS SHE SO PRETTY?
YOU CAN IMAGINE WHAT HAPPENED NEXT...
POOF
HUH?
HOW TERRIBLE! YOU ARE NOW PRETTY TOO!
WHAT'S GOING ON?
DIANA IMMEDIATELY WENT TO VISIT THE KING.
KING, I HAVE JUST FOUND OUT THAT A BEAUTIFUL PERSON LIVES IN THE VILLAGE! IT'S TRUE!
HOW IS THAT POSSIBLE?! ARE YOU SURE??
AKISSI AND BOUBOU WERE THEN THROWN INTO THE WELL, IN FRONT OF THEIR FRIENDS AND FAMILY, WHILE DIANA LOOKED ON, GLEEFULLY.
IT IS THE LAW!
AAAH
AKISSI! OH NO!
HEE HEE!
DO NOT LAUGH DIANA, OR YOU'LL BE NEXT!

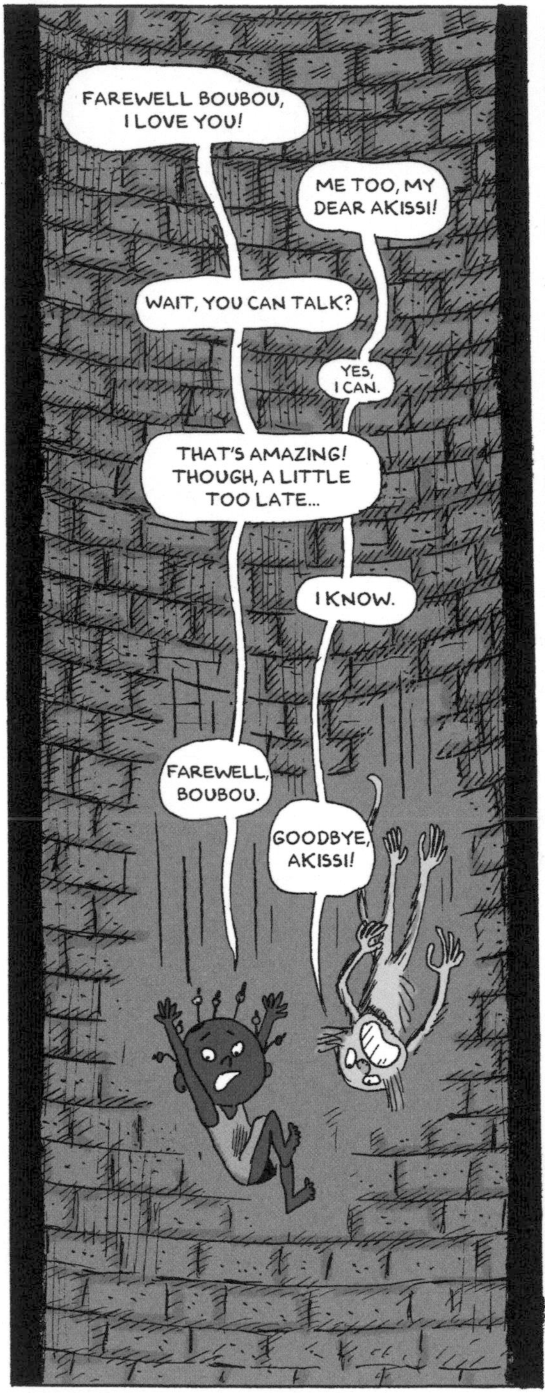
FAREWELL BOUBOU, I LOVE YOU!
ME TOO, MY DEAR AKISSI!
WAIT, YOU CAN TALK?
YES, I CAN.
THAT'S AMAZING! THOUGH, A LITTLE TOO LATE...
I KNOW.
FAREWELL, BOUBOU.
GOODBYE, AKISSI!

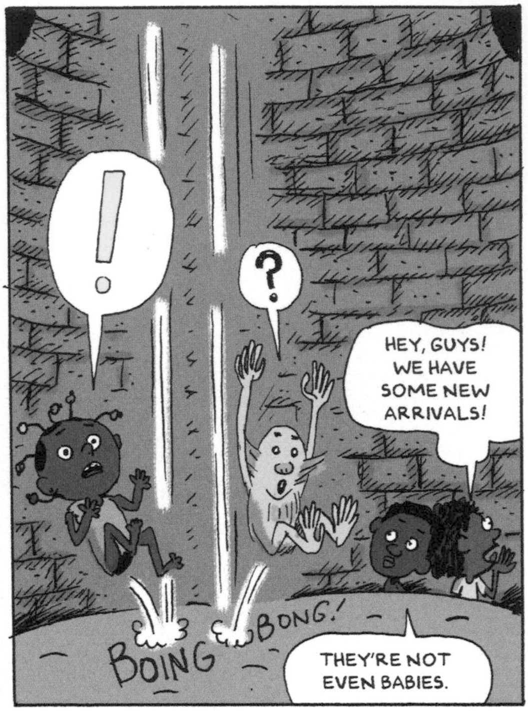
!
?
HEY, GUYS! WE HAVE SOME NEW ARRIVALS!
BOING
BONG!
THEY'RE NOT EVEN BABIES.

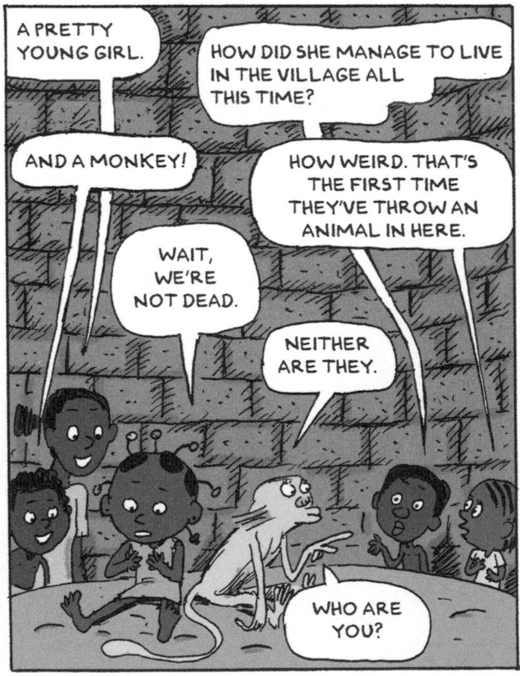
A PRETTY YOUNG GIRL.
HOW DID SHE MANAGE TO LIVE IN THE VILLAGE ALL THIS TIME?
AND A MONKEY!
HOW WEIRD. THAT'S THE FIRST TIME THEY'VE THROW AN ANIMAL IN HERE.
WAIT, WE'RE NOT DEAD.
NEITHER ARE THEY.
WHO ARE YOU?

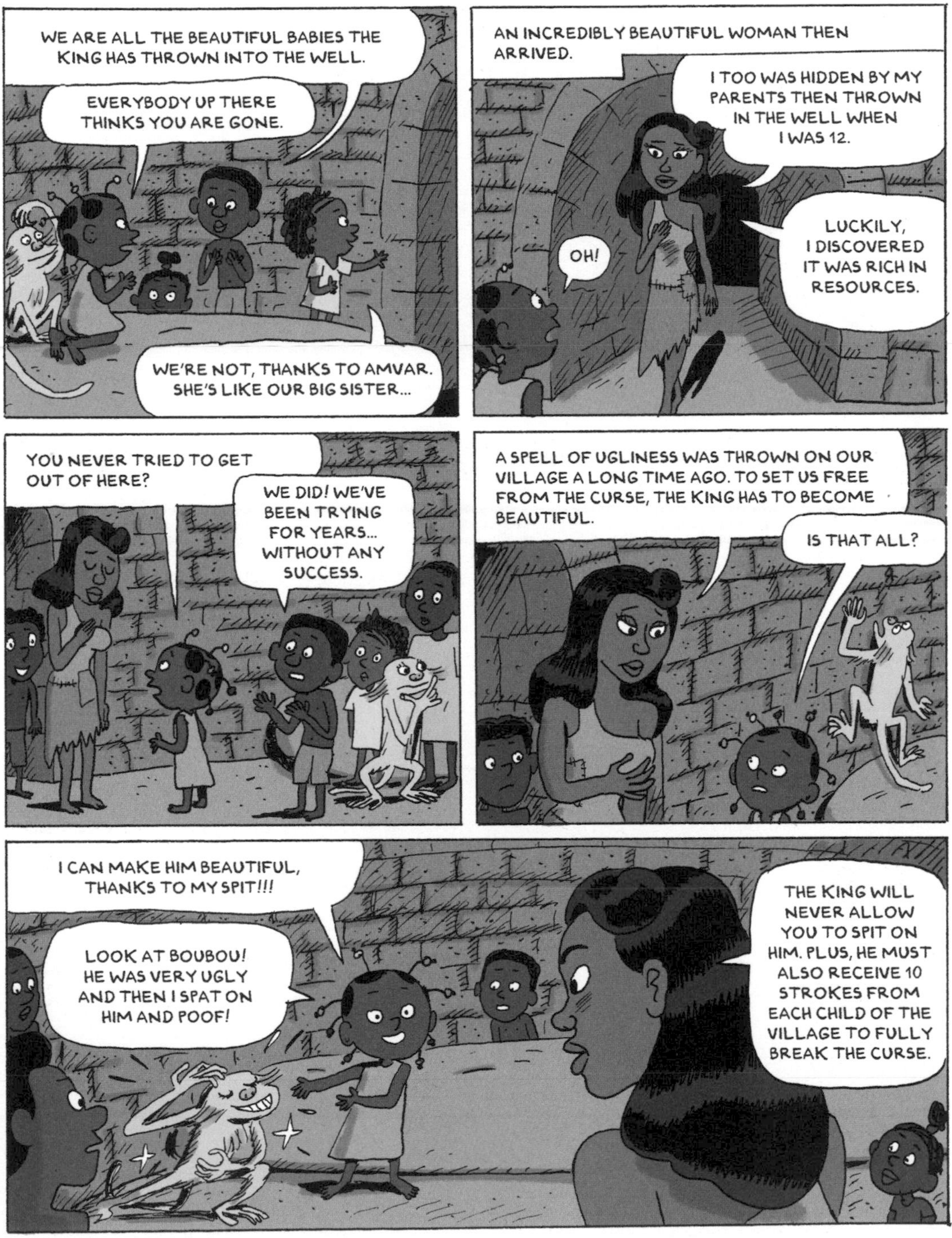

WE ARE ALL THE BEAUTIFUL BABIES THE KING HAS THROWN INTO THE WELL.
EVERYBODY UP THERE THINKS YOU ARE GONE.
WE'RE NOT, THANKS TO AMVAR. SHE'S LIKE OUR BIG SISTER...
AN INCREDIBLY BEAUTIFUL WOMAN THEN ARRIVED.
I TOO WAS HIDDEN BY MY PARENTS THEN THROWN IN THE WELL WHEN I WAS 12.
OH!
LUCKILY, I DISCOVERED IT WAS RICH IN RESOURCES.
YOU NEVER TRIED TO GET OUT OF HERE?
WE DID! WE'VE BEEN TRYING FOR YEARS... WITHOUT ANY SUCCESS.
A SPELL OF UGLINESS WAS THROWN ON OUR VILLAGE A LONG TIME AGO. TO SET US FREE FROM THE CURSE, THE KING HAS TO BECOME BEAUTIFUL.
IS THAT ALL?
I CAN MAKE HIM BEAUTIFUL, THANKS TO MY SPIT!!!
LOOK AT BOUBOU! HE WAS VERY UGLY AND THEN I SPAT ON HIM AND POOF!
THE KING WILL NEVER ALLOW YOU TO SPIT ON HIM. PLUS, HE MUST ALSO RECEIVE 10 STROKES FROM EACH CHILD OF THE VILLAGE TO FULLY BREAK THE CURSE.

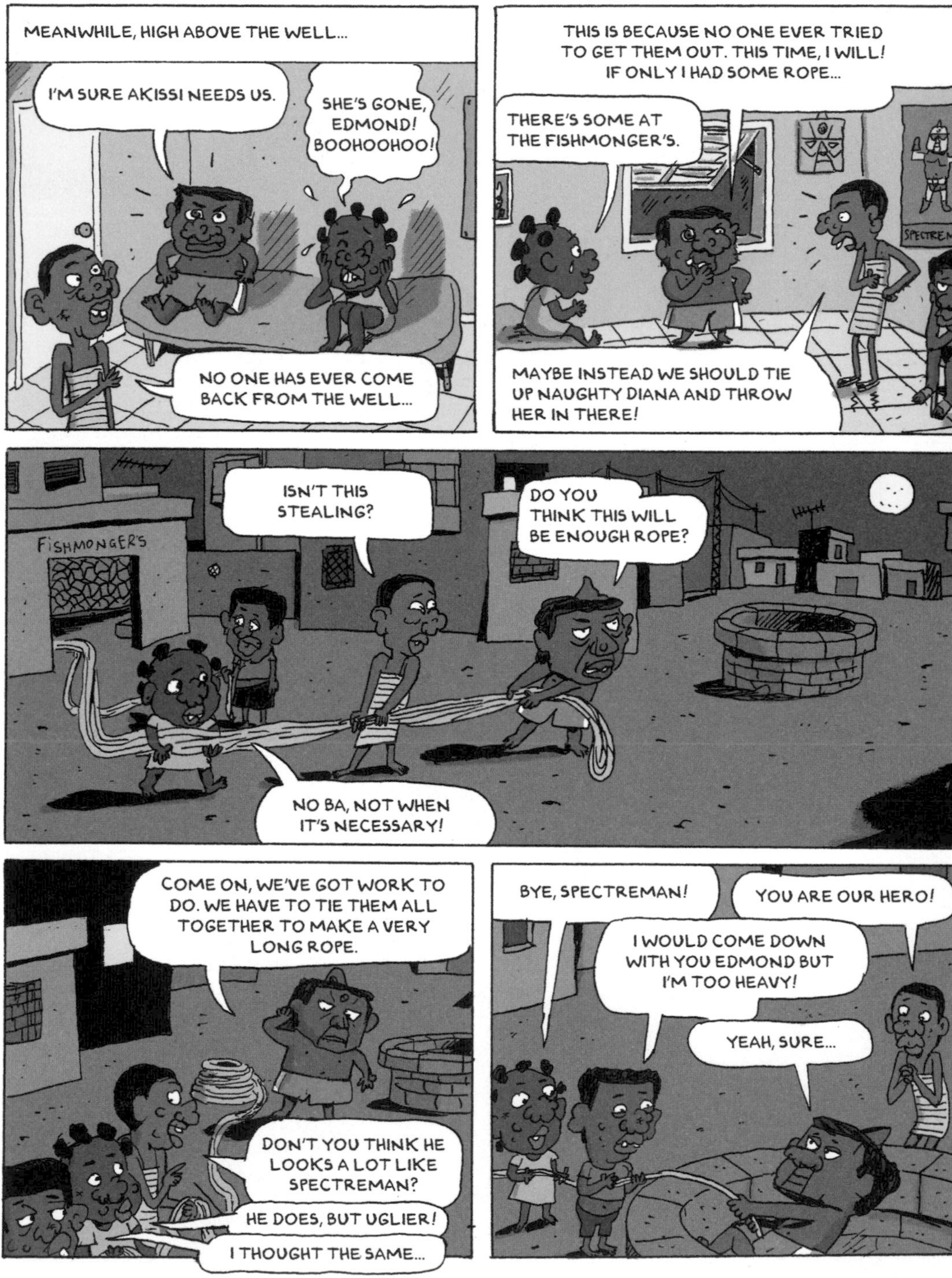
MEANWHILE, HIGH ABOVE THE WELL...
I'M SURE AKISSI NEEDS US.
SHE'S GONE, EDMOND! BOOHOOHOO!
NO ONE HAS EVER COME BACK FROM THE WELL...
THIS IS BECAUSE NO ONE EVER TRIED TO GET THEM OUT. THIS TIME, I WILL! IF ONLY I HAD SOME ROPE...
THERE'S SOME AT THE FISHMONGER'S.
SPECTREMAN
MAYBE INSTEAD WE SHOULD TIE UP NAUGHTY DIANA AND THROW HER IN THERE!
FISHMONGER'S
ISN'T THIS STEALING?
DO YOU THINK THIS WILL BE ENOUGH ROPE?
NO BA, NOT WHEN IT'S NECESSARY!
COME ON, WE'VE GOT WORK TO DO. WE HAVE TO TIE THEM ALL TOGETHER TO MAKE A VERY LONG ROPE.
DON'T YOU THINK HE LOOKS A LOT LIKE SPECTREMAN?
HE DOES, BUT UGLIER!
I THOUGHT THE SAME...
BYE, SPECTREMAN!
YOU ARE OUR HERO!
I WOULD COME DOWN WITH YOU EDMOND BUT I'M TOO HEAVY!
YEAH, SURE...

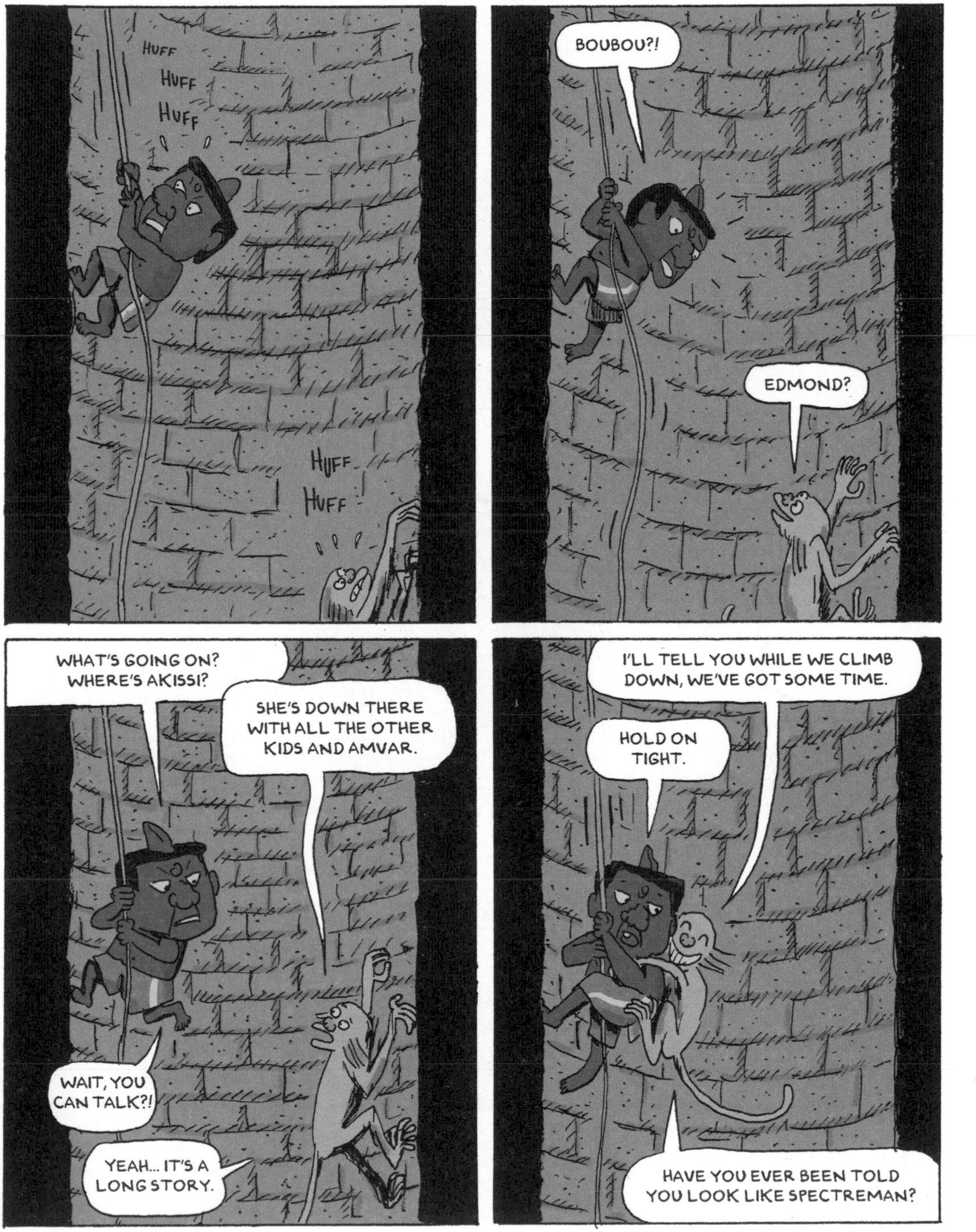
HUFF
HUFF
HUFF
HUFF
HUFF
BOUBOU?!
EDMOND?
WHAT'S GOING ON? WHERE'S AKISSI?
SHE'S DOWN THERE WITH ALL THE OTHER KIDS AND AMVAR.
WAIT, YOU CAN TALK?!
YEAH... IT'S A LONG STORY.
I'LL TELL YOU WHILE WE CLIMB DOWN, WE'VE GOT SOME TIME.
HOLD ON TIGHT.
HAVE YOU EVER BEEN TOLD YOU LOOK LIKE SPECTREMAN?

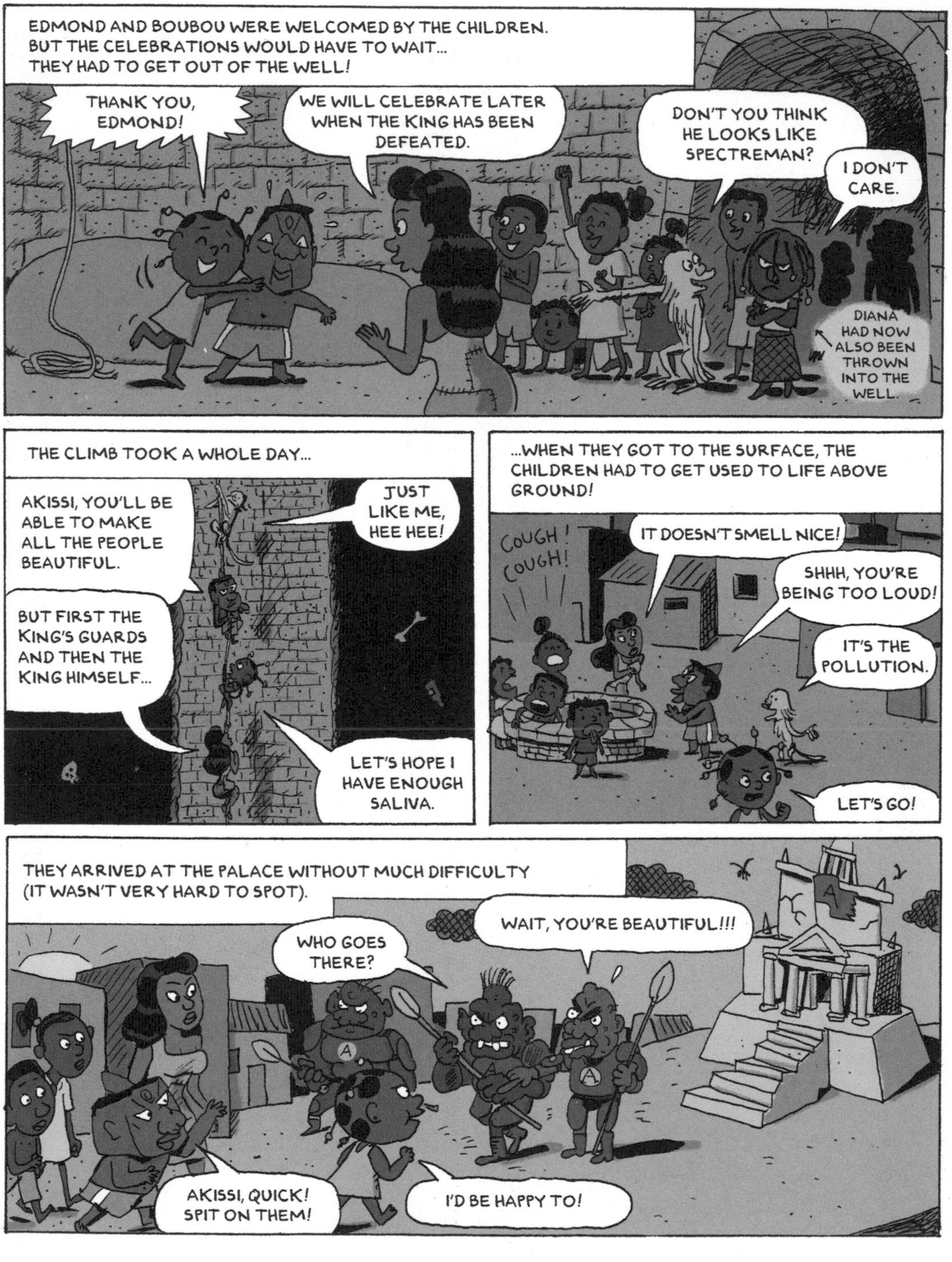
EDMOND AND BOUBOU WERE WELCOMED BY THE CHILDREN. BUT THE CELEBRATIONS WOULD HAVE TO WAIT... THEY HAD TO GET OUT OF THE WELL!
THANK YOU, EDMOND!
WE WILL CELEBRATE LATER WHEN THE KING HAS BEEN DEFEATED.
DON'T YOU THINK HE LOOKS LIKE SPECTREMAN?
I DON'T CARE.
DIANA HAD NOW ALSO BEEN THROWN INTO THE WELL.
THE CLIMB TOOK A WHOLE DAY...
AKISSI, YOU'LL BE ABLE TO MAKE ALL THE PEOPLE BEAUTIFUL.
JUST LIKE ME, HEE HEE!
BUT FIRST THE KING'S GUARDS AND THEN THE KING HIMSELF...
LET'S HOPE I HAVE ENOUGH SALIVA.
...WHEN THEY GOT TO THE SURFACE, THE CHILDREN HAD TO GET USED TO LIFE ABOVE GROUND!
COUGH! COUGH!
IT DOESN'T SMELL NICE!
SHHH, YOU'RE BEING TOO LOUD!
IT'S THE POLLUTION.
LET'S GO!
THEY ARRIVED AT THE PALACE WITHOUT MUCH DIFFICULTY (IT WASN'T VERY HARD TO SPOT).
WHO GOES THERE?
WAIT, YOU'RE BEAUTIFUL!!!
AKISSI, QUICK! SPIT ON THEM!
I'D BE HAPPY TO!

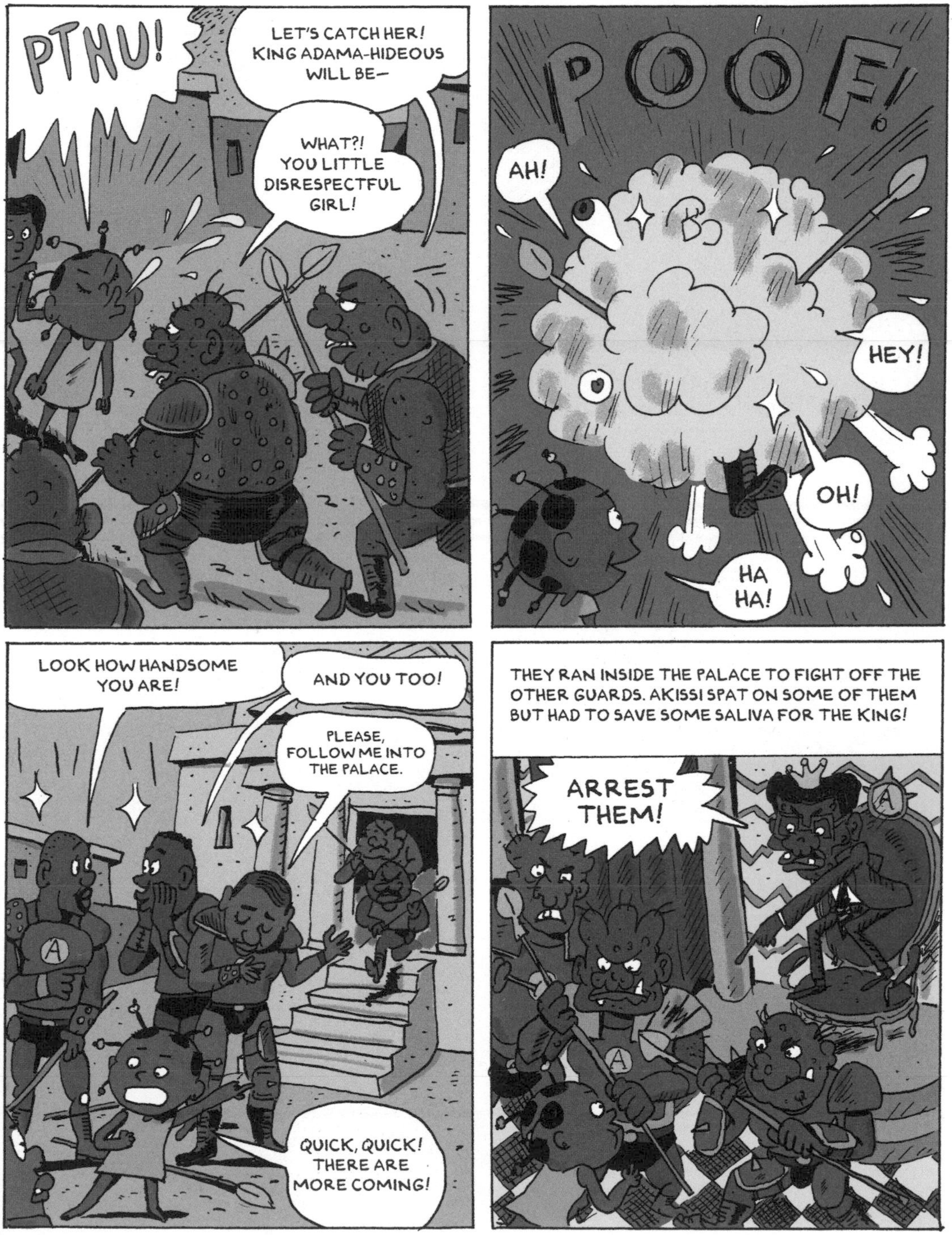
PTHU!
LET'S CATCH HER! KING ADAMA-HIDEOUS WILL BE—
WHAT?! YOU LITTLE DISRESPECTFUL GIRL!
POOF!
AH!
HEY!
OH!
HA HA!
LOOK HOW HANDSOME YOU ARE!
AND YOU TOO!
PLEASE, FOLLOW ME INTO THE PALACE.
QUICK, QUICK! THERE ARE MORE COMING!
THEY RAN INSIDE THE PALACE TO FIGHT OFF THE OTHER GUARDS. AKISSI SPAT ON SOME OF THEM BUT HAD TO SAVE SOME SALIVA FOR THE KING!
ARREST THEM!

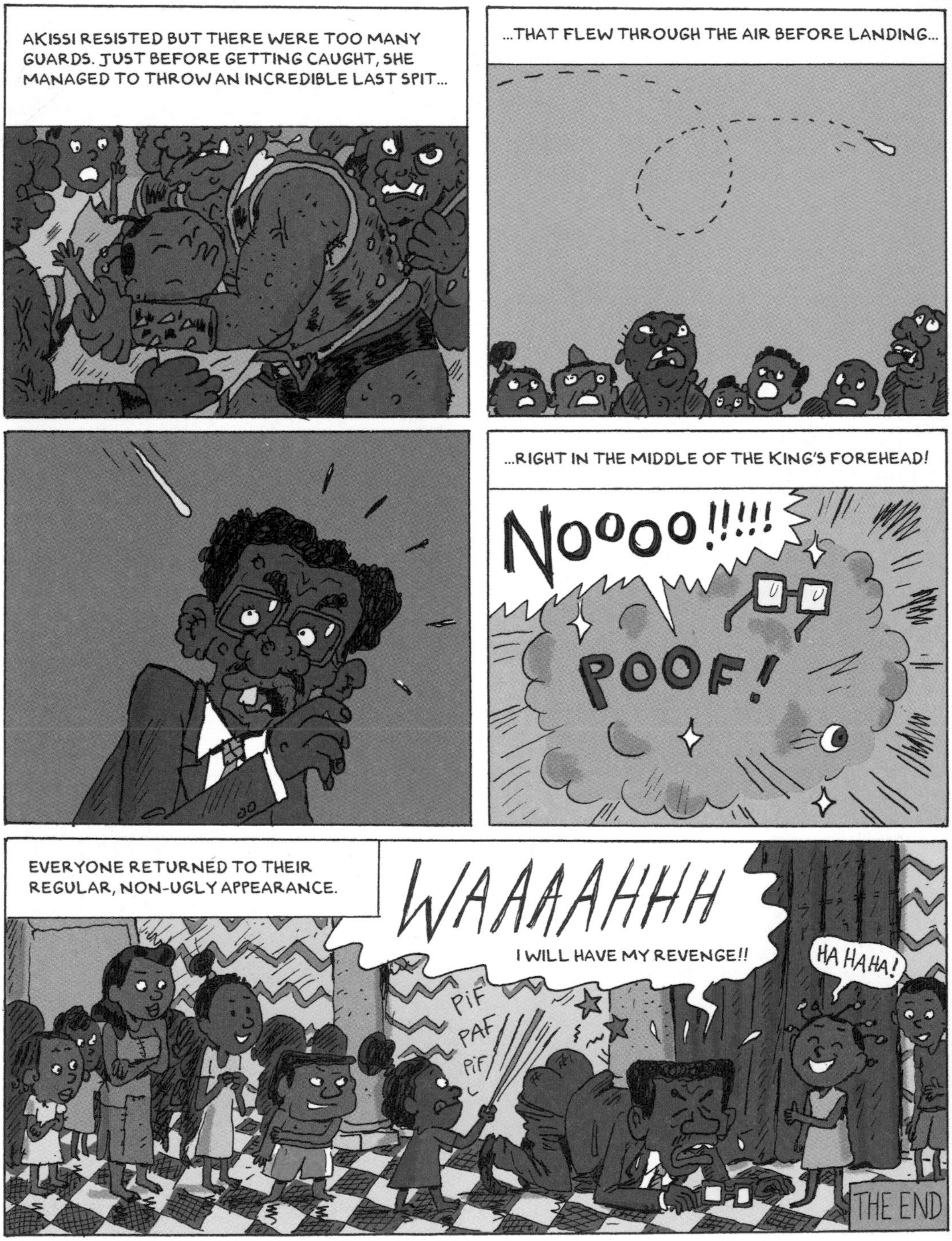
AKISSI RESISTED BUT THERE WERE TOO MANY GUARDS. JUST BEFORE GETTING CAUGHT, SHE MANAGED TO THROW AN INCREDIBLE LAST SPIT...
...THAT FLEW THROUGH THE AIR BEFORE LANDING...
...RIGHT IN THE MIDDLE OF THE KING'S FOREHEAD!
NOOOO!!!!!
POOF!
EVERYONE RETURNED TO THEIR REGULAR, NON-UGLY APPEARANCE.
WAAAAHHH
I WILL HAVE MY REVENGE!!
HA HAHA!
PIF PAF PIF
THE END

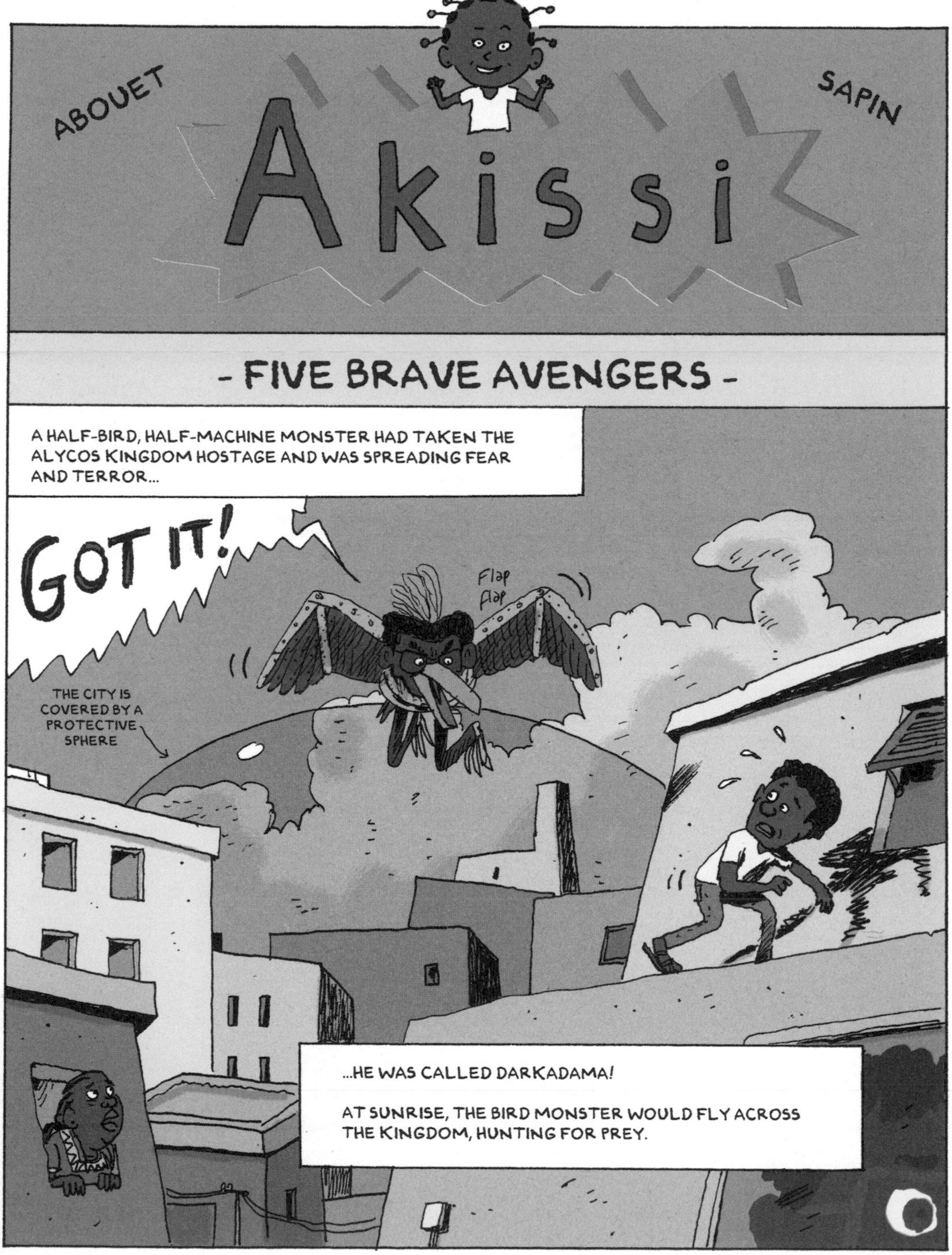
ABOUET
Akissi
SAPIN
- FIVE BRAVE AVENGERS -
A HALF-BIRD, HALF-MACHINE MONSTER HAD TAKEN THE ALYCOS KINGDOM HOSTAGE AND WAS SPREADING FEAR AND TERROR...
GOT IT!
Flap
Flap
THE CITY IS COVERED BY A PROTECTIVE SPHERE
...HE WAS CALLED DARKADAMA!
AT SUNRISE, THE BIRD MONSTER WOULD FLY ACROSS THE KINGDOM, HUNTING FOR PREY.

HE WOULD START BY GOING UP AND DOWN THE STREETS AND COURTYARDS AND LOOKING INSIDE HOUSES FOR POTENTIAL VICTIMS. HE WOULD TERRIFY THOSE HE FOUND WITH HORRIBLE LESSONS!

AM ... IS ... ARE ... BEGIN... BEGAN... BEGUN...

... MULTIPLICATIONS OF 6, 7 AND 8... GRAMMAR... IRREGULAR VERBS... PAST, FUTURE AND CONDITIONAL TENSES... SCARY STUFF!

$6 \times 1 = 6$
$6 \times 2 = 12$
$6 \times 3 = 18$
$6 \times 4 = 24$

HIS HORRIBLE LESSONS WOULD FORCE THE WHOLE POPULATION INTO A CHILDLIKE STATE. EVERYONE WAS TERRIFIED.

$6 \times 5 = 30$ $6 \times 6 = 36$
$6 \times 7 = 42$ $6 \times 8 = 48...$

HOWEVER, FIVE ADULTS DARED TO CHALLENGE THE MONSTER AND THWART HIS EVIL PLANS.

THEY WERE CALLED: THE BRAVE AVENGERS.

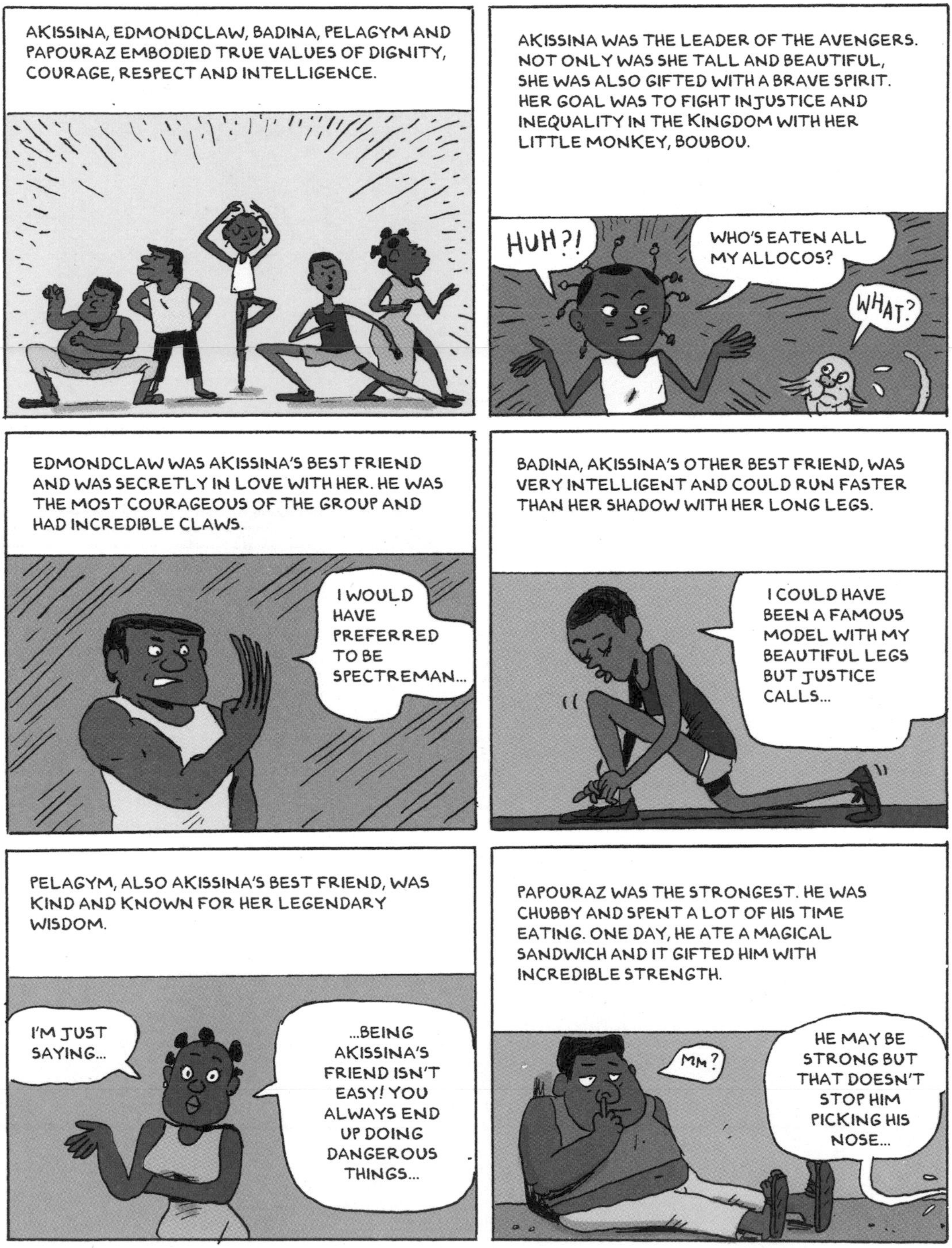
AKISSINA, EDMONDCLAW, BADINA, PELAGYM AND PAPOURAZ EMBODIED TRUE VALUES OF DIGNITY, COURAGE, RESPECT AND INTELLIGENCE.
AKISSINA WAS THE LEADER OF THE AVENGERS. NOT ONLY WAS SHE TALL AND BEAUTIFUL, SHE WAS ALSO GIFTED WITH A BRAVE SPIRIT. HER GOAL WAS TO FIGHT INJUSTICE AND INEQUALITY IN THE KINGDOM WITH HER LITTLE MONKEY, BOUBOU.
HUH?!
WHO'S EATEN ALL MY ALLOCOS?
WHAT?
EDMONDCLAW WAS AKISSINA'S BEST FRIEND AND WAS SECRETLY IN LOVE WITH HER. HE WAS THE MOST COURAGEOUS OF THE GROUP AND HAD INCREDIBLE CLAWS.
I WOULD HAVE PREFERRED TO BE SPECTREMAN...
BADINA, AKISSINA'S OTHER BEST FRIEND, WAS VERY INTELLIGENT AND COULD RUN FASTER THAN HER SHADOW WITH HER LONG LEGS.
I COULD HAVE BEEN A FAMOUS MODEL WITH MY BEAUTIFUL LEGS BUT JUSTICE CALLS...
PELAGYM, ALSO AKISSINA'S BEST FRIEND, WAS KIND AND KNOWN FOR HER LEGENDARY WISDOM.
I'M JUST SAYING...
...BEING AKISSINA'S FRIEND ISN'T EASY! YOU ALWAYS END UP DOING DANGEROUS THINGS...
PAPOURAZ WAS THE STRONGEST. HE WAS CHUBBY AND SPENT A LOT OF HIS TIME EATING. ONE DAY, HE ATE A MAGICAL SANDWICH AND IT GIFTED HIM WITH INCREDIBLE STRENGTH.
MM?
HE MAY BE STRONG BUT THAT DOESN'T STOP HIM PICKING HIS NOSE...

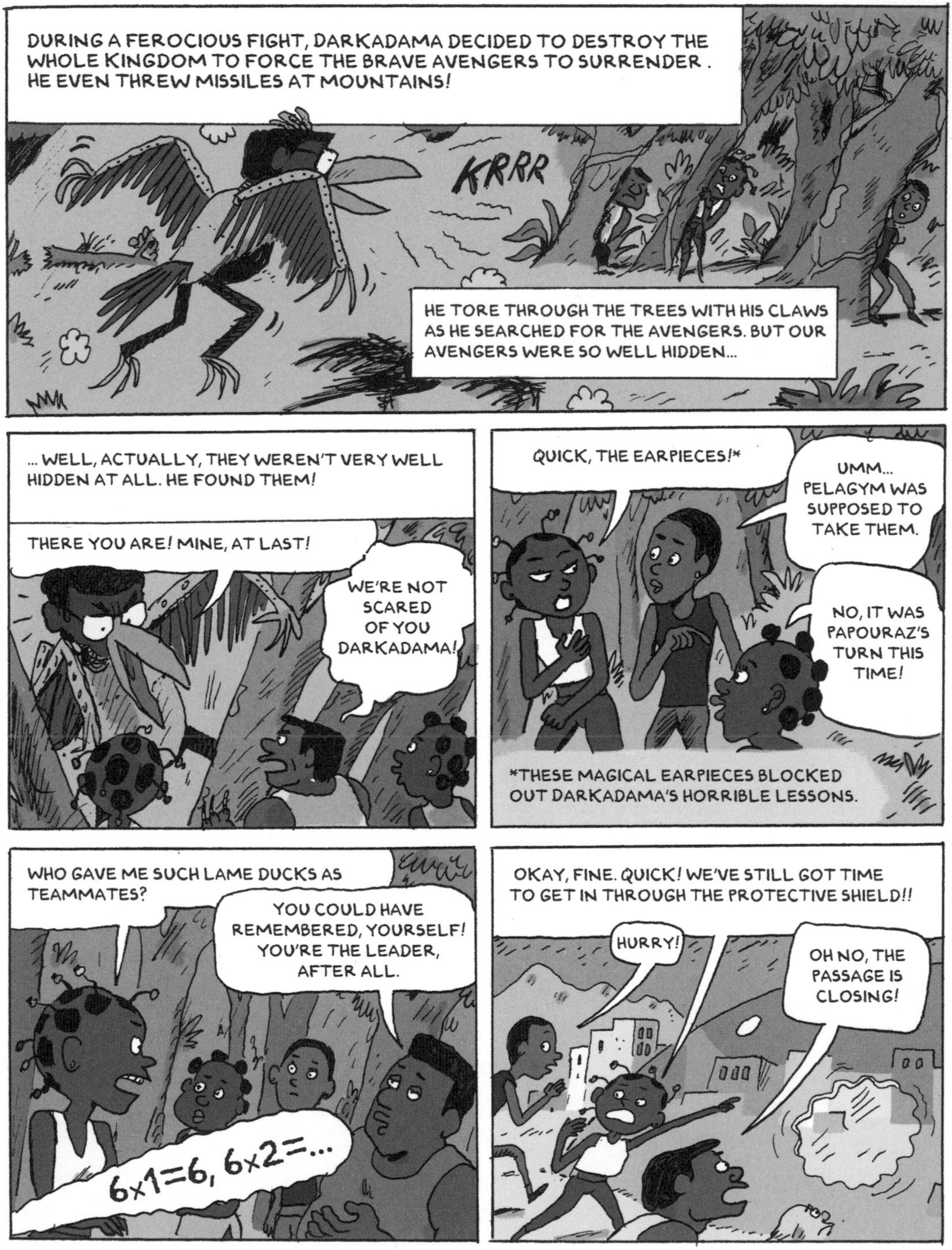
DURING A FEROCIOUS FIGHT, DARKADAMA DECIDED TO DESTROY THE WHOLE KINGDOM TO FORCE THE BRAVE AVENGERS TO SURRENDER. HE EVEN THREW MISSILES AT MOUNTAINS!
KRRR
HE TORE THROUGH THE TREES WITH HIS CLAWS AS HE SEARCHED FOR THE AVENGERS. BUT OUR AVENGERS WERE SO WELL HIDDEN...
... WELL, ACTUALLY, THEY WEREN'T VERY WELL HIDDEN AT ALL. HE FOUND THEM!
THERE YOU ARE! MINE, AT LAST!
WE'RE NOT SCARED OF YOU DARKADAMA!
QUICK, THE EARPIECES!*
UMM... PELAGYM WAS SUPPOSED TO TAKE THEM.
NO, IT WAS PAPOURAZ'S TURN THIS TIME!
*THESE MAGICAL EARPIECES BLOCKED OUT DARKADAMA'S HORRIBLE LESSONS.
WHO GAVE ME SUCH LAME DUCKS AS TEAMMATES?
YOU COULD HAVE REMEMBERED, YOURSELF! YOU'RE THE LEADER, AFTER ALL.
6x1=6, 6x2=...
OKAY, FINE. QUICK! WE'VE STILL GOT TIME TO GET IN THROUGH THE PROTECTIVE SHIELD!!
HURRY!
OH NO, THE PASSAGE IS CLOSING!

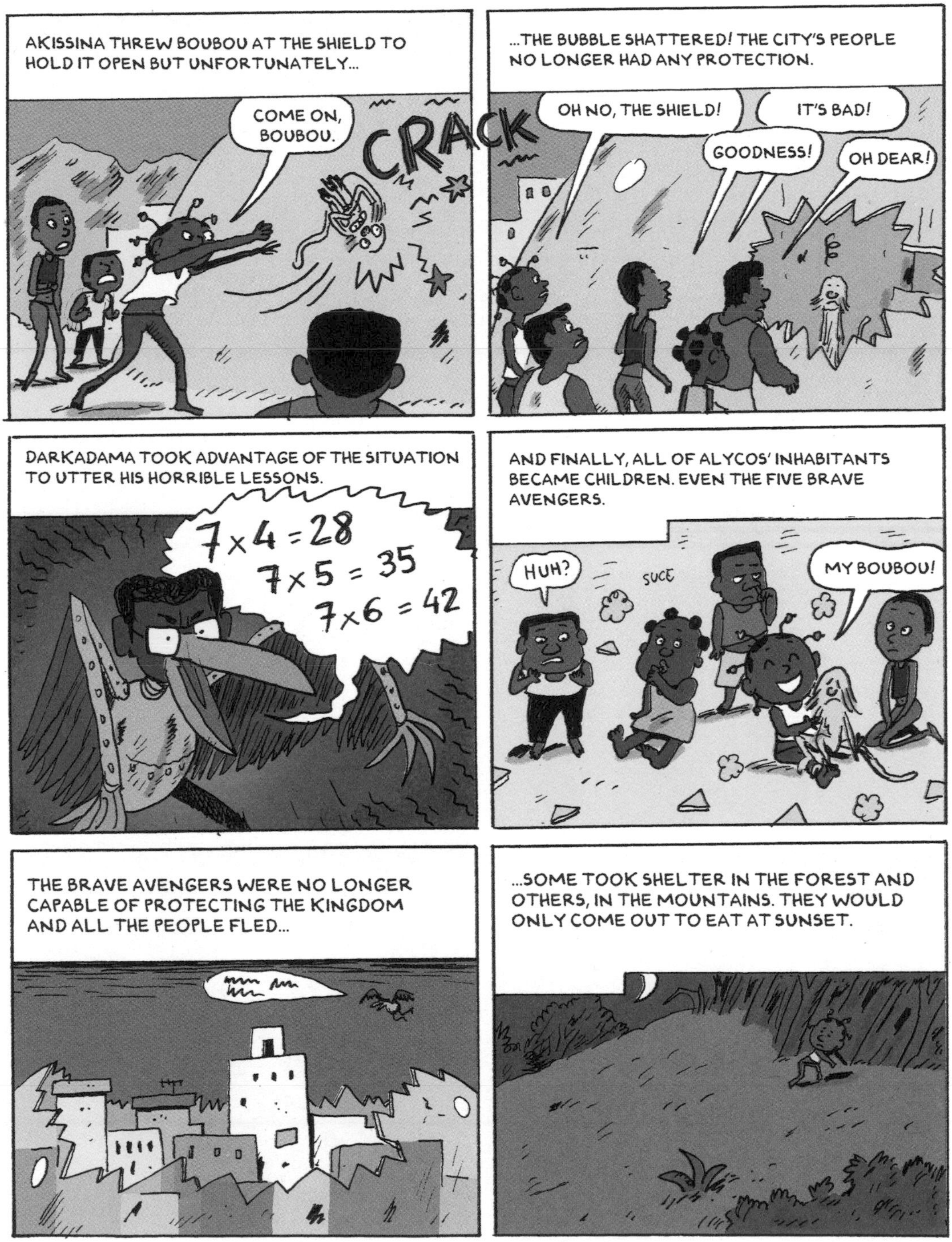
AKISSINA THREW BOUBOU AT THE SHIELD TO HOLD IT OPEN BUT UNFORTUNATELY...
COME ON, BOUBOU.
CRACK
...THE BUBBLE SHATTERED! THE CITY'S PEOPLE NO LONGER HAD ANY PROTECTION.
OH NO, THE SHIELD!
IT'S BAD!
GOODNESS!
OH DEAR!
DARKADAMA TOOK ADVANTAGE OF THE SITUATION TO UTTER HIS HORRIBLE LESSONS.
7×4 = 28
7×5 = 35
7×6 = 42
AND FINALLY, ALL OF ALYCOS' INHABITANTS BECAME CHILDREN. EVEN THE FIVE BRAVE AVENGERS.
HUH?
SUCE
MY BOUBOU!
THE BRAVE AVENGERS WERE NO LONGER CAPABLE OF PROTECTING THE KINGDOM AND ALL THE PEOPLE FLED...
...SOME TOOK SHELTER IN THE FOREST AND OTHERS, IN THE MOUNTAINS. THEY WOULD ONLY COME OUT TO EAT AT SUNSET.

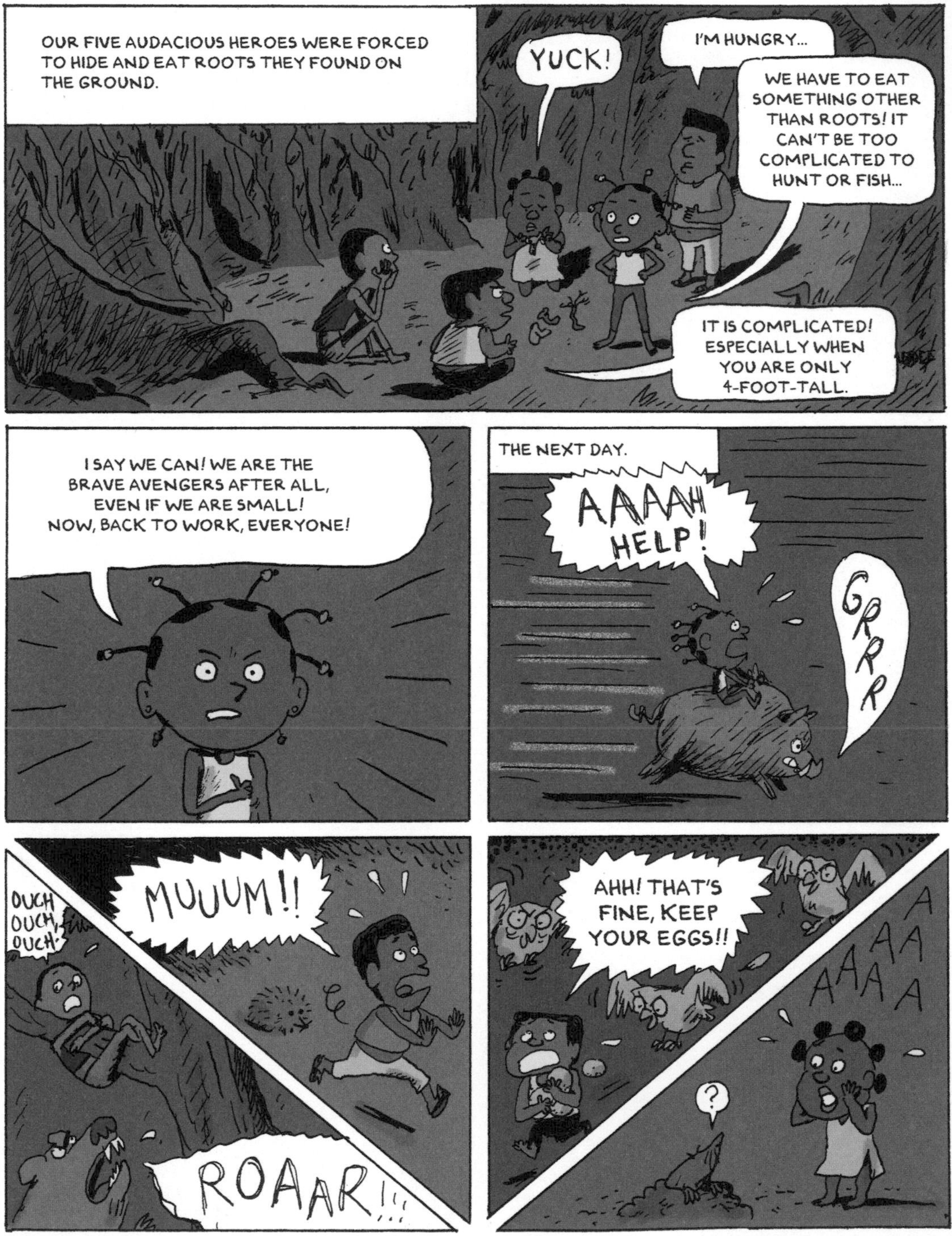
OUR FIVE AUDACIOUS HEROES WERE FORCED TO HIDE AND EAT ROOTS THEY FOUND ON THE GROUND.
YUCK!
I'M HUNGRY...
WE HAVE TO EAT SOMETHING OTHER THAN ROOTS! IT CAN'T BE TOO COMPLICATED TO HUNT OR FISH...
IT IS COMPLICATED! ESPECIALLY WHEN YOU ARE ONLY 4-FOOT-TALL.
I SAY WE CAN! WE ARE THE BRAVE AVENGERS AFTER ALL, EVEN IF WE ARE SMALL! NOW, BACK TO WORK, EVERYONE!
THE NEXT DAY.
AAAAH HELP!
GRRR
OUCH OUCH, OUCH
MUUUM!!
ROAAR!!!
AHH! THAT'S FINE, KEEP YOUR EGGS!!
AAAAAAA
?

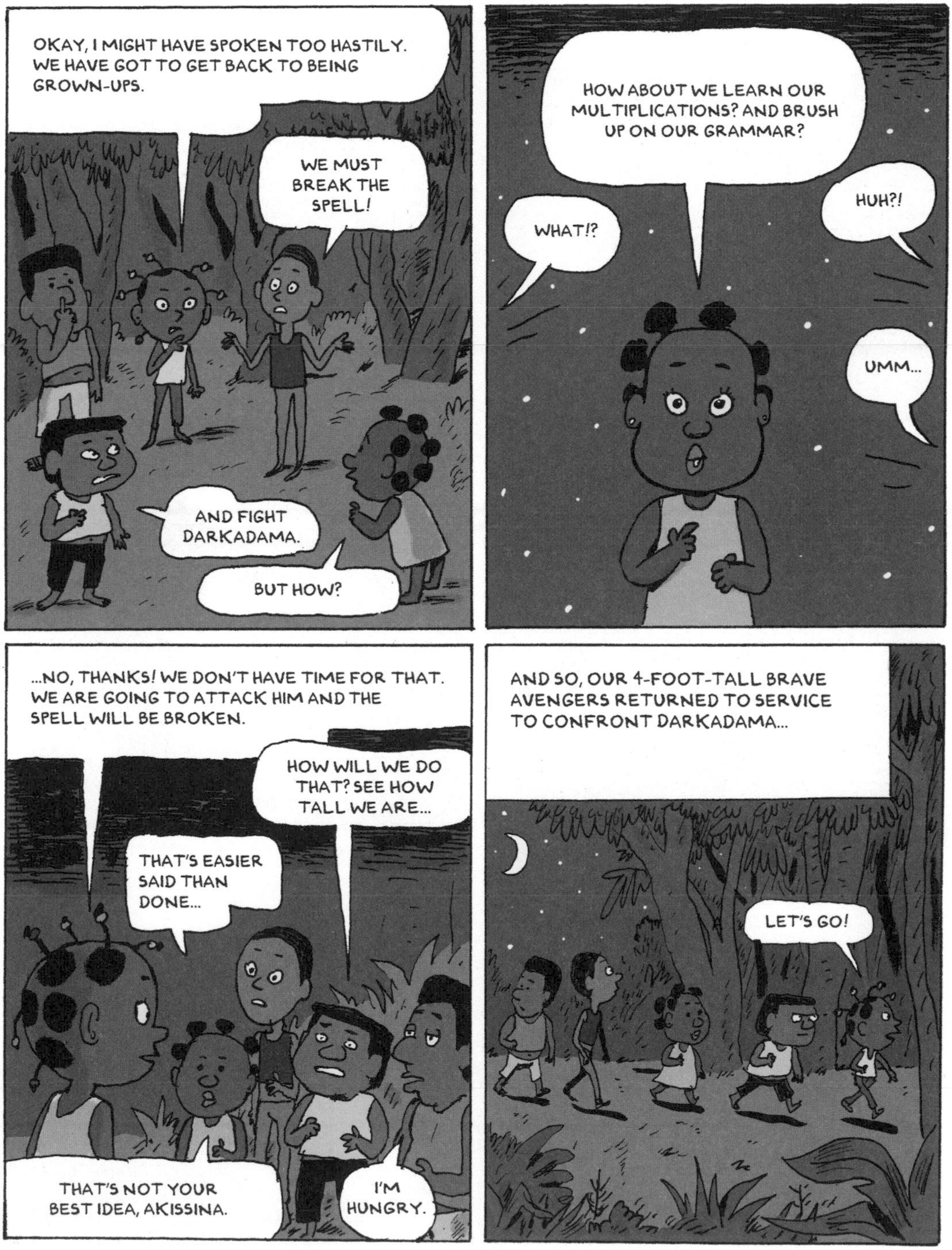
OKAY, I MIGHT HAVE SPOKEN TOO HASTILY. WE HAVE GOT TO GET BACK TO BEING GROWN-UPS.
WE MUST BREAK THE SPELL!
AND FIGHT DARKADAMA.
BUT HOW?
HOW ABOUT WE LEARN OUR MULTIPLICATIONS? AND BRUSH UP ON OUR GRAMMAR?
WHAT!?
HUH?!
UMM...
...NO, THANKS! WE DON'T HAVE TIME FOR THAT. WE ARE GOING TO ATTACK HIM AND THE SPELL WILL BE BROKEN.
HOW WILL WE DO THAT? SEE HOW TALL WE ARE...
THAT'S EASIER SAID THAN DONE...
THAT'S NOT YOUR BEST IDEA, AKISSINA.
I'M HUNGRY.
AND SO, OUR 4-FOOT-TALL BRAVE AVENGERS RETURNED TO SERVICE TO CONFRONT DARKADAMA...
LET'S GO!

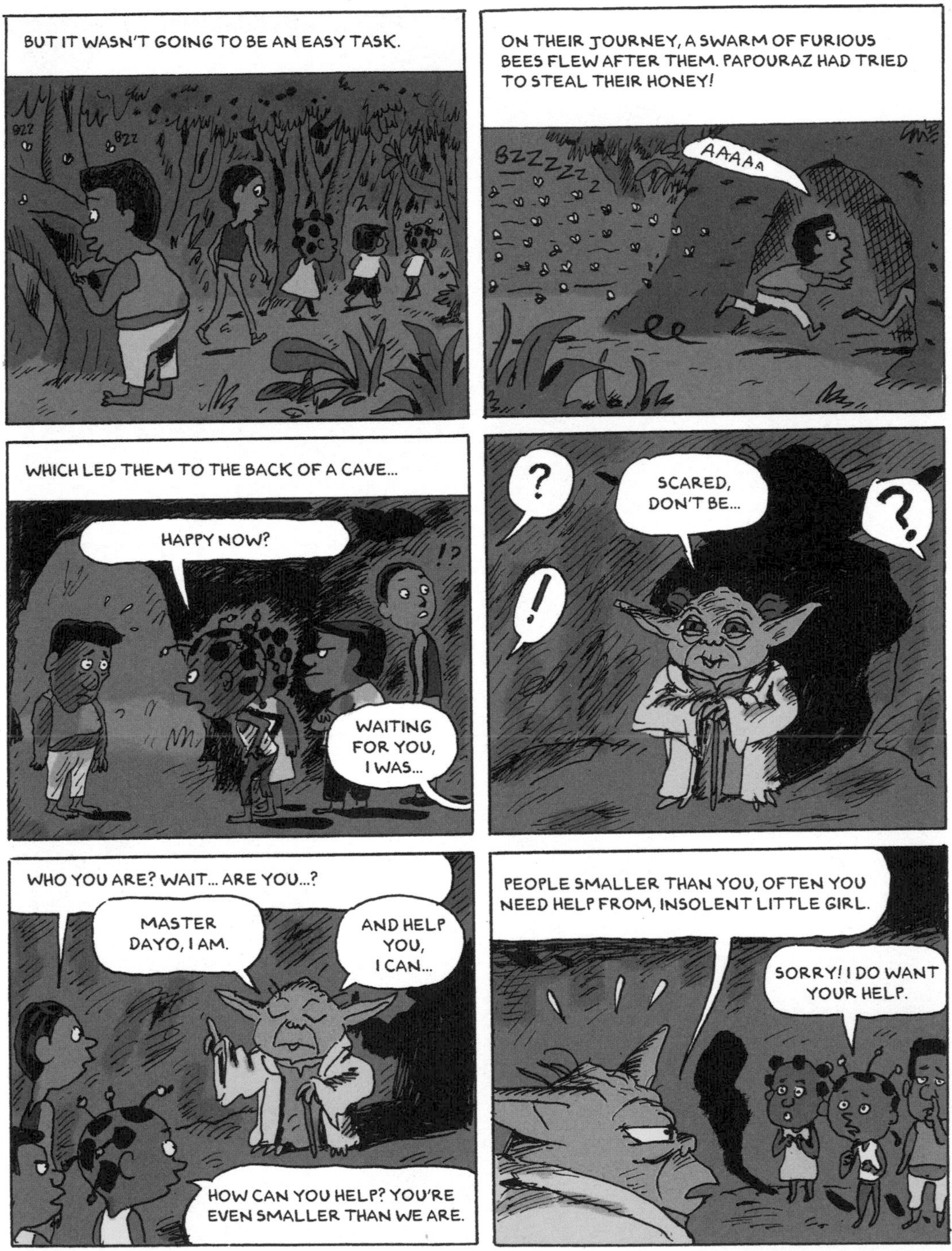
BUT IT WASN'T GOING TO BE AN EASY TASK.
BZZ
BZZ
ON THEIR JOURNEY, A SWARM OF FURIOUS BEES FLEW AFTER THEM. PAPOURAZ HAD TRIED TO STEAL THEIR HONEY!
BZZZZZZ
AAAAA
WHICH LED THEM TO THE BACK OF A CAVE...
HAPPY NOW?
!?
WAITING FOR YOU, I WAS...
?
SCARED, DON'T BE...
?
!
WHO YOU ARE? WAIT... ARE YOU...?
MASTER DAYO, I AM.
AND HELP YOU, I CAN...
HOW CAN YOU HELP? YOU'RE EVEN SMALLER THAN WE ARE.
PEOPLE SMALLER THAN YOU, OFTEN YOU NEED HELP FROM, INSOLENT LITTLE GIRL.
SORRY! I DO WANT YOUR HELP.

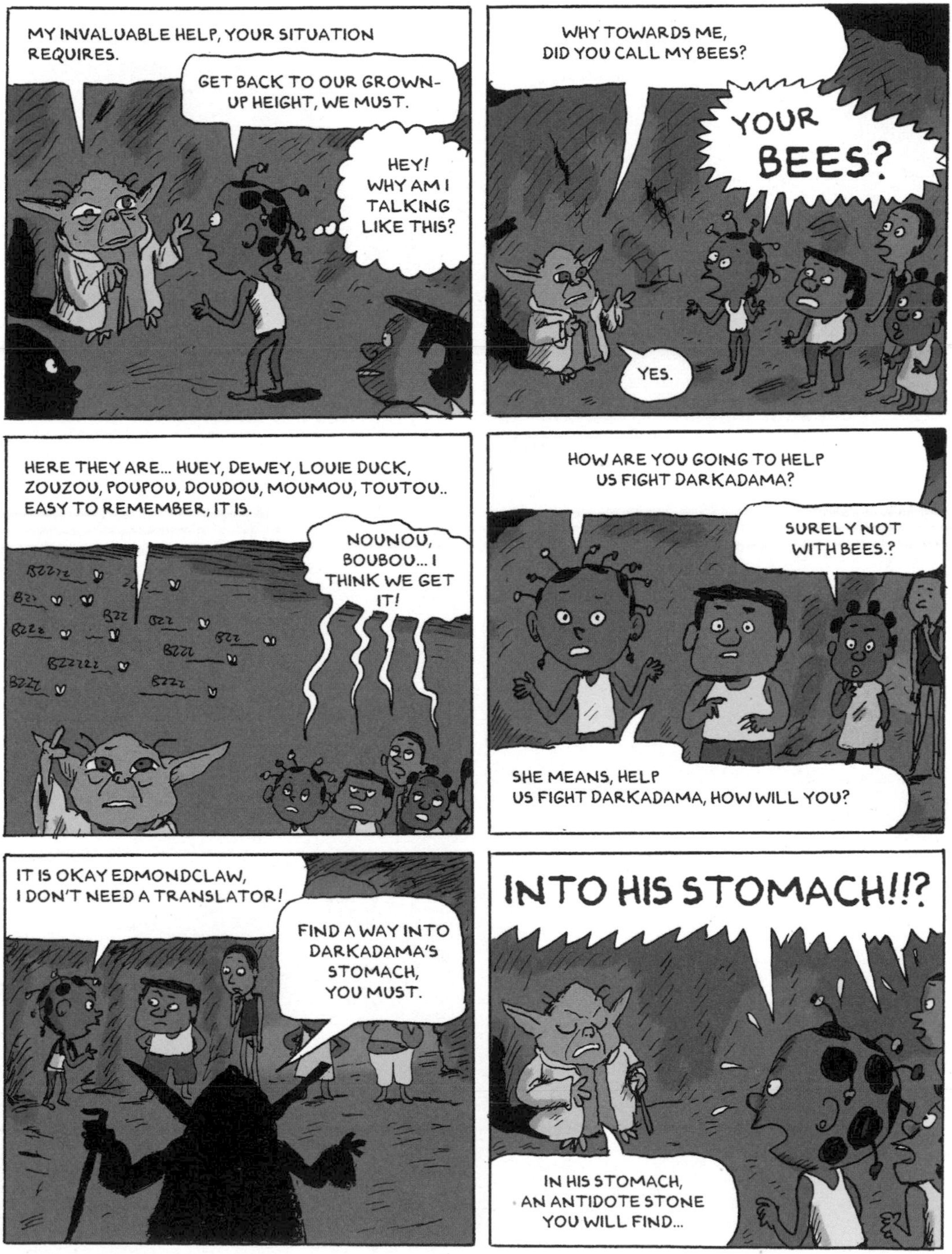
MY INVALUABLE HELP, YOUR SITUATION REQUIRES.
GET BACK TO OUR GROWN-UP HEIGHT, WE MUST.
HEY! WHY AM I TALKING LIKE THIS?
WHY TOWARDS ME, DID YOU CALL MY BEES?
YOUR BEES?
YES.
HERE THEY ARE... HUEY, DEWEY, LOUIE DUCK, ZOUZOU, POUPOU, DOUDOU, MOUMOU, TOUTOU.. EASY TO REMEMBER, IT IS.
NOUNOU, BOUBOU... I THINK WE GET IT!
HOW ARE YOU GOING TO HELP US FIGHT DARKADAMA?
SURELY NOT WITH BEES.?
SHE MEANS, HELP US FIGHT DARKADAMA, HOW WILL YOU?
IT IS OKAY EDMONDCLAW, I DON'T NEED A TRANSLATOR!
FIND A WAY INTO DARKADAMA'S STOMACH, YOU MUST.
INTO HIS STOMACH!!?
IN HIS STOMACH, AN ANTIDOTE STONE YOU WILL FIND...

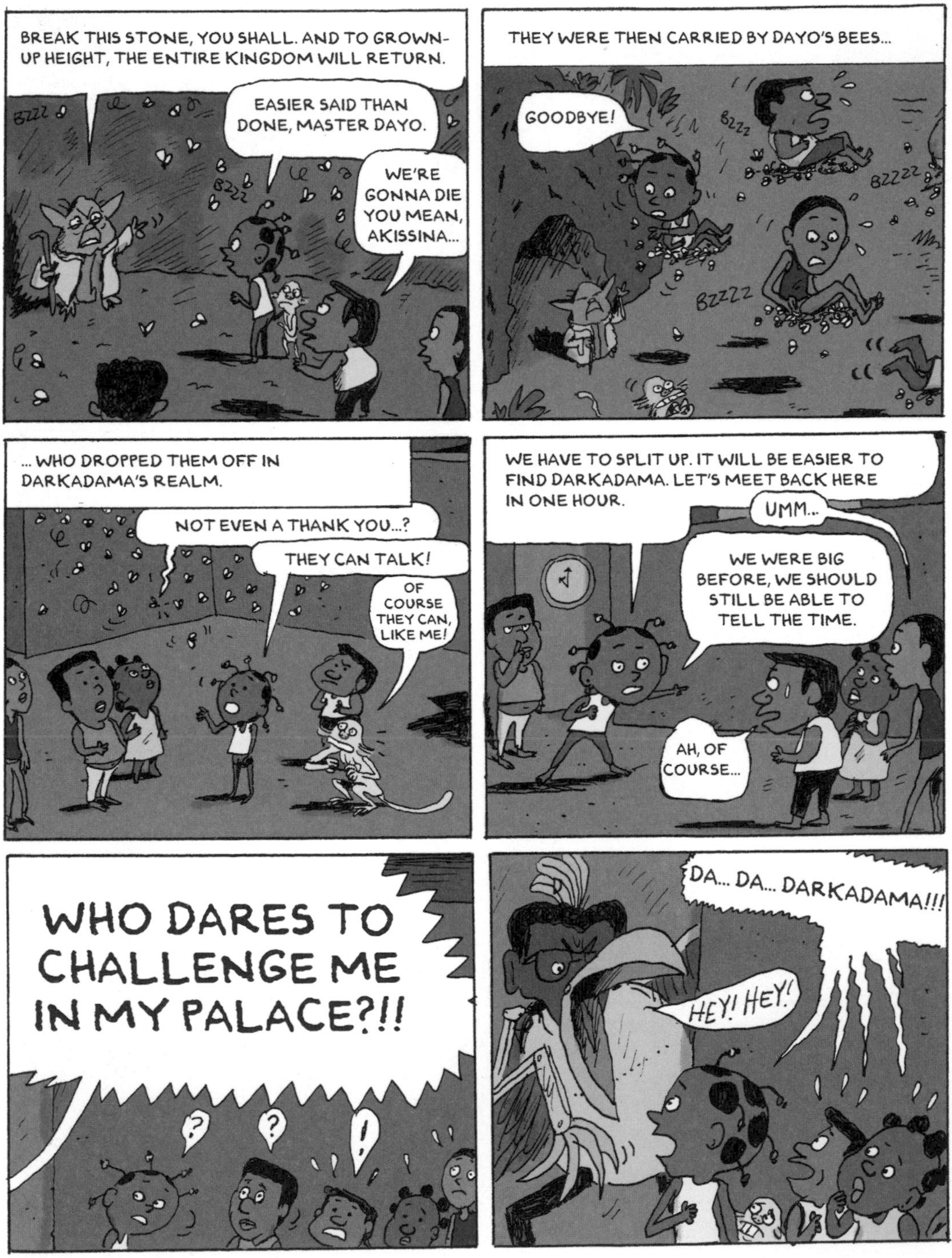
BREAK THIS STONE, YOU SHALL. AND TO GROWN-UP HEIGHT, THE ENTIRE KINGDOM WILL RETURN.
EASIER SAID THAN DONE, MASTER DAYO.
WE'RE GONNA DIE YOU MEAN, AKISSINA...
THEY WERE THEN CARRIED BY DAYO'S BEES...
GOODBYE!
... WHO DROPPED THEM OFF IN DARKADAMA'S REALM.
NOT EVEN A THANK YOU...?
THEY CAN TALK!
OF COURSE THEY CAN, LIKE ME!
WE HAVE TO SPLIT UP. IT WILL BE EASIER TO FIND DARKADAMA. LET'S MEET BACK HERE IN ONE HOUR.
UMM...
WE WERE BIG BEFORE, WE SHOULD STILL BE ABLE TO TELL THE TIME.
AH, OF COURSE...
WHO DARES TO CHALLENGE ME IN MY PALACE?!!
DA... DA... DARKADAMA!!!
HEY! HEY!

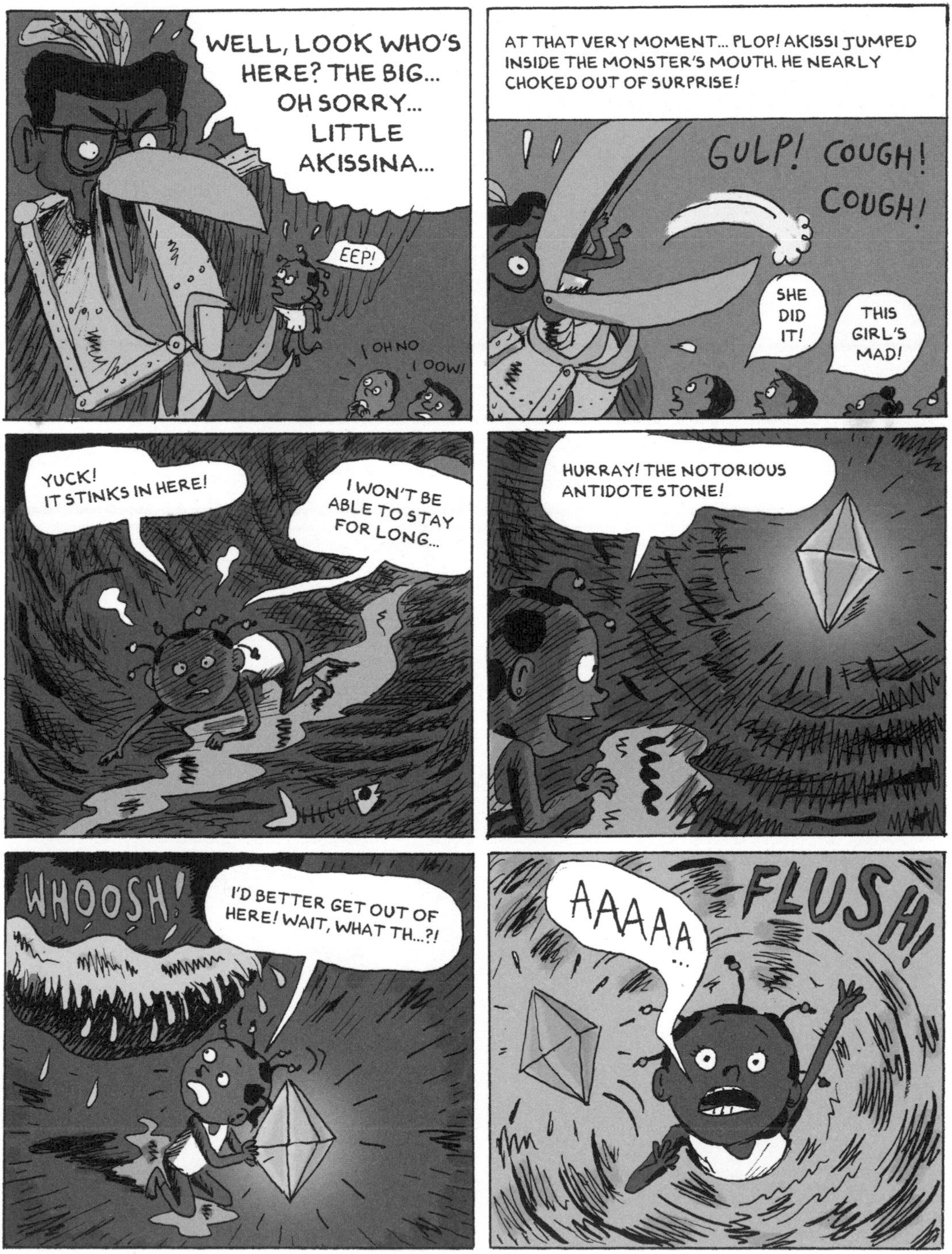
WELL, LOOK WHO'S HERE? THE BIG... OH SORRY... LITTLE AKISSINA...
EEP!
OH NO
OOW!
AT THAT VERY MOMENT... PLOP! AKISSI JUMPED INSIDE THE MONSTER'S MOUTH. HE NEARLY CHOKED OUT OF SURPRISE!
GULP! COUGH! COUGH!
SHE DID IT!
THIS GIRL'S MAD!
YUCK! IT STINKS IN HERE!
I WON'T BE ABLE TO STAY FOR LONG...
HURRAY! THE NOTORIOUS ANTIDOTE STONE!
WHOOSH!
I'D BETTER GET OUT OF HERE! WAIT, WHAT TH...?!
AAAAA...
FLUSH!

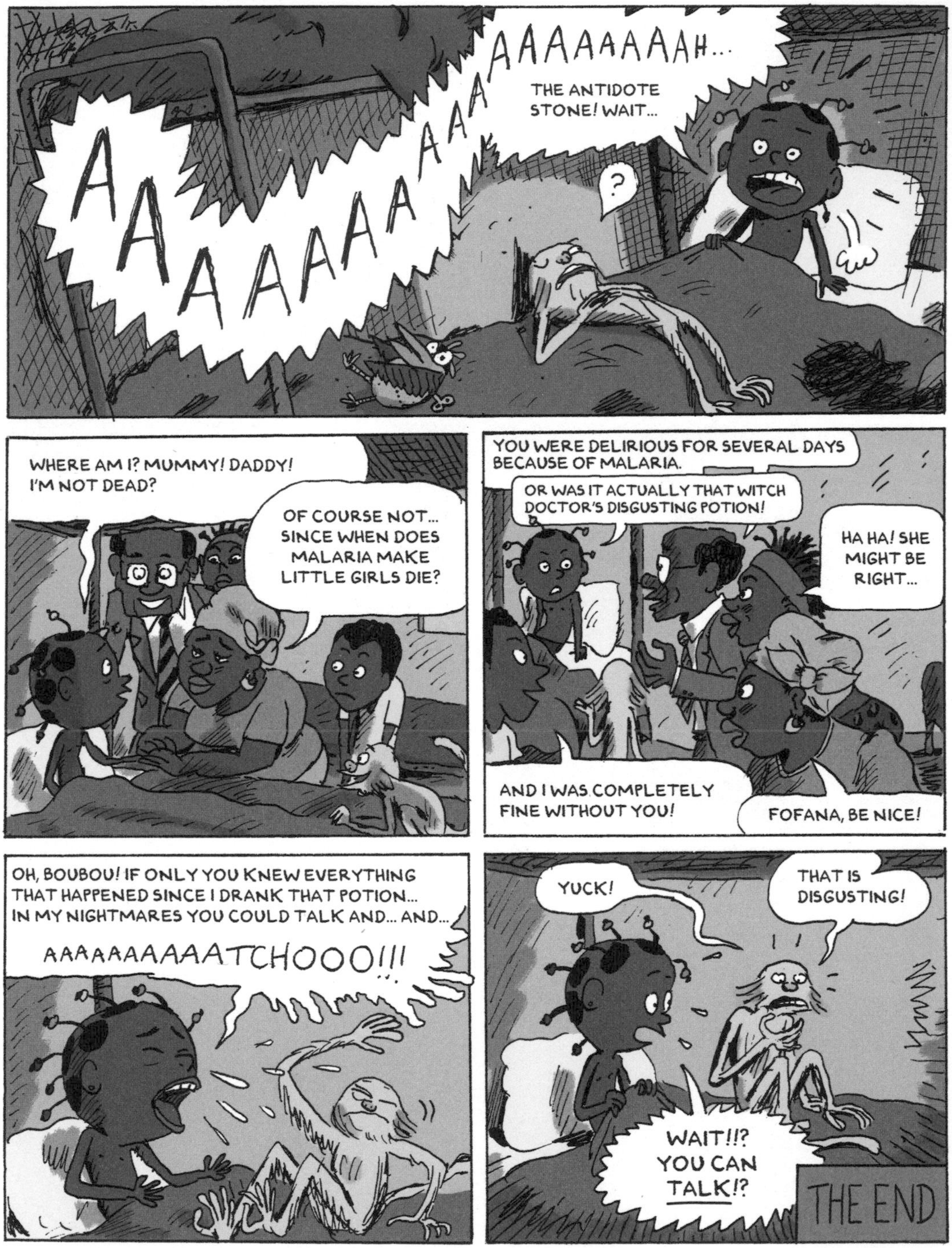
AAAAAAAAAAAAAAAAAAAAAH...
THE ANTIDOTE STONE! WAIT...
?
WHERE AM I? MUMMY! DADDY! I'M NOT DEAD?
OF COURSE NOT... SINCE WHEN DOES MALARIA MAKE LITTLE GIRLS DIE?
YOU WERE DELIRIOUS FOR SEVERAL DAYS BECAUSE OF MALARIA.
OR WAS IT ACTUALLY THAT WITCH DOCTOR'S DISGUSTING POTION!
HA HA! SHE MIGHT BE RIGHT...
AND I WAS COMPLETELY FINE WITHOUT YOU!
FOFANA, BE NICE!
OH, BOUBOU! IF ONLY YOU KNEW EVERYTHING THAT HAPPENED SINCE I DRANK THAT POTION... IN MY NIGHTMARES YOU COULD TALK AND... AND...
AAAAAAAAAATCHOOO!!!
YUCK!
THAT IS DISGUSTING!
WAIT!!? YOU CAN TALK!?
THE END

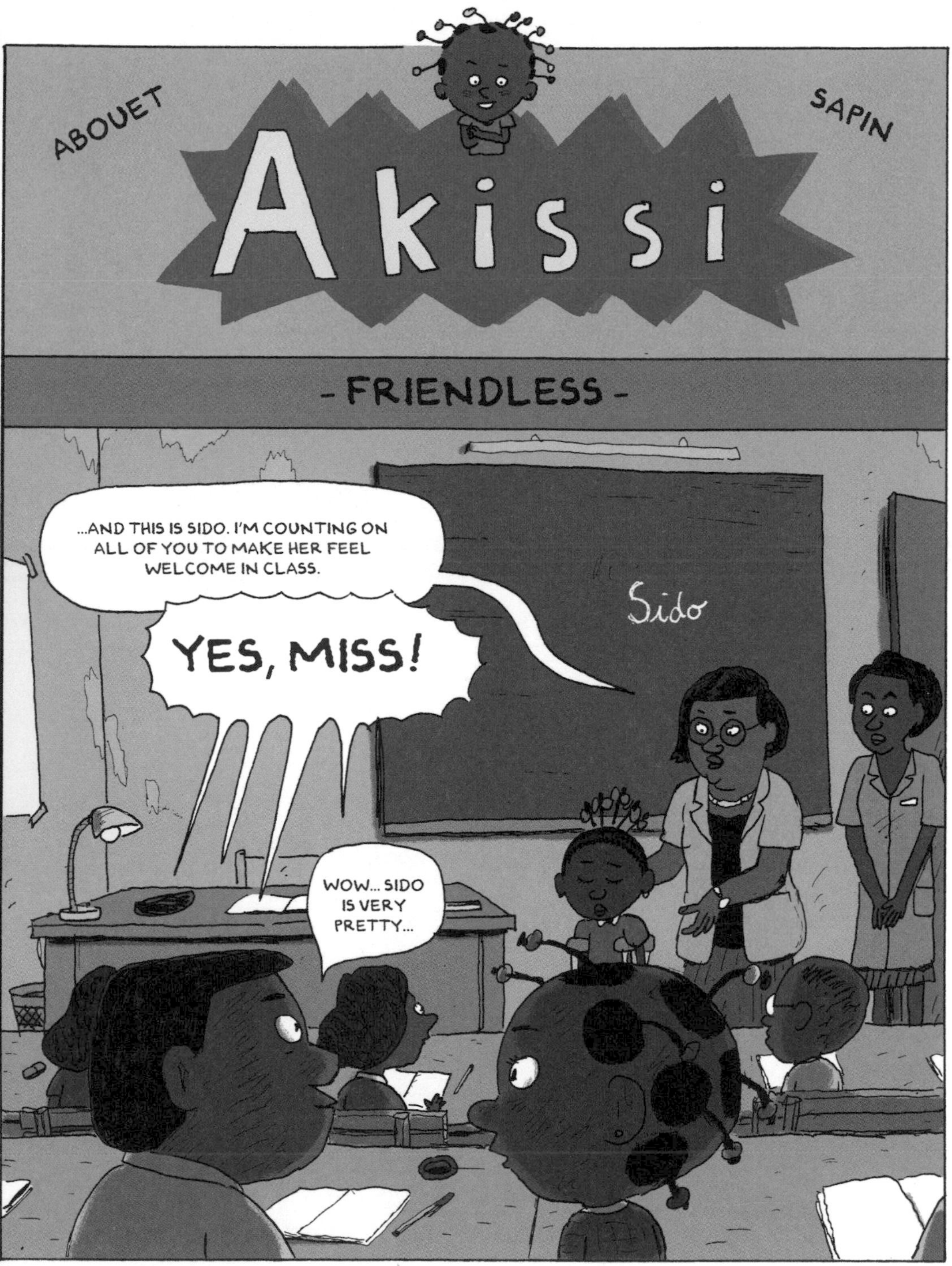
ABOUET
Akissi
SAPIN
- FRIENDLESS -
...AND THIS IS SIDO. I'M COUNTING ON ALL OF YOU TO MAKE HER FEEL WELCOME IN CLASS.
Sido
YES, MISS!
WOW... SIDO IS VERY PRETTY...

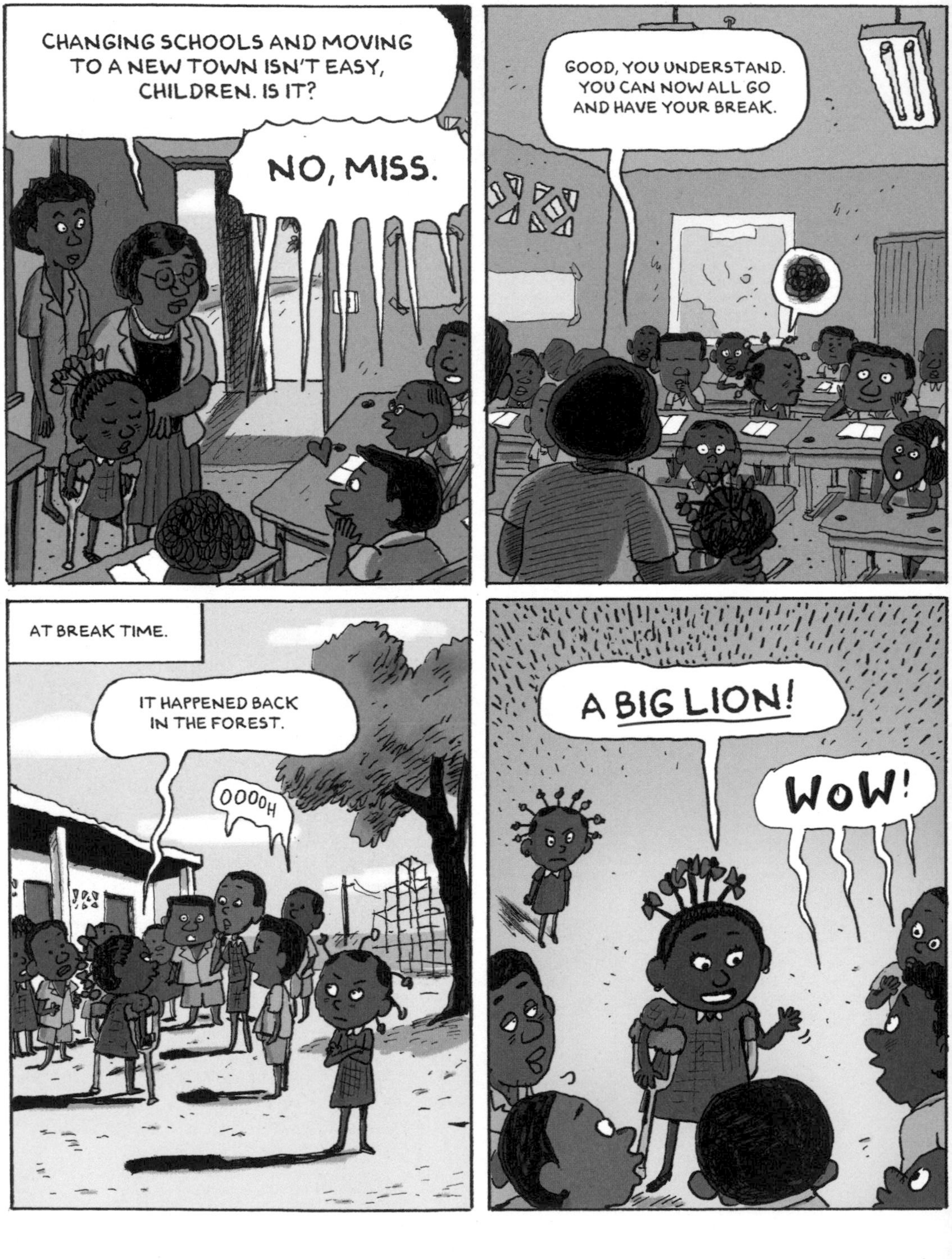
CHANGING SCHOOLS AND MOVING TO A NEW TOWN ISN'T EASY, CHILDREN. IS IT?
NO, MISS.
GOOD, YOU UNDERSTAND. YOU CAN NOW ALL GO AND HAVE YOUR BREAK.
AT BREAK TIME.
IT HAPPENED BACK IN THE FOREST.
OOOOH
A BIG LION!
WOW!

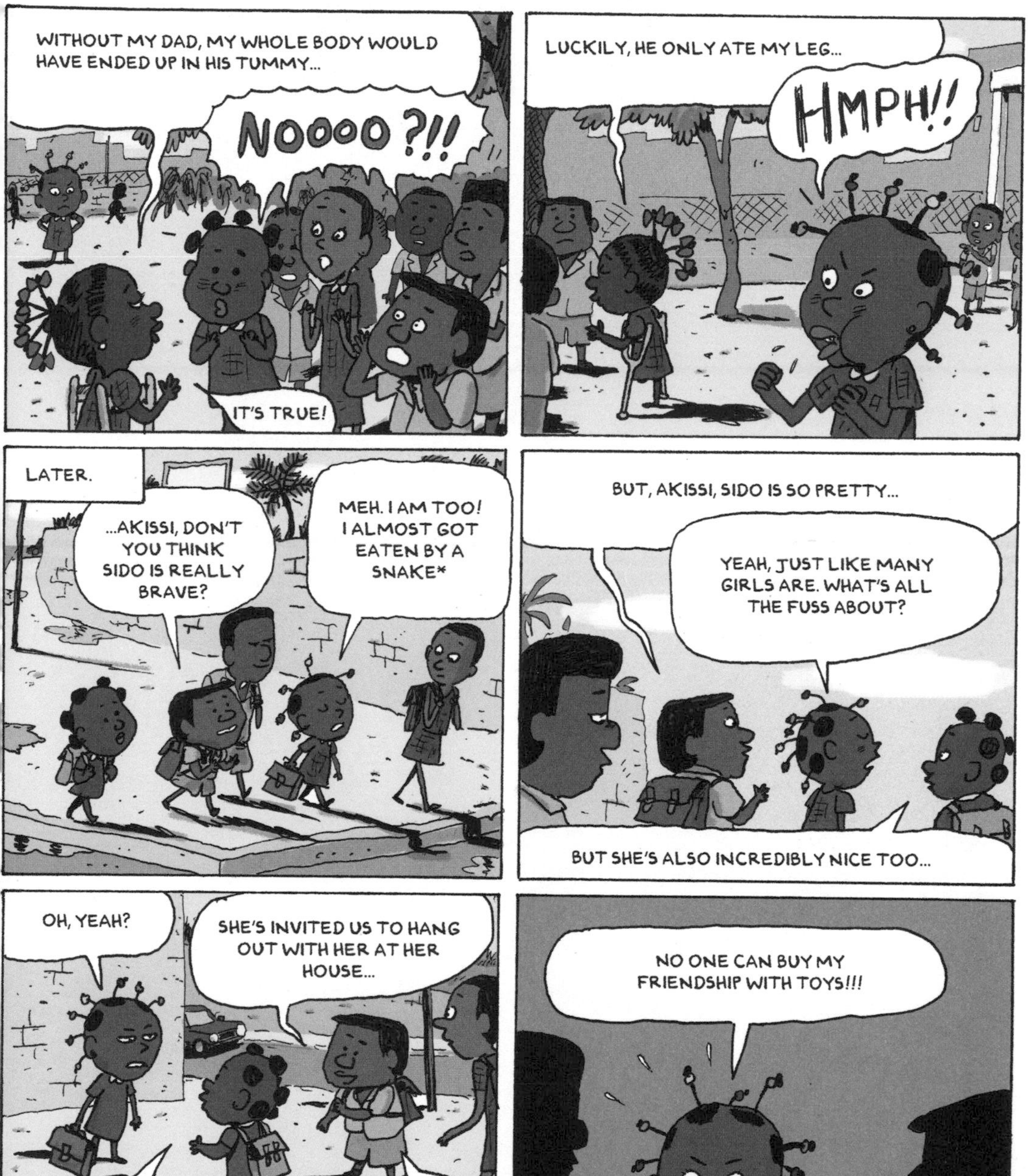
WITHOUT MY DAD, MY WHOLE BODY WOULD HAVE ENDED UP IN HIS TUMMY...
NOOOO ?!!
IT'S TRUE!
LUCKILY, HE ONLY ATE MY LEG...
HMPH!!
LATER.
...AKISSI, DON'T YOU THINK SIDO IS REALLY BRAVE?
MEH. I AM TOO! I ALMOST GOT EATEN BY A SNAKE*
BUT, AKISSI, SIDO IS SO PRETTY...
YEAH, JUST LIKE MANY GIRLS ARE. WHAT'S ALL THE FUSS ABOUT?
BUT SHE'S ALSO INCREDIBLY NICE TOO...
OH, YEAH?
SHE'S INVITED US TO HANG OUT WITH HER AT HER HOUSE...
SHE'S GOT LOTS OF TOYS FROM FRANCE. APPARENTLY, HER UNCLE BRINGS THEM BACK FOR HER!
COME ON, COME WITH US...
NO ONE CAN BUY MY FRIENDSHIP WITH TOYS!!!

*READ "AKISSI: TALES OF MISCHIEF - CASSAVA PANIC."

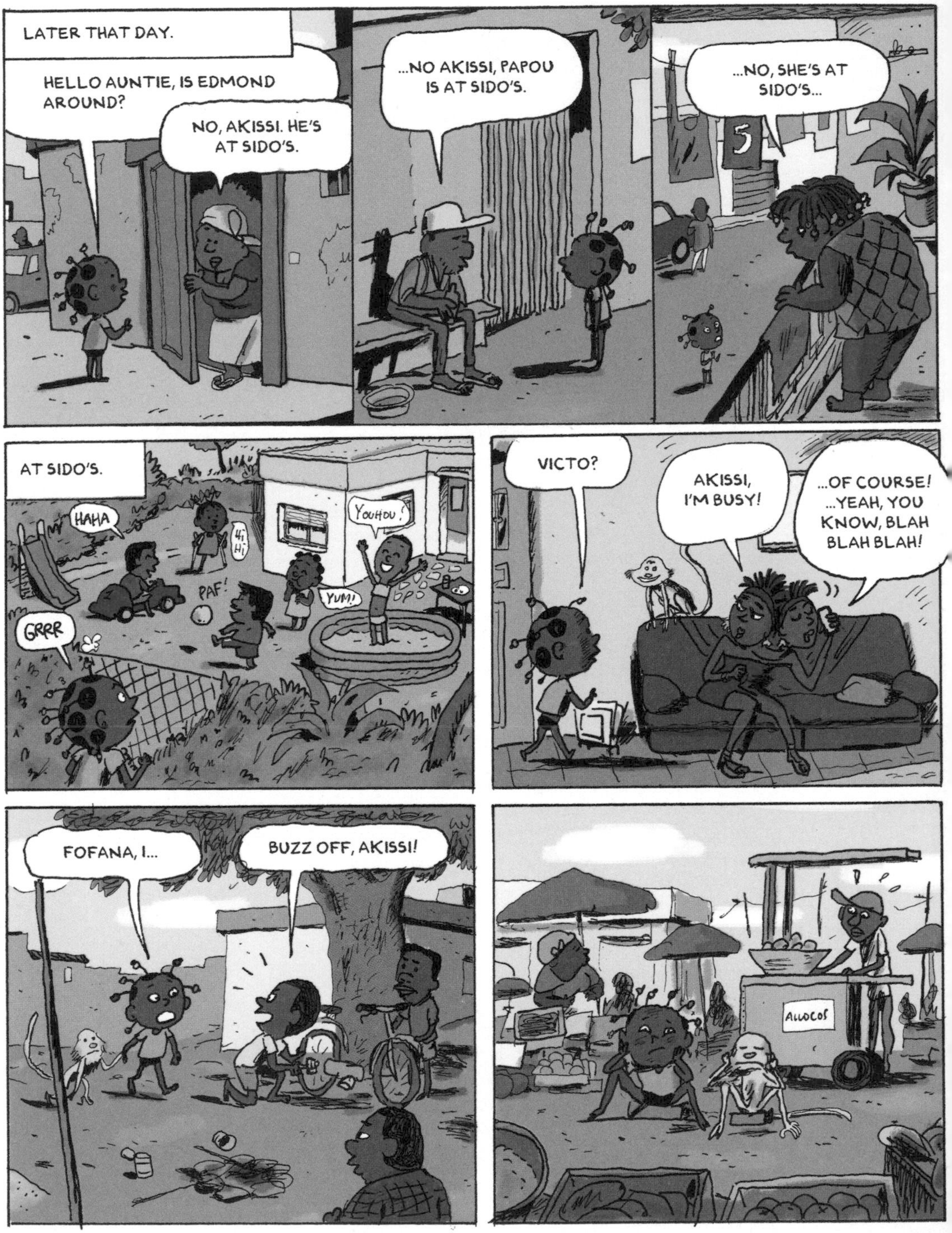
LATER THAT DAY.
HELLO AUNTIE, IS EDMOND AROUND?
NO, AKISSI. HE'S AT SIDO'S.
...NO AKISSI, PAPOU IS AT SIDO'S.
...NO, SHE'S AT SIDO'S...
AT SIDO'S.
HAHA
HI HI
YOUHOU!
PAF!
YUM!
GRRR
VICTO?
AKISSI, I'M BUSY!
...OF COURSE! ...YEAH, YOU KNOW, BLAH BLAH BLAH!
FOFANA, I...
BUZZ OFF, AKISSI!
ALLOCOS

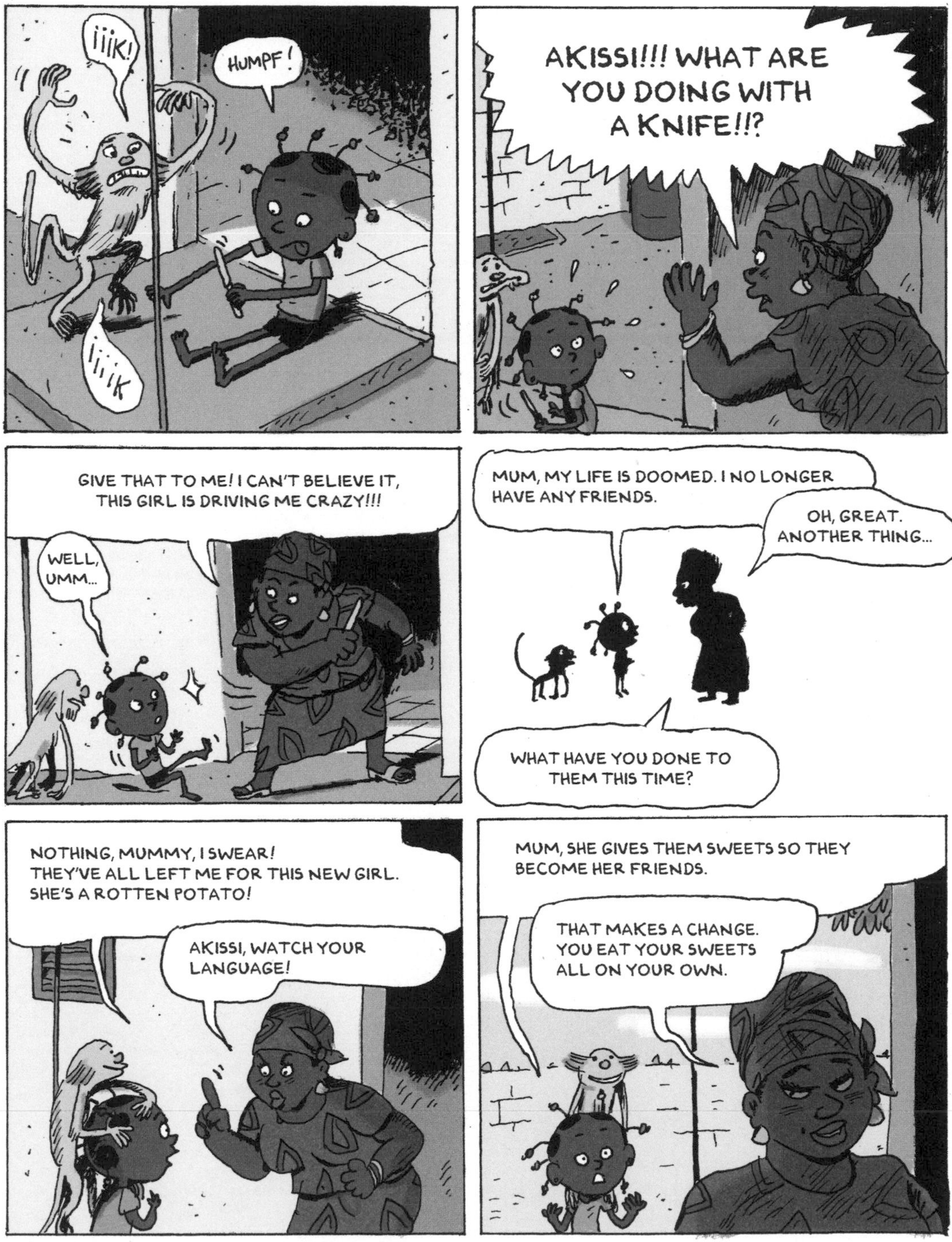

IIIK!
HUMPF!
IIIIK
AKISSI!!! WHAT ARE YOU DOING WITH A KNIFE!!?
GIVE THAT TO ME! I CAN'T BELIEVE IT, THIS GIRL IS DRIVING ME CRAZY!!!
WELL, UMM...
MUM, MY LIFE IS DOOMED. I NO LONGER HAVE ANY FRIENDS.
OH, GREAT. ANOTHER THING...
WHAT HAVE YOU DONE TO THEM THIS TIME?
NOTHING, MUMMY, I SWEAR! THEY'VE ALL LEFT ME FOR THIS NEW GIRL. SHE'S A ROTTEN POTATO!
AKISSI, WATCH YOUR LANGUAGE!
MUM, SHE GIVES THEM SWEETS SO THEY BECOME HER FRIENDS.
THAT MAKES A CHANGE. YOU EAT YOUR SWEETS ALL ON YOUR OWN.

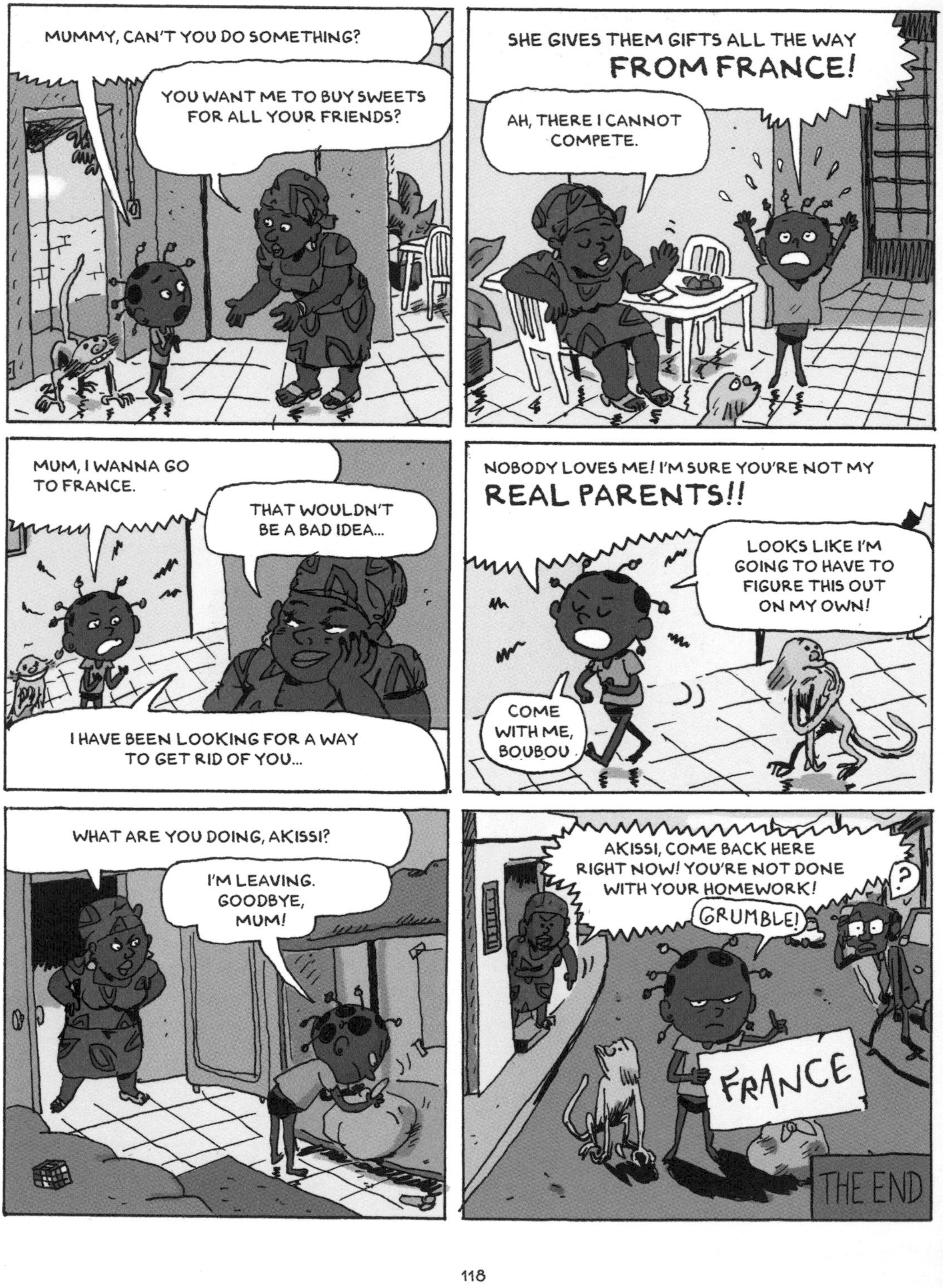
MUMMY, CAN'T YOU DO SOMETHING?
YOU WANT ME TO BUY SWEETS FOR ALL YOUR FRIENDS?
SHE GIVES THEM GIFTS ALL THE WAY FROM FRANCE!
AH, THERE I CANNOT COMPETE.
MUM, I WANNA GO TO FRANCE.
THAT WOULDN'T BE A BAD IDEA...
I HAVE BEEN LOOKING FOR A WAY TO GET RID OF YOU...
NOBODY LOVES ME! I'M SURE YOU'RE NOT MY REAL PARENTS!!
LOOKS LIKE I'M GOING TO HAVE TO FIGURE THIS OUT ON MY OWN!
COME WITH ME, BOUBOU.
WHAT ARE YOU DOING, AKISSI?
I'M LEAVING. GOODBYE, MUM!
AKISSI, COME BACK HERE RIGHT NOW! YOU'RE NOT DONE WITH YOUR HOMEWORK!
?
GRUMBLE!
FRANCE
THE END

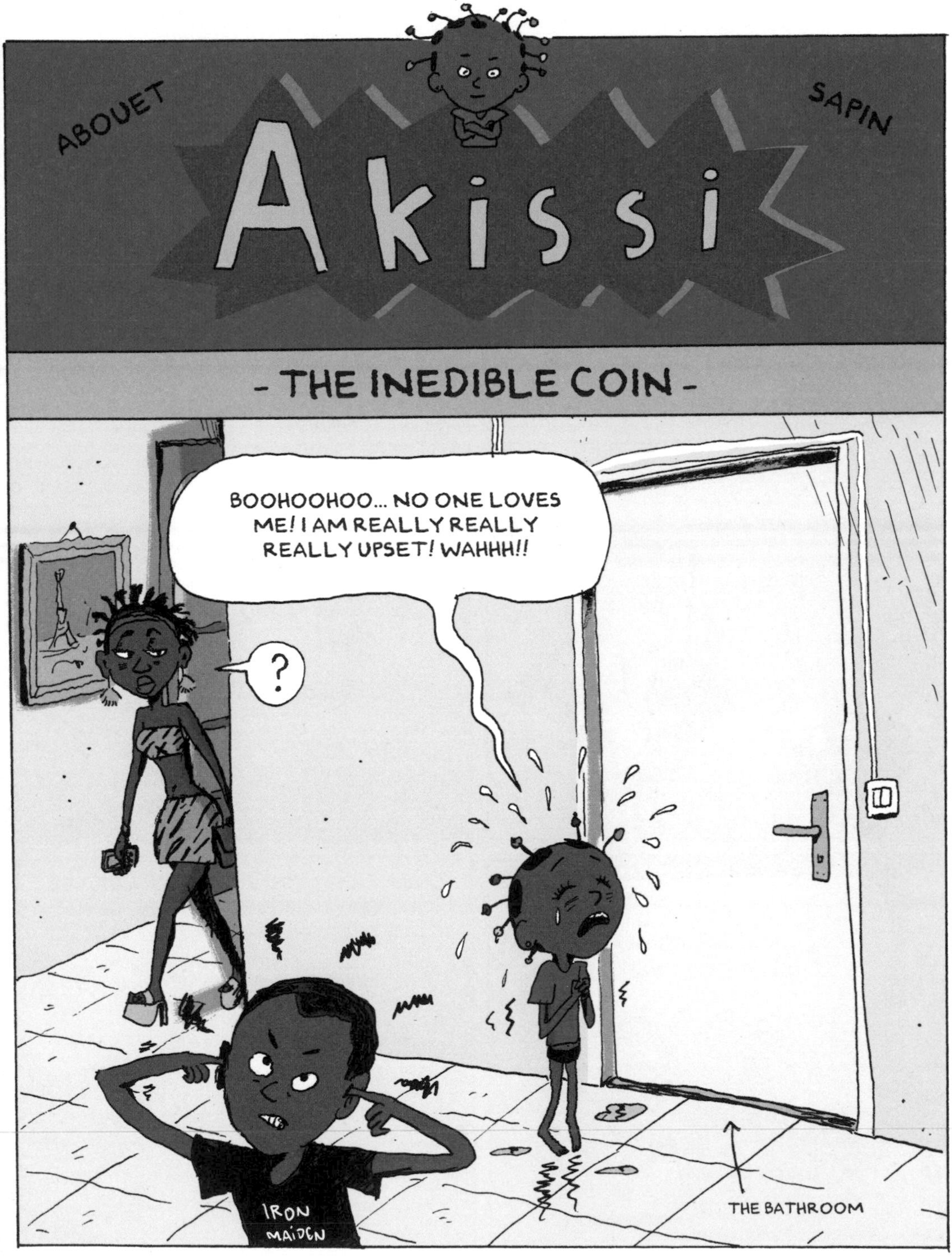
ABOUET
SAPIN
Akissi
- THE INEDIBLE COIN -
BOOHOOHOO... NO ONE LOVES ME! I AM REALLY REALLY REALLY UPSET! WAHHH!!
?
IRON MAIDEN
THE BATHROOM

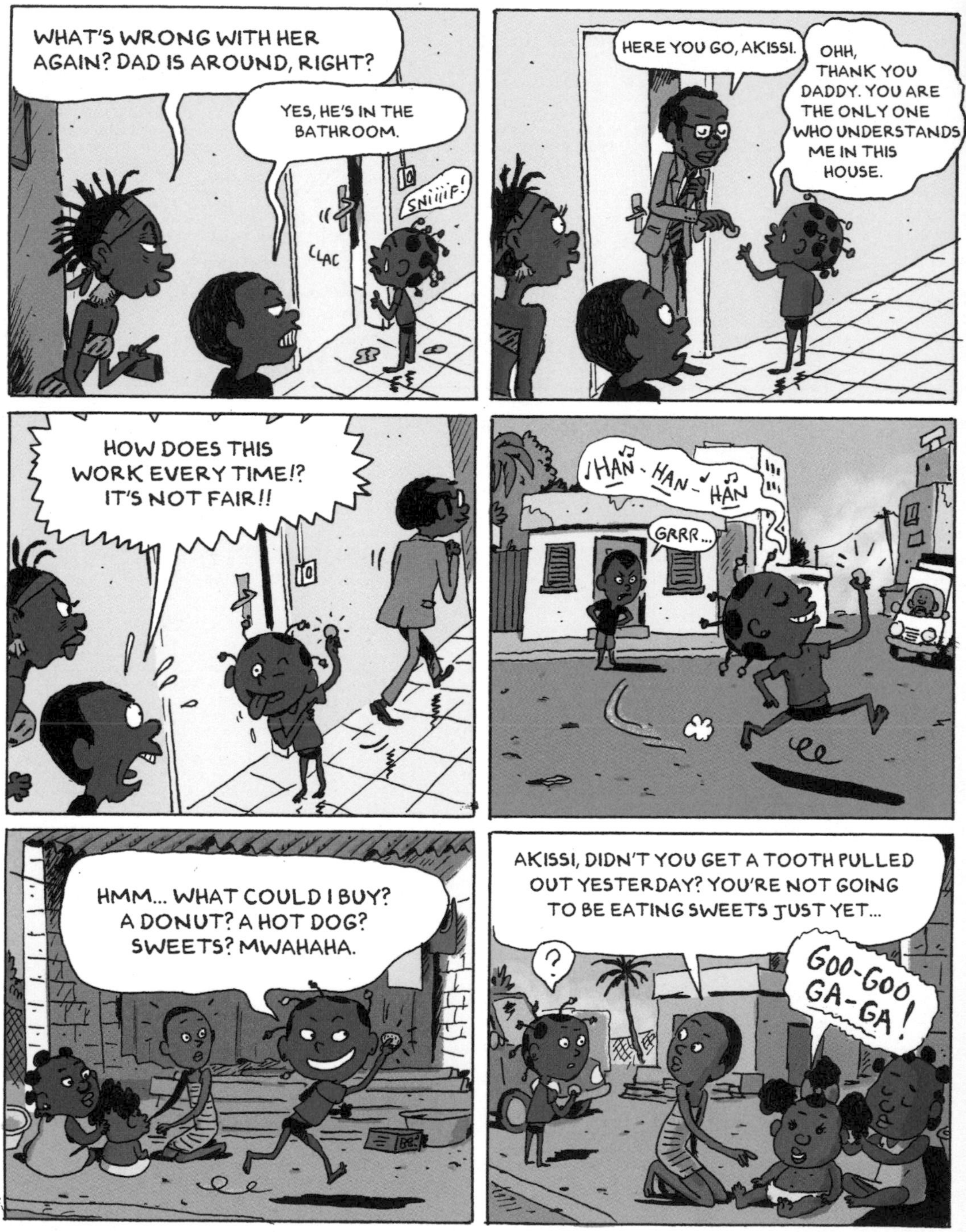

WHAT'S WRONG WITH HER AGAIN? DAD IS AROUND, RIGHT?
YES, HE'S IN THE BATHROOM.
CLAC
SNIIIIIF!
HERE YOU GO, AKISSI.
OHH, THANK YOU DADDY. YOU ARE THE ONLY ONE WHO UNDERSTANDS ME IN THIS HOUSE.
HOW DOES THIS WORK EVERY TIME!? IT'S NOT FAIR!!
HAN - HAN - HAN
GRRR...
HMM... WHAT COULD I BUY? A DONUT? A HOT DOG? SWEETS? MWAHAHA.
AKISSI, DIDN'T YOU GET A TOOTH PULLED OUT YESTERDAY? YOU'RE NOT GOING TO BE EATING SWEETS JUST YET...
?
GOO-GOO GA-GA!

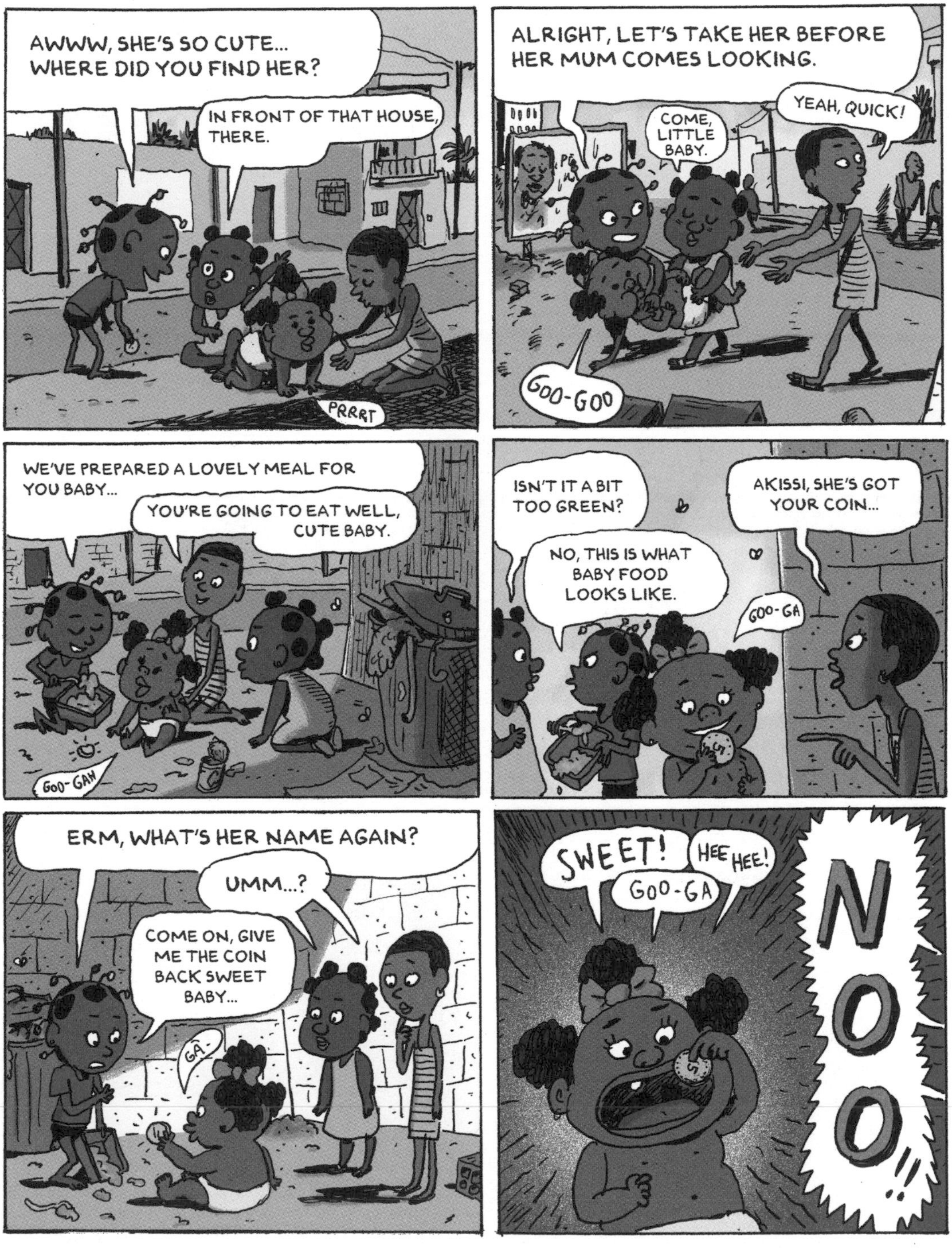
AWWW, SHE'S SO CUTE... WHERE DID YOU FIND HER?
IN FRONT OF THAT HOUSE, THERE.
PRRRT
ALRIGHT, LET'S TAKE HER BEFORE HER MUM COMES LOOKING.
COME, LITTLE BABY.
YEAH, QUICK!
GOO-GOO
WE'VE PREPARED A LOVELY MEAL FOR YOU BABY...
YOU'RE GOING TO EAT WELL, CUTE BABY.
GOO-GAH
ISN'T IT A BIT TOO GREEN?
NO, THIS IS WHAT BABY FOOD LOOKS LIKE.
AKISSI, SHE'S GOT YOUR COIN...
GOO-GA
ERM, WHAT'S HER NAME AGAIN?
UMM...?
COME ON, GIVE ME THE COIN BACK SWEET BABY...
GA-
SWEET!
HEE HEE!
GOO-GA
NOO!!

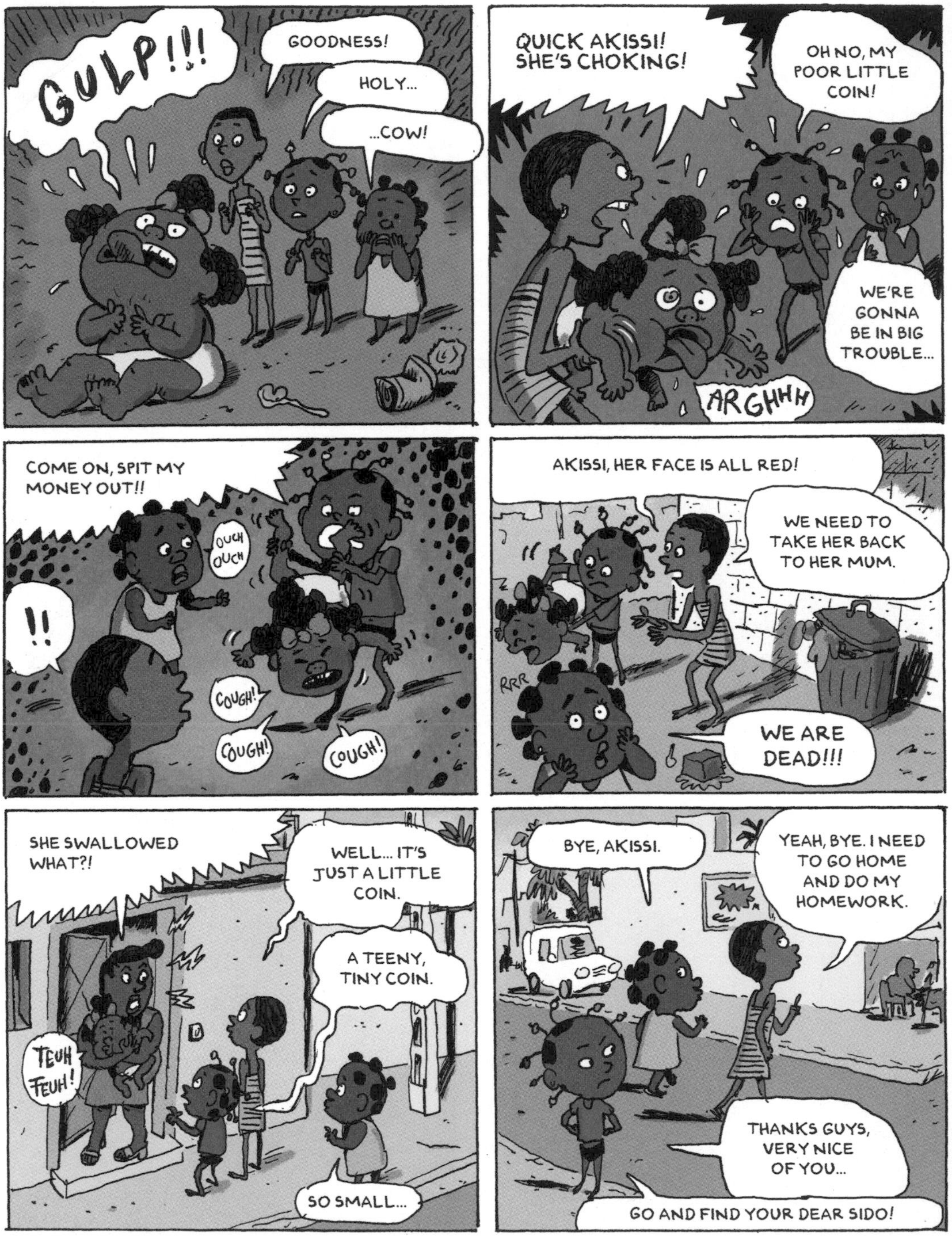
GULP!!!
GOODNESS!
HOLY...
...COW!
QUICK AKISSI! SHE'S CHOKING!
OH NO, MY POOR LITTLE COIN!
WE'RE GONNA BE IN BIG TROUBLE...
ARGHHH
COME ON, SPIT MY MONEY OUT!!
OUCH OUCH
!!
COUGH!
COUGH!
COUGH!
AKISSI, HER FACE IS ALL RED!
WE NEED TO TAKE HER BACK TO HER MUM.
RRR
WE ARE DEAD!!!
SHE SWALLOWED WHAT?!
WELL... IT'S JUST A LITTLE COIN.
A TEENY, TINY COIN.
TEUH FEUH!
SO SMALL...
BYE, AKISSI.
YEAH, BYE. I NEED TO GO HOME AND DO MY HOMEWORK.
THANKS GUYS, VERY NICE OF YOU...
GO AND FIND YOUR DEAR SIDO!

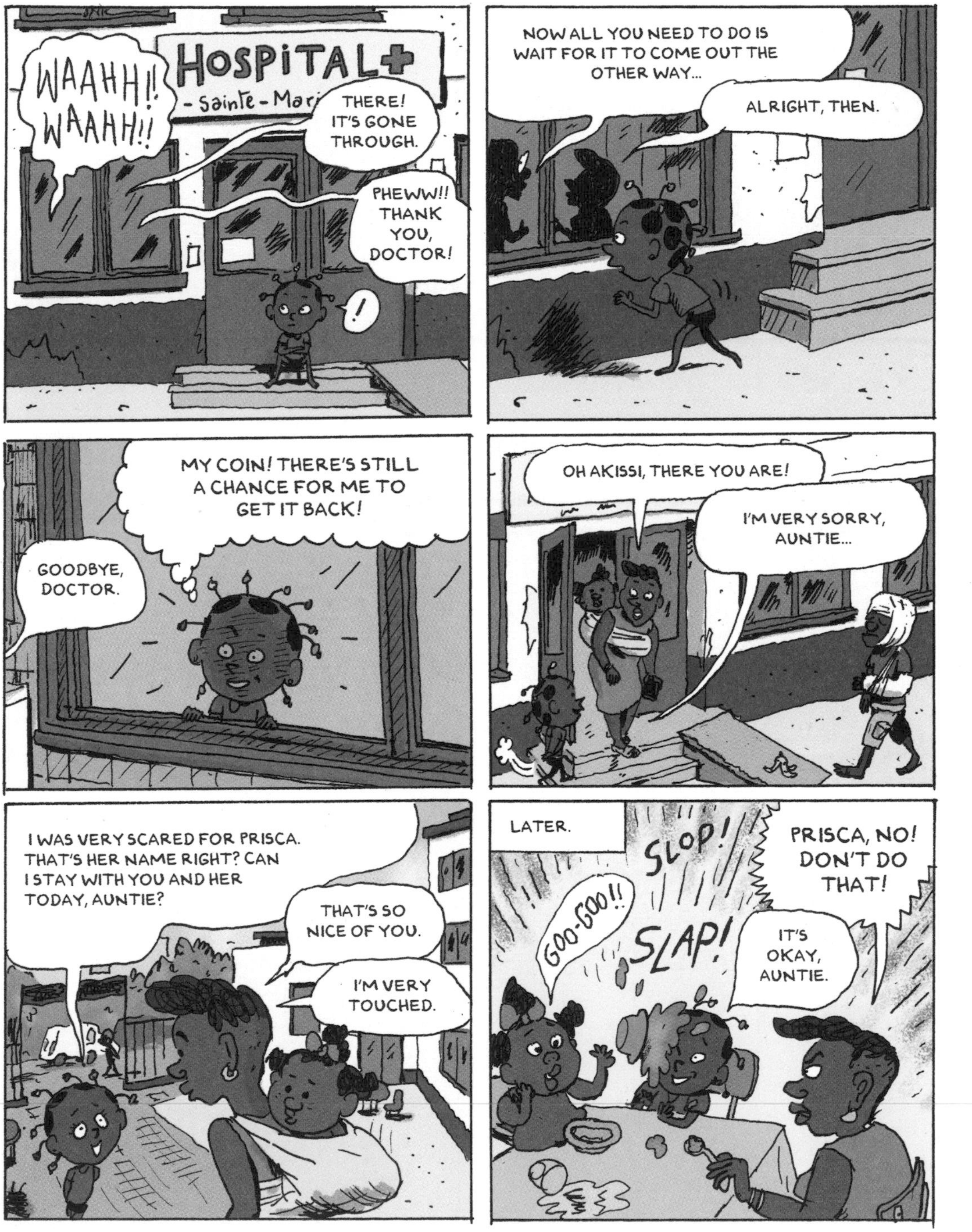
HOSPITAL
- Sainte - Mari
WAAHH!! WAAHH!!
THERE! IT'S GONE THROUGH.
PHEWW!! THANK YOU, DOCTOR!
!
NOW ALL YOU NEED TO DO IS WAIT FOR IT TO COME OUT THE OTHER WAY...
ALRIGHT, THEN.
MY COIN! THERE'S STILL A CHANCE FOR ME TO GET IT BACK!
GOODBYE, DOCTOR.
OH AKISSI, THERE YOU ARE!
I'M VERY SORRY, AUNTIE...
I WAS VERY SCARED FOR PRISCA. THAT'S HER NAME RIGHT? CAN I STAY WITH YOU AND HER TODAY, AUNTIE?
THAT'S SO NICE OF YOU.
I'M VERY TOUCHED.
LATER.
SLOP!
PRISCA, NO! DON'T DO THAT!
GOO-GOO!!
SLAP!
IT'S OKAY, AUNTIE.

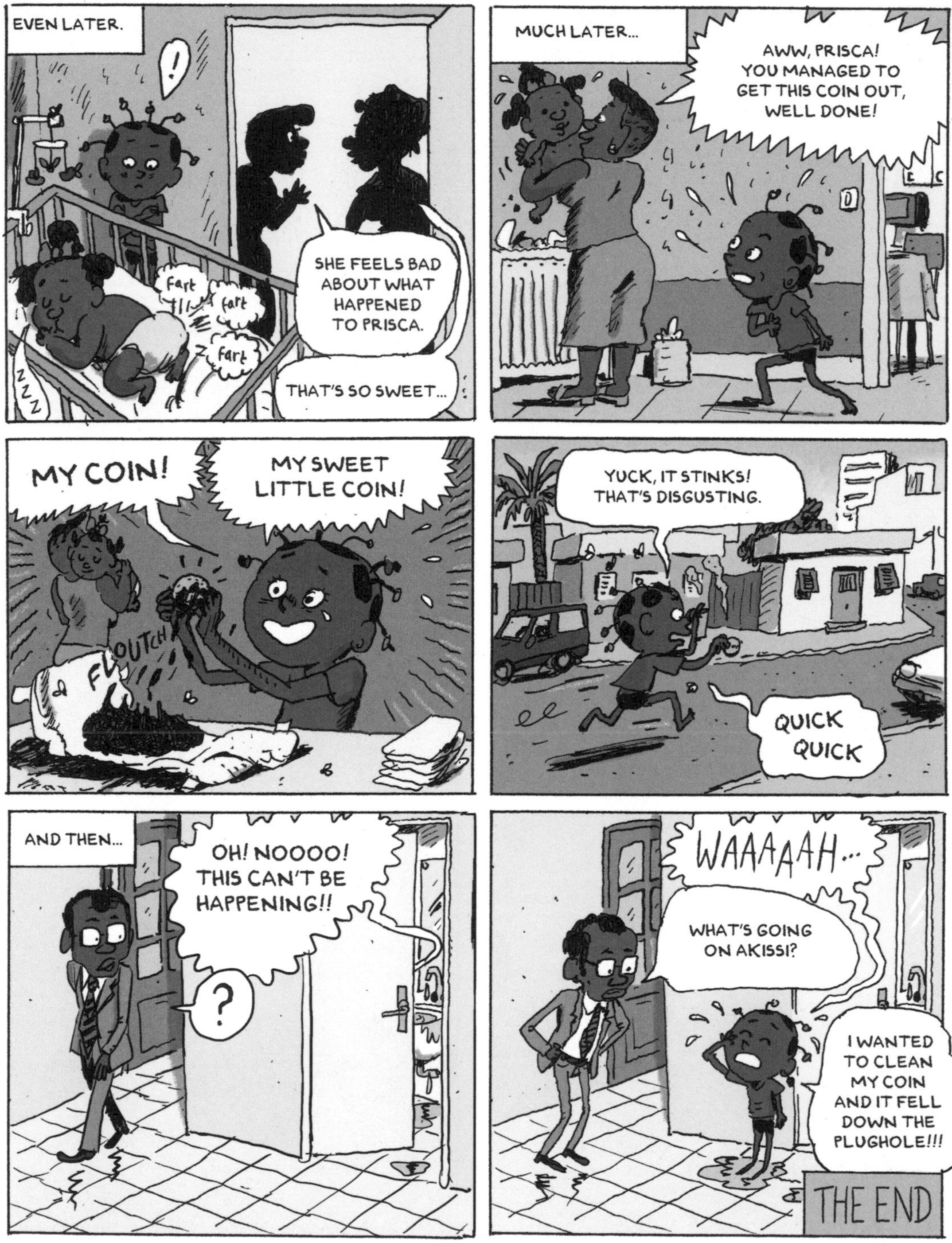
EVEN LATER.
!
fart
fart
fart
ZZZ
SHE FEELS BAD ABOUT WHAT HAPPENED TO PRISCA.
THAT'S SO SWEET...
MUCH LATER...
AWW, PRISCA! YOU MANAGED TO GET THIS COIN OUT, WELL DONE!
MY COIN!
MY SWEET LITTLE COIN!
FLOUTCH
YUCK, IT STINKS! THAT'S DISGUSTING.
QUICK QUICK
AND THEN...
OH! NOOOO! THIS CAN'T BE HAPPENING!!
?
WAAAAAH...
WHAT'S GOING ON AKISSI?
I WANTED TO CLEAN MY COIN AND IT FELL DOWN THE PLUGHOLE!!!
THE END

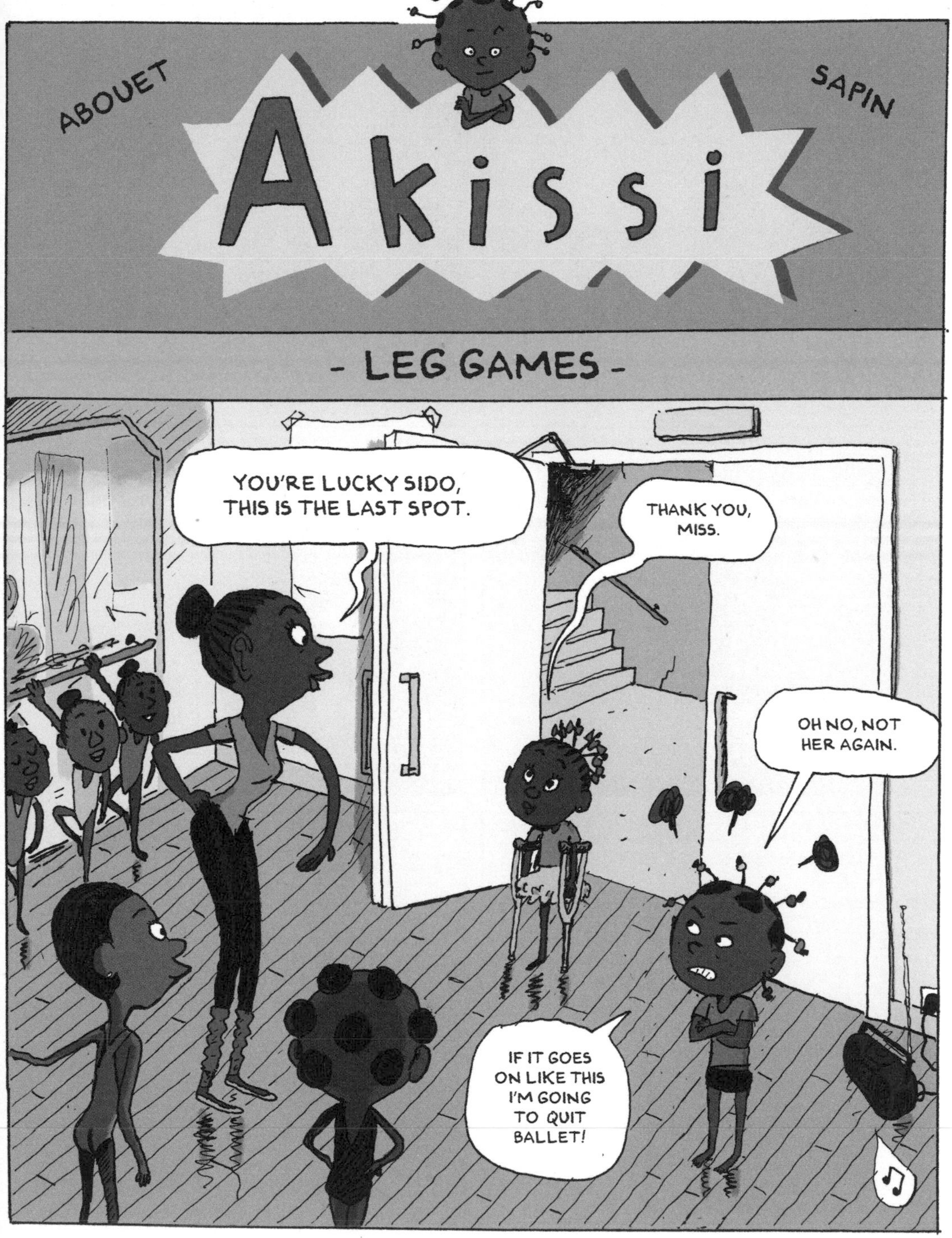
ABOUET
SAPIN
Akissi
- LEG GAMES -
YOU'RE LUCKY SIDO, THIS IS THE LAST SPOT.
THANK YOU, MISS.
OH NO, NOT HER AGAIN.
IF IT GOES ON LIKE THIS I'M GOING TO QUIT BALLET!

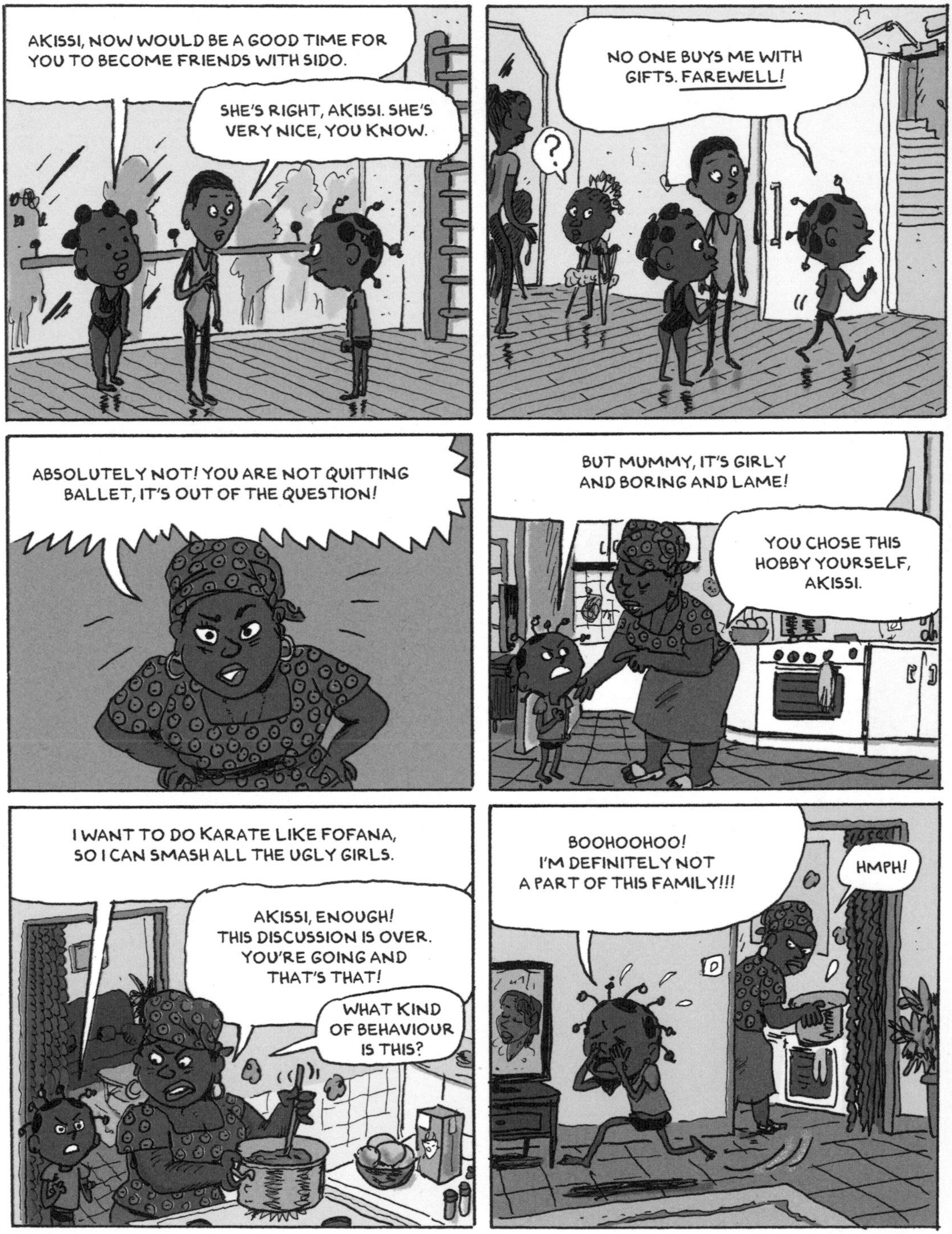
AKISSI, NOW WOULD BE A GOOD TIME FOR YOU TO BECOME FRIENDS WITH SIDO.
SHE'S RIGHT, AKISSI. SHE'S VERY NICE, YOU KNOW.
?
NO ONE BUYS ME WITH GIFTS. FAREWELL!
ABSOLUTELY NOT! YOU ARE NOT QUITTING BALLET, IT'S OUT OF THE QUESTION!
BUT MUMMY, IT'S GIRLY AND BORING AND LAME!
YOU CHOSE THIS HOBBY YOURSELF, AKISSI.
I WANT TO DO KARATE LIKE FOFANA, SO I CAN SMASH ALL THE UGLY GIRLS.
AKISSI, ENOUGH! THIS DISCUSSION IS OVER. YOU'RE GOING AND THAT'S THAT!
WHAT KIND OF BEHAVIOUR IS THIS?
BOOHOOHOO! I'M DEFINITELY NOT A PART OF THIS FAMILY!!!
HMPH!

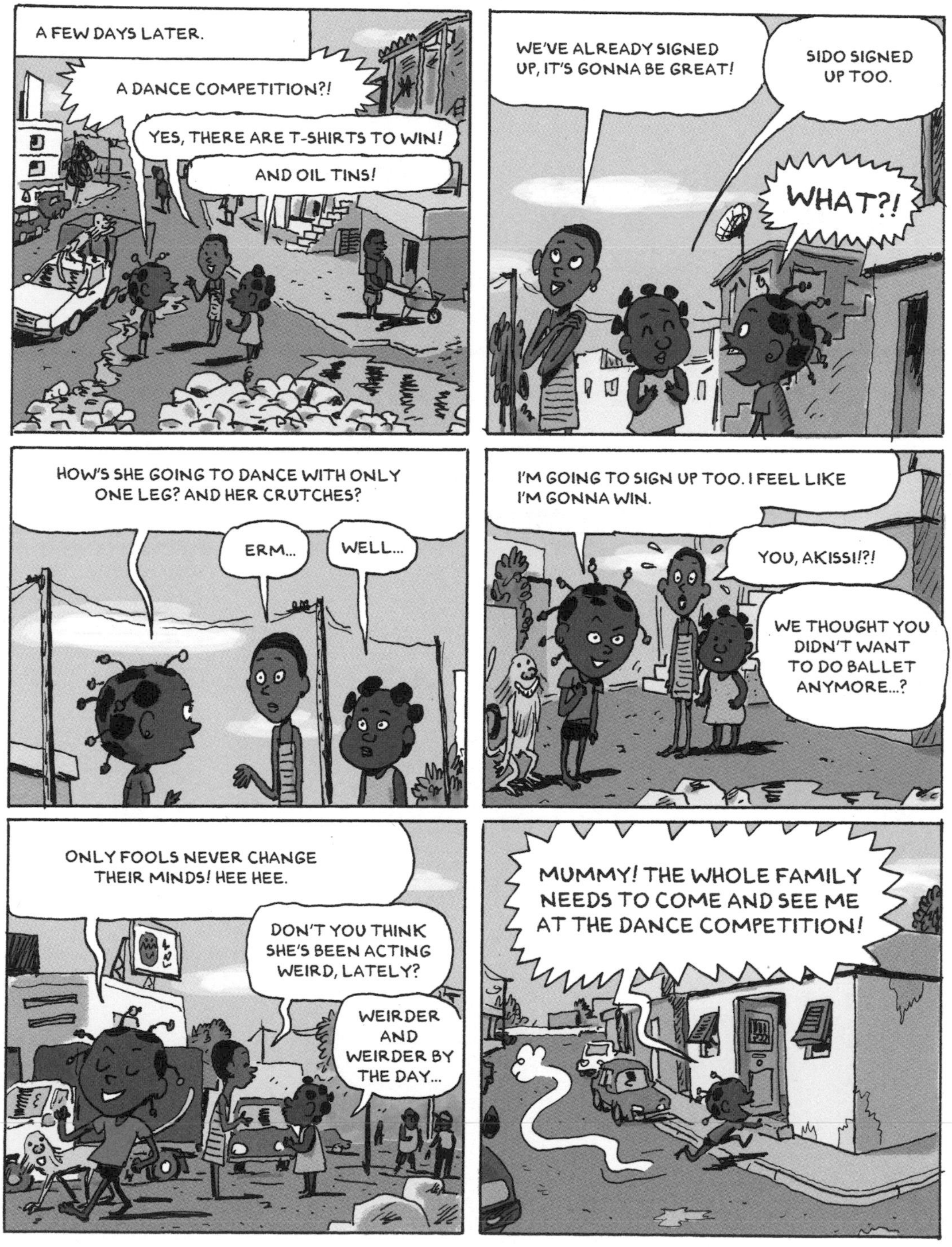
A FEW DAYS LATER.
A DANCE COMPETITION?!
YES, THERE ARE T-SHIRTS TO WIN!
AND OIL TINS!
WE'VE ALREADY SIGNED UP, IT'S GONNA BE GREAT!
SIDO SIGNED UP TOO.
WHAT?!
HOW'S SHE GOING TO DANCE WITH ONLY ONE LEG? AND HER CRUTCHES?
ERM...
WELL...
I'M GOING TO SIGN UP TOO. I FEEL LIKE I'M GONNA WIN.
YOU, AKISSI!?!
WE THOUGHT YOU DIDN'T WANT TO DO BALLET ANYMORE...?
ONLY FOOLS NEVER CHANGE THEIR MINDS! HEE HEE.
DON'T YOU THINK SHE'S BEEN ACTING WEIRD, LATELY?
WEIRDER AND WEIRDER BY THE DAY...
MUMMY! THE WHOLE FAMILY NEEDS TO COME AND SEE ME AT THE DANCE COMPETITION!

I THOUGHT YOU NO LONGER WANTED TO BE A DANCER, YOUNG LADY...
TRUE! BUT I'M GOING TO WIN THIS, I'M TELLING YOU!
YOU SEEM PRETTY SURE OF YOURSELF. YOU DO KNOW IT'S A COMPETITION?
OF COURSE. BUT YOU SHOULD SEE WHO I AM COMPETING AGAINST...
AC DC
AKISSI, YOU ASKED TO COMPETE AGAINST SIDO?!
sign up
YEAH, SO WHAT? SHE SIGNED UP FOR THE COMPETITION...
WOW, BUT SHE'S CRAZY GOOD!!
YEAH, SIDO IS AN AMAZING DANCER!
YOU ARE STARTING TO GET ON MY NERVES WITH ALL YOUR SIDO TALK!
SIDO THIS, SIDO THAT... I GET IT! YOU GUYS ARE BETTER FRIENDS WITH HER THAN WITH ME!
BUT, AKISSI...
WE'RE STILL YOUR FRIENDS... WE'RE TELLING YOU BECAUSE WE LOVE YOU.
YOU'D BETTER START TRAINING YOU KNOW, INSTEAD OF UNDERESTIMATING HER...
THAT'S IT. FAREWELL, FORMER FRIENDS!

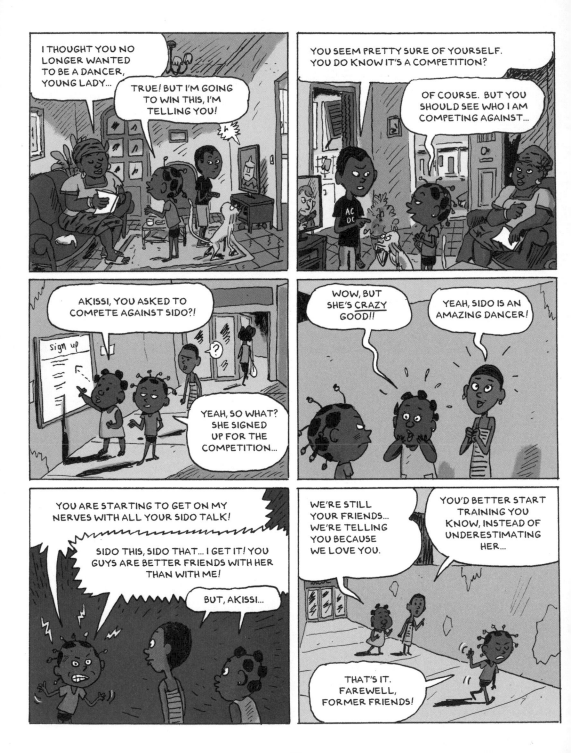

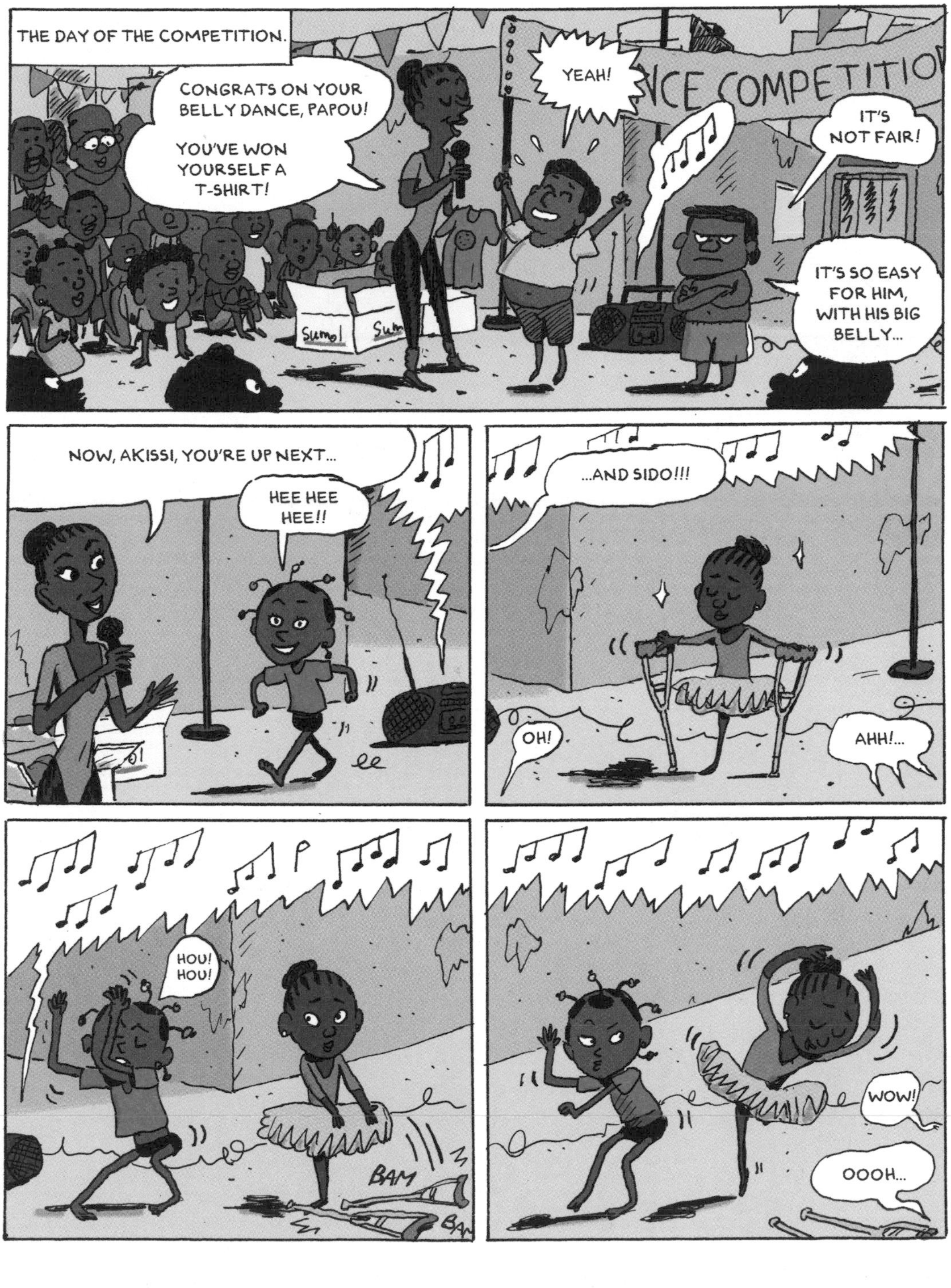
THE DAY OF THE COMPETITION.
CONGRATS ON YOUR BELLY DANCE, PAPOU!
YOU'VE WON YOURSELF A T-SHIRT!
YEAH!
NCE COMPETITIO
IT'S NOT FAIR!
IT'S SO EASY FOR HIM, WITH HIS BIG BELLY...
NOW, AKISSI, YOU'RE UP NEXT...
HEE HEE HEE!!
...AND SIDO!!!
OH!
AHH!...
HOU! HOU!
BAM
WOW!
OOOH...

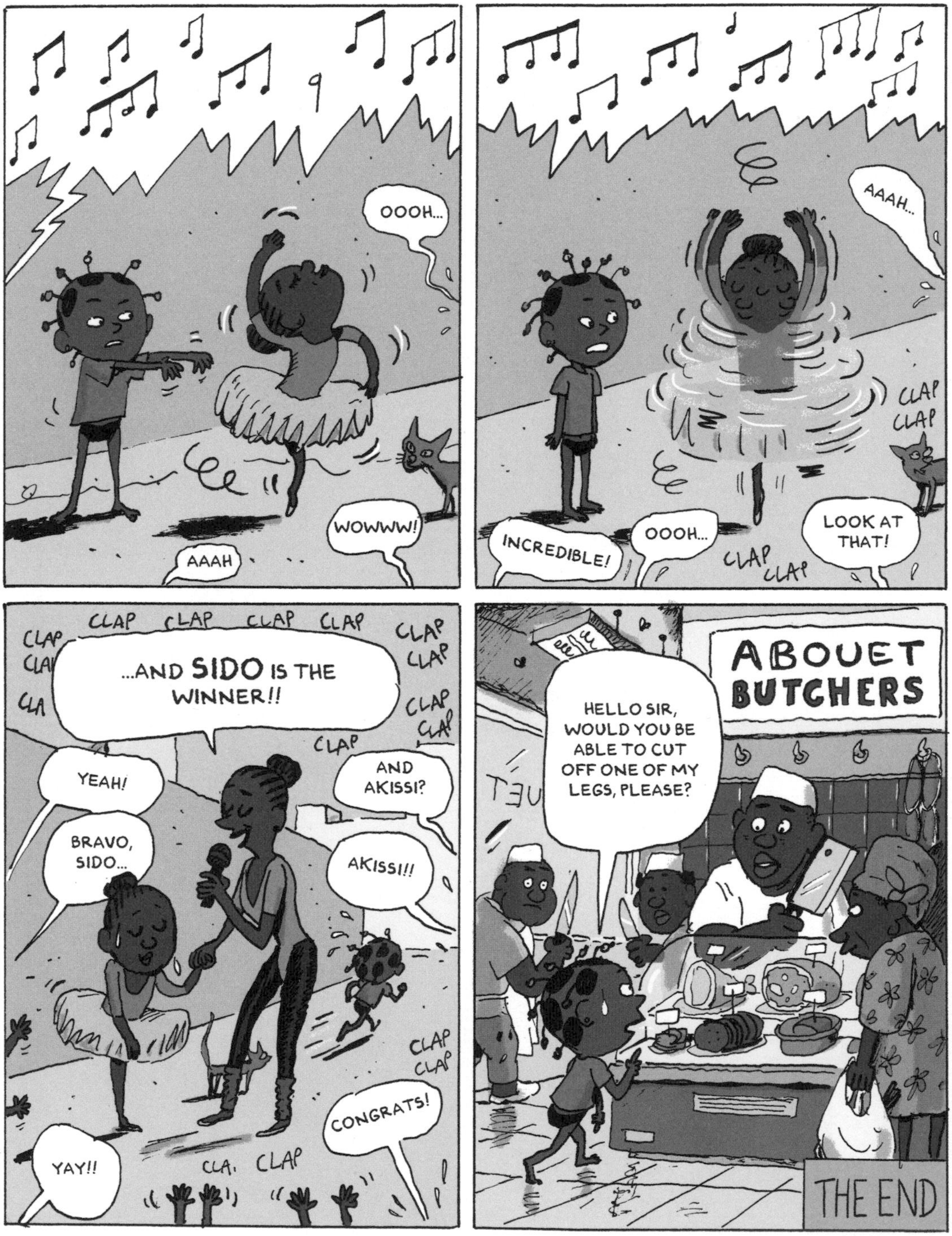
OOOH...
WOWWW!
AAAH
AAAH...
CLAP
CLAP
INCREDIBLE!
OOOH...
CLAP
CLAP
LOOK AT THAT!
CLAP CLAP CLAP CLAP CLAP CLAP
CLAP CLAP
...AND SIDO IS THE WINNER!!
CLAP CLAP
CLAP
YEAH!
AND AKISSI?
BRAVO, SIDO...
AKISSI!!
CLAP CLAP
CONGRATS!
YAY!!
CLA. CLAP
ABOUET BUTCHERS
HELLO SIR, WOULD YOU BE ABLE TO CUT OFF ONE OF MY LEGS, PLEASE?
THE END

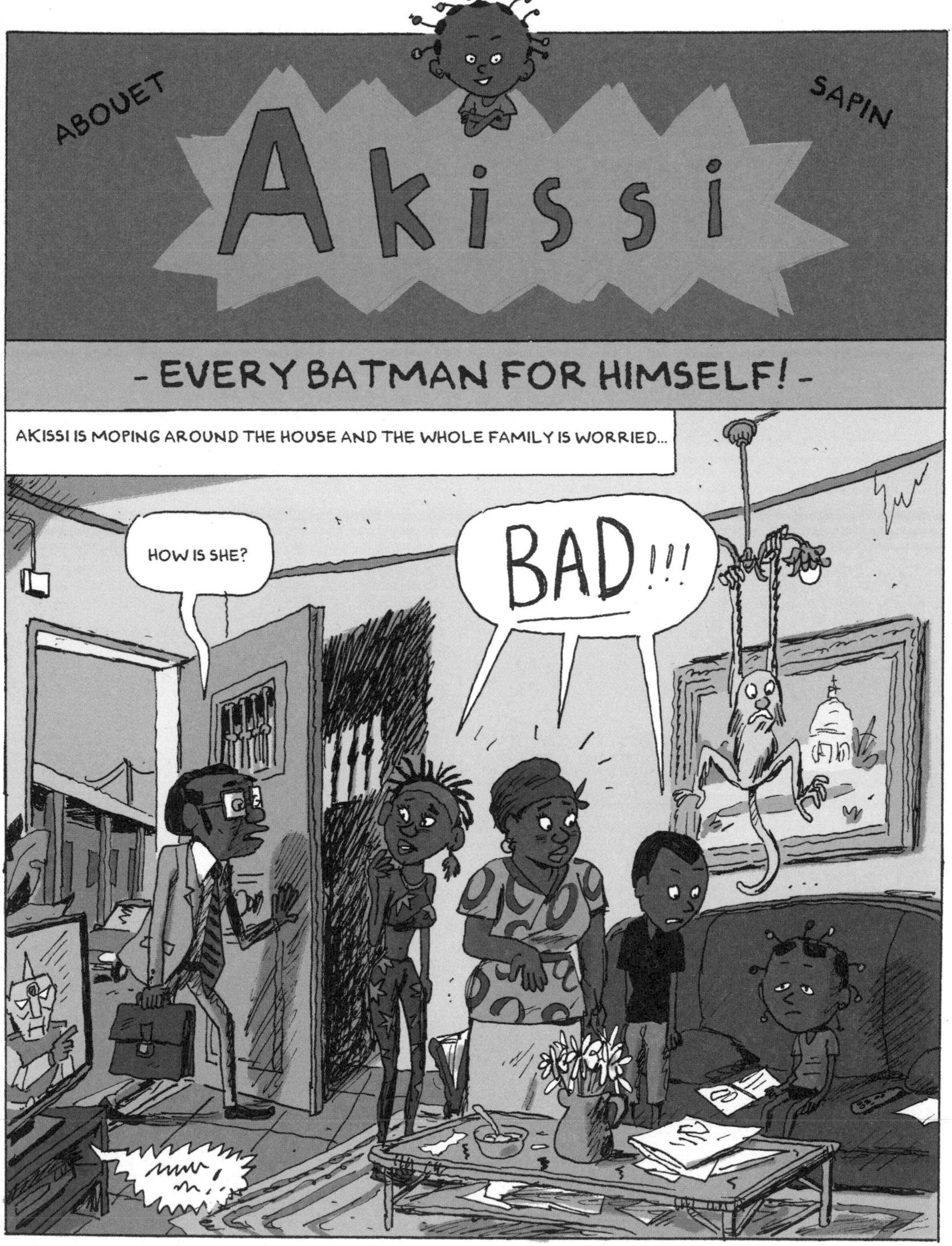
ABOUET
Akissi
SAPIN
- EVERY BATMAN FOR HIMSELF! -
AKISSI IS MOPING AROUND THE HOUSE AND THE WHOLE FAMILY IS WORRIED...
HOW IS SHE?
BAD!!!

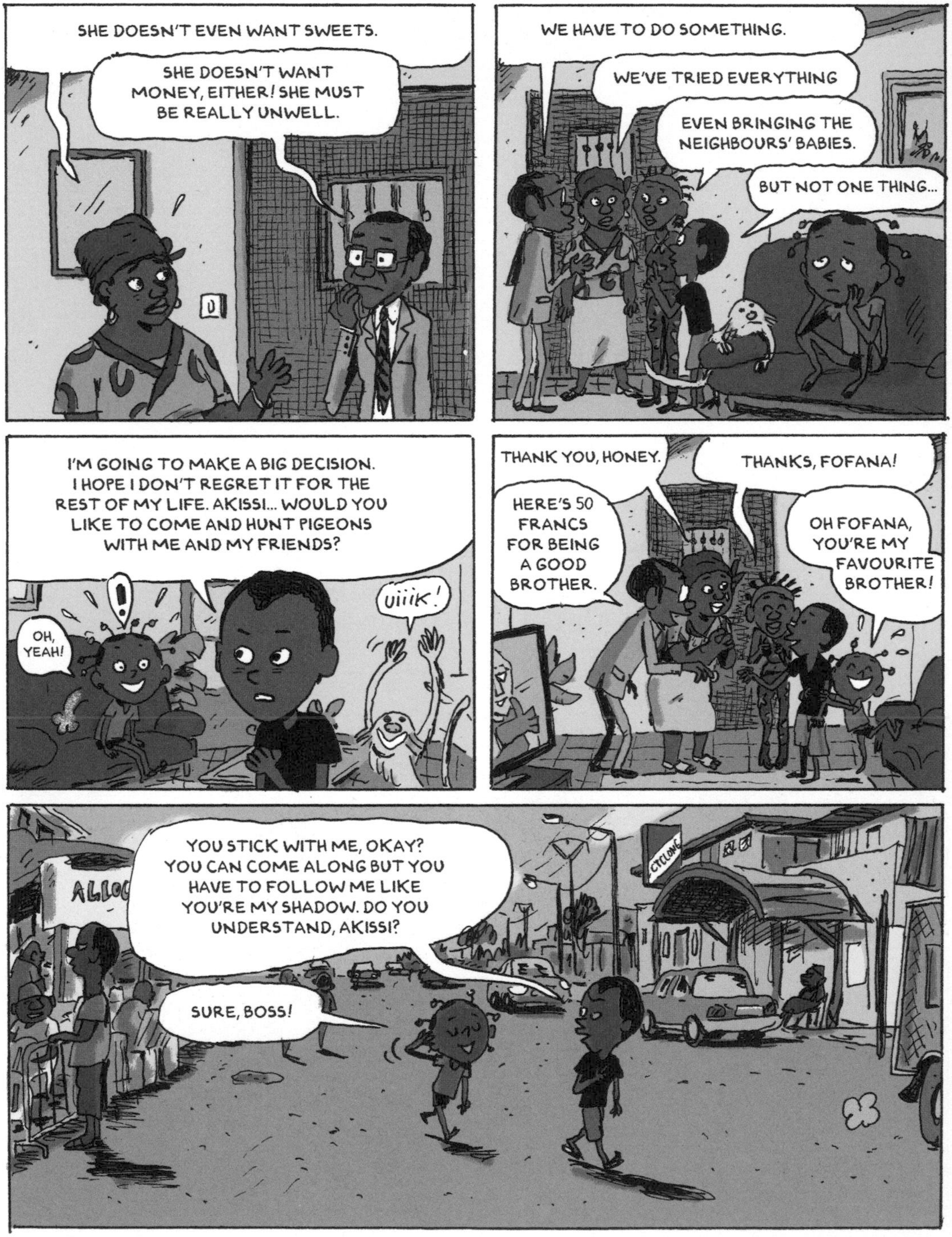
SHE DOESN'T EVEN WANT SWEETS.
SHE DOESN'T WANT MONEY, EITHER! SHE MUST BE REALLY UNWELL.
WE HAVE TO DO SOMETHING.
WE'VE TRIED EVERYTHING
EVEN BRINGING THE NEIGHBOURS' BABIES.
BUT NOT ONE THING...
I'M GOING TO MAKE A BIG DECISION. I HOPE I DON'T REGRET IT FOR THE REST OF MY LIFE. AKISSI... WOULD YOU LIKE TO COME AND HUNT PIGEONS WITH ME AND MY FRIENDS?
OH, YEAH!
UIIIK!
THANK YOU, HONEY.
HERE'S 50 FRANCS FOR BEING A GOOD BROTHER.
THANKS, FOFANA!
OH FOFANA, YOU'RE MY FAVOURITE BROTHER!
YOU STICK WITH ME, OKAY? YOU CAN COME ALONG BUT YOU HAVE TO FOLLOW ME LIKE YOU'RE MY SHADOW. DO YOU UNDERSTAND, AKISSI?
SURE, BOSS!
CYCLONE

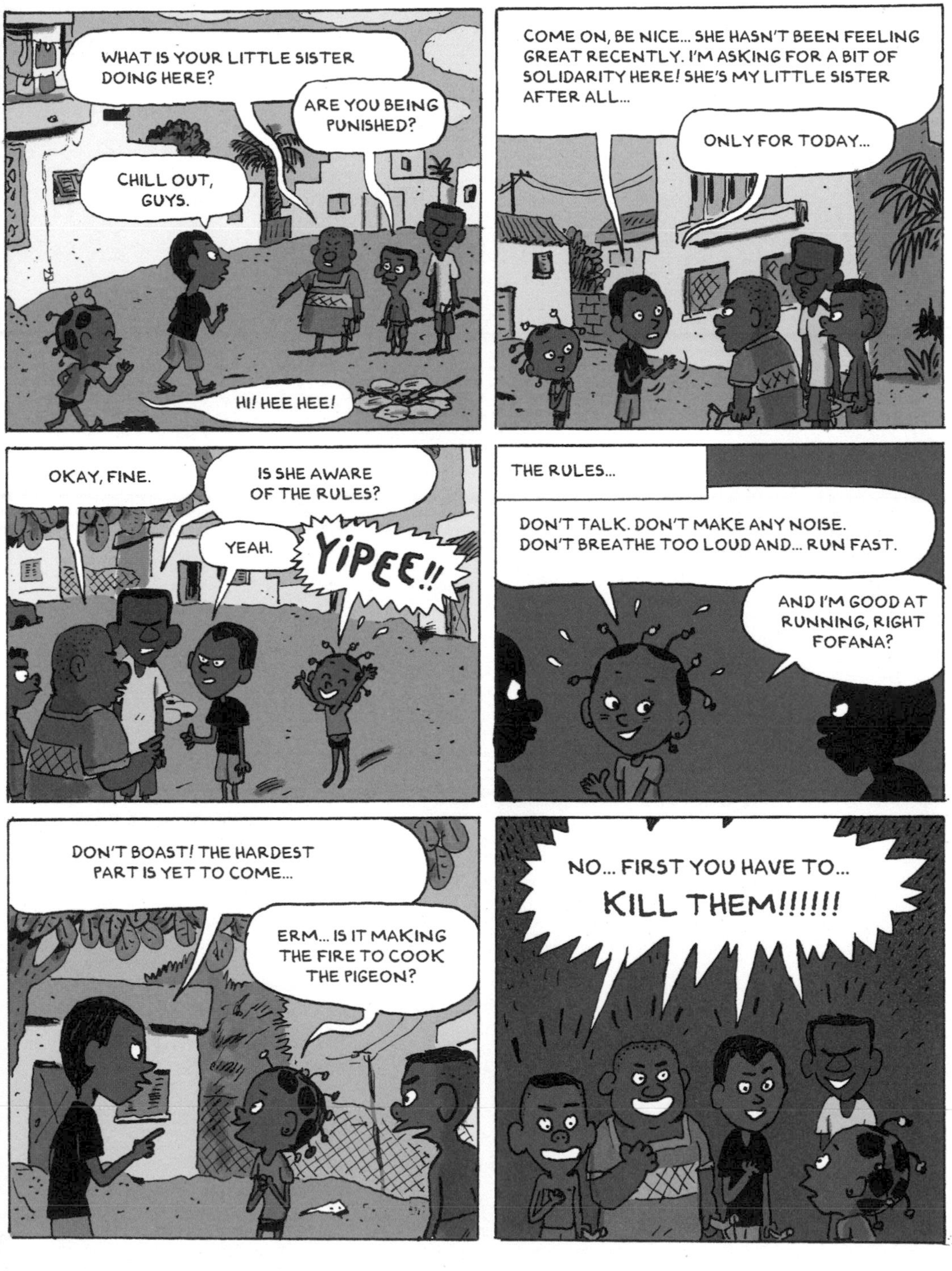
WHAT IS YOUR LITTLE SISTER DOING HERE?
ARE YOU BEING PUNISHED?
CHILL OUT, GUYS.
HI! HEE HEE!
COME ON, BE NICE... SHE HASN'T BEEN FEELING GREAT RECENTLY. I'M ASKING FOR A BIT OF SOLIDARITY HERE! SHE'S MY LITTLE SISTER AFTER ALL...
ONLY FOR TODAY...
OKAY, FINE.
IS SHE AWARE OF THE RULES?
YEAH.
YIPEE!!
THE RULES...
DON'T TALK. DON'T MAKE ANY NOISE. DON'T BREATHE TOO LOUD AND... RUN FAST.
AND I'M GOOD AT RUNNING, RIGHT FOFANA?
DON'T BOAST! THE HARDEST PART IS YET TO COME...
ERM... IS IT MAKING THE FIRE TO COOK THE PIGEON?
NO... FIRST YOU HAVE TO... KILL THEM!!!!!!

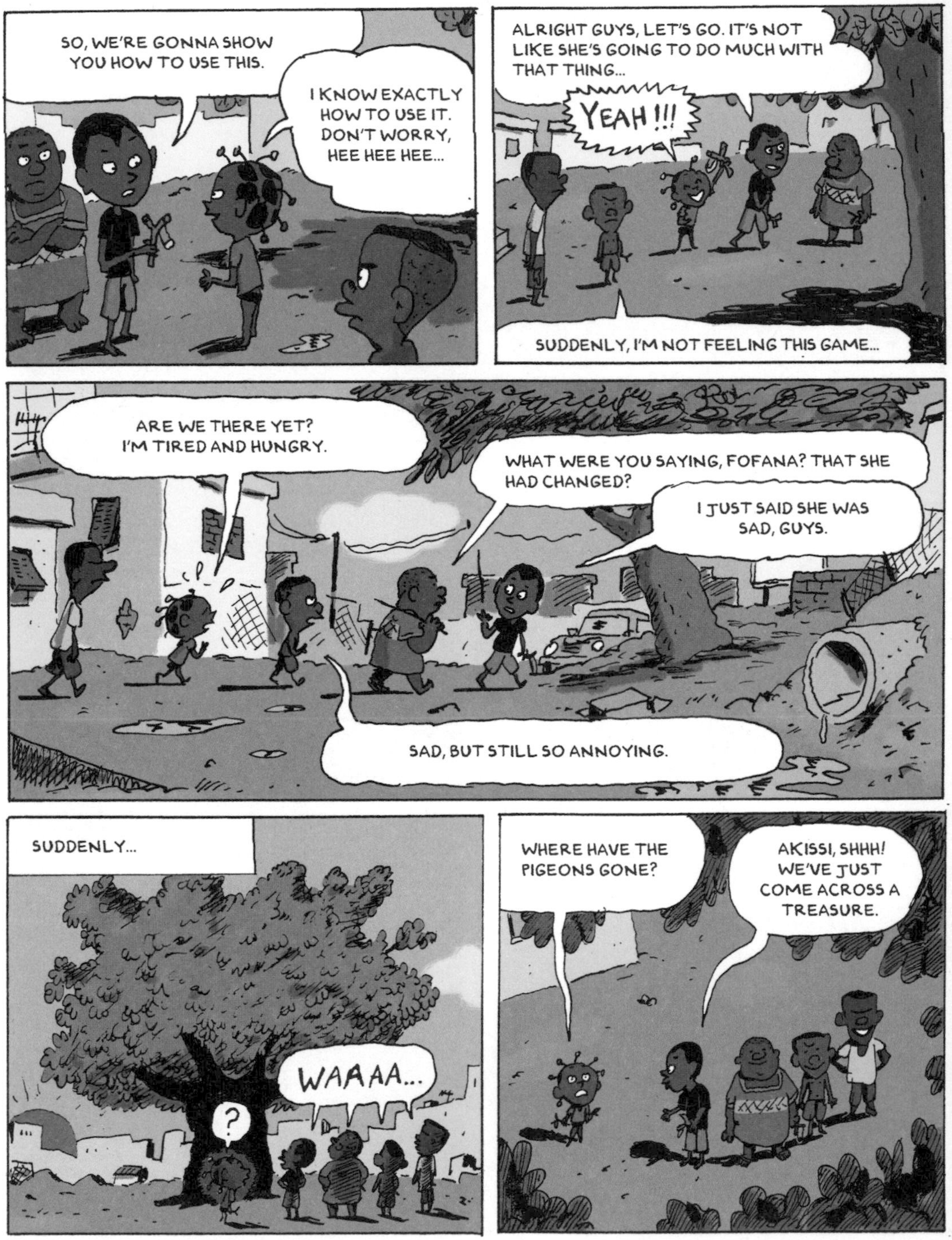
SO, WE'RE GONNA SHOW YOU HOW TO USE THIS.
I KNOW EXACTLY HOW TO USE IT. DON'T WORRY, HEE HEE HEE...
ALRIGHT GUYS, LET'S GO. IT'S NOT LIKE SHE'S GOING TO DO MUCH WITH THAT THING...
YEAH !!!
SUDDENLY, I'M NOT FEELING THIS GAME...
ARE WE THERE YET? I'M TIRED AND HUNGRY.
WHAT WERE YOU SAYING, FOFANA? THAT SHE HAD CHANGED?
I JUST SAID SHE WAS SAD, GUYS.
SAD, BUT STILL SO ANNOYING.
SUDDENLY...
WAAAA...
?
WHERE HAVE THE PIGEONS GONE?
AKISSI, SHHH! WE'VE JUST COME ACROSS A TREASURE.

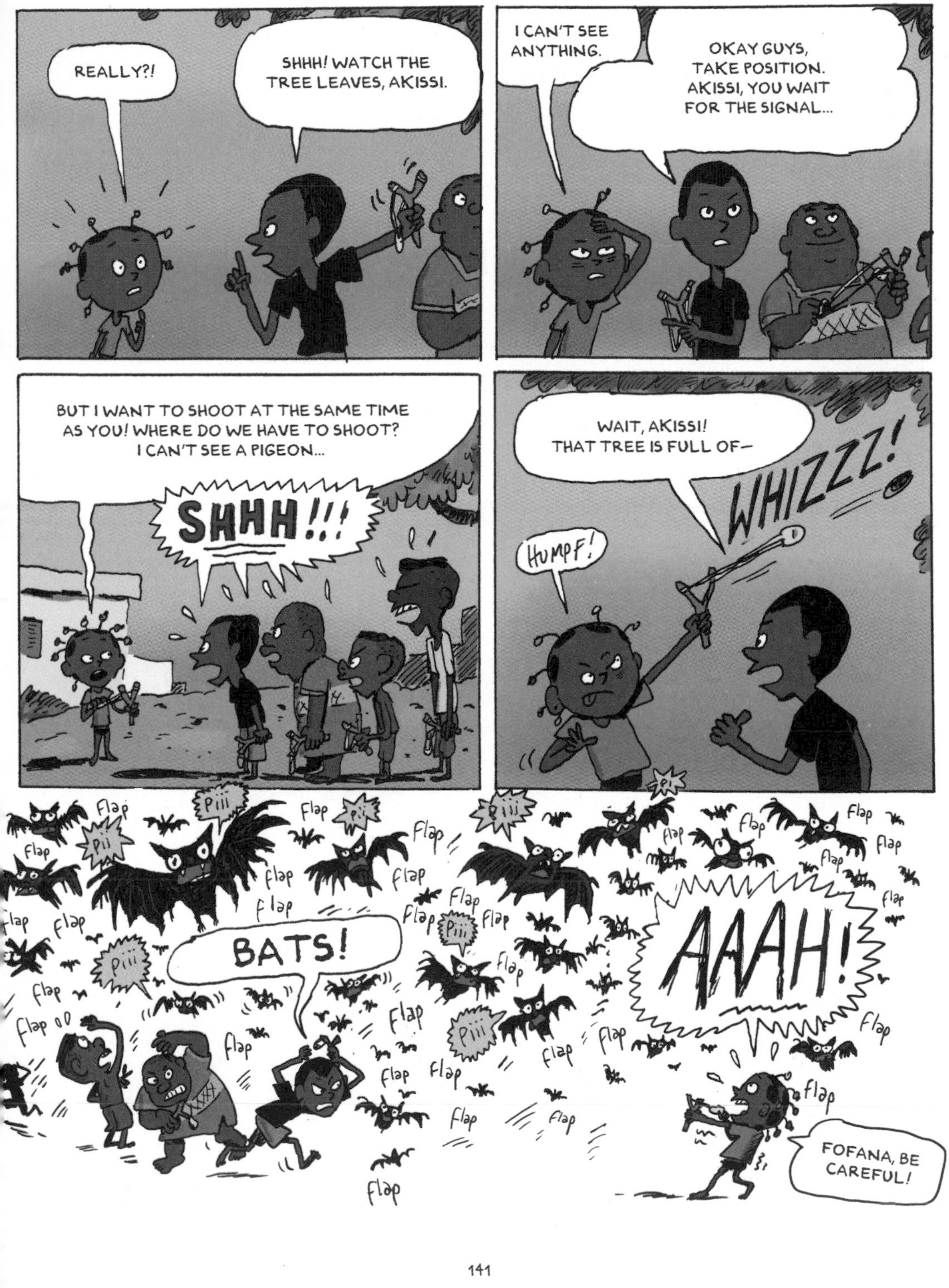
REALLY?!
SHHH! WATCH THE TREE LEAVES, AKISSI.
I CAN'T SEE ANYTHING.
OKAY GUYS, TAKE POSITION. AKISSI, YOU WAIT FOR THE SIGNAL...
BUT I WANT TO SHOOT AT THE SAME TIME AS YOU! WHERE DO WE HAVE TO SHOOT? I CAN'T SEE A PIGEON...
SHHH!!!
WAIT, AKISSI! THAT TREE IS FULL OF—
HUMPF!
WHIZZZ!
Flap
Piii
BATS!
AAAH!
FOFANA, BE CAREFUL!

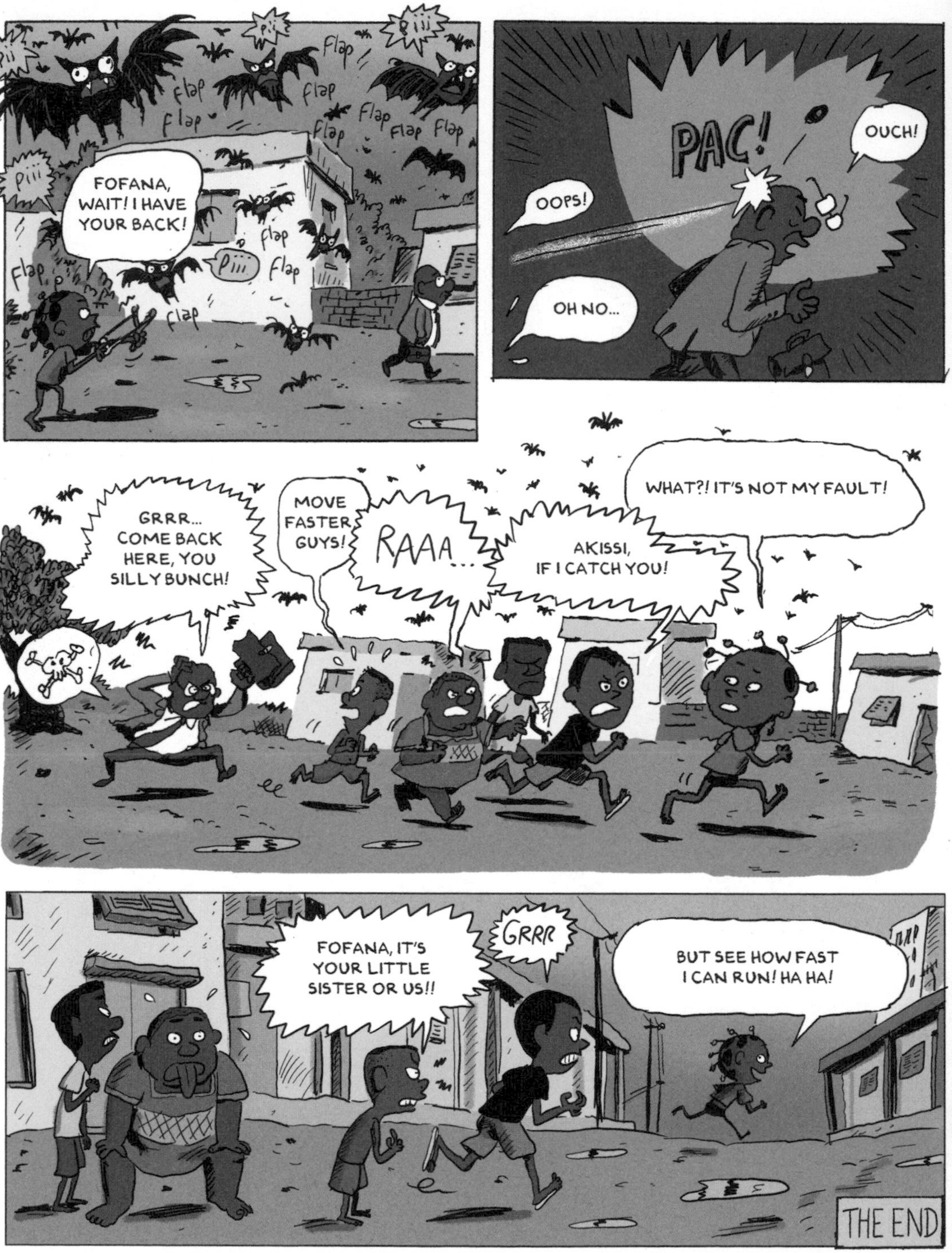
Pii
Pii
Piii
Flap
Flap
Flap
Flap
Flap
Flap
Flap
Flap
Piii
FOFANA, WAIT! I HAVE YOUR BACK!
Piii
Flap
Flap
Flap
Flap
PAC!
OUCH!
OOPS!
OH NO...
GRRR... COME BACK HERE, YOU SILLY BUNCH!
MOVE FASTER GUYS!
RAAA...
AKISSI, IF I CATCH YOU!
WHAT?! IT'S NOT MY FAULT!
FOFANA, IT'S YOUR LITTLE SISTER OR US!!
GRRR
BUT SEE HOW FAST I CAN RUN! HA HA!
THE END

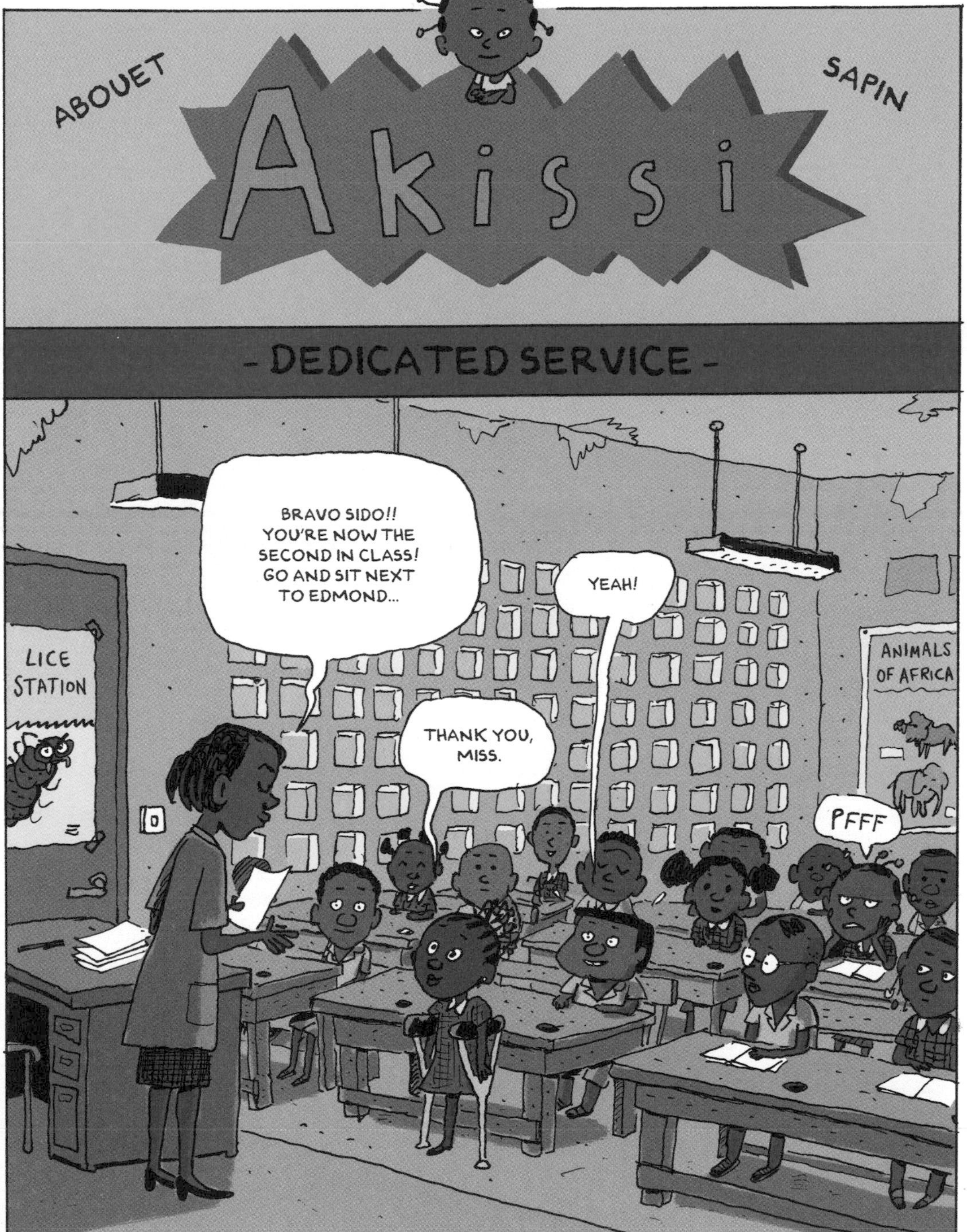
ABOUET
Akissi
SAPIN
- DEDICATED SERVICE -
BRAVO SIDO!! YOU'RE NOW THE SECOND IN CLASS! GO AND SIT NEXT TO EDMOND...
THANK YOU, MISS.
YEAH!
PFFF
LICE STATION
ANIMALS OF AFRICA

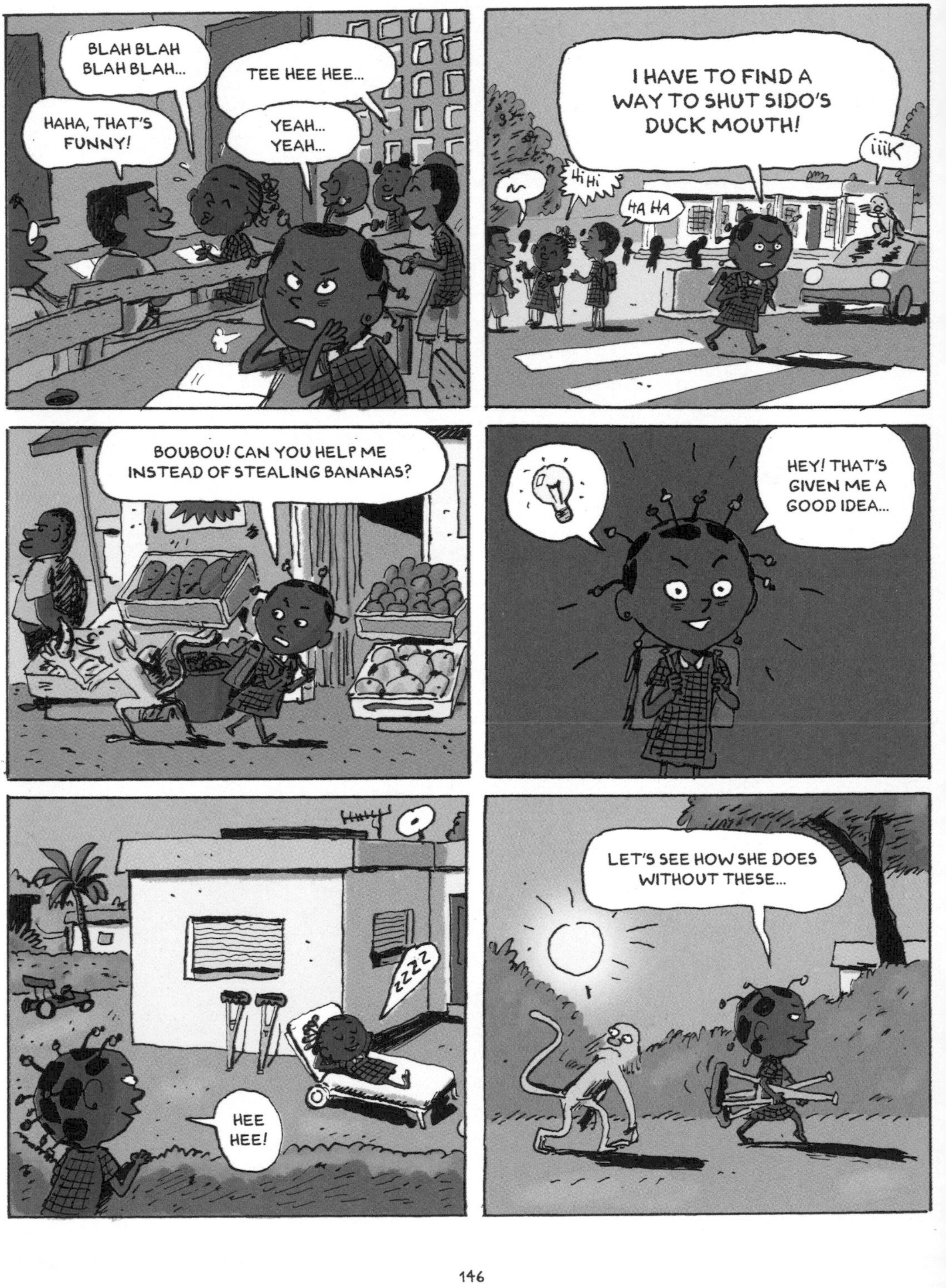

BLAH BLAH BLAH BLAH...
TEE HEE HEE...
HAHA, THAT'S FUNNY!
YEAH... YEAH...
I HAVE TO FIND A WAY TO SHUT SIDO'S DUCK MOUTH!
Hi Hi
HA HA
iiiK
BOUBOU! CAN YOU HELP ME INSTEAD OF STEALING BANANAS?
HEY! THAT'S GIVEN ME A GOOD IDEA...
ZZZZ
HEE HEE!
LET'S SEE HOW SHE DOES WITHOUT THESE...

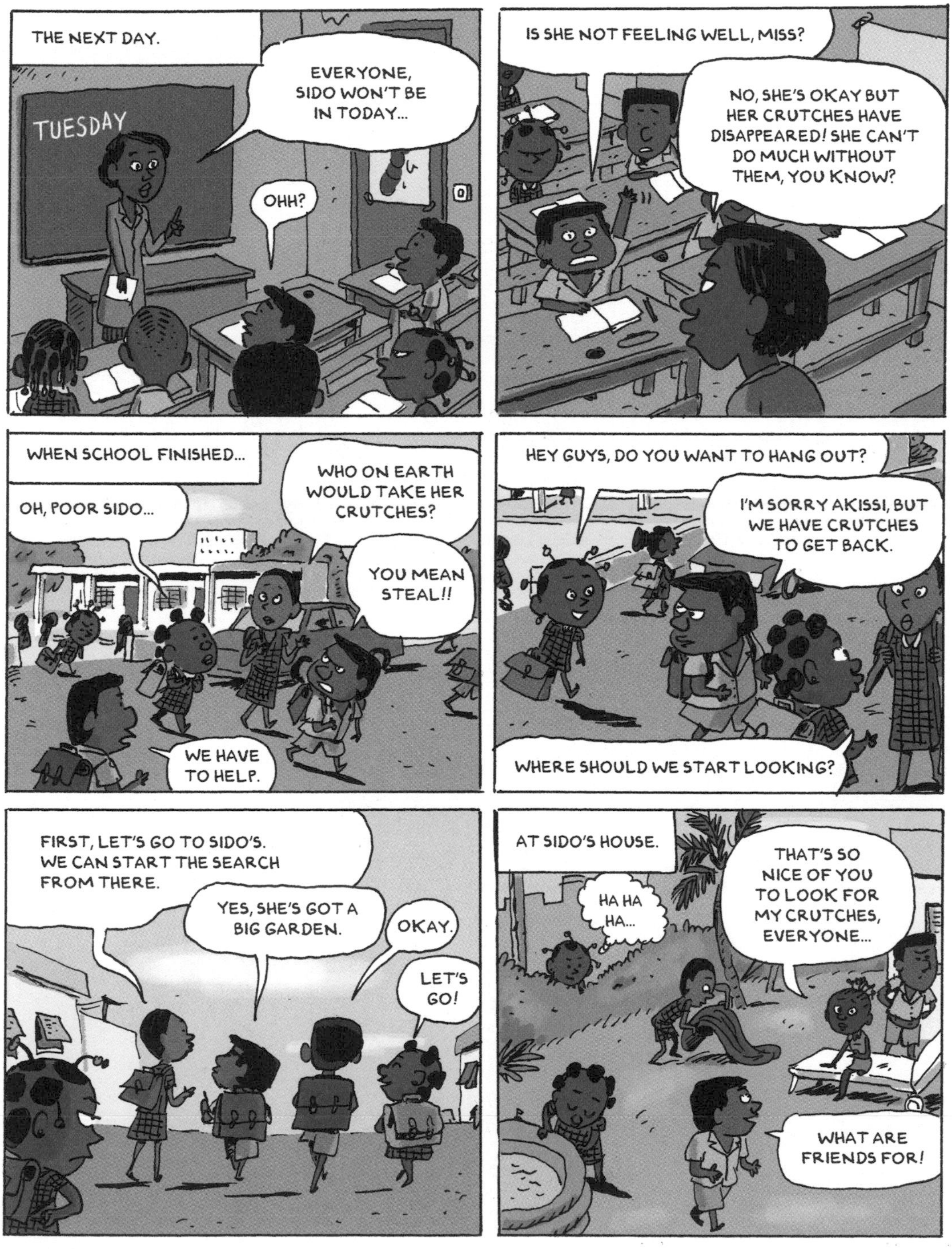
THE NEXT DAY.
EVERYONE, SIDO WON'T BE IN TODAY...
TUESDAY
OHH?
IS SHE NOT FEELING WELL, MISS?
NO, SHE'S OKAY BUT HER CRUTCHES HAVE DISAPPEARED! SHE CAN'T DO MUCH WITHOUT THEM, YOU KNOW?
WHEN SCHOOL FINISHED...
OH, POOR SIDO...
WHO ON EARTH WOULD TAKE HER CRUTCHES?
YOU MEAN STEAL!!
WE HAVE TO HELP.
HEY GUYS, DO YOU WANT TO HANG OUT?
I'M SORRY AKISSI, BUT WE HAVE CRUTCHES TO GET BACK.
WHERE SHOULD WE START LOOKING?
FIRST, LET'S GO TO SIDO'S. WE CAN START THE SEARCH FROM THERE.
YES, SHE'S GOT A BIG GARDEN.
OKAY.
LET'S GO!
AT SIDO'S HOUSE.
HA HA HA...
THAT'S SO NICE OF YOU TO LOOK FOR MY CRUTCHES, EVERYONE...
WHAT ARE FRIENDS FOR!

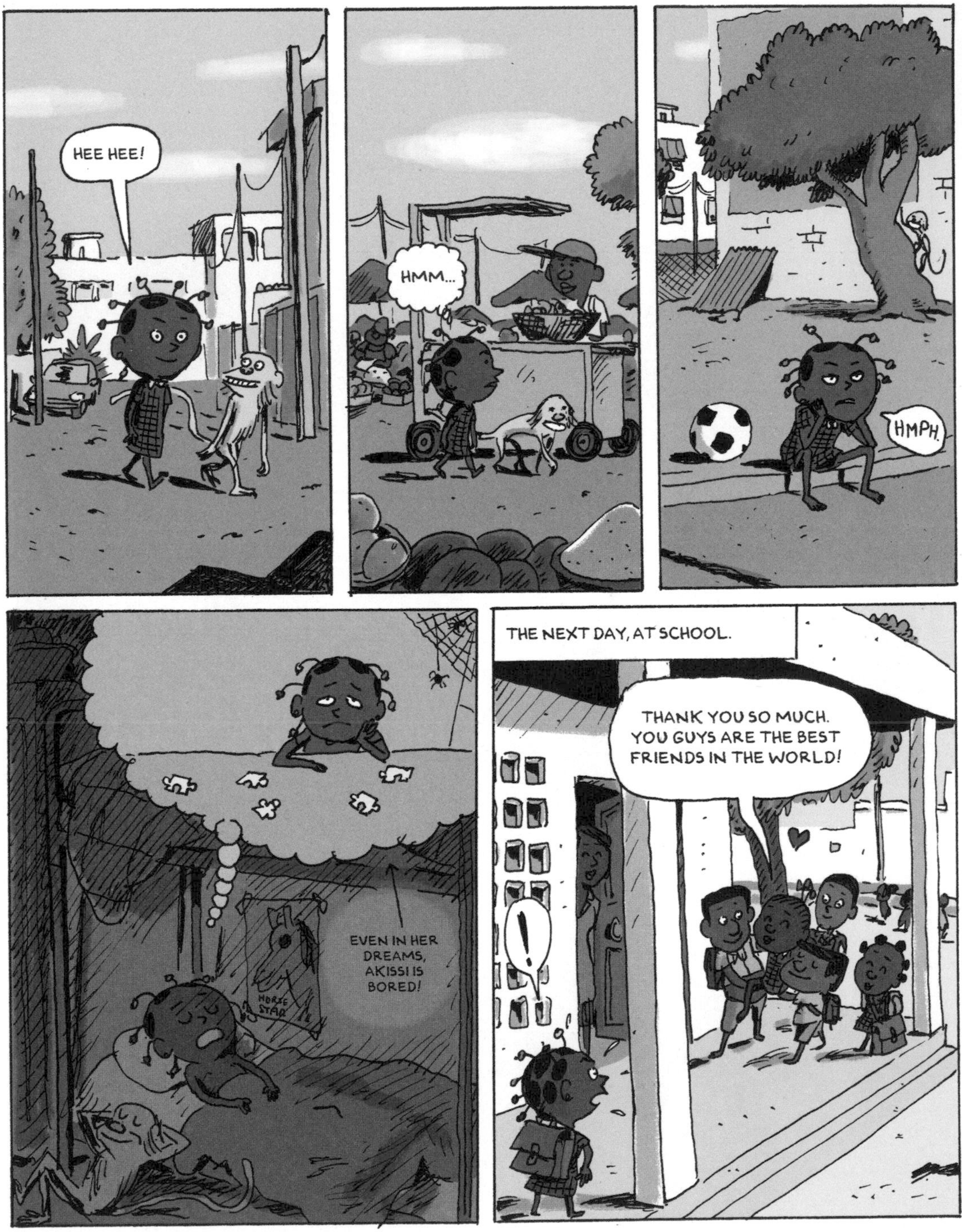
HEE HEE!
HMM...
HMPH.
EVEN IN HER DREAMS, AKISSI IS BORED!
HORSE STAR
THE NEXT DAY, AT SCHOOL.
THANK YOU SO MUCH. YOU GUYS ARE THE BEST FRIENDS IN THE WORLD!
!

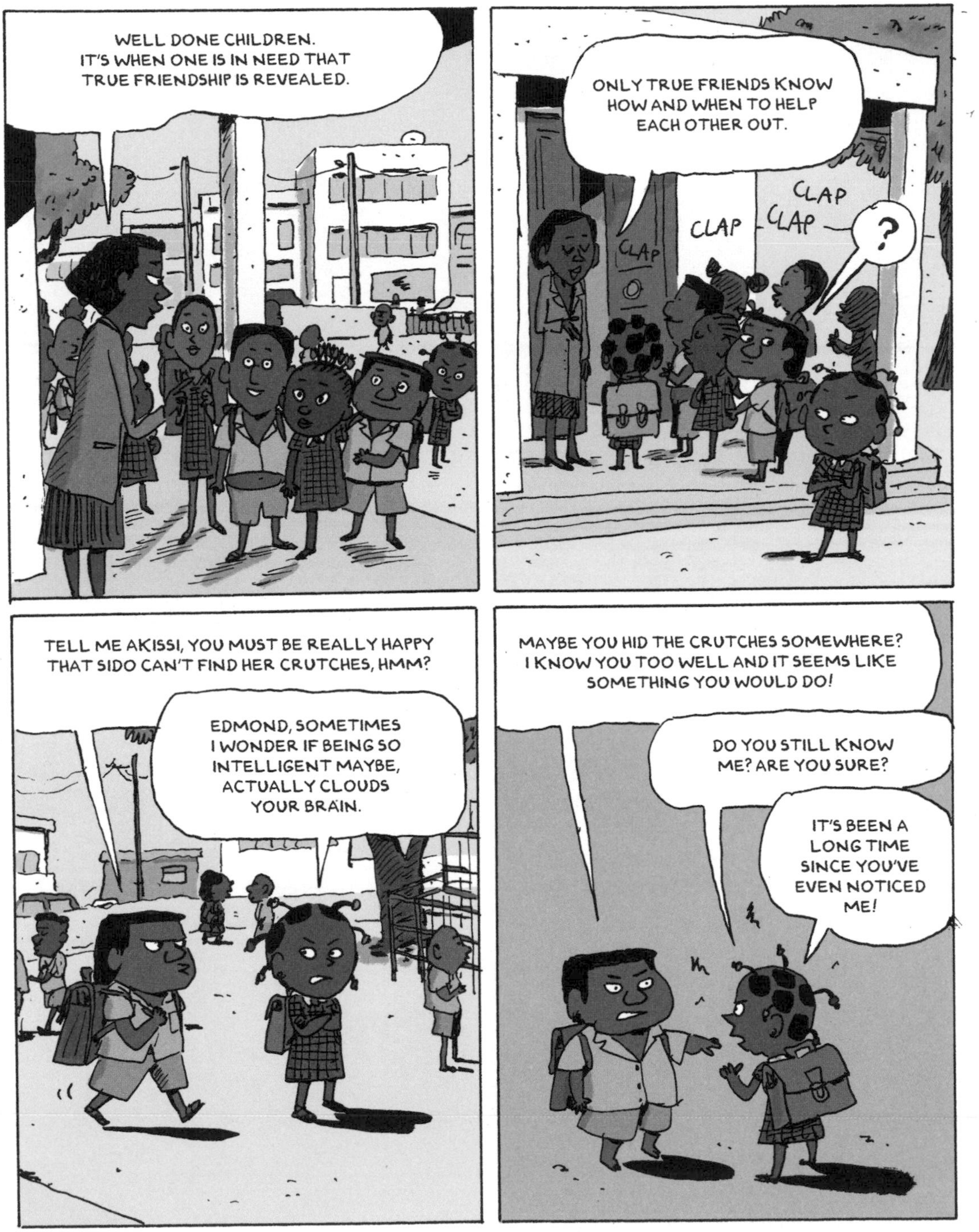
WELL DONE CHILDREN.
IT'S WHEN ONE IS IN NEED THAT TRUE FRIENDSHIP IS REVEALED.
ONLY TRUE FRIENDS KNOW HOW AND WHEN TO HELP EACH OTHER OUT.
CLAP
CLAP
CLAP
CLAP
?
TELL ME AKISSI, YOU MUST BE REALLY HAPPY THAT SIDO CAN'T FIND HER CRUTCHES, HMM?
EDMOND, SOMETIMES I WONDER IF BEING SO INTELLIGENT MAYBE, ACTUALLY CLOUDS YOUR BRAIN.
MAYBE YOU HID THE CRUTCHES SOMEWHERE? I KNOW YOU TOO WELL AND IT SEEMS LIKE SOMETHING YOU WOULD DO!
DO YOU STILL KNOW ME? ARE YOU SURE?
IT'S BEEN A LONG TIME SINCE YOU'VE EVEN NOTICED ME!

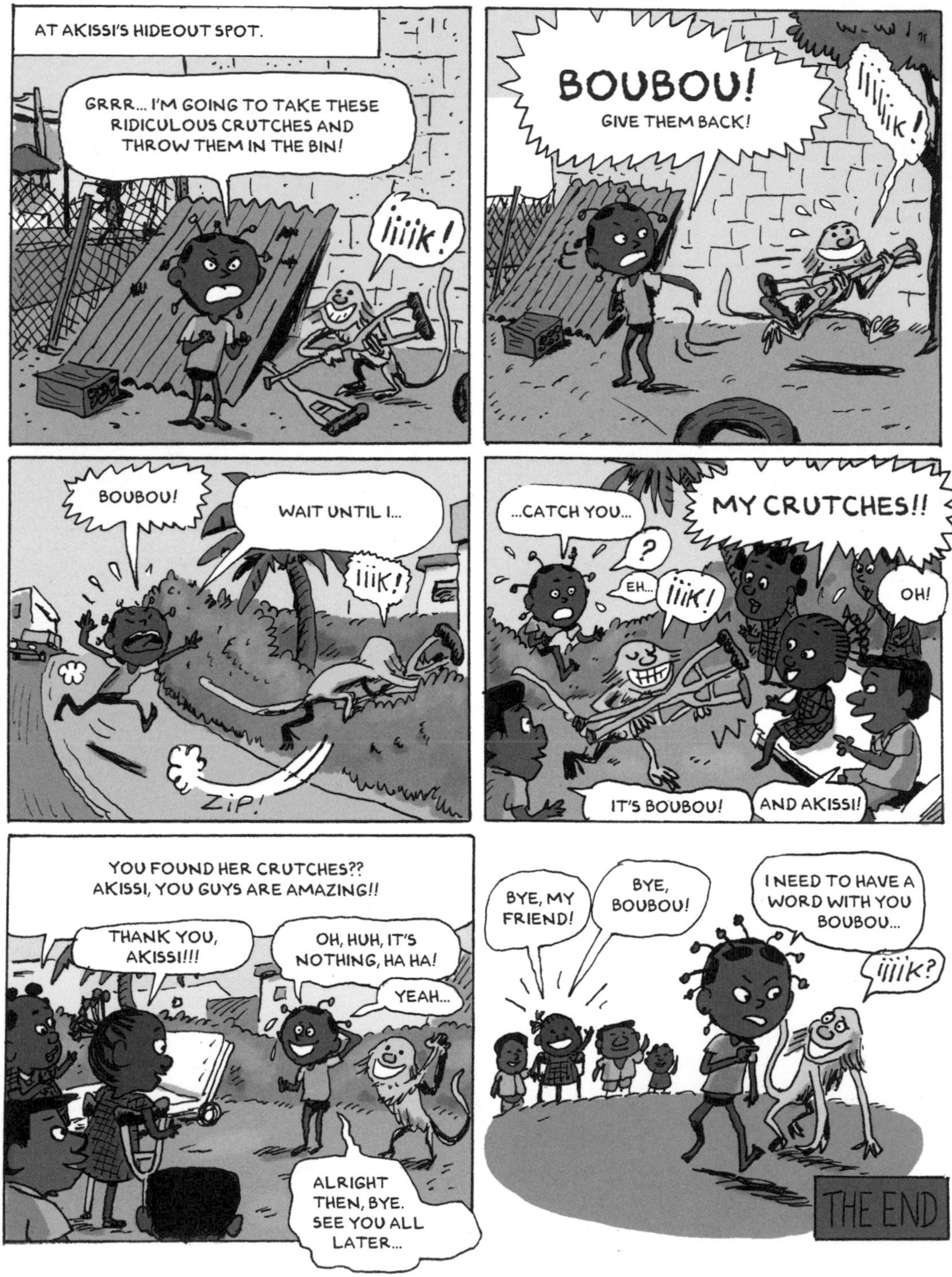
AT AKISSI'S HIDEOUT SPOT.
GRRR... I'M GOING TO TAKE THESE RIDICULOUS CRUTCHES AND THROW THEM IN THE BIN!
iiiik!
BOUBOU! GIVE THEM BACK!
iiiiiik!
BOUBOU!
WAIT UNTIL I...
iiiK!
ZIP!
...CATCH YOU...
MY CRUTCHES!!
?
EH...
iiiK!
OH!
IT'S BOUBOU!
AND AKISSI!
YOU FOUND HER CRUTCHES?? AKISSI, YOU GUYS ARE AMAZING!!
THANK YOU, AKISSI!!!
OH, HUH, IT'S NOTHING, HA HA!
YEAH...
ALRIGHT THEN, BYE. SEE YOU ALL LATER...
BYE, MY FRIEND!
BYE, BOUBOU!
I NEED TO HAVE A WORD WITH YOU BOUBOU...
iiiik?
THE END

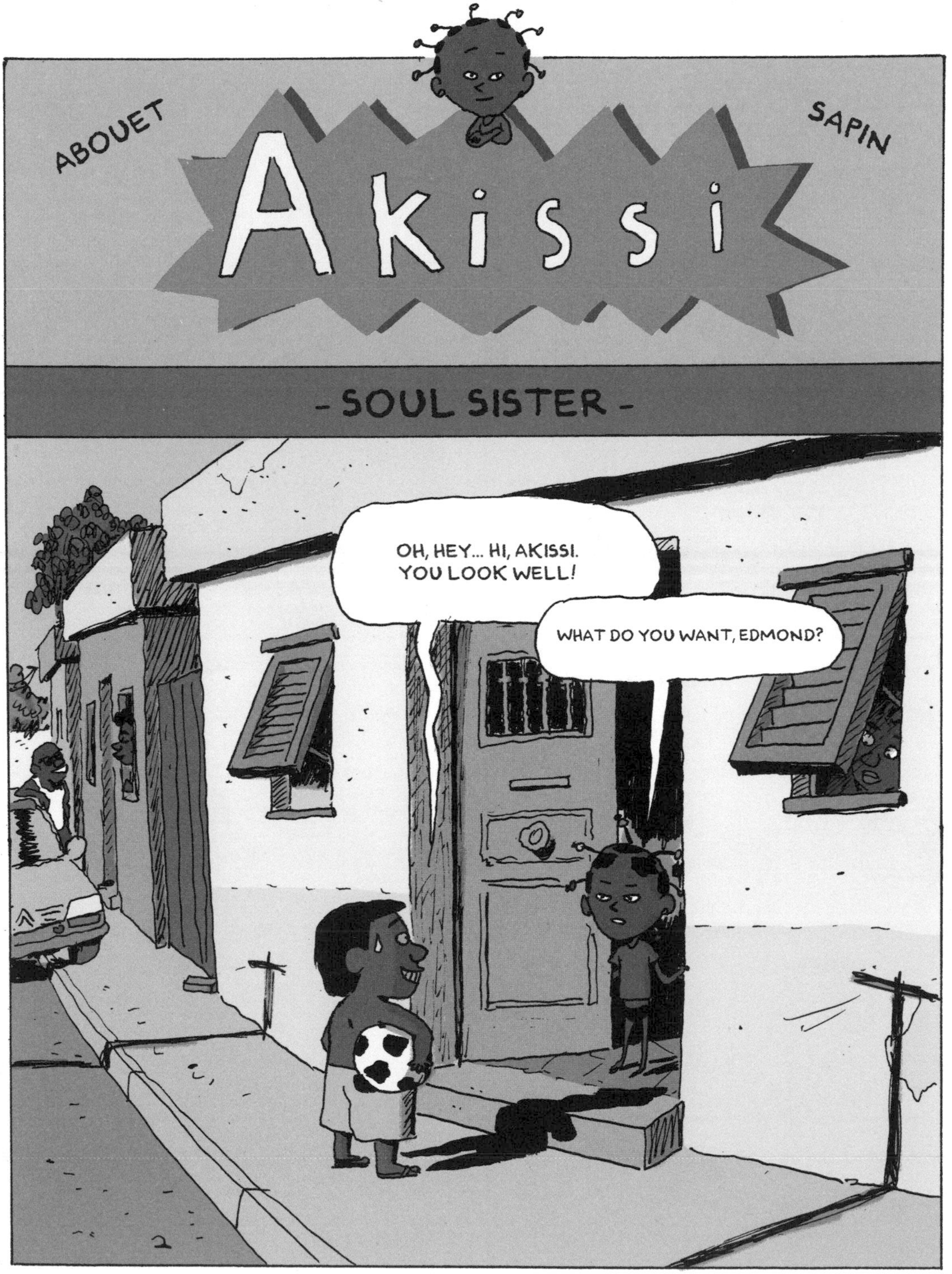
ABOUET
Akissi
SAPIN
- SOUL SISTER -
OH, HEY... HI, AKISSI. YOU LOOK WELL!
WHAT DO YOU WANT, EDMOND?

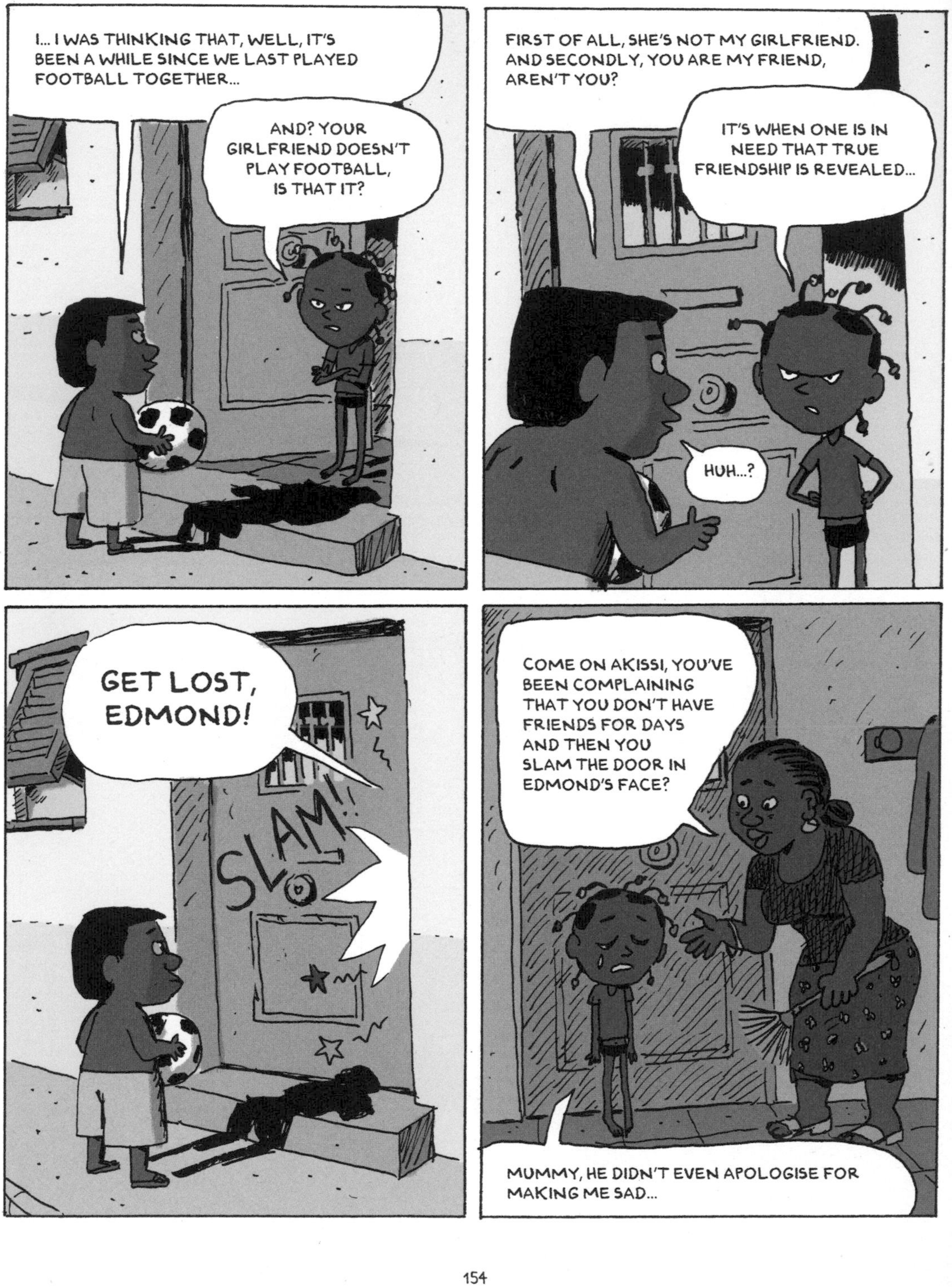
I... I WAS THINKING THAT, WELL, IT'S BEEN A WHILE SINCE WE LAST PLAYED FOOTBALL TOGETHER...
AND? YOUR GIRLFRIEND DOESN'T PLAY FOOTBALL, IS THAT IT?
FIRST OF ALL, SHE'S NOT MY GIRLFRIEND. AND SECONDLY, YOU ARE MY FRIEND, AREN'T YOU?
IT'S WHEN ONE IS IN NEED THAT TRUE FRIENDSHIP IS REVEALED...
HUH...?
GET LOST, EDMOND!
SLAM!
COME ON AKISSI, YOU'VE BEEN COMPLAINING THAT YOU DON'T HAVE FRIENDS FOR DAYS AND THEN YOU SLAM THE DOOR IN EDMOND'S FACE?
MUMMY, HE DIDN'T EVEN APOLOGISE FOR MAKING ME SAD...

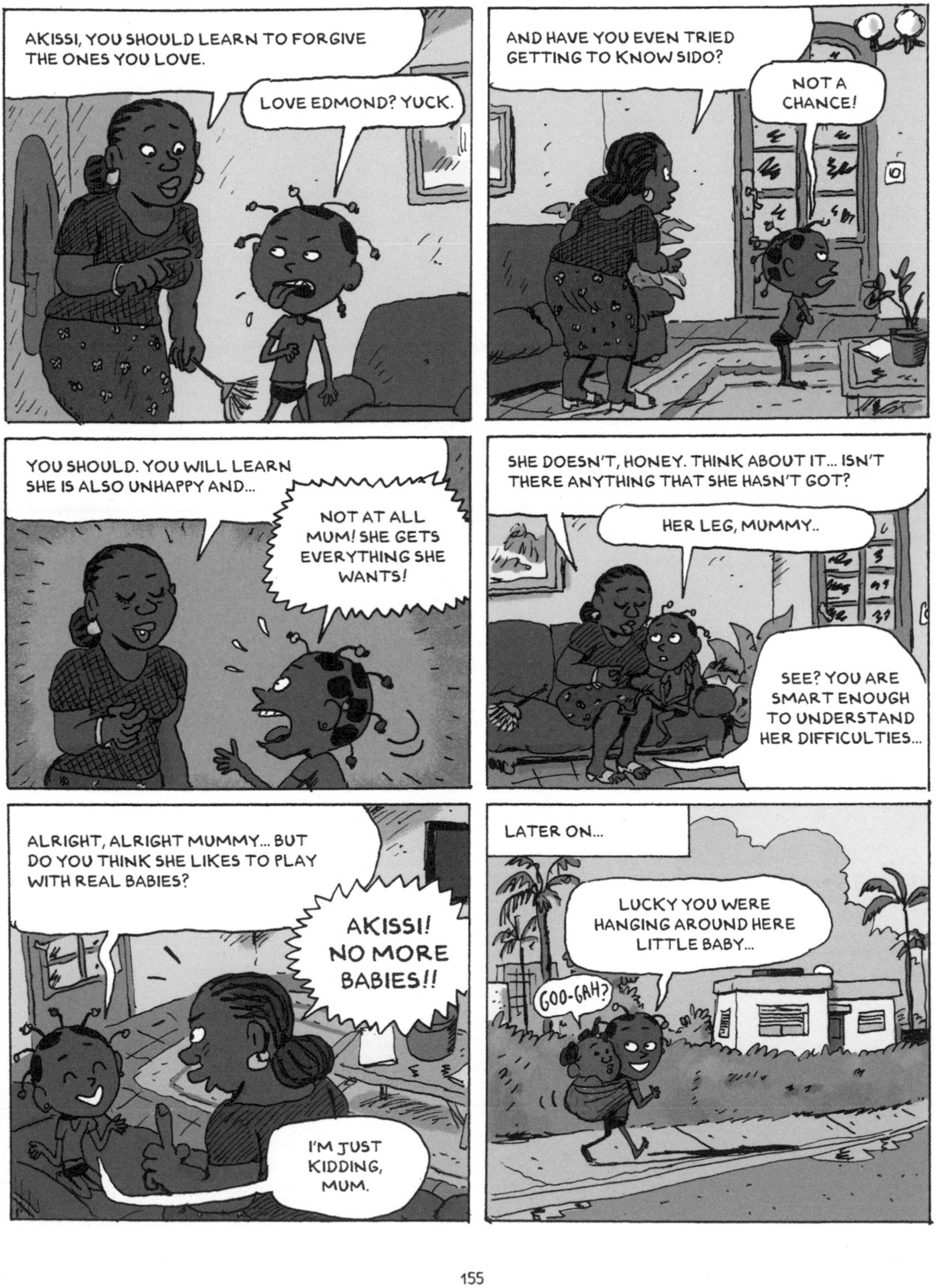
AKISSI, YOU SHOULD LEARN TO FORGIVE THE ONES YOU LOVE.
LOVE EDMOND? YUCK.
AND HAVE YOU EVEN TRIED GETTING TO KNOW SIDO?
NOT A CHANCE!
YOU SHOULD. YOU WILL LEARN SHE IS ALSO UNHAPPY AND...
NOT AT ALL MUM! SHE GETS EVERYTHING SHE WANTS!
SHE DOESN'T, HONEY. THINK ABOUT IT... ISN'T THERE ANYTHING THAT SHE HASN'T GOT?
HER LEG, MUMMY..
SEE? YOU ARE SMART ENOUGH TO UNDERSTAND HER DIFFICULTIES...
ALRIGHT, ALRIGHT MUMMY... BUT DO YOU THINK SHE LIKES TO PLAY WITH REAL BABIES?
AKISSI! NO MORE BABIES!!
I'M JUST KIDDING, MUM.
LATER ON...
LUCKY YOU WERE HANGING AROUND HERE LITTLE BABY...
GOO-GAH?

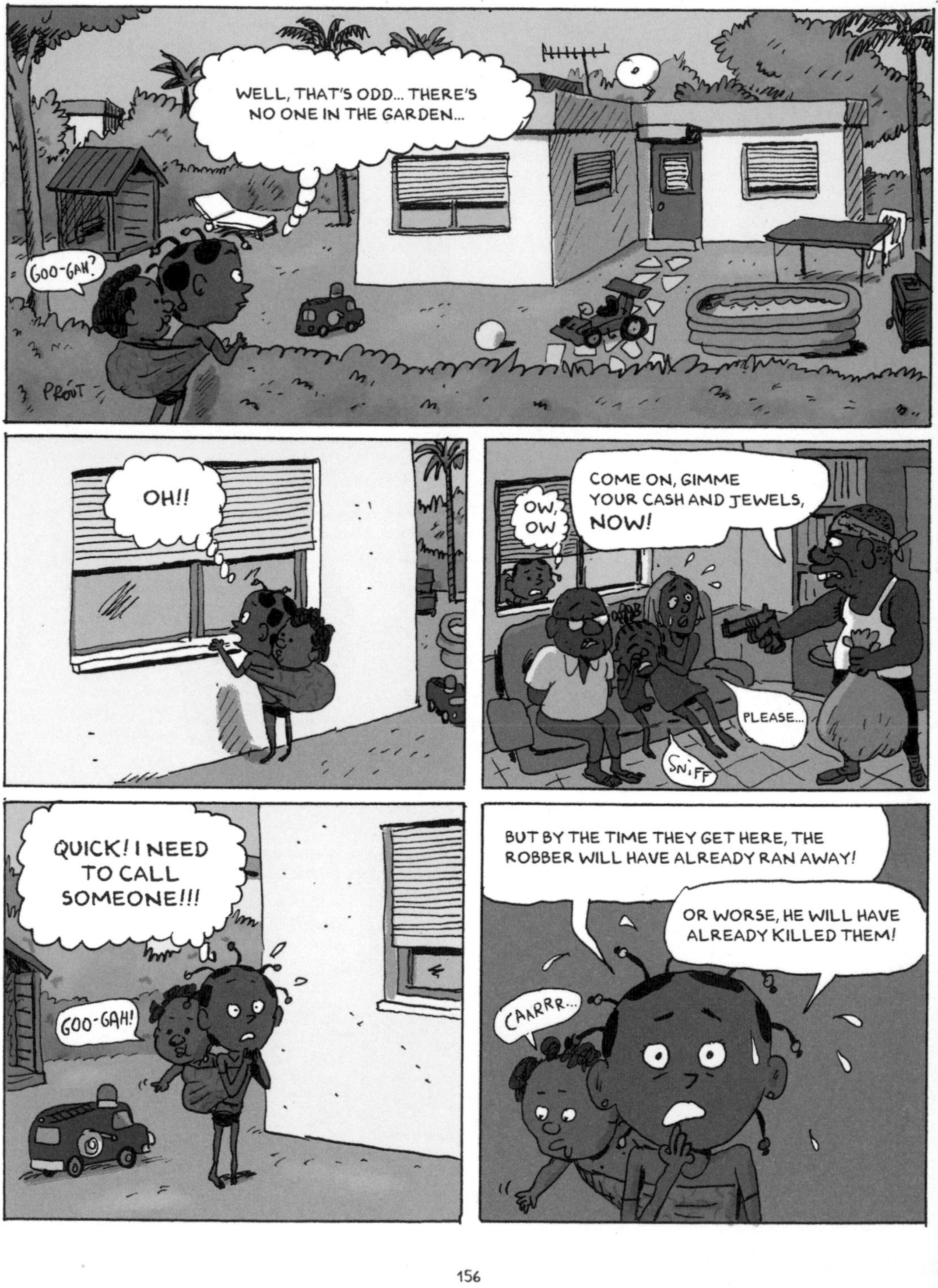
WELL, THAT'S ODD... THERE'S NO ONE IN THE GARDEN...
GOO-GAH?
PROUT
OH!!
COME ON, GIMME YOUR CASH AND JEWELS, NOW!
OW, OW
PLEASE...
SNIFF
QUICK! I NEED TO CALL SOMEONE!!!
GOO-GAH!
BUT BY THE TIME THEY GET HERE, THE ROBBER WILL HAVE ALREADY RAN AWAY!
OR WORSE, HE WILL HAVE ALREADY KILLED THEM!
CAARRR...

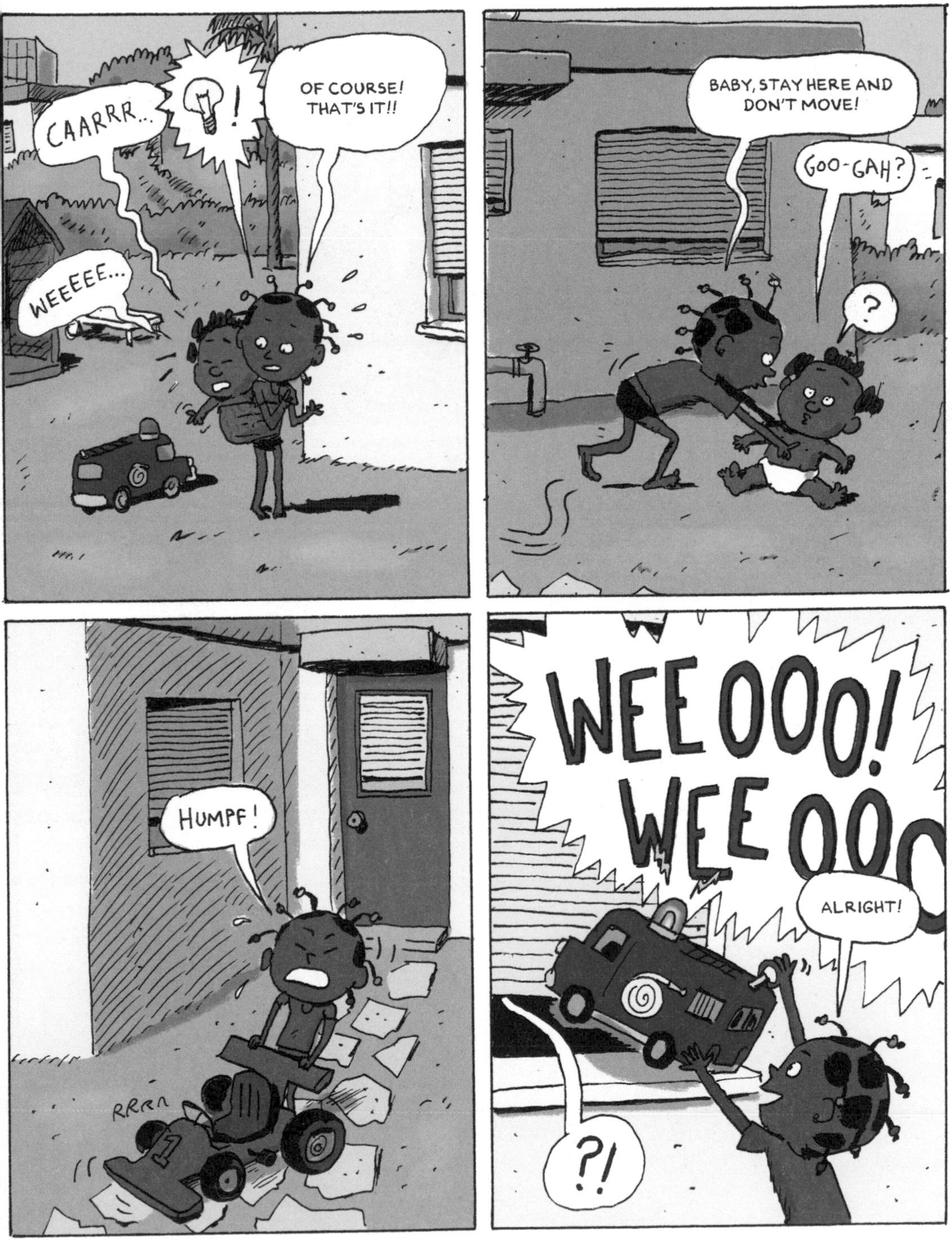
CAARRR...
!
OF COURSE! THAT'S IT!!
WEEEEE...
BABY, STAY HERE AND DON'T MOVE!
GOO-GAH?
?
HUMPF!
RRRR
WEE OOO! WEE OOO
ALRIGHT!
?!

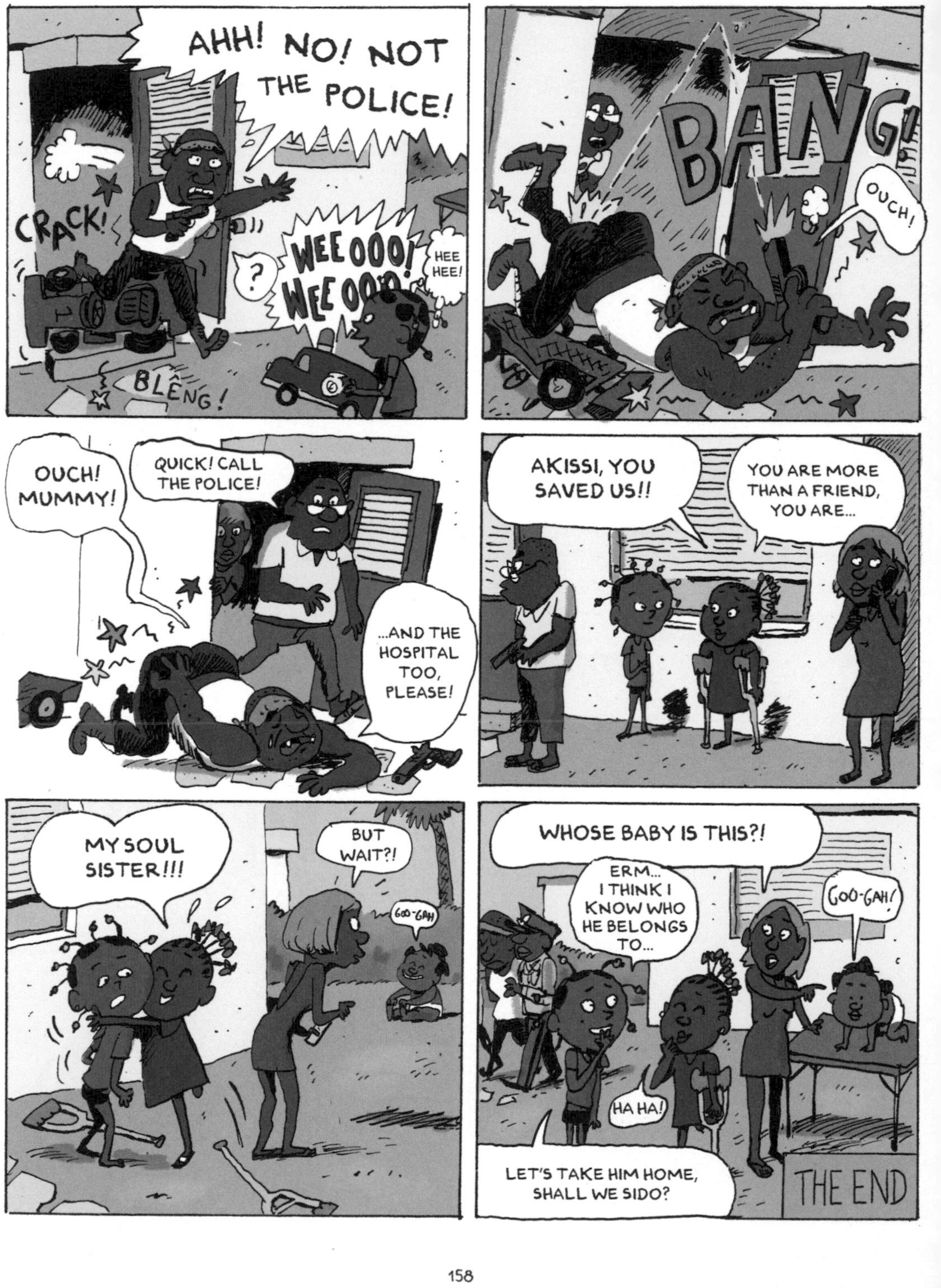
AHH! NO! NOT THE POLICE!
CRACK!
?
WEE OOO! WEE OOO!
HEE HEE!
BLÊNG!
BANG!
OUCH!
OUCH! MUMMY!
QUICK! CALL THE POLICE!
...AND THE HOSPITAL TOO, PLEASE!
AKISSI, YOU SAVED US!!
YOU ARE MORE THAN A FRIEND, YOU ARE...
MY SOUL SISTER!!!
BUT WAIT?!
GOO-GAH
WHOSE BABY IS THIS?!
ERM... I THINK I KNOW WHO HE BELONGS TO...
GOO-GAH!
HA HA!
LET'S TAKE HIM HOME, SHALL WE SIDO?
THE END

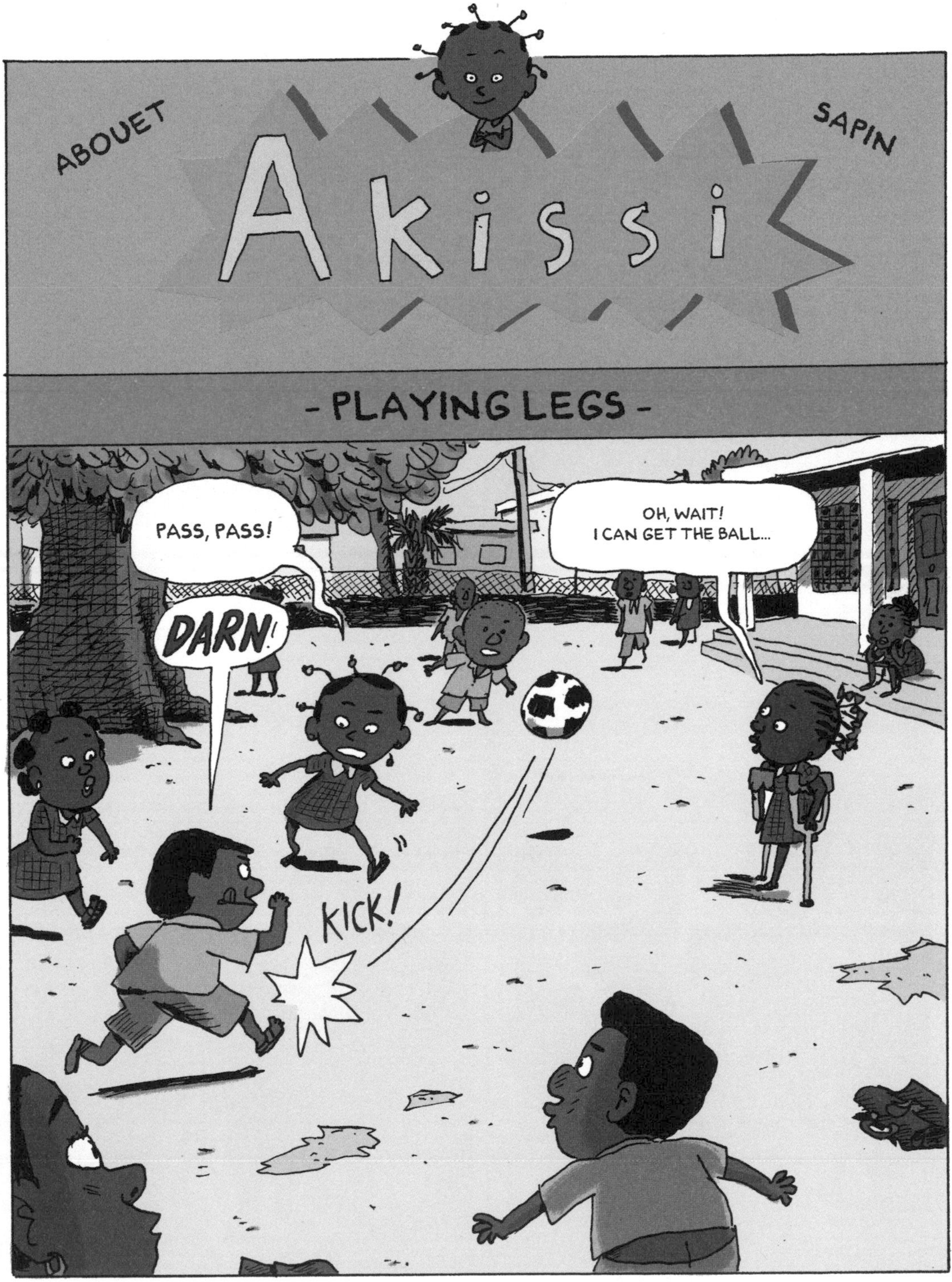
ABOUET
Akissi
SAPIN
- PLAYING LEGS -
PASS, PASS!
DARN!
OH, WAIT! I CAN GET THE BALL...
KICK!

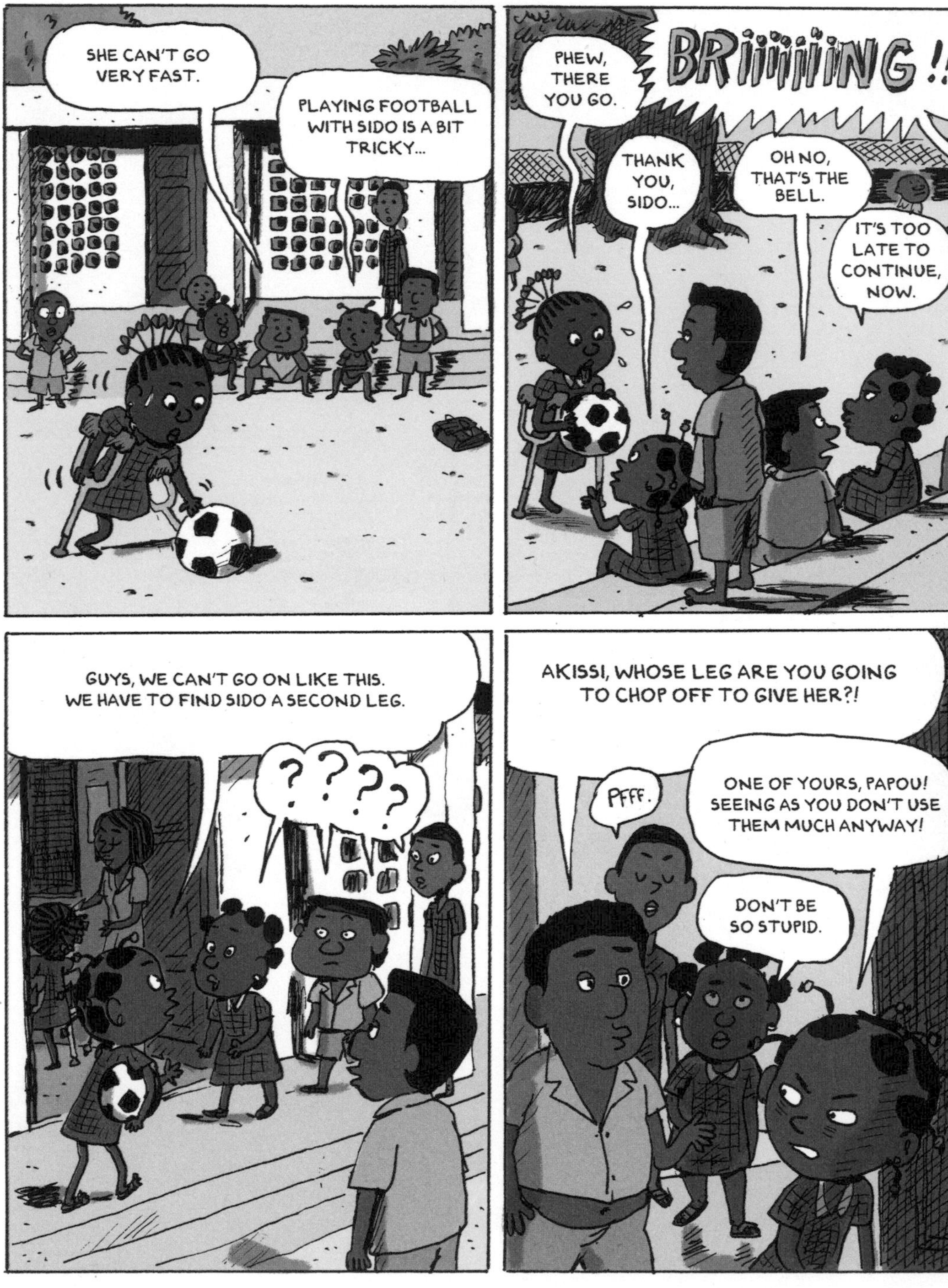
SHE CAN'T GO VERY FAST.
PLAYING FOOTBALL WITH SIDO IS A BIT TRICKY...
PHEW, THERE YOU GO.
BRiiiiiiiNG!!
THANK YOU, SIDO...
OH NO, THAT'S THE BELL.
IT'S TOO LATE TO CONTINUE, NOW.
GUYS, WE CAN'T GO ON LIKE THIS. WE HAVE TO FIND SIDO A SECOND LEG.
????
AKISSI, WHOSE LEG ARE YOU GOING TO CHOP OFF TO GIVE HER?!
PFFF.
ONE OF YOURS, PAPOU! SEEING AS YOU DON'T USE THEM MUCH ANYWAY!
DON'T BE SO STUPID.

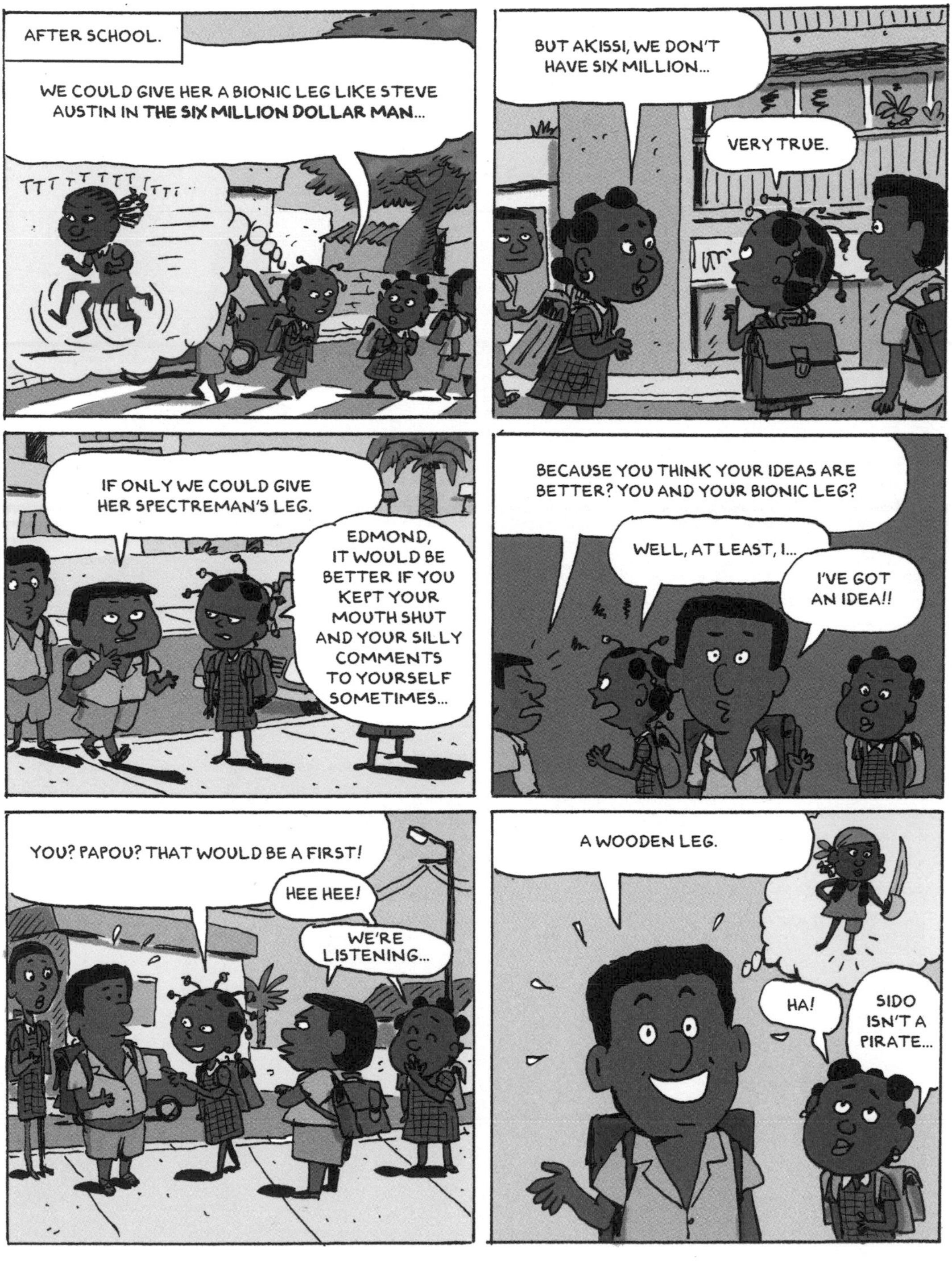

AFTER SCHOOL.
WE COULD GIVE HER A BIONIC LEG LIKE STEVE AUSTIN IN THE SIX MILLION DOLLAR MAN...
TTTTTTTTTTTT
BUT AKISSI, WE DON'T HAVE SIX MILLION...
VERY TRUE.
IF ONLY WE COULD GIVE HER SPECTREMAN'S LEG.
EDMOND, IT WOULD BE BETTER IF YOU KEPT YOUR MOUTH SHUT AND YOUR SILLY COMMENTS TO YOURSELF SOMETIMES...
BECAUSE YOU THINK YOUR IDEAS ARE BETTER? YOU AND YOUR BIONIC LEG?
WELL, AT LEAST, I...
I'VE GOT AN IDEA!!
YOU? PAPOU? THAT WOULD BE A FIRST!
HEE HEE!
WE'RE LISTENING...
A WOODEN LEG.
HA!
SIDO ISN'T A PIRATE...

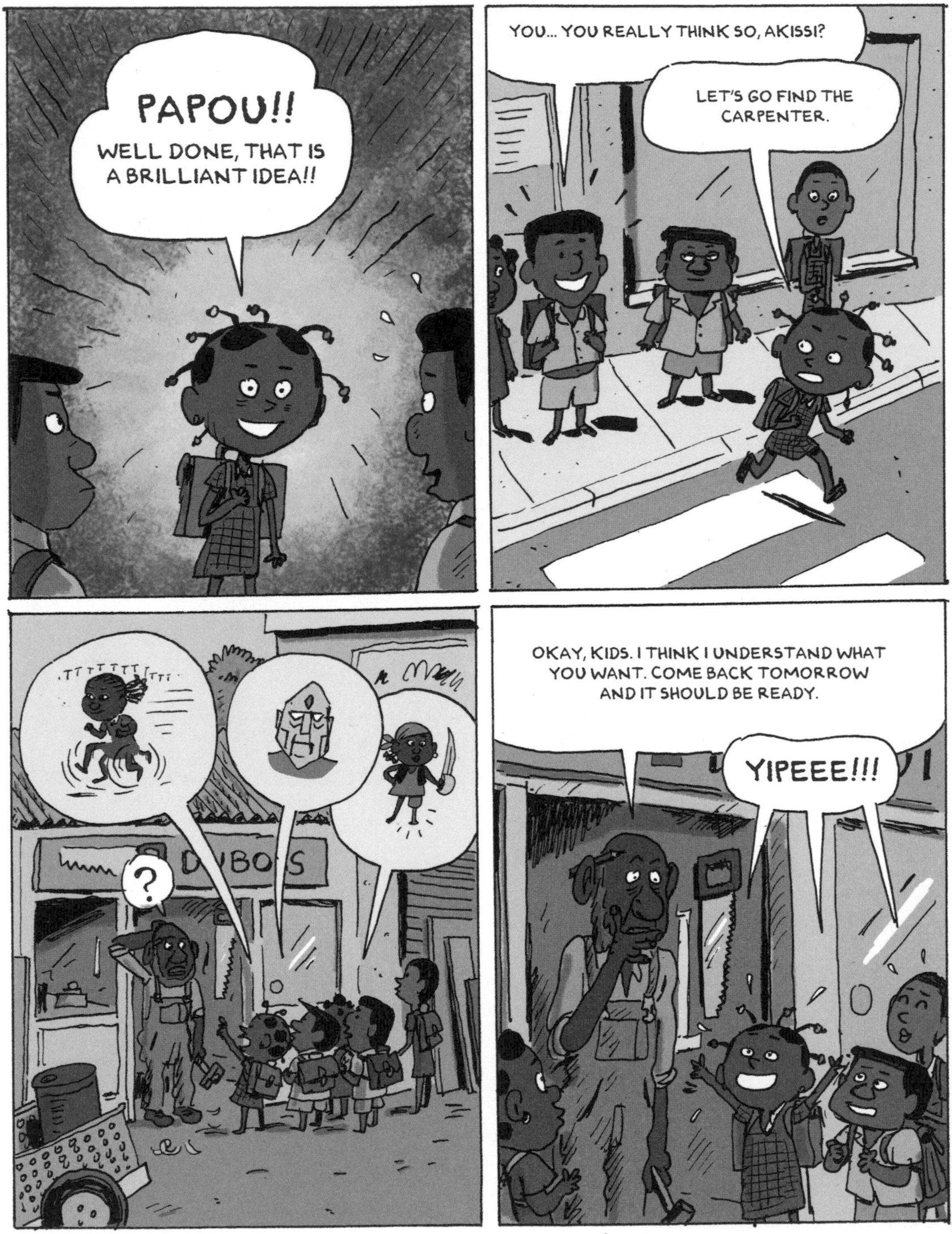
PAPOU!!
WELL DONE, THAT IS A BRILLIANT IDEA!!
YOU... YOU REALLY THINK SO, AKISSI?
LET'S GO FIND THE CARPENTER.
DUBOIS
OKAY, KIDS. I THINK I UNDERSTAND WHAT YOU WANT. COME BACK TOMORROW AND IT SHOULD BE READY.
YIPEEE!!!

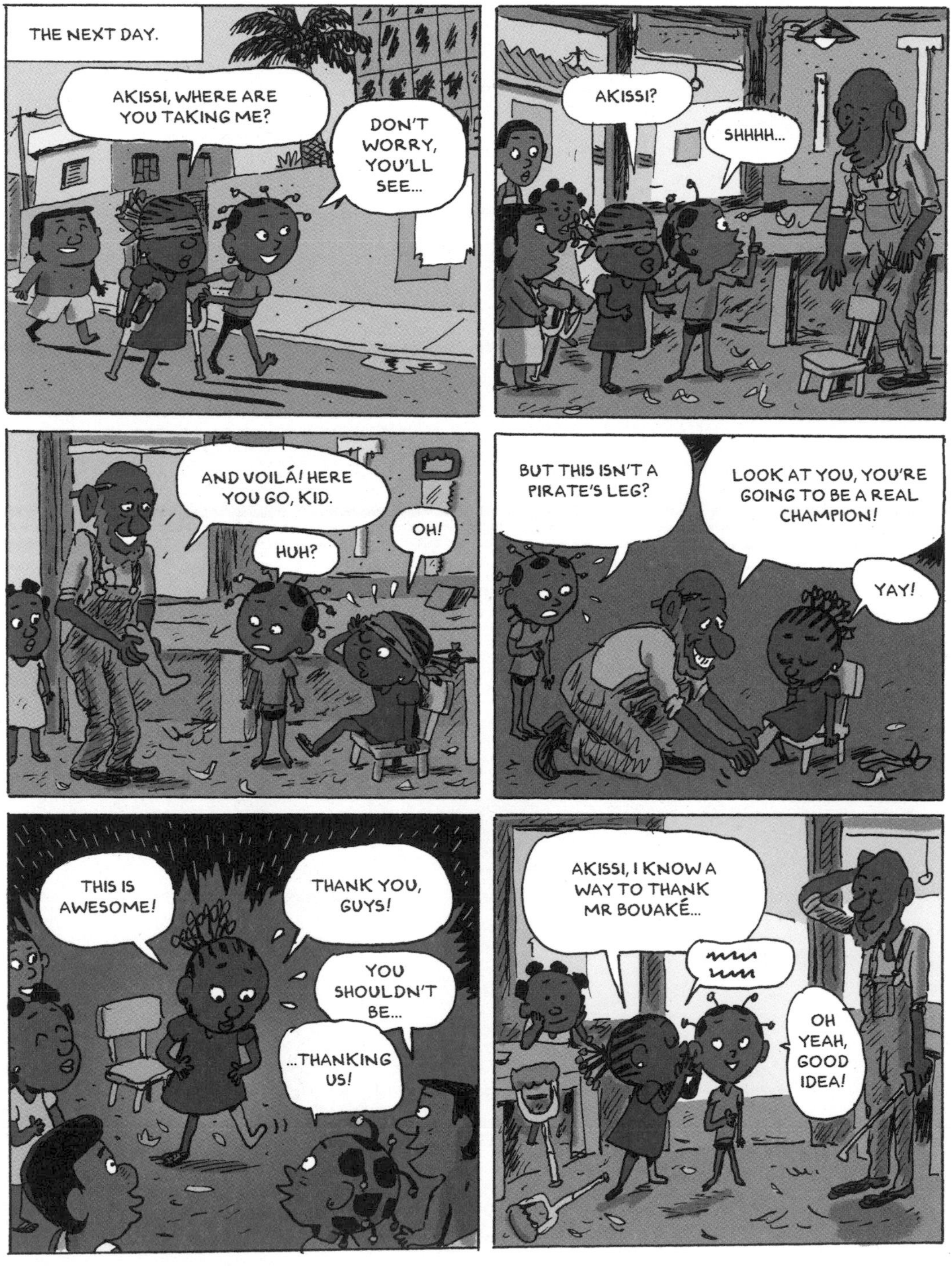
THE NEXT DAY.
AKISSI, WHERE ARE YOU TAKING ME?
DON'T WORRY, YOU'LL SEE...
AKISSI?
SHHHH...
AND VOILÁ! HERE YOU GO, KID.
HUH?
OH!
BUT THIS ISN'T A PIRATE'S LEG?
LOOK AT YOU, YOU'RE GOING TO BE A REAL CHAMPION!
YAY!
THIS IS AWESOME!
THANK YOU, GUYS!
YOU SHOULDN'T BE...
...THANKING US!
AKISSI, I KNOW A WAY TO THANK MR BOUAKÉ...
OH YEAH, GOOD IDEA!

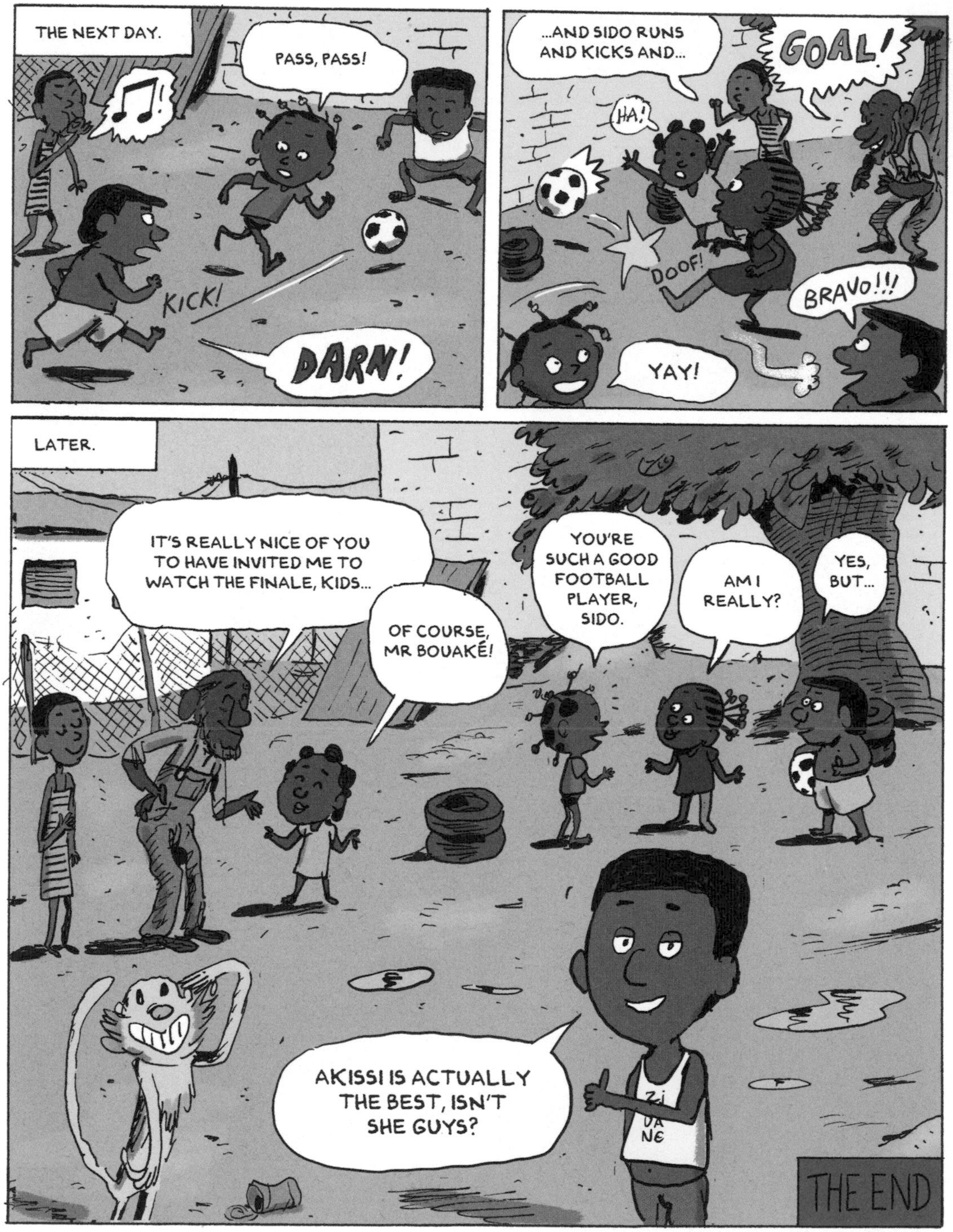

THE NEXT DAY.
PASS, PASS!
KICK!
DARN!
...AND SIDO RUNS AND KICKS AND...
GOAL!
HA!
DOOF!
BRAVO!!!
YAY!
LATER.
IT'S REALLY NICE OF YOU TO HAVE INVITED ME TO WATCH THE FINALE, KIDS...
OF COURSE, MR BOUAKÉ!
YOU'RE SUCH A GOOD FOOTBALL PLAYER, SIDO.
AM I REALLY?
YES, BUT...
AKISSI IS ACTUALLY THE BEST, ISN'T SHE GUYS?
ZI DA NE
THE END

BONUS
pages

LEARN HOW TO DRAW

AKISSI'S HEAD

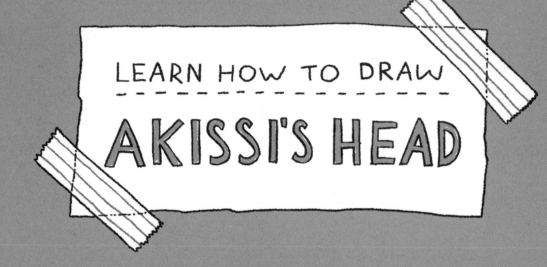

LEARN HOW TO DRAW AKISSI'S HEAD

① START BY DRAWING A NOT-SO-ROUND CIRCLE...

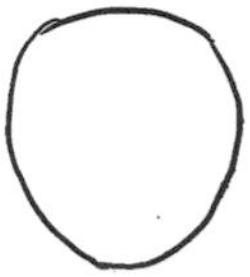

② TWO OVALS AND A DOT IN EACH FOR THE EYES...

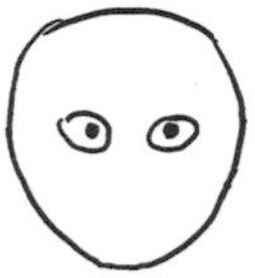

③ A SMALL COMMA FOR THE NOSE...

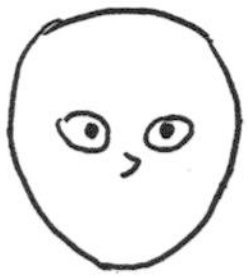

④ THEN TWO SMALL LINES FOR THE EYEBROWS AND A LITTLE BEAN FOR THE MOUTH!

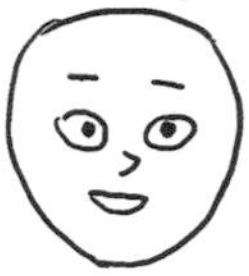

⑤ DON'T FORGET TWO HALF-MOONS FOR THE EARS.

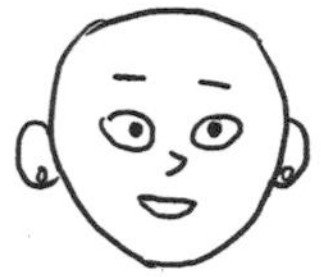

⑥ ALL YOU NEED TO DO NOW IS DRAW THE BRAIDS!

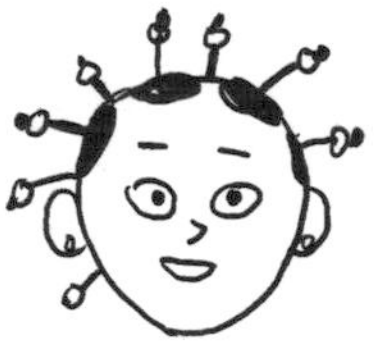

DID YOU KNOW YOU CAN CHANGE FACIAL EXPRESSIONS JUST BY PLAYING WITH THE WAY YOU DRAW EYES, EYEBROWS AND MOUTHS?

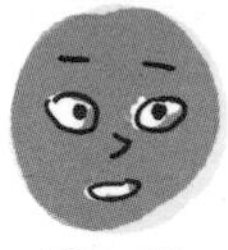

NORMAL

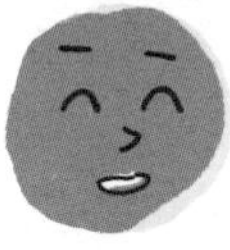

HAPPY

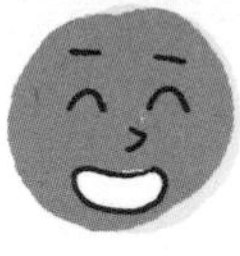

OVERJOYED

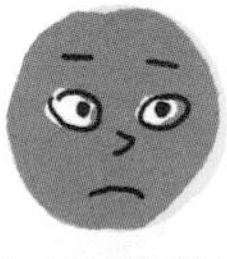

DISAPPOINTED

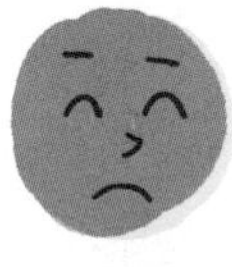

SAD

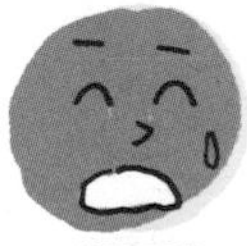

UPSET

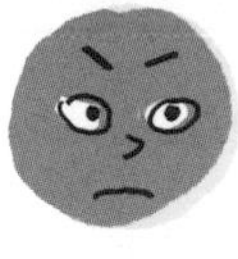

ANNOYED

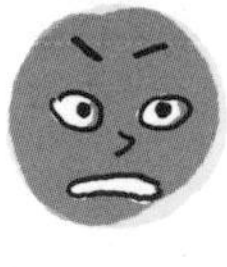

VERY IRRITATED

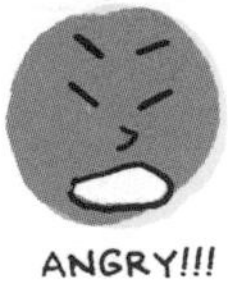

ANGRY!!!

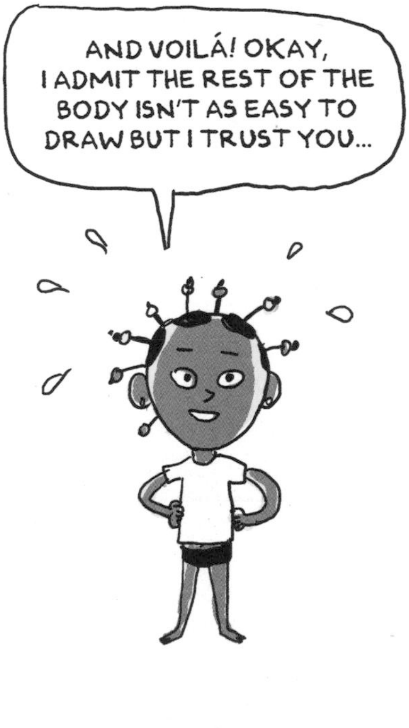
AND VOILÁ! OKAY, I ADMIT THE REST OF THE BODY ISN'T AS EASY TO DRAW BUT I TRUST YOU...

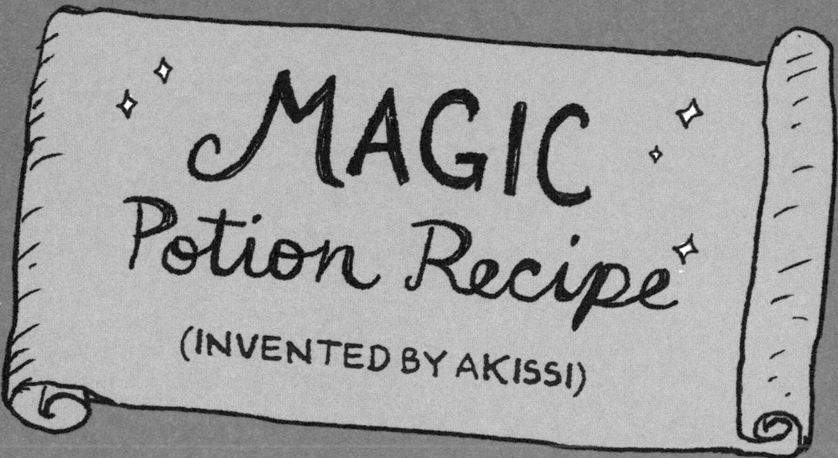
MAGIC
Potion Recipe
(INVENTED BY AKISSI)

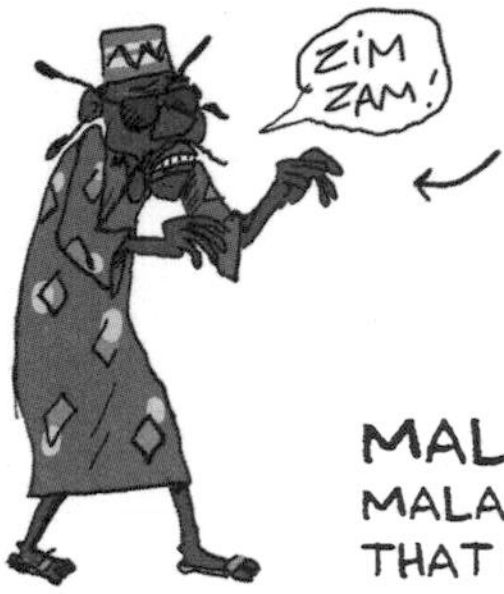
ZIM ZAM!

WITCH DOCTOR
THIS CAN MEAN SEVERAL THINGS BUT IN THIS BOOK IT MEANS A WIZARD OR A MAGICIAN WHO OFFERS HIS SERVICES TO SOLVE ALL KINDS OF PROBLEMS.

MALARIA
MALARIA IS A TERRIBLE CONDITION THAT COMES FROM PARASITES TRANSMITTED TO PEOPLE THROUGH INFECTED MOSQUITOES' BITES.

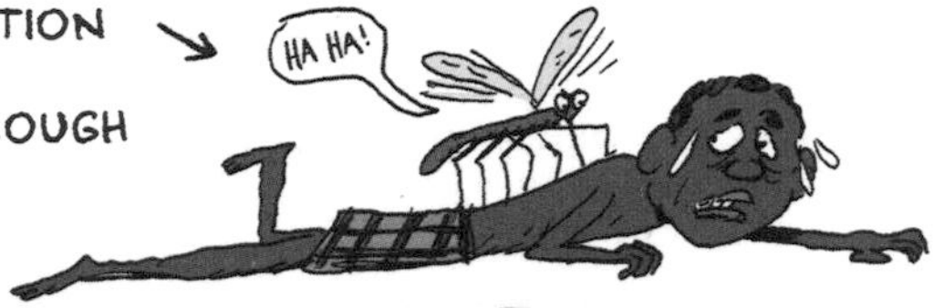
HA HA!

MAGIC Potion Recipe

(INVENTED BY AKISSI)

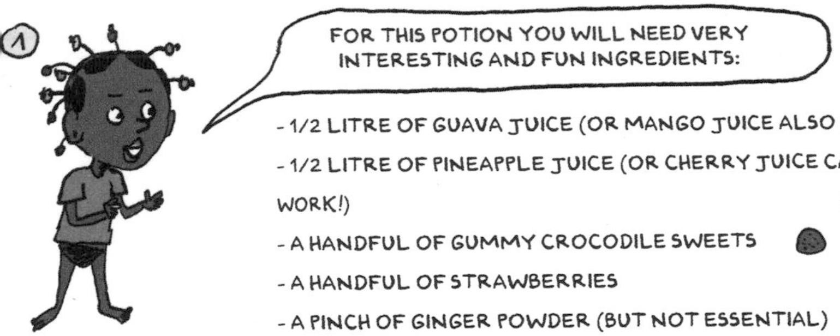
1
FOR THIS POTION YOU WILL NEED VERY INTERESTING AND FUN INGREDIENTS:

- 1/2 LITRE OF GUAVA JUICE (OR MANGO JUICE ALSO WORKS!)
- 1/2 LITRE OF PINEAPPLE JUICE (OR CHERRY JUICE CAN ALSO WORK!)
- A HANDFUL OF GUMMY CROCODILE SWEETS
- A HANDFUL OF STRAWBERRIES
- A PINCH OF GINGER POWDER (BUT NOT ESSENTIAL)
- THREE GRAINS OF SALT (EXTREMELY ESSENTIAL!)

+ A BIG COOKING POT, A WOODEN SPOON AND A GLASS.

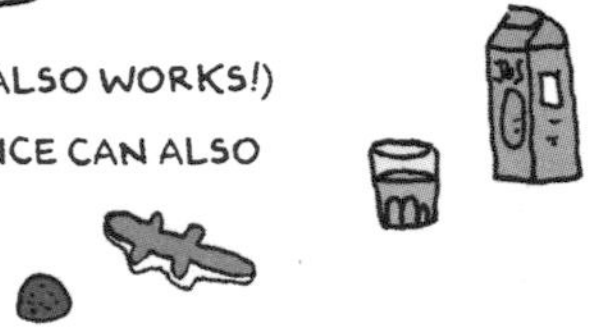

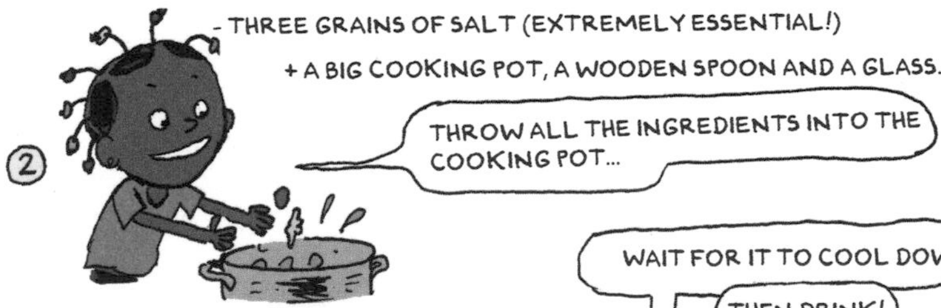
2
THROW ALL THE INGREDIENTS INTO THE COOKING POT...

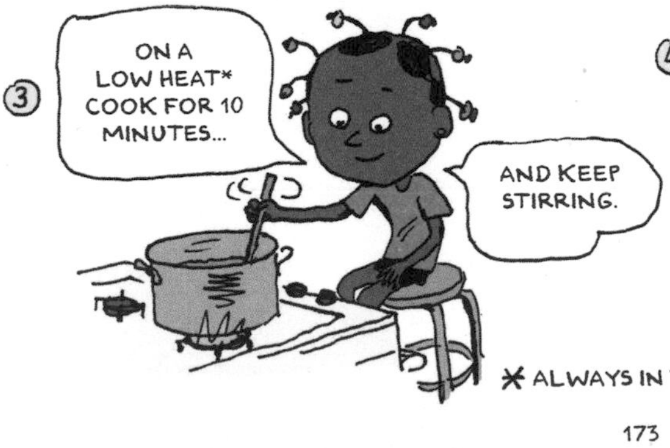
3
ON A LOW HEAT* COOK FOR 10 MINUTES...
AND KEEP STIRRING.

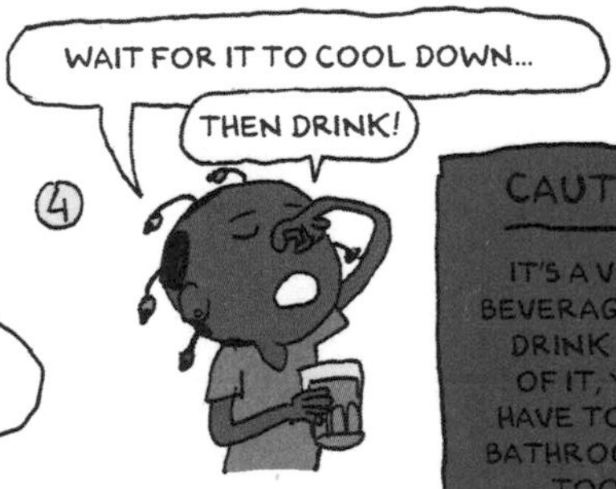
4
WAIT FOR IT TO COOL DOWN...
THEN DRINK!

CAUTION ⚠

IT'S A VERY TASTY BEVERAGE BUT IF YOU DRINK TOO MUCH OF IT, YOU MIGHT HAVE TO GO TO THE BATHROOM A LITTLE TOO OFTEN.

* ALWAYS IN THE PRESENCE OF AN ADULT!

Marguerite Abouet was born in Abidjan, Ivory Coast, in the neighbourhood of Yopougon. At the age of 12, she moved to Paris, where she discovered wonderful libraries and developed a passion for books. In 2005, she published *Aya de Yopougon*, which won the Best Album prize at the Angoulême Comics Festival. In 2010, Marguerite Abouet and Mathieu Sapin published the first volume of Akissi, which is inspired by Abouet's childhood memories. When she is not busy writing stories, Marguerite Abouet helps build libraries throughout Africa through her charity, Des Livres pour Tous.

Mathieu Sapin was born in 1974. After attending the School of Decorative Arts in Strasbourg, he spent two years working at the International Center for Comic Strips and Images, where he illustrated children's literature. In 2003, he began to devote himself entirely to making comics. Today, his list of works includes over 30 titles, including the Akissi series.

THE MISCHIEF NEVER ENDS!
READ MORE LAUGH-OUT-LOUD TALES
IN THE WONDROUS AKISSI SERIES:

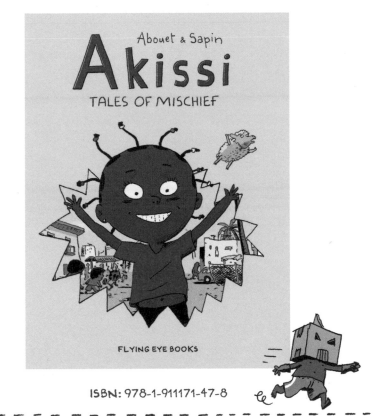

Abouet & Sapin

Akissi
TALES OF MISCHIEF

FLYING EYE BOOKS

ISBN: 978-1-911171-47-8

PRAISE FOR AKISSI:

"AN UNFORGETTABLE, BOUNDARY-BUSTING, FALLING-OVER-FUNNY COLLECTION...
WE STAND DESPERATELY IN NEED OF MORE AKISSI AND MORE ABOUET."
- KIRKUS REVIEWS, STARRED REVIEW

"[AKISSI] FILLS A GAP IN CHILDREN'S COMICS FEATURING AFRICAN CHARACTERS AND
SETTINGS. HIGHLY RECOMMENDED FOR MIDDLE GRADE GRAPHIC NOVEL COLLECTIONS."
- SCHOOL LIBRARY JOURNAL, STARRED REVIEW

WWW.FLYINGEYEBOOKS.COM

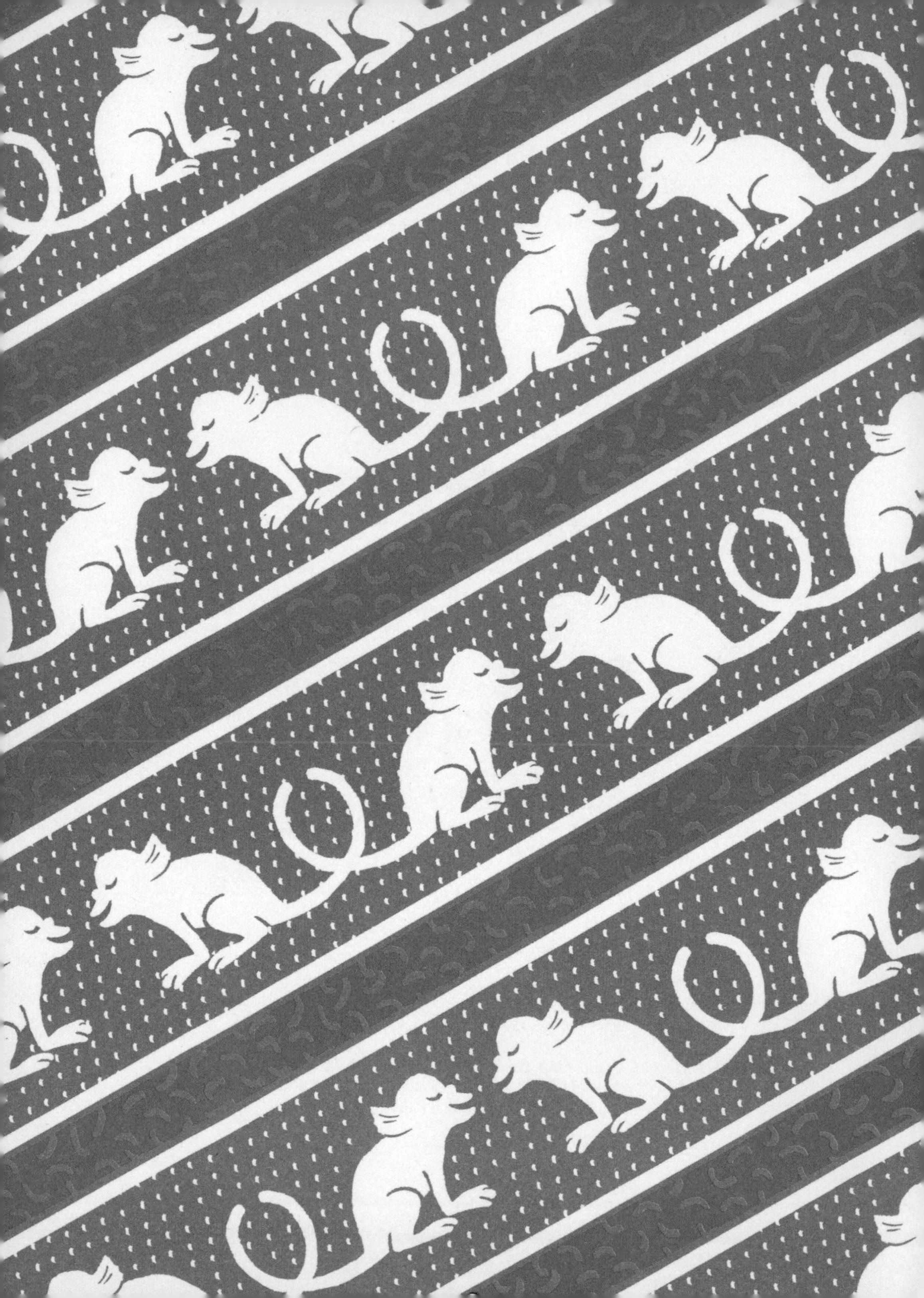